THE CLAWS OF CHAOS

CURSING HIMSELF FOR a fool, Kurt rose and ran. He heard a roar from behind him and glanced back to see the troll lumbering forward before dropping to all fours and bounding through the snow with surprising speed.

'This way!' he shouted out, plunging through a snow-drift and almost losing his footing. Ursula raced out of the darkness, her pale face twisted with fear. They were barely ten yards apart when a massive shape loomed up behind her, three long arms held high, one clawed hand gripping a crude club.

'Watch out!' screamed Kurt as he hurled himself forward even faster, his lungs fit to burst. Ursula dived forwards and rolled through the snow, the club thumping down in a shower of snow and frozen dirt.

More Warhammer from the Black Library

· GOTREK & FELIX ·

TROLLSLAYER by William King
SKAVENSLAYER by William King
DAEMONSLAYER by William King
DRAGONSLAYER by William King
BEASTSLAYER by William King
VAMPIRESLAYER by William King

· THE VAMPIRE GENEVIEVE NOVELS ·

DRACHENFELS by Jack Yeovil
GENEVIEVE UNDEAD by Jack Yeovil
BEASTS IN VELVET by Jack Yeovil

· THE TALES OF ORFEO ·

ZARAGOZ by Brian Craig
PLAGUE DAEMON by Brian Craig

· THE KONRAD TRILOGY ·

KONRAD by David Ferring
SHADOWBREED by David Ferring
WARBLADE by David Ferring

· WARHAMMER NOVELS ·

ZAVANT by Gordon Rennie
HAMMERS OF ULRIC by Dan Abnett,
Nik Vincent & James Wallis
GILEAD'S BLOOD by Dan Abnett & Nik Vincent
THE WINE OF DREAMS by Brian Craig

More Gav Thorpe from the Black Library

13th LEGION, a Last Chancers novel
KILL TEAM, a Last Chancers novel

A WARHAMMER NOVEL

Slaves to Darkness · Book One

THE CLAWS OF CHAOS

GAV THORPE

To Dennis, for all his help and inspiration

A BLACK LIBRARY PUBLICATION

First published in Great Britain
in 2002 by The Black Library,
an imprint of Games Workshop Ltd.,
Willow Road, Lenton,
Nottingham, NG7 2WS, UK

10 9 8 7 6 5 4 3 2 1

Cover illustration by Adrian Smith
Map by Nuala Kennedy

A CIP record for this book
is available from the British Library

ISBN 1 84154 257 1

Set in ITC Giovanni

Printed and bound in Great Britain by
Cox & Wyman Ltd, Cardiff Rd, Reading, Berkshire RG1 8EX, UK

See the Black Library on the Internet at
www.blacklibrary.com

Find out more about Games Workshop
and the world of Warhammer at
www.games-workshop.com

THE CLAWS OF CHAOS

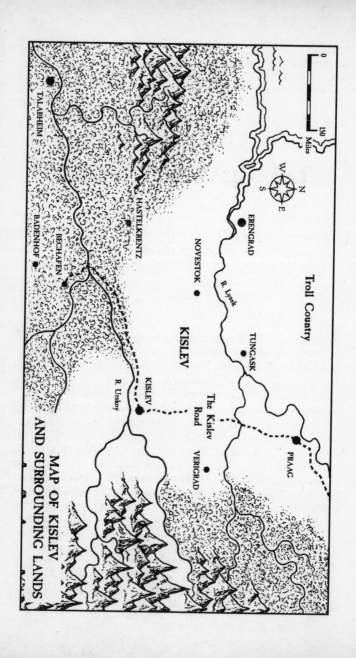

MAP OF KISLEV AND SURROUNDING LANDS

Author's Note

THE EVENTS OF this book took place during a time of great strife and upheaval in the lands known as the Empire. Following the death of Emperor Mandred at the hands of inhuman assassins, the states of the Empire could not elect a new ruler, and war broke out between several Imperial provinces. This continued for several hundred years, and the period in which the following events took place was known as the Time of Three Emperors, because three of the provincial elector counts had declared themselves rightful Emperor – Stirland, Talabecland and the city state of Middenheim.

Assailed from outside and divided within, the Empire was all but shattered, the once united states now operating as separate nations. Suspicion and politicking became the rule of the day in the Imperial courts, while the people tried to eke out a living amidst the ruins of the former Empire. Anarchy prevailed, brigands roamed the wilds, vile beastmen stalked the forest roads and the once cosmopolitan people of the Empire became introverted and parochial. With the rulers of the elector states bickering amongst themselves, towns and villages were left to defend themselves, and the purges of orcs, mutants, skaven and other foul *creatures fell by the wayside, allowing much of the realm to be overrun. Apocalyptic cults ran rife in the cities, bands of flagellants roamed the countryside with their own doom-laden religions and prophecies. Shrines to Sigmar found their congregations dwindling as the disaffected populace sought salvation from the older gods – Taal, Ulric and even darker powers.*

All dates are in the Imperial calendar, which began with the crowning of Sigmar as the first Emperor.

PROLOGUE

THE BODIES OF the dead littered the snow-covered ground. In half a day of bitter fighting, twenty thousand already lay dead or wounded and still the battle raged. Sutenvulf Daemonkin surveyed the carnage with a smile twisting his inhuman lips. The daemon prince stretched out his leathery wings and leapt into the air, his mighty pinions beating slowly, carrying him down the slope where he had been standing. All around was the din of war, a pleasing melody of battle cries and screams: the ring of metal on metal, and his unnatural ears delighted in the sound of axe blade in flesh and sword through bone. The battle had ebbed and flowed for seven hours now, and as the cold northern sun dipped over the eastern mountains, the daemonic general felt it was time to finish off the upstart warriors from the Empire of the south.

He looked with great pride over the army that he had gathered. Warbands of the gods' champions fought side by side with legions of daemons he had brought forth with his own powerful magic, alongside the savage, undisciplined beastmen, bull-headed minotaurs, scaled dragon

9

ogres and other monsters of the Chaos Wastes. This was his all-conquering force, and when the incursion of the foolish mortals was dealt with, he would sweep further south, sacking and burning, offering up thousands in sacrifice to the Dark Gods who had granted him such power and his immortality.

Looking with his daemonsight, Sutenvulf could sense the emotions that swirled across the bloodied glacier: the rage of the champions of Khorne; the fear of the Imperial Knights as the daemon prince swept towards them; the loathing of the weakling Sigmarite priest who hid behind the armour-clad horsemen; the ferocious, instinctual blood-thirst of the beastmen who hacked and slashed at the halberdiers protecting the Imperial clergyman.

The daemon prince savoured it all, landing in front of the knights with a great bellow. Opening up his immaterial form to the magical winds that poured from the north, Sutenvulf pulled the power of raw Chaos into himself, feeling invigorated and strengthened. He drew his sword, taller than a man and forged with runes in the Dark Tongue that twisted in on themselves when seen by mortal eyes, and held it above his head. Exerting some of the energy that coursed through his unnatural form, he pushed his power outwards, causing the blade of his daemon weapon to explode with flame. It seemed such a petty feat now, requiring the smallest amount of his power, but the thrill of dread that flowed from the knights and the surge of exaltation from his followers was justification enough for the simple parlour trick.

The knights spurred their horses forward, lances levelled, their steeds whinnying in terror yet hurtling at him under the unkind urging of their riders. Growling, Sutenvulf pivoted slightly on the ball of his right foot, balancing himself like the practiced swordsman he once had been, his wings furling behind him out of harm's way. He raised his sword to the guard position in a mock salute of the knights thundering towards him, then leapt forward with a gargantuan stride, his clawed feet churning up red-stained snow. Lances shattered on his black-scaled hide, failing to pierce his immortal flesh, and with the speed of a lightning bolt, the daemon prince struck back, a snarl of satisfaction issuing from his throat.

The flaming blade carved off the head of the first knight, whose horse buckled and fell, passed through the upraised arm and then the chest of the next, the magical flames cauterising the wounds instantly. The sweet aroma of charred flesh filled the daemon prince's nostrils. The backhand sweep sliced a horse in half from shoulder to spine, its head and forelegs spinning into the air, the rider's thigh cleaved in two by the blow, his armour no defence against Sutenvulf's daemonblade. Sword cuts and mace blows glanced harmlessly from the daemon's arms and torso, failing to cause even the lightest of wounds on his magical flesh. Two dozen more knights were carved to pieces by his fell sword; parts of them flung yards into the air, to topple amongst their comrades, panicking the knights and their warhorses.

Feeling their panic building, Sutenvulf extended his will once more, pushing out a wave of pure malevolence and hatred that washed over the Imperial soldiers in a tide of terror, causing them to falter. One leapt from his horse screaming, clawing at his visored face. Another was crushed as his horse reared and fell backwards, while the man next to him slipped from his saddle to his knees and began gibbering a prayer to his upstart god, Sigmar.

The knights routed en masse, fleeing before the daemon prince, whose guttural laughs echoed after them.

The daemon turned his fiery gaze to the halberdiers and the priest who was mounted upon a fine white horse in their midst. He pointed his sword at the priest and uttered a command in the Dark Tongue. Either side of him, the animal-headed beastmen renewed their attacks, hurling themselves forward in a flurry of wild axe blows, flailing maces, gouging horns and biting fangs.

Then something stirred on the edge of Sutenvulf's daemon vision, drawing his attention away from the hapless priest and his bodyguard. The stench of impure faith was rank in the air as he looked about the battlefield, locating a white glow from which it emanated. Here was their champion, the Sigmarite lapdog who dared to defy the will of the Northern Gods. He would rip the upstart's head from his shoulders with his bare hands and crush his skull with taloned fingers made strong by the power of the Chaos gods. He would teach the soft-bellied southerners which gods ruled the lands, and what manner of warriors fought for them.

With spiteful glee in his heart, Sutenvulf once more took to the skies on black-skinned wings and drifted on the waves of hate and fear, swiftly gliding over the mounds of the fallen. The Empire soldiers and their fawning Kislevite allies fled before his wrath, but the glowing figure of the Sigmarite champion remained. Anger flared through Sutenvulf's being at the audacity of the mortal, and he plunged down through the air, his sword ready for the killing blow.

Throwing up fountains of earth, ice and blood, the daemon prince landed before the Imperial leader and snarled a curse in the Chaos tongue; words which lashed the soul to the core. Yet the shining figure that confronted him remained unaffected, standing resolutely, a two-handed hammer in its grasp. The daemon prince towered above his foe, fully three times taller, and spread his wings with a noise like the clap of thunder. He once more exerted his immortal power in a pulse of terror-inspiring magic, but still the figure remained motionless. Sutenvulf was intrigued, wanting to know more about this courageous mortal who glowed with unholy light. Leaving behind his gift of daemonsight, Sutenvulf regarded his foe with mortal eyes. Looking at the pale, determined faced that regarded him coolly, there was a flicker of remembrance.

BOOK ONE

CHAPTER ONE
Farewells
Badenhof, autumn 1708

THE EARLY MORNING sun was crisp and bright, shining pale and white in a clear sky. The oaks and sycamores in the shrine's yard had all but shed the last of their leaves, carpeting the grass in a layer of golden yellows, russet and brown. There was a touch of frost on the autumn leaves, a glimmer across the grounds that spoke of the bitter winter fast approaching. There had been much talk in Badenhof about the weather, and the old folk shook their heads and claimed that they had never seen such a short summer. Old stories resurfaced of mighty blizzards and harsh winters; the favoured subject of such elderly raconteurs being the famine and winter of 1586, when whole villages starved or froze to death, and the army of Sevir the Blood-terror marched across the Urskoy and attacked the Ostermark. These are troubling times, they complained, a warning from the gods of worse things to come.

The leaders of the town were worried too, for news had arrived a few months before of a great warband of orcs rampaging in the south. Solland had been all but destroyed, and the army of Stirland, whose rulers were seen as uneasy allies by the people of the Ostermark where Badenhof was found, had been scattered in battle. Now Ostermark stood alone, desperately clinging to independence against the warlike intentions of Talabecland to the west.

Talabecland's ruler, the Ottila, had all but declared war on the neighbouring states, and fear gripped the lands, just as uncertainty and outright war had waxed and waned for the last three hundred and fifty years.

Yet these weighty matters and worldly events did not occupy the thoughts of Ursula Schek as she picked her way through the fallen leaves that morning. The nineteen year old was troubled by news far worse, and far more personal. Her betrothed was leaving again that very morning, to return to Ostermark's capital, Bechafen. It could be months, perhaps the whole winter if it was as bad as expected, before she would see him again. So it was with a heavy heart that she walked along the path that meandered through the dishevelled gardens towards the chapel.

It was not the largest shrine she had ever seen, nor the most welcoming, but the old stone and timber building lent her confidence that morning. She looked up at the twin steeples, and the golden hammer emblazoned across the east door as she approached. The church was about twice the size of the townhouses that surrounded it, situated within a wide compound of gardens, which in turn were encircled by a shoulder-high brick wall overgrown with moss. The grounds were similarly overgrown, the commemorative stones and weathered statues thick with mouldering vegetation, the grass knee high after months of neglect. Behind her were the outhouses where she lived, three half-abandoned wooden barns supposedly used to store food for the poor, but now empty except for the rough dwelling Ursula had made for herself.

Scraping what mud she could from the plain shoes she wore, Ursula opened the shrine's doors and stepped inside, kicking off the offending footwear without much thought. She looked down at her toes, stained slightly by the walk from the outhouse just across the yard, and sighed. Flicking a few rebellious strands of long red curls from her face, she looked down the shrine towards the altar. There, in dark stone, was the life-size statue of Sigmar. He exuded strength and confidence, and Ursula smiled to herself, feeling the love of her god in her heart. Stepping lightly between the benches, she walked reverently towards the effigy; its right hand outstretched towards her, holding the great warhammer Ghal-maraz, the Skull Splitter. Sigmar Heldenhammer's handsome bearded face was stern but kind as he watched his approaching worshipper. Ursula liked the statue, it was much nicer than some she had seen, even though they had been gilded or carved from exotic marble or alabaster. It embodied how she saw Sigmar: benevolent yet strong; caring but proud; father and protector.

Picking up the hem of the blue woollen dress she wore, Ursula knelt before the altar and bowed her head.

'Great Sigmar, founder and lord of our great lands, I humbly offer my love to you,' she prayed. 'I thank you for keeping me safe in the night and for guarding my soul against the darkness. I give thanks for the water I shall drink and the bread I shall eat today, and for guarding the lives of those who provide it for me.'

She paused, thinking she had seen a flicker of movement out of the corner of her eye. Seeing nothing, she dismissed the distraction; it was probably one of the rats that had infested Badenhof since the poor harvest a couple of months earlier. To make matters worse, she had heard that rot had gotten into the grain stores, and now everyone was feeling the pinch just a couple of short months after the harvest.

'Great Sigmar, forgive my intrusion into your eternal watchfulness,' Ursula said softly. 'I pray that you keep my love safe while he is away, and that my heart remains pure for him while he is gone. I pray that he does brave deeds and acts with honour, just as you did. I also pray that you see fit to speed him back to my arms, for though I love and adore you above everything, on this world he is my only care.'

Ursula stood, and took from the pocket of her dress a ring of flowers, freshly picked and woven by her own hand into a delicate wreath. Blues and yellows of the last summer flowers mixed with whites and reds of early blossoming winter blooms. She stepped forward, kissed the hammer and laid

the wreath about the head, pushing it down so it slid
around Sigmar's wrist. It was a ritual she had performed
every day of her life that she could remember. When she had
been a child, and her grandparents had beaten her, she had
sought refuge in the shrine of Sigmar. It had been warm and
comforting, and she had seen a wreath about Sigmar's hammer just like the one she had placed today. In thanks for the
comfort and succour his shrine had given her, Ursula had
sworn that she would repay him with such a gift every day.

That had been ten years ago, barely months after the death
of her parents by the black spite, their lungs rotted, their
faces pale and yellow before the shrouds covered them.
Every day since, she had kept that promise when she could.
Even in the wilds, when she had run away from her tyranni-
cal grandparents, she had made a wreath and laid it on the
branch of a tree or a farm hedge to honour Sigmar.

Looking up from the flowers, troubled by the memory of
her orphaned wandering from village to village, and from
town to town, she caught sight of the candles behind the
altar. They were almost burnt out, but Brother Theobald
would be here within the hour to refresh them. He did not
mind her small flower offerings, but always shooed her away
from performing any of the other tasks. Ursula knew that
Theobald tolerated her presence in the outhouse because of
his sacred duty, rather than because he felt any genuine sym-
pathy for the foundling.

The flame on the candle seemed to be growing larger, and
Ursula was mesmerised by its flickering and dancing. The
burning light grew in her vision, and the rest of the shrine
dropped away out of sight. Voices came to her – hoarse cries
and fierce bellowing. She saw flames enveloping everything,
roaring in their hunger, smoke billowing in massive dark
clouds. Bestial figures appeared in the smoke-wreathed fire.
Hunched things with shaggy fur and long fangs and wicked
claws. There was war and terror in the air, and terrible fear
gripped Ursula as the vision grew in clarity. The burning was
painfully close, and for a moment, she thought she was on
fire and panicked, gasping aloud, though there was no one
else in the shrine to hear her. She mumbled to herself, staring at the candle flame, and swayed slightly, her head dizzy.

Amidst the burning, Ursula could make out a single figure. It was a man, tall and broad, and the flames seemed not to touch him. She thought he was the source of the flames and tried to see his face, but could not make out any details. He strode through the inferno, a long sword in one hand, and a shield in the other. A sudden great wailing arose from the flames themselves, as if the stranger caused the fire itself pain and fear. Terror swept over Ursula, the need to turn tail and run washed through her, making her physically shake in the grip of her second sight.

Suddenly, the vision ended and Ursula slumped forwards, grabbing the outstretched arm of Sigmar for support. She looked at his face again and for a moment thought she saw flames flickering in those carved eyes.

'My love?' she heard a familiar voice from behind her and spun quickly, ignoring her sudden dizziness. 'Are you well?'

Grinning broadly, the vision pushed from her mind, Ursula ran down the aisle towards the main doors, her feet flapping on the wooden floor, her long plaited hair slapping against her back. Kurt smiled back at her and she all but threw herself into his arms, planting a long kiss on his forehead as she stretched up on tiptoe. His arms encircled her and she closed her eyes for a moment, enjoying his closeness. Realising something was amiss – she could feel the cold touch of metal – Ursula opened her eyes and stood back.

Kurt was dressed in full plate armour, though she had not noticed it before, still giddy from the vision and her delight at seeing him. She looked up at his face, drinking in the softness of his eyes, his dark hair, his handsome, chiselled features. She ran a finger down the slight cleft in his chin, and then stroked his left cheek with the back of her hand.

'You're leaving now?' she asked, knowing the answer, her voice quiet.

'Once I have said goodbye to you, my love,' Kurt replied, his own smile now gone too, but it returned after only a moment. 'The farrier is still readying Heldred, walk with me back to the town square.'

* * *

URSULA WALKED DOWN the muddy, rutted street in comfortable silence with Kurt, and her thoughts turned back to the vision she'd just experienced. It was not the first time, but it had been two years since the last one, ever since she had arrived in Badenhof in fact. The first had been when she was only twelve years old, when she had been hiding out in a small shrine to Sigmar in Kellenbad, in northern Stirland.

She had seen a small band of beastmen attacking the sheep on the high pasture and told the priest. He had dismissed it as a young girl's fancy at first, but when news reached him that half the flock had been slaughtered he came for Ursula in the night, getting the truth out of her with a birch switch. She had run away again the next day, still bruised and bloody.

And so for the next five years, Sigmar had spoken to her on occasion. Sometimes she just heard his voice, warning her, telling her to get away. Like the time she had left Lessenburg just a week before an army of the Ottila had crossed the border and burnt it to the ground.

Sometimes, like today, Sigmar sent her visions of events, such as the assassination of the elector heir Prince Fredrick four years ago, or more personal ones as in the time she foresaw a hellish storm three years ago, and managed to seek shelter in a derelict barn before the rain and lightning lashed down for four whole days and nights.

The vision today scared her. It had been more terrifying than any before, and yet felt like one of the personal warnings, as if it were really only a threat to her. She could still feel the fear within herself, and shuddered. She hoped Kurt had not noticed, as she could not afford for him to find out. Or anyone else for that matter, more importantly. Kurt was a knight of the Osterknacht, bodyguard to the count, and if it was found out that he was due to marry a seer, or possibly a witch, it would be very bad for him. So Ursula had stayed silent, though it cut her to her soul to lie to her love. And why had the visions suddenly returned, after two years of peace and calm? Ursula fretted inside, afraid that great turmoil was about to upset her life once again.

* * *

KURT WAS WORRIED too, for when he had entered the shrine he had seen Ursula almost faint, holding herself up on the statue to Sigmar. He hoped that she was not falling sick. When he had last travelled to Bechafen four weeks ago, he had heard tales of the red pox reappearing in the Ostermark. And if she were ill, the cruel winter that was coming would severely lessen her chances of fighting off any plague or fever, and Kurt would be away, perhaps for several months, unable to tend to his beloved. The priest might care for her, but the rest of Badenhof's inhabitants were ignorant, rural folk who would sooner burn a plague victim alive then try to tend to their ills.

Not for the first time, Kurt longed to have enough money to take Ursula to Bechafen, away from this place, and to leave behind the long separations that his duty imposed on them. But he was not a wealthy man, what little he had, was scraped together from his monthly pay and added to the small bequest that Lord Gerhardt had left him in his last testament two years ago. Gerhardt had been kind, and for that Kurt thanked the ghost of the old knight, wishing him peace. But the life that Gerhardt's patronage had allowed him to build was in danger of unravelling, and without funds it would be impossible to marry Ursula and give her the stable, loving home she craved and deserved.

So the two of them were sombre in their thoughts as they passed between the two and three-storey wooden buildings either side, some of them with timbers still showing, others crudely plastered. The slick grey of the slate roofs stood out against the crisp sky, and the smoke of early morning fires began to drift intermittently from chimney holes and brick stacks. The first sounds of life began to grow louder as they approached the square at the centre of Badenhof. The town was waking up to the noise of barking dogs, the shouts of children and the clatter of shutters banging against walls as windows were thrown open to air musty rooms.

A goat that had strayed from its pen trotted out into the middle of the Sigmarstrasse in front of Kurt and Ursula. It had odd-coloured eyes, one of them yellow, the other blue, and it regarded them calmly. It reminded Ursula of the beasts in the vision, indistinct as it had been, and she wondered if it was beastmen again, like her first gifted sight. A small girl, perhaps no more than eight years old, came running out from the same direction, in a plain woollen smock that dragged through the mud and threatened to trip her up. She grabbed the goat around the neck and then appeared to notice Ursula and Kurt for the first time. She stared at Kurt in his polished full plate armour, her mouth open in amazement. Blushing heavily, she dragged the goat away, muttering into its ear.

It was another half a mile until they reached the square, where the market was just being set up. A handful of stalls were already there, but pitifully few were being wheeled in or assembled, compared to the bustling commerce that had kept Badenhof thriving only a decade ago. There was little gold around these days, and brass and bronze pennies were seen more often than silver coins.

One of the stallholders, Herr Schamp, lifted his battered hat in greeting to Kurt, but his gaze avoided Ursula. The spindly little man turned and shouted at his wife, who was struggling across the square, her arms filled with old, brown-looking cabbages. Not only was the grain poor, blight had descended on many of the farms, further complicating the local food shortage.

The clang of metal began to reverberate around the square as smith Klein began his day's work, the glow from his furnace clear in the open front of his shop opposite the decaying town hall. Next to Klein's smithy were the stables and farrier, and Kurt led Ursula between the market stalls, nodding in greeting to those they passed, receiving many a 'Good morning' and 'Fine day to you' in return.

When Kurt pushed open the door of the stables and he and Ursula stepped inside, the stable boy, a sandy-haired lad called Mika, gave a start and pulled himself to his feet. He had been napping against a hitching post.

'Knacht Leitzig!' the boy blurted, straightening out his tunic and hose. 'Heldred's just out the back being saddled.'

'Bring him out to the square soon as you like,' Kurt replied sternly, but as the boy scurried off the knight gave a wink to Ursula and led her back outside. A few more people had started to gather, waking early to try and buy the best of the meagre supplies available. They shuffled about in their heavy cloaks and furs, trying not to appear too eager, but subtly jostling each other to get to the front of the growing queues. The growing whispers of plague did little to help the demand for fresh food, though these were put down to gossip and rumour. Still, there were worried glances whenever someone gave a sneeze or cough, and the gathering people would move slightly further away from such unfortunate individuals.

The square was dominated by the town hall, which stretched four storeys above the heads of the people at the market. Built entirely of dark stone, pierced by scores of narrow windows, it looked as much a bastion of defence as a civil building. Gargoyles around its many slanted roofs spat thin dribbles of water from the previous day's drizzle onto the cobbles, splashing those below. The main doors stood twice the height of a man, but the hinges and locks were so rusted it had been nearly half a century since they had been opened. Glistening moss and tendrils of ivy crawled across the ancient stonework, obscuring the worn carvings and faded murals that had once decorated the most important building in Badenhof.

Neither Kurt nor Ursula spoke. There was no need to, the conversation would run the same way it had done the first few times Kurt had to leave.

'Must you go so soon?' Ursula would ask.

'I wish I did not have to, but I must be back in Bechafen by the end of the week,' Kurt would reply.

'Then I'll come with you,' Ursula would state firmly.

'There's no place to stay, and you do not have a horse,' Kurt would respond evenly.

'Then I shall run after you!' Ursula would assure him.

'I know you would,' Kurt would agree, half believing her.

'Be careful, say your prayers,' Ursula would demand, running a hand down his cheek, with a tear in her eye.

'I will, and you stay out of trouble,' Kurt would reply, stroking her long red hair with his gauntleted hand.

Now there was nothing more to say, more than a year after their first meeting. Now they simply stood next to each other. Kurt pulled off one armoured gauntlet and held her

hand in his, bending down to kiss her hair, delighting in the
flowery scent of her plaited locks. She craned her head back
and to the side to catch his lips on hers, and they kissed for
a moment, eyes closed.

The clip-clop of hooves broke the spell as the farrier, Herr
Struben, led Heldred out onto the cobbles of the square.
Kurt's horse, another bequest from Lord Gerhardt, was a
broad and powerful stallion, nearly sixteen hands high,
black as pitch with a grey mane, tail and socks. Named after
the founder of the Osterknacht, Lord Heldred Orcbane, he
was not the finest horse Kurt had ever seen, but he was fast
when spurred, placid when led and the two of them shared
a bond of battle with each other.

Heldred nuzzled the knight affectionately, nipping at
his dark hair, which brought a laugh from Ursula even as
she wiped the tears from her cheeks with the back of her
hand.

'Ride with me to the edge of town,' Kurt said suddenly,
pulling his gauntlet back on. Ursula paused for a moment,
taken aback by the change in routine.

'What?' she stammered.

'Ride with me. I'll go by the western road first, back past
the shrine and drop you off by the gatehouse.' Kurt
explained. 'I feel like showing you off today, a fine sight
you'll be on the back of Heldred! It won't be a long walk
back.'

As Mika tied the saddlebags to Heldred and Herr Struben
tightened the cinch of the saddle, Kurt mounted, and then
pulled Ursula up across his lap, where she sat precariously
in a side-saddle position, his arms around her holding the
reins.

'I've never ridden a thing in my life before,' Ursula said
nervously. 'I'm going to fall off and break my arm!'

'I'll keep a tight hold, we'll not go fast,' Kurt comforted
her. Heldred's head came up and he whinnied, taking a clattering step to the left.

'Good journey!' Herr Struben wished Kurt, patting
Heldred's flanks.

'Will you be hunting orcs?' Mika asked, his smile beam-
ing.

'If I do, I'll bring you back a head in a sack!' Kurt promised the youth, before gently kicking his heels into Heldred and setting off at a walk.

They had been gone for no more than a few minutes, Kurt's arms clasped tightly around Ursula's waist, when she leant backward and whispered in his ear.

'You can go a little faster if you like,' she urged him.

Without saying anything, the knight pushed Heldred into a trot, and Ursula squealed as she slipped to her left, and he hugged her tighter, the unforgiving metal of his armour chafing slightly against her.

'Faster still?' he asked, smiling down at her.

'Yes, faster still!' she laughed back, slapping his shoulder and pulling him forwards.

With a shout, Kurt dug in his heels and Heldred leapt into a gallop, causing Kurt to laugh and Ursula to shriek girlishly. The horse thundered along the mud throwing up great clods of dirt with his freshly shod hooves. There were few people in the streets as the pair sped across Badenhof, though they had to swerve quickly at the crossroads of Sigmarstrasse and Lernrod when a miller's horse and cart appeared in front of them. His angry shout echoed in their ears, as they laughed together and sped on. They raced back past the Sigmarite church, and Ursula gave a wave to Brother Theobald as he made his way up the steps to the shrine. Heldred galloped on, taking them towards the outskirts, passing Kurt's small two storey townhouse as they turned onto the Bechafenstrasse and towards the town walls. Another part of Lord Gerhardt's bequest, it had once been part of the Gerhardt estate, but now Kurt lived there as a free tenant. The house was small but well appointed, allowing Kurt to live in a small measure of comfort when he visited Ursula. Kurt only wished Ursula could live there while he was away, but it was better not to fuel the wagging tongues of the townsfolk.

It was on the Bechafenstrasse, just as they were storming up the hill towards the east well, that Ursula saw Frau Linde. Walking back towards them, a yoke laden with two brimming buckets across her shoulders, Kurt's neighbour gave an angry snarl as Heldred ran past. Ursula couldn't suppress the

laugh which burst from her lips as she looked back over her
shoulder and saw Frau Linde roundly cursing them.

It was only a short while before they reached the gatehouse, the crumbling towers covered with ivy, the shutters
on the windows mildewed and broken. The town could no
longer afford to employ permanent watchmen, and mainte-
nance of this gatehouse, just like the other on the opposite
side of Badenhof, had ceased a few years ago. The town leaders claimed vehemently that prosperity would return soon,
but few believed their promises of fortune and wealth.

Kurt slowed Heldred to a trot as they passed under the
rusting iron portcullis, and then pulled him to a stop.
Ursula slipped off the horse's back, almost losing her footing on the uneven ruts of the road. Kurt did not dismount,
but pulled the horse round so that he could bend down and
kiss Ursula on the cheek. He did not say anything, but
kicked Heldred into a walk again and rode away, not looking back. He had told her once that he would never look
back, lest he change his mind and never leave. Ursula had
laughed, saying that he always put his duty first. He had
protested that she was the most important thing in his life,
but she assured him that if it were any other way, she would
probably love him less.

She stood there for a long while and watched the receding
shape of horse and rider become nothing more than an
indistinct blob, which then passed out of sight over the
brow of a hill. With a heavy sigh, Ursula turned on her heel
and paced slowly back through the gateway.

It was a long trudge back up the Bechafenstrasse for
Ursula, her heart heavy with loneliness. With Kurt gone
again, she was going to have to fend for herself. It was nothing new to her, even since they had met. She would do what
she always did: spend her time tending the shrine and gardens to earn her board in the outhouse. She would attend
prayer sessions held by Brother Theobald and perform her
own morning ritual. And she would spend her other waking
hours counting down the time until Kurt returned.

She longed for the time when they could marry and move
to Bechafen and live in the Ostermark's capital. Over all the
years of her wandering from town to village to town, she

had felt herself inexorably drawn northwards towards that great city. She had felt that somehow Sigmar had guided her along some path he had laid down for her. Always fuelled by the belief, she had pressed on. Whenever she had been cast out, chased from her many homes, or accused of witchcraft, she had turned to Sigmar time and time again and he had led her onwards. And now that faith and patience was paying off. She had come here to Badenhof and by chance encounter, or perhaps the will of Sigmar, she had met Kurt.

Ursula remembered that day as she walked slowly back towards the shrine, passing the well where they had nearly run down Frau Linde. It had been cold, blustery and she had been pulling weeds from the flowerbeds in the eastern consecrated gardens. She could picture herself, slightly damp and dishevelled, her long, wind-tossed hair stuck to her face, her hands covered in dirt and her long grey woollen skirt patched and stained.

The creak of the gate opening had cut through her idle thoughts and she had turned to see who it was. There, under the natural arch formed by the two yew trees that flanked the gate, stood a handsome young knight, his horse tethered to the post just outside. She had thought she was dreaming at first, as he stood there gazing along the path towards the shrine. Like most young girls, when she had been small she had often daydreamed about a brave, virtuous knight falling in love with her, and she laughed to herself at the memory. Looking at Kurt, he had seemed slightly confused. She had stood up, dusted herself down as best she could and walked over to him. He was even more handsome up close, with dark eyes, a strong chin, and a stern expression on his face.

He had not noticed her at first, but as she got closer, his gaze moved from the church to her face and she was trapped in that instant. Looking back, Ursula wondered what it was that had instantly attracted her to Kurt. Naturally suspicious from her harsh life, she had trusted nobody, but looking into the knight's face she had been filled with the urge to tell him everything about herself, even though they had just met. He had asked, in his quiet polite way, if this was the shrine of Brother Theobald, and she had said yes. She had later found out that the priest's older brother had been a knight in the Osterknacht, alongside Kurt, and he had been sent to bring news of the death of Theobald's kin.

'You wretched child!' Frau Linde's voice cut through Ursula's thoughts like a saw through a rusted nail, grating on her nerves immediately. The middle-aged woman was glaring at Ursula over the low wall surrounding the Linde cottage that sat next to the shrine, a black shawl wrapped tightly around her head and shoulders, giving her thin, pinched face the appearance of a crow's.

'And good morning to you, Frau Linde,' Ursula replied curtly, turning her look of agitation away and continuing towards the church. She knew exactly where the exchange would go, the two of them having long since dropped any pretence of civility. This morning, Ursula simply was not in the mood for one of Emerelde's haranguing outbursts.

'Don't ignore me, you worthless strip of a girl,' rasped Emerelde Linde, pointing a thin finger at Ursula, the finger-nail blackened and cracked. 'I see the way you've bewitched that man! There's many a hard-working lass in this town deserves a fine young man like him, and yet it's you, wastrel and harlot that you are, who turns the handsome head of Knacht Leitzig.'

'You speak, of course, of your own daughter, the enchanting Gelda,' Ursula responded. Like many of the town's womenfolk, Gelda had seen Kurt several times and made plans for wedlock, but her ruddy complexion, wide hips and second chin were less than appealing to the handsome knight.

Though she knew she should not bite on the bait dangled by the meddling housewife, Ursula could not stop herself. She turned back towards the cottage and strode up to the wall to stand face to face with her critic. It was nothing new, at least once a week they would have these vitriolic exchanges, and on more than one occasion Ursula had felt like pulling out the interfering woman's hair and gagging her with it. 'Perhaps the smell of a fish is not quite the perfume Kurt wishes to wake to every morning.'

'She's loyal and steady, just what a man needs to warm his hearth and bed, not a flighty bed-hopper like you,' Frau Linde replied venomously. 'I see your strange ceremonies, I see you talking to yourself. You're tainted – tainted by dark things.'

'The only dark thing is this town is its hospitality,' Ursula argued back. 'You've never shown me any charity or kindness since I arrived.'

It was an old argument, and Ursula resented it every time, and yet could not help herself been drawn into it whenever she met Emerelde Linde.

'Kindness and respect is earned,' sniped Frau Linde. 'You come to this town, drift in and expect to make a life here without working for it. You, a stranger from Taal knows where. You and your strange ways, your sly looks, pouting lips and wicked tongue. We can do without your type of loose morals.'

'My ways may be strange to you,' Ursula said hotly, 'but at least I worship our Lord Sigmar, not one of your old gods. You call on Taal, here outside a shrine to benevolent Sigmar, and you wonder why life has gifted me with love? Perhaps you should look to lay your blame closer to home before you point your accusing finger at me.'

'Blasphemous wench!' Emerelde spat back, with vehemence that shocked even Ursula, who was used to her baseless tirades. 'You dare talk of the gods, you who have perverted the teaching of the holy church? It's not Sigmar that guides your life, it's the darkest witchery, a curse upon those around you from the dark gods.'

With a look of utter disgust, Frau Linde spun on her heel and stalked back into the cottage, the heavy door slamming shut behind her. Ursula stood there for a moment looking at the portal, stunned by the turn of events. Even though she had argued many times with Emerelde, these latest accusations were getting dangerous. Shaking off the daze, she carried on up the road, her thoughts turning back to the vision that had plagued her this morning.

Frau Linde's accusations of witchcraft had shaken her, and she was glad of her decision not to disclose her gift to Kurt. No matter how understanding he might be, he had been brought up by the petty minds of provincial yokels like Linde, and even Ursula could not tell what his reaction would be.

CHAPTER TWO
Purge
Hastelkrentz, Autumn 1708

MARIUS WAS NOT often scared, but he was worried as the sun sank over the rooftops of the fishing village, dipping towards the great lake Krentz, which provided the settlement with its lifeblood. For three weeks he had been in Hastelkrentz, brought here by the auguries of the seer Filandantis. In those three weeks, cultists had made four separate attempts on his life, one even getting so close as to scratch a new scar across his already battered face. And here he was, only twenty men with him, torch in hand, about to storm what might well be the cultists' main hideout. The dockyards stank of fish, unsurprisingly, and the burning torch he held did little to combat the long shadows of the autumn evening. He could hear the men talking quietly amongst themselves and the deep breathing of his trusted lieutenant, Ruprecht, just behind him.

Nightfall was never a good time for a battle, and it was made all the worse by his ignorance of what they might face. His investigations into the missing people and the mutilated bodies found in the village had proved fairly fruitless, and his only lead had brought him in desperation

to the supposedly abandoned warehouse he was now view-
ing. The building was low and long, built of ill-fitting
wooden planks that were slimy with moss and mould.
Someone was definitely inside though, he had seen lights
passing through the cracks between the planks, and shadowy figures coming and going while he had watched. There
was at least one sentry they could see. He was half-hidden
behind a pile of rotting barrels a little further ahead.

'We should wait 'til morning,' Ruprecht said, cutting
through Marius's reverie. 'We have no idea what awaits us in
there.'

The man was soft-spoken for his size. Known by the men
as The Bear, Ruprecht was barrel-chested, broad and well
over six feet tall. Marius had once seen him push a horse cart
over onto a pack of ghouls, when they had uncovered a vile
necromancer in the town of Lowein.

'They might hear word that we have located them,' Marius
argued. 'By dawn, they might vanish. Even now, they might
be waiting for us, gathering their strength. No, we strike
now, and strike hard!'

With that, the witch hunter turned and signalled the rest
of the band forward. He wished he had been able to draw
troops from the village militia, but he had no idea if the offi-
cers of the local watch could be trusted. No, he told himself,
he would have to rely on the handpicked men who had
been loyal to him for years.

They began to run along the street, down the hill
towards the warehouse, quickly but with surprisingly little
noise. They had done this many times before; too many
times in Marius's eyes, for the darkness that now welled
up within the Empire seemed to grow every month,
despite the work of warrior bands like his that moved
from town to town, rooting out the evil creatures of the
world. Some of the men were faster than him, pulling
slightly ahead, but he let them go. Speed and impetus
would carry them inside better than any intricate plan. He
trusted their discipline, and was proved right when the
sentry suddenly stood up, eyes comically wide. Three
arrows flitted through the air almost instantly, two burying themselves into the barricade of barrels, but one

found its target, catching the man high in the chest and pitching him backwards without even a groan.

They were less than a dozen yards from the big double doors of the loading gate when there was a cry from their left. Another sentry sprinted for safety from under a pile of mouldy sacks, heading for a small door at the corner of the dilapidated building. Without pause, Marius and his men surged forward, and the witch hunter drew out his sword, its oiled blade gleaming red in the flames of the brand.

Ruprecht was ahead of the witch hunter, a warhammer clenched tightly in his left hand, a shield gripped in his right. With a thunderous crash he charged the gate, ripping the weak wood from its hinges, and pushed on inside, the others streaming after him. Marius heard a bellow from his second-in-command, and as he passed through the gap with two more men just behind him, he saw the giant warrior striking left and right with the hammer, smashing skulls and bones.

At first glance, Marius guessed they were facing over a score of cultists, men of all ages dressed in tattered rags, wielding rusty knives and short swords. They would be little match for his trained soldiers, who were already cutting into the ranks of the enemy with merciless efficiency.

The witch hunter joined the attack, parrying a wild sword thrust from a teenager with sores down one side of his face, thrusting the torch into the boy's face. The youth leapt backwards screaming, his sword falling from his grasp as he clutched at his seared eyes, and Marius ran his sword through his gut without a second thought. Turning, he leapt after a man even older than he, who was hobbling away towards a flight of stairs to the right. He caught the man at the bottom of the steps and drove the point of his sword between his shoulder blades, the weapon sticking slightly as it caught in the cultist's ribs. Marius glanced up as he struggled to pull the sword free and gave a gasp of horror at what he saw coming down the stairs.

'Sigmar's mercy,' he muttered to himself.

With a ragged black cloak swirling behind it, a skaven leapt down the full length of the stairwell with a single bound of inhuman agility. Nearly as tall as Marius, the rat-man hissed malevolently as it landed just to his side, two notched blades in its hands, its tail whipping left and right. Its fur was matted and mangy, its sharp fangs glistened yellow in the poor light. Marius threw himself backwards as the twin swords lashed out, pulling his own blade free just in time to parry the blow. Without pause, the skaven continued its ferocious attack, forcing Marius back step after step with a flurry of lightning-quick blows.

More of the ratmen were pouring forth from the shadows, their clawed feet scratching on the wooden floor, their chittering screeches filling the warehouse. Marius had no time to see how his men were faring; all his attention was focussed on the creature attacking him. The witch hunter tried a riposte, but his blow was easily turned aside by one of the creature's swords, the other ripping through the black cloth of his shirt across the belly, scoring the toughened leather armour he wore beneath.

With a yell, Marius threw himself forward suddenly, thrusting the burning brand into the midriff of the creature. Its cloak burst into flames instantly, and the fire leapt across its body filling the witch hunter's nostrils with the stench of burning hair. Shrieking, the skaven flailed around wildly, barrelling into its fellow creatures in its panic. Ruprecht appeared from the left, his shield smashing the beast away before the heavy head of the hammer swung down and shattered its skull.

'I want prisoners!' Marius bellowed over the din of the fighting, glancing around to see his men battling with the rat-things. The presence of the skaven boded something far more sinister than he had first realised and he needed answers. Remembering the stairway, Marius hacked the head off a ratman and ran through the throng towards the steps. Leaping up them two at a time, he found himself in a small attic that extended over half the length of the warehouse. There was barely room for him to stand straight, and in the flickering of the torchlight, he could see nothing in the gloom. Making his way forward cautiously, aware that more Chaos ratmen might be waiting in the darkness, he tried to filter out the noise of the fighting below. He thought he heard the chink of metal to his right, in the far corner, and stepped slowly forwards.

Sure enough, trying to hide behind a water cistern, were two men. One was young and fat, and his flabby cheeks were flushed red. The other was a little older, and wiry, his thin face and pointed nose making him look almost as rat-like as his skaven masters. Neither of them seemed armed and they held up their hands in surrender. Below, the noise of the fighting was dying out and he heard Ruprecht calling his name.

There was a creak on the stairs behind Marius and he stepped back so that he could keep his prisoners in view and watch the stairs at the same time. He relaxed when the bulky form of Ruprecht came into view, stooped under the low beams of the ceiling, squeezing his bulk into the attic.

'The skaven fled through the sewer grates,' the burly man reported, shuffling through the gloom. 'I've got the men guarding the entrances in case they come back, but thought it unwise to follow them down there.'

'You did the right thing,' Marius assured him. 'No need to pursue them tonight, no need at all to fight them on their home ground. We have more pressing matters.'

He turned to the two men and motioned them to their feet with his sword. Both had fear on their faces, their eyes were fixed on the grim-faced witch hunter.

'Search them,' Marius told Ruprecht, prodding the two forwards with the point of his blade, absently rubbing at the cut leather across his stomach.

Ruprecht worked efficiently, stripping out their pockets and searching their clothing with his large but nimble hands. Pushing them to their knees, he handed over what he had found to Marius. There were two pouches of coins, gold crowns and silver shillings amounting to a fairly substantial amount of money. There was also a letter, the wax seal broken. Handing the money back to Ruprecht, the witch hunter read the contents. It was addressed to Karl Schullig, apparently a wealthy local merchant. It seemed innocuous enough, a simple bill of lading for a barge, annotated with an invoice for payment.

'Which of you is Schullig?' demanded Marius, thrusting the letter at the captured pair. The younger one raised his hand cautiously.

'This says you shipped a variety of goods along the Talabec. What were you sending, where was it going?' Marius asked.

Schullig remained silent, and his companion's expression changed from fear to angry resentment.

'Who are you to question our business dealings?' the thin man demanded.

'When you consort with foul creatures of Chaos, then your business dealings are open to the scrutiny of any defender of the Empire,' Marius retorted. 'And who are you?'

'I am Klaus van Wenckel,' the man replied, as if his name would mean something.

'Head of the Stevedores' guild,' added Ruprecht. 'He runs half of the warehouses on the dock.'

'And I would bet the content of those pouches that you own this one, don't you?' Marius suggested to Schullig, who nodded mutely, earning himself a scowl from van Wenckel. 'So which of you is pulling the strings?'

Before either replied, a grunt from Ruprecht drew Marius's attention. At a glance from the big mercenary Marius went and stood next to him. Ruprecht passed him one of the coins taken from the men.

'This was minted in Bechafen,' whispered the giant. 'It's from the Ostermark.'

'Trading across the border? I thought the Ottila had banned that?' Marius replied, turning the coin between his fingers.

'Perhaps that was the deal with the skaven?' suggested Ruprecht. 'Their goods would only go along the river as far as the Urskoy, but with some help from our underground friends that would be no problem. What I don't understand is what the ratmen get out of it.'

'Agents within our towns,' Marius replied bluntly. 'You can be sure that Schullig and van Wenckel were more than happy to perform the odd errand or favour in return. You can also be sure that there may be more of them here in Hastelkrentz.'

'And someone must be at the other end receiving the cargo...' realised Ruprecht. 'It seems our two merchants here will have a lot of talking to do tonight.'

'Take them back to the Swan's Wing, quietly,' Marius said. 'Who knows how many others are party to this conspiracy.'

'I'll start heating the tongs,' Ruprecht replied with a grin.

CHAPTER THREE
Honour
Bechafen, Late autumn 1708

KURT WAS LESS than joyful as he crested a hill in the early morning mist and saw the dark shape of Bechafen on the horizon. Pulling Heldred to a stop he sat there for a moment, looking at the city. Just coming into view from beyond the horizon was the great mount on which the Ostermark's capital was built, rising several hundred feet above the fields, farms and villages that clustered around the city like children hanging on the skirts of a protective mother. The high walls and dark towers of Bechafen stood out against the Ostermark Marches; where the forbidding forests that dominated most of the Empire's landscape gave way to treacherous fens and bogs, slowly rising eastwards into a maze of foothills which sat beneath the jagged, ancient peaks of the World's Edge Mountains some two hundred miles from where Kurt sat looking at the city.

Kurt was in a sombre mood on two accounts. Firstly, he already missed Ursula and her happy, selfless presence. Secondly, and in total contrast, he was returning to the chapterhouse of the Osterknacht, a bleak and dreary place where he was held by many of the knights as an upstart. Though he

had some noble lineage – it was impossible to become a
knight without some hereditary claim – many of them
treated him as little more than a commoner who had been
lucky enough to be squired by an ageing and eccentric
knight. He had little time for them either, many were the
pretentious young sons of local nobles playing at soldiers.
Men with real military ambition went westwards to Ostland,
Middenheim or Talabecland, where the state armies were
still well funded and provisioned. Or they sold their services
as dogs of war, their sword arms going to the highest bidder.
The Ostermark could not afford mercenaries, and the pay
for knights was woeful compared to what the claimants to
the Emperor's throne could offer.

Once the Osterknacht had been the pride of the eastern
Empire, rivalling the White Wolves of Middenheim and the
Reiksguard who protected the princes of Altdorf. Now, as the
long years of turmoil took their toll, corruption and nepo-
tism had set in, and there were too few fighting soldiers left
in the ranks of the Osterknacht. The mighty Osterknacht
had once been the protectors of the Empire, watching the
northern borders for foes, and acting as a bulwark against
marauding bands from the mountains to the east. Now they
were little more than an honour guard for a teenage count,
kept in storage to be wheeled out to add a tarnished glitter
to the decaying pomp and ceremony of holidays and
parades.

Realising his foul mood would do little good, Kurt tried to
lift his spirits. Nudging his horse into a walk again, he gazed
along the muddy road that wound its way to the capital and
let his thoughts wander to better times to come. Perhaps by
the summer, he would have enough money to bring Ursula
to Bechafen and wed her. His pay from the Osterknacht,
though good by the standards of many of the Empire's citizens, was only just enough to sustain a knight and his wife
in the capital in a manner that would be deemed fitting.
Ursula deserved the fine clothes and good food of the best
hostelries that the wives of other knights took for granted.
With the small bequest left him by Lord Gerhardt, he could
find a small but well appointed apartment in one of the less
fashionable districts of the city – enough for him and Ursula

to feel comfortable. But before they could do that they needed to be wed, for not only were Ursula and Kurt both reluctant to live outside of wedlock, the laws of the Osterknacht strictly forbade such arrangements. And to be married would cost money, but Kurt felt confident that come summer he would have enough in the guardhouse treasury for a small, dignified service, even if it meant that for now he was forced to endure the heartache of leaving Ursula for three months out of every four while he was on duty. With these happier thoughts, Kurt let the miles pass him by without undue concern.

The hour had just passed midday when Kurt approached the gatehouse at the foot of the road leading up to Bechafen. The gates were thrown wide open as a steady stream of carts and people passed both ways along the road, which for the last mile had been paved with cracking flags and edged with brick. If the legends were to be believed, the road had once all been maintained in similar fashion for some 600 miles, along the old dwarf road from the mountains to Talabheim. Now the count's wealth was so diminished the east-west highway had fallen into disarray barely out of sight of his palaces atop the mount in the centre of Bechafen.

As Kurt joined the line of people making their way slowly through the gateway, the knight looked up the massive hill. Around the base of the mount was the outer curtain wall, the Dragon Wall. Pierced only by this single gate, it rose twenty feet and was hewn from solid mountain rock brought the many leagues here back when the Empire was still growing and the bond with the dwarfs was at its strongest. Some half a mile outside the wall were small makeshift villages of tents and roughly constructed wooden buildings. No building was allowed closer for fear of providing cover to approaching enemies, and so those who had come to the city to find solace, refuge, fortune and fame, but had failed, now hung about its outskirts, looking up at the glories they could no longer afford and which would no longer tolerate their presence. They were the flotsam of life in Ostermark, drawn to the capital but spat out with contempt.

Covered in long grass and bracken, the fell stretched upwards steeply, the inner wall some hundred feet higher than the Dragon Wall, allowing war machines in the many emplacements to fire over the first line of defence. It was within the secondary wall that the city proper began, hidden from view at the moment by the black granite of the formidable defences. But the odd steeple peeked higher above the mighty Griffon Wall, and rising up towards the clouds were the towers and battlements of the central keep, where the count's palace was founded on the ruins of the original longhouse of the Thuringian tribe from whose stock were born the original inhabitants of the Ostermark.

Kurt could not deny that the city was steeped in great tradition. It was here that Count Vandel had held out against the northern horde of Sevir the Blood-terror; from here had marched the great army of Count Hurkon on their way to victory at the Battle of Waldenhof; here that the same Count Hurkon had wedded Mariella of the Reik and founded one of the great alliances of the Empire before the strife had come.

Perhaps great days would come again, Kurt pondered, but he doubted it would be in his lifetime, or in the lifetime of his children, should he and Ursula be blessed with offspring. The likes of Hurkon were near myth nowadays, and his bloodline had dwindled over the centuries. Kurt doubted that the Ostermark would hold out again against the likes of the Blood-terror, nor would the Osterknacht lead out the army in relief of their neighbours. When the orcs had descended on Stirland, the count's orders had been to patrol the borders and turn back the thousands of refugees seeking food and shelter. Here in the north it was as if the troubles of the world were a distant problem, and the co-operation that had built the Empire had turned to self-service and denial.

It was at that moment, as Heldred walked slowly between the pedlars and hawkers, that Kurt realised how much he yearned for a return to those glories. He wished he could ride out with the sun gleaming on his armour, holding aloft the banner of the Ostermark, declaring to the world that the Osterknacht had returned and would right the wrongs of the world. A fanciful, romantic notion, he admonished himself lightly, but perhaps a little more romance and passion was

what the lands needed now. Perhaps heroes were not just
the stuff of legend, but necessary for all people to look up to
and inspire them to increase their own efforts. Where had all
the heroes gone, he wondered?

Passing through the southern gate of the Griffon Wall, its
shadow chilling him after the moderate warmth of the noon
sun, Kurt entered what was considered the true boundary of
Bechafen. Now, at the height of the day, all was business and
bustling crowds. Farmers from the outlying settlements
stocking the stalls of the markets; merchants from other
towns bartering in the streets over furs, pots, silverware and
countless other commodities; cutpurses and pickpockets
stalking the unwary through the throng, plying their villain-
ous trade; beggars holding out palsied limbs, asking for
succour; ladies of low repute offering their services to the
lonely; urchins dressed in rags offering to run errands, looking after horses and belongings, or just haggling for scraps
of food or a copper coin. All of it washed around Kurt as he
urged Heldred through the crowds, the lower end of humanity here in the capital. As he rode into the centre of the city
the crowds thinned and then disappeared, and the square
outside the keep gates was all but deserted.

Kurt rode across the square, noting the four armed knights
standing at the keep gates, his eyes flicking to the flagstaff
atop the central tower. The flag of the Ostermark was flying
high in the sharp winter breeze and beneath it the standard
of the Osterknacht, showing that the elector count was in
residence, and that Lord Lothar, head of the knightly order,
was in attendance today. This did not trouble Kurt unduly;
quite often he had returned to find their commander here in
the capital, having travelled from the chapterhouse in the
southern town of Helsburg.

Kurt dismounted as he approached the eastern gate that
led through to the stables of the guardhouse. The young
man-at-arms on watch was stood to one side, halberd held
casually across the small door at the middle of the gate. At
Kurt's approach, he banged three times on the gate and it
swung open ponderously, accompanied by the grinding of
hidden gears as the old dwarven mechanism squealed into
life inside the keep itself.

Passing through the gate, Kurt dismounted and led Heldred from the sun into a shadowy world lit by countless flickering torches and lanterns. The keep itself was a massive castle, its wall encompassing over a hundred halls, some of them like the courtyard Kurt now entered, merely open spaces linking the other chambers beyond. A wiry, ageing servant with drooping moustaches ambled over and took Heldred's reins and led him toward the stables, while Kurt headed across the flagged ground towards the sentry house to report to the officer on watch. He could hear the faint ringing of metal as the knights and squires practised their swordplay in the hall beyond the sentry chamber, magnified by the high walls and all-encompassing ceiling.

The knight on watch was Karsten, a stocky fellow, ten years Kurt's senior and a member of the Osterknacht since he was eight years old. Karsten was one of Kurt's few allies in the order; a man after his own heart who bemoaned the dilapidation of their quarters and the general decline of the knightly order. When Kurt entered, the sergeant was berating a squire in the sentry room for some real or perceived misdeed. Karsten looked up as Kurt's spurs jingled lightly and his booted feet scraped on the flagstones. Sending the young squire on his way with a clip round the back of his head, Karsten's scowl turned to a grin.

'So the young hero returns to our bosom once more,' he laughed, gesturing Kurt to sit down on one of the padded high-backed seats dotted around the otherwise sparse chamber. 'I take it you were recalled early like me?'

'Yes,' Kurt replied, pulling off his armoured gauntlets and lowering himself carefully into a chair next to the empty fireplace. 'I got word yesterday morning. I wasn't supposed to be back for another five days. Is something happening, I see the commander is here?'

'I fear it's no coincidence,' confirmed Karsten. 'Bayen tells me that he escorted a messenger from Kislev to the count last week. That can't bode well.'

For long centuries, the people of the Ostermark had been close allies with their neighbours in the northern nation of Kislev. Many were the times they had fought side-by-side against a common threat, and few the occasions of conflict.

The Kislevites were a proud people, fearless defenders of their independence from the much larger Empire, but all too often it was they who fell beneath the blade when an army gathered in the northern wastes and set about rampaging southwards through more civilised lands.

A messenger could mean many things. Perhaps it was just a courtesy, a routine diplomatic mission. Perhaps it was more though. It might be a warning, or a summons for aid. If that were the case, given the recall of the Osterknachts' warriors from their homes, it seemed likely that the knightly order would be marching north to fight again.

'And how is our count?' asked Kurt.

'Still young enough to rely on the advice of his counsellors, thank Ulric,' replied Karsten. 'A year or two more though, and I fear he will start to want to flex his political muscles, and he is not ready for it.'

'A boy of thirteen on the throne of Ostermark,' sighed Kurt, gazing into the fireplace. 'Perhaps one day he'll grow up to be a great leader, but will the Ostermark survive long enough to see it?'

'Aye, of course it will,' grinned the other knight. 'With good iron, and some will behind it, we can hold back Ostland, the marauders, orcs and whatever else is thrown at us. You're in a pessimistic mood today, I'd snap yourself out of it before the commander makes his inspection this evening.'

'Perhaps I'm just a little tired from riding,' Kurt covered up his misgivings with a shrug. With a nod to Karsten, he stood up and left, pacing hurriedly across the stone floor towards the knights' quarters. Passing through an archway he walked out onto a landing at the top of the stairs that led down into the main chamber. Here, the arrayed knights and squires took part in mock battle with each other in a vast cavernous space that stretched nearly ten times the height of a man above their heads and some quarter of a mile square. Hewed from the rock of the mount itself, the massive hall was held aloft by thirty mighty pillars, which were now hung with the battle honours of the order. Shields and banners captured as trophies from vanquished enemies hung alongside the colours of the Osterknacht itself and scrolls of merit and commendation from a succession of elector counts, each mounted upon an ornate wooden plaque.

As he walked down the stone steps, Kurt watched as three knights were encircled by twice their number of squires, who jabbed them into a circle back-to-back with their long spears. Hacking away at the tips of their enemies' weapons with their wooden swords, the knights counter-attacked, forming up into a small wedge that drove through the squires and allowed them to break free. No longer confined, the knights set about the squires with a vengeance, despatching bruises and cuts with their mock swords as a physical reminder to the young students.

Reaching the bottom of the stairway, Kurt was confronted by Bayen, another knight not much older than himself, though with many years more service in the order. Bayen and Kurt did not get along well. Kurt thought the distant cousin of the count was a spoilt snob, while Bayen frequently bemoaned Kurt's dubious origins and cursed him for being a foolish country boy.

'So good of you to return to the fold, though I don't know why you bother coming back,' sneered Bayen, wiping the sweat from his long blond hair with a towel. He held his practice sword loosely in one hand, his armour glistening in the light of the hundreds of torches that lit the hall.

'When the call comes, I answer,' Kurt replied quietly, mustering what politeness he could. He took a step to the side to walk around Bayen, but the other knight shifted as well, blocking his route.

'I know why you don't live in Bechafen. Just because she's out of the city, doesn't mean we don't know about your trollop,' Bayen hissed accusingly. 'You bring shame to the order. Sigmar knows why Gerhardt even gave you a second glance, never mind giving you a squirehood.'

'Perhaps he was tired of fighting alongside toads like you,' snapped Kurt in return, instantly regretting his outburst as a hate-filled scowl creased Bayen's boyish looks.

'The only toad around here is that warty creature you've been bedding this last year,' spat Bayen, noticing a number of knights gathering around the pair of them. He cast his glance around the audience as he spoke. 'It's disgusting, but

I suppose we cannot expect better from a dishonourable pig like you. Why don't you leave us? Go back to the sty that you were spawned in, to fornicate to your heart's content and produce more litters.'

'One more word and I'll break your jaw,' warned Kurt. 'You really are a distasteful, spiteful little worm, Bayen, and one of these days it'll be the runts like you that are cast out of the order.'

'Did you hear that?' Bayen said to the knights, his face a mask of indignation. 'He insults me to my face. He actually threatens me in front of witnesses, and then claims it is *I* who am dishonourable. This, from a man who stoops so low as to bed farmers' wenches on his leave and then comes crawling back here with his tail between his legs like a whipped mongrel, when his master calls for him. Is this the type of knight we wish the Osterknacht to be famed for?'

'Ursula is my betrothed,' snarled Kurt in return. 'She is my lady and you would do well to show more respect. Slight her again and I will demand reparation.'

At that point Master Sergeant Viksson intervened, the burly veteran shouldering his way through the crowd to stand between the two young knights, his heavily whiskered face red with anger.

'You're a damnable disgrace, the pair of you!' he bellowed. 'Bickering like school children, and with the commander in the same building no less. Now, make your apologies and get out of my sight before I punish the pair of you.'

'I demand satisfaction,' Kurt growled quietly, drawing a hushed silence from the murmuring crowd. Duelling was a relatively new concept in Bechafen, but was growing in popularity amongst the gentry. By the ancient rites of the order, any knight was allowed to seek judgement by a trial of arms, but rarely was it ever used to accuse a fellow knight.

'What?' Viksson rounded on Kurt. 'Are you tainted? Did you hear what I said? The commander himself is upstairs now, preparing for an inspection in a few short hours time. I'll have none of this on my watch, now take it back.'

'I cannot unsay something which I have said,' Kurt replied stubbornly. 'It is my right as a knight, and my duty as a future husband, to protect the honour of this order and that of my wife to be. I demand to face Bayen this evening in front of the commander himself!'

Viksson glanced at the young knight, Bayen, who was staring incredulously at Kurt. Noticing the old knight's gaze, Bayen regained his composure and shrugged.

'Fine,' he said flippantly, 'if Leitzig is fool enough to face me, then I accept.'

'And if I win, you will apologise publicly for any slight against myself and my lady?' Kurt insisted.

'Of course. If the trial of arms proves you correct, I will offer my most sincerest apology,' agreed Bayen, before turning away. The knight took a few steps before turning to look Kurt straight in the eye.

'But if I win, then my case is proven,' Bayen said slyly. 'If you lose, then you must renounce your pledge of loyalty, leave the Osterknacht and never come back to Bechafen.'

'You go too far!' shouted Kendil Hark, one of the knights watching the exchange.

'Apologising to this guttersnipe would be an equal disgrace,' retorted Lord Helfen, who never made any attempts to hide the fact that he was one of Bayen's sycophantic lackeys, though he was nearly ten years the young knight's senior.

'What's it to be, Leitzig?' Viksson demanded, betraying his own loyalty to the royal blood that flowed within Bayen's veins. 'Withdraw now and apologise, or face the consequences? The demands have been laid out in true accordance with the laws of the order. What's it to be?'

Kurt thought for a moment. In all honesty he had nothing to lose, he thought at first. Most of the knights were against him here anyway, many of them as bad as Viksson and Helfen in their favouritism. If he lost, he would be shamed and dishonoured, but a small part of him was glad at the thought that he might be forced to leave the order and walk away from all these troubles. He could return to Badenhof and marry Ursula.

He could also see the disappointment in her eyes at the news. He could hear the sly talk and gossip behind his back from the petty-minded townsfolk. What good would it do Ursula? She was already hounded and mistrusted, and to be associated with a dishonoured knight would probably break her. All he had to do was withdraw his claim to judgement and none of it would be at risk. It would mean losing face in front of the knights, but he had little enough respect from them as it was.

Kurt looked at Bayen's eager face, one blond eyebrow raised in question. He thought of the horrid things the count's cousin had said about Ursula, a woman he had never met, and of all the small slights and slurs that had come before and would come after. Yes, if he retracted now, he was not only condemning himself to more torment, but also approving of Bayen's insults against Ursula. Kurt's rashness and enmity with Bayen had finally got him into a tight spot, and he could see no way out. There was only one way this could be put right. He had to fight and beat Bayen.

'I will face you tonight on the terms we have agreed,' Kurt said finally. 'And I will be the victor, for right, justice and the gods are on my side.'

'I bloody hope they are,' whispered Hark in his ear as Kurt pushed his way through the throng, the veteran falling into step beside him. 'Bayen's quick as viper, you know that.'

'I can beat him,' Kurt said confidently, glancing across at Hark's concerned face. 'I have to.'

THE MOOD INSIDE the great hall was subdued as Kurt entered through the great double doors at the eastern end. The immense fire pit to Kurt's left blazed with a flame reaching high towards the ceiling, bathing the rough stone walls in a ruddy glow. Around the edges of the chamber stood the assembled knights of the Osterknacht, resplendent in full ceremonial armour, standing beside them their squire holding aloft their colours. With no squire of his own, Kurt's colours were held by Jakob, the manservant who had taken Heldred from him earlier, a half-Kislevite by birth. It was yet another example of the low esteem in which Kurt was held, that no other knight had come forward to bear his banner. The pale blue blazon, with a simple silver crown motif at its centre, hung limply from its plain oaken staff. They were not the traditional colours of House Leitzig, but that was Kurt's secret, for if the purple and gold of

Leitzig was ever remembered it was with memories of shame and anger. Kurt had hidden his origins for the last fourteen years, claiming to be from a distant branch of the family that had moved across the border to Stirland. If the truth ever came out, it would not only guarantee his expulsion from the Osterknacht, but could well see him on trial for treason and witchcraft. Those secrets were best left buried.

In contrast, the master sergeant Viksson bore Bayen's banner on the opposite side of the hall to Kurt, a long pennant edged with gold thread, with crossed swords against a field of deep purple, the royal colour of the Ostermark. Bayen himself wore his battle armour, but even so, the full plate mail suit was chased with fine veins of silver and gold, which glittered in the firelight. He held his helmet beneath one arm, its purple plume hanging to the floor, and lazily stroked his long hair with his free hand, chatting quietly with Viksson.

'I heard you called him coward,' whispered Jakob from behind Kurt, his voice tinged with a northern accent. Kurt turned to the retainer, his face impassive. Jakob's eyes flitted keenly between Viksson and Bayen. His narrow face gave him a rodent-like appearance, and he wore long drooping moustaches in the manner of the northern tribes, something that had fallen out of fashion in the Empire several centuries ago. The man's thin fingers fidgeted on the banner staff, and he seemed on edge. Kurt also noted fresh bruising on the servant's knuckles.

'No, but I should have done,' Kurt answered after a moment. 'He insulted my lady, I seek judgement to clear her sullied name.'

'That's what I said, I said it was your lady's honour,' Jakob answered earnestly. 'They didn't take kindly to me saying, some trouble started, nothing much to mind.'

'Thank you anyway,' Kurt said, turning back to look at Bayen. Their gaze met and the smile faded from the blond knight's lips and was replaced by a curling sneer.

At that moment, the main doors to Kurt's left opened and there was a metallic ringing as the assembled knights and squires saluted, banging their fists against their chestplates.

Through the door walked Lord Lothar, Commander of the Osterknacht, flanked by the Lords Militant, Trevigar and Steinlend. He was dressed in a flowing robe trimmed with black fur, and about his neck on a thick golden chain hung the badge of his office, a shield emblazoned with two rearing dragons. He was old but sturdy, his face lined with the years but his body showing that there was much strength and vigour left in his old frame. Nearly sixty, Lothar had served as the commander for twenty years, well respected by the knights and the count's advisors, he was possibly the most powerful man in the Ostermark. To Kurt's eyes he looked displeased, and as well he might, he considered ruefully. He was here in the city on important military or state matters, and now he had to come down here to officiate a petty squabble between two of his junior knights.

Striding to the centre of the room, midway between all of the assembled knights, Lord Lothar looked at Kurt, then at Bayen.

'We are in grim times,' he said, voice booming, used to bellowing commands to his men over the din of battle. 'This very week I have arrived from the southern borders to hear news of a new enemy threatening the Ostermark. I come here to build an army, and what do I find? My own household riven with domestic discord. My men-at-arms growing fat and lazy. My knights, my proud and noble Osterknacht, fighting amongst themselves like old maids.'

He paused and his eyes scanned the circumference of the hall, spending no more time on Kurt and Bayen than any other individual there. It was clear that Lord Lothar's displeasure stretched far wider than Kurt's run-in with Bayen.

'In just a few short days we will be marching from this keep to do battle with a dreaded foe, and yet I must put aside my plans, my orders of march, my provisioning rosters and my mustering records. I must delay my next consultation with our count and his wise counsellors. And why must I do this?' Lord Lothar's expression was like a thundercloud and his next words were shouted at a volume as deafening as a storm. 'I must do this because my knights can no longer discipline themselves! Heed my words well, this campaign we are about to embark on is vital to the defence of our homes. The man who falls out of line, the man who fails to bear his burden of duty, the man who does not do his utmost in the coming war will fall beneath my blade, and good riddance to him.'

Once more he paused, and this time he looked directly at Kurt.

'You have asked for a judgement, is that correct?' the commander asked.

'I have asked for a trial by arms, my lord commander,' acknowledged Kurt with a nod. 'I challenge that the honour of my betrothed has been besmirched by Hans Bayen, and I demand full apology if my cause be proven right.'

'Very well,' Lord Lothar responded before turning to Bayen. 'And you too accept this judgement?'

'Aye, my lord commander, I do,' Bayen replied confidently. 'If I am proved in the right, then Kurt Leitzig shall quit the order with full dishonour and be banished from the city and regions of Bechafen.'

'Very well,' Lord Lothar said again. 'Then by the right invested in me as Commander of the Osterknacht, I hereby pledge that the following trial by arms be conducted according to the laws and traditions of our order. The trial shall be with blunted weapons and to submission. The victor's cause is proven aright, and the submitter will face the full penalty of his false case. Proceed.'

As Lord Lothar strode back towards the doors, a great noise shook the chamber as the assembled squires began to bang the hafts of their banners on the stone floor. The crashing echoed around Kurt, but was muffled as he placed his helmet over his head. Jakob leaned forward and handed him a long hand-and-a-half sword, its edges very obviously filed down and dull. He glanced at the monogram on the pommel and realised it had once belonged to Lord Gerhardt. Glancing at Jakob, his inquiring look was answered by a sly wink.

'Thought it appropriate,' Jakob confessed with a mutter. 'Hope I did no wrong by it.'

'You did well,' Kurt assured the manservant, looking back at Bayen, who was now stepping across the floor of the hall, his shield on his left arm, a single edge cavalry sword in his right hand.

Kurt started towards Bayen, swinging the blade back and forth a little to get its weight and balance. It was a good blade, and Kurt thought it a cruel irony that it had been reduced to a mere training weapon now. Perhaps the memory of Lord Gerhardt was fading quicker than Kurt realised. That memory had served him well on occasion, but if the old knight's patronage was now falling out of favour it could mean nothing more than greater difficulties for Kurt in the future. Putting aside these thoughts, Kurt concentrated on Bayen.

The count's cousin moved quickly and with calm assurance. He almost strutted towards Kurt, glancing left and right at his supporters. He stopped ten feet away and raised his sword to his visor in salute. Kurt copied the action before dropping the blade down and assuming a fighting stance, his weight on his back foot, sword held forward. Bayen turned slightly to present his shield arm towards Kurt and took a couple of quick steps forward and to his opponent's right.

Kurt began to move to his left, and the two of them circled each other warily. Bayen may have been arrogant, but he was a good fighter and knew better than to underestimate any opponent. His eyes were locked on Kurt's, dark within the visor of his helm. Kurt was also concentrating fully on his opponent, watching the weaving tip of his blade, seeking some weak point in his defence.

Without warning, Bayen stepped back to his right and lunged forward with a harsh shout, his sword tip thrust towards Kurt's abdomen. With a pace back, Kurt parried the quick blow to the left, rolling his wrists and bringing his own sword around and up towards Bayen's groin. With a clang, the other knight's shield intercepted the attack, deflecting Kurt's sword upwards. Bayen thrust again beneath Kurt's raised sword, forcing him to jump to the left and bring the pommel of his sword down onto Bayen's outstretched arm. The two separated after the exchange of blows, putting a few yards between each other. The thunderous banging of the banner poles by the squires continued to echo around the hall, and Kurt could feel his heart beating hard in his chest, his body surging with energy. He could see that Bayen was breathing heavily too, and pushed himself forward towards the blond knight, sword held low and to the right, swinging it across at head height.

Again, Bayen's shield blocked the strike but the force of the blow knocked him back a step, allowing Kurt to reverse the direction of the sweeping attack and come in from his left. The other knight's sword crashed against his own, pushing the blade down towards the floor. Bayen threw himself forward, his shield slamming into Kurt and pushing him backwards. Kurt back-stepped quickly to retain his balance, but Bayen launched a series of blistering attacks with his sword, aiming first at his head, then his midriff and then a downward cut towards Kurt's chest, each blow parried aside by Kurt's bastard sword.

Having weathered Bayen's offensive, Kurt strove to retake the initiative. He feinted a blow to Bayen's legs, before releasing one hand from the sword and punching him full in the face. However, Bayen was fast to recover and by the time Kurt had got both hands back on the sword for a powerful downward stroke, the count's cousin had his shield raised to ward away the attack.

Kurt realised his best hope of winning was to wear Bayen down – the heavy blows from his bastard sword kept the blond knight off balance and unable to counter-attack, although every time he prepared to swing, Kurt was leaving himself open for a swift thrust by Bayen. The two of them duelled in this manner for several more minutes until the sweat was pouring off Kurt inside his armour, stinging his eyes and clogging his nose. Both of them were gasping for breath and their blows became slower and heavier. It was then that a cunning ploy occurred to Kurt. Bayen was the sort who was so centred on himself it was not likely he had paid much attention to Kurt during practice sessions. He was unlikely to know that Kurt could fight equally well with his left or right hand, and that could prove an advantage.

Dodging to his right, Kurt manoeuvred Bayen so that the other knight was standing to Kurt's left hand side. Bayen, fooled by the trick, attacked against what he thought was

Kurt's weaker side. Kurt swapped his grip on the hilt of his broadsword and reversed the direction of his parry, forcing Bayen's sword across his body and overbalancing him. Kurt once more let go of his sword, this time with his right hand, grabbed Bayen's shield and smashed it back into his helmeted face. A split second after, Kurt's sword crashed against the back of Bayen's right knee, buckling his leg and sending him toppling to the ground. Kurt followed up relentlessly, kicking away the other knight's shield and ramming the point of his sword into the gap between breastplate and helm. Pulling the blow at the last moment, the tip of the sword hovered over Bayen's neck. Even blunted, it could crush his windpipe with ease.

'Yield?' snarled Kurt, stamping down on Bayen's sword arm, pinning it to the flagstones.

'I yield...' hissed Bayen, letting go of his sword, which clattered beside Kurt's foot.

'I look forward to your apology,' Kurt replied, smiling grimly inside his helmet.

CHAPTER FOUR
Suspicion
Badenhof, Late winter 1708

URSULA LOOKED BACK at her footprints in the snow and wrapped her woollen cloak more tightly around her shoulders. Already they were beginning to fill up with fresh snow as the heavy fall continued. For three weeks blizzards and winds had enveloped the town, confirming earlier fears that the winter would be harsh. Hooking her basket further up her arm, she forged through the blustery wind, determined to buy fresh bread today after putting off her visit to the bakers for several days, eking out the few stale scraps from her last visit.

The town was blanketed in snow, a stark whiteness against the black timbers that made up many of the buildings. Smoke drifted along the Sigmarstrasse as it billowed from every home, combining with the snow to cut down the distance she could see to just a few feet. The walls of houses and shops were dim shadows on the edge of her vision, as were the occasional dark silhouettes of the few other souls who braved the bitter weather.

Every sound was muffled too, adding to the feeling of isolation that Ursula felt. The town had closed in on itself, cut off from even the nearby farms by blocked roads. The few merchants still with fresh stock had hiked their prices beyond the means of someone as poor as her, and bread was all she could afford to eat except for the broth she made from the mouldering vegetables she had, supplemented occasionally by the meagre strips of gristly meat that Brother Theobald brought to her at the start of each week. Her stomach growled with hunger as she walked through the heavy snow, her legs dragging, and she unconsciously rubbed a hand across her empty belly.

The poor food and bitter weather meant that disease was already beginning to take a grip on Badenhof. Frequently she had seen people with pinched, sallow faces, and many youngsters were said to be suffering from 'horse cough' – a virulent, but so far not deadly infection that attacked the lungs and throat. Ursula had stayed in good health, mainly due to her isolation, but others were afflicted with scabrous rashes and prominent boils.

If the weather persisted then soon it would be pickled vegetables and what was left of the salted meat, and with that would come more poxes. She had seen it before, when she was just a girl and the red famine had plagued southern Ostermark. She had seen the desperation in the villagers' eyes, and they had taken to eating horses, dogs and even the rats that had gorged themselves on what little grain had remained. Half of the village had died from disease and starvation, people had been killed by their neighbours, and the survivors had deserted the town.

She was scared. In fact, when she sat on her rough pallet at night and listened to the howling wind outside the loft she lived in, she was terrified and lonely. She fretted about Kurt's absence, and longed for him to return, but it was not likely. More than that, she had felt the townsfolk becoming even more distant from her than normal. Though she had lived there for two years, she was still considered a stranger. When belts had to be tightened, she knew the charity of Brother Theobald would wear thin and there would be no hospitality offered by any of the town's other inhabitants.

As she approached the main square, she could make out more figures around her. Approaching through the blizzard, she saw a milling crowd at the foot of the steps leading up to the town hall. There was angry murmuring, and she was roughly shouldered aside and shoved as she tried to pick her way through. Recognising Herr Fleischkemp, the baker, she pushed through the crowd towards him.

'What's all the commotion?' she asked him, tugging on the sleeve of his heavy, snow-covered coat. He had obviously been stood there for quite a while.

'Body's been found, up near the Stein grain store,' he replied shortly, giving her a glance from under his deep red hood.

'A body?' Ursula asked incredulously. 'Who found it? Who's died?'

'That's the damnedest thing,' the baker said, turning fully to her. 'It was Michel Stein himself, and he died two months ago!'

'What?' gasped Ursula.

'Yes, you heard me right,' said Fleischkemp. 'Somebody checked the graveyard, body was dug up right out of the ground.'

Ursula shuddered and stepped away, glancing over the others. Looking around, she saw that the macabre news was spreading fast, and more people were hurrying in to the square despite the foul weather. There was movement near the town hall doors and someone trod on her foot as the crowd surged forward before two of the guild watchmen appeared and shoved the mob back with the shafts of their halberds.

Ludwig Kirche, guildmaster of Badenhof, emerged from the door. Tall and skinny, he looked a lot heavier swathed in a sheepskin cloak, his pointed nose poking out from under the brim of a black hat.

'Get back!' he snapped, making shooing gestures with his right hand, each finger adorned by a gold ring. 'Get back and give me space!'

Pulling himself up to his full height, he towered a head above everyone else in the square, He glowered at the crowd, casting his gaze to the left and right, and a hush fell.

'Go back to your homes,' he snarled. 'Go back to your warm hearths, out of this foul weather. You have no business haranguing us here.'

'What are you doing about the strange goings-on?' a voice called from near the back of the crowd. 'Ain't safe to walk the streets!'

'The food stores are running low. What will we have to eat come the end of the week?' another voice chipped in.

'What's happened to the boy, Timold?' came a woman's voice.

Ursula darted a quizzical glance at Herr Fleischkemp. The baker bent down to whisper in her ear.

'Three children have gone missing in the last two weeks,' he told her quietly. 'All three from around the Bergmund.'

'The Bergmund, that's where the Stein houses are,' Ursula replied, getting a nod from Fleischkemp in confirmation. 'Do you think there is some kind of connection?'

'Not for us to say, is it?' the baker replied pointedly, looking back at Herr Kirche, who was conferring with one of the guards.

'Investigations are still inconclusive,' the guildmaster declared after a moment.

'Still inconclusive?' barked a short, thickset man just behind Ursula. 'No surprise there, when you've stripped the watch down to a couple of retired militia men.'

'We will review the present strength of the watch at our guild meeting in two days' time,' growled Kirche. 'Stop this scare-mongering and get on with your lives.'

'Where's Burgomeister Koln?' the man demanded. 'We want to see the man we voted for, not the guilds' spokesman!'

'Burgomeister Koln is currently indisposed with a head cold, brought on by the inclement climate,' Kirche replied smoothly, obviously using a well-rehearsed phrase. 'I will convey your concerns to him shortly, and when he is well enough he will call an open meeting of the town councillors.'

With no further word, and ignoring the angry shouts hurled at his back, Kirche disappeared back in to the town hall.

'I don't envy him,' muttered Fleischkemp as the crowd began to disperse. Ursula fell in step beside him as they began to trudge through the snow back towards his shop, which was a short way off the main square.

'How so?' Ursula countered. 'He's the richest man in Badenhof, and if some of the gossip is to be believed, the most powerful too. It seems that he has control of the council as well as the guilds.'

'Yes, and a winter like this one could destroy him,' explained the baker, pulling his hood tighter around his cheeks and rubbing his hands together. 'He made most of his money and power by bringing the guilds together, but to do that he poured in his own family's funds to provide assurances and backing for many of the smaller merchants and artisans.'

'So?' Ursula asked. 'Prices are rising rapidly, surely he is getting his share of the profits?'

'Aah, but that's the rub isn't it?' Fleischkemp replied with a grimace. 'The prices go up but profits are down. The food is running out, we're totally ill prepared for this, and that will be blamed on the guilds. Kirche lined his pockets over the last years when the going was not too bad, but now he's going to have to pay back on those assurances when businesses close because we have nothing to sell, and there's no love for the guilds amongst many of the common people.'

They reached the shop and the baker shouldered open the door, kicking the snow off his boots before stomping inside and pulling his cloak off. Ursula followed suit, taking the cloth off the top of her basket and shaking the snow onto the low step. Inside it was warm and welcoming, filled with the smell of freshly baked bread, the oven glowing ruddily from behind the counter. The racks that flanked the door to the oven room were almost bare, the few loaves on the shelves were small and misshapen.

'I'm eking out the flour as long as I can,' Fleischkemp explained after noticing Ursula's look. 'I've got three and a half sacks left, but if the weather doesn't ease there'll be no more from the mills for a while yet.'

'I heard there were rats in Stein's store,' Ursula commented, placing her basket on the counter.

'That's the real rub,' Fleischkemp replied with a sad shake of his head. 'That's been the real disaster, and there's no explaining it. The granaries over on the other side of town have had no problems, but like everyone else they've raised their prices. The rich folk don't want to come out in this snow and I can't afford to keep a delivery boy, so they go elsewhere. That means I can't afford more flour, and I pay good money to keep a shop here so close to the market square.'

'Well, here's a little custom, thought not much I'm afraid,' Ursula said with a rueful smile, picking a handful of pennies from the pocket of her coat and dropping them on to the counter top. Kurt always gave her a little money while he was away, but she was loth to spend too much, as she had no idea when he would return. At the same time, she hated living on charity, whether it was Brother Theobald's or Kurt's.

'I feel a little bad, putting prices up and taking more money from people at a time like this, ' the baker told her, but he still swept the coins into his hand and placed them in a drawer beneath the counter. He took a loaf from the shelves and deftly wrapped it in the cloth proffered by Ursula. 'But I guess it helps nobody if I starve as well.'

'You're too kind-hearted to be a merchant,' joked Ursula, receiving a woeful nod in reply. Placing the loaf in her basket, she took a step towards the door before turning back to the baker.

'I could do with a couple of shillings to add to what I have,' she said. She preferred not to talk about the money Kurt left her; the townsfolk would no doubt twist the meaning behind it to something sordid. 'I could make deliveries for you if you like, and I'll be cheaper than anyone else.'

Fleischkemp avoided her gaze and busied himself under the counter for a moment.

'What's wrong with that?' Ursula demanded, feeling her temper rising. 'Why not?'

'Well,' the baker replied without meeting her eye, 'I'd lose more customers than I gained.'

'How so?' Ursula asked, striding back to the counter. 'You said yourself you'd get more of the households from around the square.'

'Yes, and lose the ones on the Sigmarstrasse and Bechafenstrasse,' he replied defensively. 'There's families round here asked me for jobs for their sons or daughters who I've had to turn down, and they'd not come back if they see I've given one to you. You know you're not the most popular lass in the town, and some folks would turn their backs on me too. And besides, those that can afford delivery can afford to send servants out, and people with money prefer not to spend more than they have to.'

Ursula's anger subsided and was replaced by sadness. Without further word, she turned and started to walk out. As she pushed open the door, she looked back at Fleischkemp.

'In two years here, no one has given me a chance,' she said bitterly. 'How long am I going to be the outsider, the stranger? Kurt wasn't born here, yet he's welcomed like a long lost son.'

'I'm afraid that's people for you,' the baker said after a moment. 'He's a knight, he makes them feel like Badenhof is important. What do you do for them?'

IT WAS THREE more weeks of tension, arguments and recriminations before things came to a head. More bodies had gone missing from the graveyards, the weather had let up slightly and news had arrived from outside the town. The news was not encouraging. Livestock had died in droves out on the farms, and many were still cut off by the extremely harsh conditions. The roads were still too clogged with snow for carts and what little food that came in was carried on horseback. These meagre supplies had been quickly snapped up by the richer town inhabitants, who offered more money for fresh meat than the bulk of the population could even dream of matching.

There was also news from further afield. With the sporadic arrival of merchants and farmers came growing rumours that a small army was currently moving across the north of the Ostermark, led by the witch hunter Marius van Diesl. Some speculated that he was going to the capital, Bechafen, but others claimed that his route was more southerly, and that he was on his way to Badenhof. This caused mixed reactions. There were those who said the witch hunter would be welcome, and that he would root out the cause of the grave-robbing and missing children. The town leaders argued against this, claiming that outside interference was the last thing that was needed, and that the perpetrators of the ghastly crimes would go to ground if such a force arrived. The more suspicious of the townsfolk began to point accusing fingers at their neighbours, and under pressure from the merchants and craftsmen, three dozen more men had been drafted into the town watch to patrol the richer neighbourhoods and the market square. This in itself had caused upset, since they were all guild members currently out of work due to the collapsing economy of the town.

In that time Ursula had tried to keep to herself, out of harm's way and the ever more spiteful accusations of Emerelde Linde. Despite this, she went to the shrine every day and prayed. She prayed for the people of Badenhof to show patience and tolerance, even though she cursed them inwardly for their narrow-mindedness and superstitious natures. It was during her morning ritual that trouble caught up with her.

Ursula was kneeling before the statue of Sigmar as usual, having placed her garland about his arm. The main doors slammed open and the tramp of booted feet caused the young woman to turn and look to see what the commotion was. Four men marched into the church. They wore red ribbons tied around their left arms, identifying them as deputised watchmen. Behind them, Ursula could see Frau Linde.

'That's her, she's the one!' the housewife called out in her shrill voice, pointing at Ursula.

As the men approached closer, Ursula stood, annoyed at the interruption.

'Leave me to pray in peace!' Ursula snapped, tossing her head in agitation, wisps of red hair falling across her face.

'You're Ursula Schek?' one of the men demanded, an unshaven and unkempt fellow only a little older than Ursula herself.

'Who are you?' Ursula shot back, jabbing a finger at the four of them. 'Who are you to barge into Sigmar's house and disturb his worshippers?'

'I'm Klaus Kurntz, town watch,' the man replied, stepping forward. 'Accusations have been made, and I've orders to take you to the watch house to answer some questions.'

'Accusations?' Ursula replied, fighting to keep her temper. She looked at Emerelde. 'From her?'

'Look, just come with us and it'll be sorted out, alright?' said the portly man just behind Kurntz. He was an ex-joiner she knew, called Fredrick Bille, who had been out of work for a year at least. He seemed embarrassed to be there, and when she looked at the others, she could tell that she had been overly harsh on them. They looked plaintively at her, obviously not at ease with what they had to do, silently willing her to come quietly with them.

'Wait for me outside while I finish my prayers,' she told them. When they hesitated, she crossed her arms and gave them a withering stare and they started to walk away.

'What are you doing?' shrieked Emerelde. 'Arrest her like you were told to!'

The group of men ignored her, one of them grabbing her gently by the arm and guiding her outside. Ursula took a moment to calm herself, breathing deeply to regain some composure. She would go when she was good and ready.

THE OLD WATCH house had been very busy of late with the growing troubles of the town. It was situated at the northeastern corner of the town hall, on the opposite side to the market square. Cut into the street where the cobbles met the watch house wall were a dozen small cell windows, each a semicircle in shape and roughly a foot across, unglazed and barred with wire mesh. The smell of effluent wafted out from the cells beyond, tainting the crisp winter air. The clink and rattle of chains and echoing murmur of voices broke the early morning silence.

As Klaus opened the heavy iron door to the watch house, a wave of noise washed over the group. Babbling voices competed with shouts, sobs, bellows of anger and wailing children. With two watchmen in front and two behind her, Ursula was shepherded into the building into the roiling crowd.

The hall in which they stood was a low and wide square. Just overhead the wooden ceiling was supported by thick beams that brushed the top of people's heads, and at its centre the town's arms were carved out in age-worn relief. The stone walls were blackened by smoke from torches in open sconces, and the air was thick with the smell of people and

guttering brands. Packed between the bare stone brickwork
was a sea of people. The red flashes of the watchmen's armbands were everywhere; scuffling with surly-looking youths,
comforting crying women, arguing with their charges and
each other. Behind a counter built up out of the stone floor
itself, three watch captains vainly tried to instil some form
of order; alternating between outright threats and
unashamed pleading. Ursula's group shouldered their way
through the throng until they were stood in front of one of
the captains.

'Ah, Kurntz,' exclaimed the man, a bleary-eyed fellow in his
middle age, with a distinctive jagged scar running from his
chin across his right cheek. Ursula recognised him as one of
the regular watchmen who used to patrol the Bechafenstrasse
near the shrine, who had obviously been promoted to try to
control the recent influx of inexperienced recruits. 'Yes, this is
the Schek woman. Take her to the magistrate!'

Before she could say anything, Ursula was pulled by the
arm through an archway to the right of the counter and
pushed unceremoniously down the corridor beyond into a
small antechamber. There she was made to sit on a bench
ornately carved from dark red wood and told to wait until
she was called for, the door slamming shut behind the
guards as they left. She heard a cough and the scraping of
boots, which indicated that at least one of the men was
stood just outside the door.

Two doors led off from the room, flanking an alcove con-
taining a statue of Verena, goddess of justice and law. It was
bronze, about twenty inches high and depicted a tall, beautiful woman, with thick hair, swathed in a long robe. On her
right shoulder sat on owl, its head inclined towards her as if
whispering in her ear. In her right hand she held a thin
sword by her side, while in her left she carried a set of scales.
It was plain and not particularly well sculpted, and the
bronze was tarnishing in many places. Ursula hoped it was
not a bad sign that the goddess of fairness and wisdom was
allowed to fall into decay.

Growing bored, Ursula started tapping her foot on the
plain stone floor. She turned her attention to the bench she
was sitting on.

With a disgusted gasp, Ursula jumped to her feet, staring at the piece of furniture in horror. What she had taken to be ornate scrollwork was in fact a design wrought from the intertwining bodies of writhing daemons, in all manner of violent and lascivious poses. Horned beasts consorted with serpent-like devils, alongside winged faeries grappling against many-breasted birds. Horrified that such a grotesque thing could be found in the centre of the courthouse, she looked pointedly at the statue instead, trying to push the images from her mind. It was typical, she thought, that this kind of blasphemous art could be allowed to exist, while churches were left bare, impoverished and dilapidated.

Ursula found herself shaking, and a shiver ran through her body. She could not explain what was happening to her. Surely, the images carved into the bench were not that shocking. Examining her feelings, she concluded that there was something familiar about the twisting, perverted images, like a half-remembered dream, or perhaps a scene from a vision she could no longer recall.

The sound of the door to her right creaking open snapped Ursula from her contemplation. Magistrate Fenster stalked through, muttering to himself. Despite his advanced years, he stepped nimbly enough across the flagstones, neck craned forward like a carrion bird, his sharp eyes darting around the room before settling on Ursula. His face was painfully thin, the skin hanging in folds over sunken cheeks and around deep eye sockets. Only a few wisps of pure white hair sprouted at irregular angles from his bald scalp, mottled with liver spots, warts and scars. A small fleck of spittle moved at the corner of his mouth as he smiled grimly at Ursula. He beckoned to her with an emaciated hand, his long, pointed fingernails yellowing and cracked. As he moved, the layers of the severe black robes he wore swung heavily, hanging limply off his frail frame.

'Come with me,' he told her in a hoarse whisper, before breaking into a rasping cough that caused him to almost double up. Gasping for breath, he leant against the open door and instinctively Ursula moved forward a step in case he needed help, though she was reluctant to get any closer to the withered wreck of a man. Straightening up after a while, eyes watering and with blood-flecked saliva spattered on his chin, Fenster snarled wordlessly and pointed through the door.

Ursula followed the silent command and walked through, finding herself in a cramped but lushly appointed study chamber. One wall was covered with a bookshelf from floor to ceiling, filled with mouldering tomes of law and precedents. A high desk dominated the study, a small bell hanging on a stand next to it. Ursula felt a bony finger prod her in the back and she stumbled forward. Fenster shuffled quickly around the room, his hands flicking out to pluck a parchment from a stand to the door's left, before he dropped down into the overstuffed armchair behind the desk, wheezing gently.

As he peered at the parchment held in his left hand, Fenster's right hand seemed to act with a life of its own. Fascinated, Ursula watched as it crawled its way across the desk to pick up a leather pouch. Opening the pouch, Fenster's single-minded fingers pulled out a short clay pipe, independent of attention from the magistrate who now looked at Ursula from under drooping eyelids. The hand plucked free a wad of pipeweed, then rubbed it for a while between thumb and forefinger before tamping it down into the bowl of the pipe.

All of the time Fenster's attention focussed on the young woman. Raising the pipe to his lips, Fenster turned in his chair and leaned to his left, opening the shutter on the lantern in the corner of the room and plucking the candle out. Lighting the pipe with the candle's flame, he placed it back in the lantern and closed the shutter with a loud snap that made Ursula jump.

'Frau Linde has levelled charges of witchcraft... heresy, kidnapping... child murder and immoral living against you,' croaked the magistrate between puffs on the pipe.

'That's complete nonsense!' Ursula blurted out incredulously. 'What proof does she have?'

'Oh, we'll come to that at your trial, young woman,' Fenster admitted with a dismissive wave of the pipe. Leaning forward, he jabbed the stem of the smoking pipe towards her.

'What laws have I broken?' demanded Ursula before Fenster could speak, crossing her arms.

'What am I to do with you?' he asked quietly, eyeing up Ursula like a piece of meat. She went to reply but a raised hand quelled her arguments. 'You are a stranger here, who I am told has turned out to be a frequent disturber of the peace, perpetrator of unorthodox religious practices, and general troublemaker. You are a corrupting influence on one of our fine sons, the knight Kurt Leitzig, and in the two years you have been in Badenhof you have done nothing to contribute to the well-being of our citizens or the peace and calm of our quiet society.'

'And who told you this?' asked Ursula. 'Emerelde?'

'For two years she has complained incessantly to her sister,' the lawmaker said quietly, as if talking to himself. 'And for those two years her sister has complained daily, loudly and vociferously to her husband, in turn making his life a misery. Unfortunately, young lady, that means that for two years I have had to sit down to my breakfast hearing every detail of your life, I go to bed learning every nuance of every slight you have levelled against my sister-in-law. A pox on all women I say, they should leave me in peace, but do they?'

'I'm here because you're Emerelde Linde's brother-in-law?' Ursula butted in, but Fenster did not appear to notice and continued his diatribe.

'They chatter incessantly, they smell funny and my wife has all the cooking skills of a drooling simpleton,' he continued with his rant. 'She cannot even keep a clean house without me paying out a small fortune for a maid. And now she's left, driven away by that vindictive bitch of a sister's lash of a tongue and so it's rancid cold meat on the table for me.'

'This is ridiculous, I'm not standing around listening to this nonsense any longer!' snorted Ursula, spinning on her heel.

'You walk out that door and I'll have you clapped in irons!' snapped Fenster, his voice cracking with anger. Ursula turned back to face him, fuming.

'I came to this town and offered to do any work, for little money, and they all turned me down,' Ursula spat, striding across the room, glaring at the magistrate. 'I've been treated as an outsider and freak ever since I came here. The hospitality of your quiet town leaves a lot to be desired, and if it wasn't for Kurt, I would have left this dismal, petty-minded, superstitious hole a long time ago.'

'Your tone is completely at odds with the respect my position demands, young woman,' Fenster hissed back, before being wracked by a coughing fit. 'Your ill-tempered nature and unnatural beliefs confirm the tainted nature of your birth evidenced by your daemon-tinted locks.'

'What does my hair have to do with this?' Ursula asked, taken aback.

'All learned men know,' the magistrate said with the assurance of one who considers himself such a scholar, 'that orange or red hair shows a child to be of wayward temperament and ill fortune. Your behaviour has proven that beyond doubt.'

Ursula stared open-mouthed at Fenster. She was dumbstruck by the magistrate's prejudice.

'I was prepared to give you a chance earlier,' the magistrate continued relentlessly. 'I was simply going to give you a short flogging in the square as a public example. However, I now see that your behaviour is entirely anti-social and you are indeed a menace and a violent incident cannot be far away, I fear. In these troubled times, you are a lit tinder next to a blackpowder keg and I cannot risk the consequences. As for the more spiritual charges of witchcraft and heresy, I was going to simply dismiss them but now I see that there is cause for concern. However, I shall leave that to the judgement of others.'

'Witchcraft? What do you mean?' demanded Ursula, a chill creeping up her spine.

'I shall confine you to the gaol to await the inquiry of the respected witch hunter, Marius van Diesl who is, I am led to believe, even now on a journey to this town.'

'Gaol?' shrieked Ursula lunging across the desk, and grabbing the magistrate's robes at the front.

'Harm me and you'll hang before nightfall!' rasped Fenster, unperturbed. Ursula let go and stepped back, her head spinning. This was worse than she had thought. Charges of heresy and witchcraft were far beyond the spitefulness of Frau Linde, or so she had thought. Fenster reached out and picked up a small silver hammer from his desk, and struck the hanging bell twice. 'The guards will be here shortly to take you to your new accommodation.'

URSULA STUMBLED DOWN the spiralling steps, the pommel of the guard's sword nudging her between the shoulder blades. Reaching the bottom she found herself in a small hallway, with an iron gate to the right and a half-open door to the left past which she could see an untidy rough wooden desk littered with scraps of parchment, a set of manacles and a half-eaten apple. The clank of metal drew her attention back to the iron gate.

Creaking the gate open, the prison warden stepped through. He was quite handsome, with a thin moustache and goatee beard that gave him a slightly dashing appearance. He was dressed well but not lavishly, with a short red jerkin, tight black breeches and knee-high leather boots that glistened with polish in the dim light from the lantern hung from the centre of the ceiling. The guard stepped forward and proffered a small slip of parchment, which the warden took, glanced at and then crumpled into the pocket of his jerkin.

'Ursula Schek,' he said quietly, his voice deep and confident. 'Disturbing the peace, jailed awaiting trial.'

'I haven't done anything wrong!' protested Ursula.

'The piece of paper in my pocket says otherwise,' the man pointed out. 'I am Dirk Lowl, the gaol warden. How much money do you have?'

'I'm sorry?' Ursula barked. 'What does that have to do with anything?'

'It's three pennies a week for a straw mattress,' Lowl told her placidly. 'I give you bread and water, you can have stew for another two pennies a week. You go into the communal cell unless you want to pay two shillings a month for your own chamber, and you can swap water for beer for another shilling a month. It's also five pennies a month for a blanket.'

'You charge people for being imprisoned?' Ursula asked incredulously, having had no real experience of law and justice. Whenever she had been in trouble when she was younger, she had always been quick and nimble enough to give her pursuers the slip. She could barely believe what was happening to her. Her thoughts were in turmoil, it all seemed somehow unreal. It was still only mid-morning and now she was being locked up because of the gossiping of her vengeful neighbour, for Sigmar knew how long.

'The council pays me barely enough to run the gaol,' Lowl explained without rancour. 'I clean the cells out every other week, I pay a rat-catcher to come in twice a week, and I won't brutalise you, or take advantage of you. No chains, no manacles, no thumb locks or scold's bridle for you. You have free roam of the cell block and exercise yard between sunrise and sunset, and if you like I will organise for a priest to visit you on whatever is your holy day.'

'Sigmar,' muttered Ursula.

'A Sigmarite?' confirmed Lowl. 'Then you're in luck, because this is the town gaol and there's still what's left of a shrine out on the other end of the exercise yard. I'm supposed to pay to have it maintained but perhaps we can sort out something else.'

'What do you have in mind?' said Ursula.

'If you want to renovate it for me, I'll give you a shilling a week in perks,' explained Lowl. 'If you want more money, you can also get a penny back for every rat you kill. The rat-catcher's a drunken swine, and I've got two terriers that have the run of the place, but the last six months we've been knee-deep in the vicious little buggers.'

'There's rats in here?' Ursula asked with a shiver of apprehension.

'Oh, every gaol has rats, but it seems like we've become a bit of a haven for them lately,' the warden explained casually, opening the gate again and leading Ursula gently through by the arm. A corridor flanked by cell doors stretched into the darkness. 'Look, I'm not a bad warden, don't look so frightened. It'll take some getting used to, but you'll get by.'

Ursula looked down the dank corridor, heard the coughing and groans of some poor inmate and the skittering of clawed feet. A wave of sickness swept through her and she blacked out.

CHAPTER FIVE
Battle
North of Erengrad, Late winter 1708

THE ROAD TO the north-east was clogged with a line of refugees, trudging disconsolately through the slush and snow. Kurt looked out at the river of people from his vantage point atop Heldred. Swathed in blankets, cloaks and furs, the miserable line of Kislevites was made up of men and women of all ages, from young mothers carrying babes cradled in their arms to bewhiskered old boyars who could barely take another step.

Three northern towns had fallen to the predations of the Norsemen, many of the inhabitants slain or enslaved. The thousands who had made the exodus south were the lucky few who had fled before the storm of war had fallen onto their homes. The army of the barbaric northmen had swept out of Norsca with no warning. Driving down the coast, they had been supplied and reinforced by longships making the daring crossing of the storm-tossed Sea of Claws. The quickly mustered force sent by the Tsar had been swept aside after a single bloody battle, and that was when the messengers had been sent southwards.

Looking back, Kurt watched the Osterknacht making camp beside the rough road. Four hundred and fifty knights had been assembled in the past two months, three hundred squires and twice as many men-at-arms, all drawn from chapter houses across the Ostermark. Some thirty leagues ahead were the scattered Kislevite forces, and Lord Lothar had made it his priority to link up with their commanders and help them form into a fighting army once more. However, the whereabouts of the northmen had not been known for several days. Lothar's scouts either had failed to return or had come back with no sighting to report. There was quiet debate as to whether the missing scouts had simply fallen foul of the harsh northern climate or been killed or captured. If it were the latter, then the enemy force might be within a day's march.

Since they had crossed the river Urskoy, Lord Lothar had pushed them hard: they had been forced to march every two nights out of three to cover the vast snow-covered plains of southern Kislev. They had turned westwards to Erengrad to great celebration, the populace welcoming them as the old allies they were. From Erengrad the column had marched northwards along the coast, in the hope that the northmen had not turned east and headed for Praag or the capital Kislev. If that was the case, there was little they could do except perhaps arrive in time to lift the resulting siege. Now the snows had closed in again with a vengeance, the blizzard forcing the Imperial force to camp down for the night.

Since his duel, Kurt had kept himself busy with training and readying for the march. Bayen had made a stilted apology at the great banquet held in honour of the count's birthday three weeks later, an occasion that had further delayed the army setting off. Bayen and his cronies had kept clear of Kurt, and an uneasy truce had been tacitly agreed in the preparations for battle. On the march itself, he had only seen Bayen once, as Kurt was in the vanguard with Lord Lothar, while Bayen was part of the main body.

THAT EVENING KURT was riding back from patrol duty to the north, and as Heldred pushed through the thick snow, the sun was dipping over the horizon. Kurt thought he heard something in the distance over the howling wind. Pausing to listen more carefully, he heard it again. It was a muffled shout. More than one, he realised as the wind slackened briefly. In the next lull, the shouts were louder and clearer and there was a distinctive ring of metal on metal. There was fighting back at the camp!

Kurt kicked in his spurs, and Heldred leapt into a gallop. The knight could see nothing through the swirling snow, but as he rode on, he could hear the fighting even over the noise of Heldred's panting and the whirl of wind around his head. Dragging his sword free from its scabbard, he slowed his mount to a trot as he started to make out the glow of campfires in the twilight. The tents were spread out over several wide concentric circles, and fires were burning at regular intervals around the circles. At the centre were the kitchens and arms store, and it was towards this that he rode.

As he came closer, Kurt could make out more detail. It wasn't just the campfires that were burning; there were also several of the large tents ablaze. The din of fighting grew louder and Kurt saw men running back and forth against the flames, and heard hoarse shouts in a foreign language. Realising that the Norse marauders were attacking, he spurred Heldred again and galloped into the fray.

Everything was confusion but Kurt picked out the distinctive shape of horned helmets and fur-clad warriors and steered Heldred between the rows of tents, sword ready. He chose his first target, a tall barbarian wielding a double-headed hammer in whirling arcs, keeping three spearmen at bay. Guiding Heldred to the left, Kurt struck downward with his sword, the blade cleaving through the back of the marauder's head. The men-at-arms leapt aside as Heldred sprang between them, kicking up snow as Kurt hauled him further left towards a knot of knights who were still struggling to strap on their armour. Amongst them was Viksson, who waved Kurt in the direction of the main fighting.

'Just grab a sword and follow me!' Kurt bellowed, racing past. Ahead he could see a thicket of spears as a group of thirty or more men-at-arms hastily assembled. They were still milling around when a shrieking war cry sounded out and a score of Norse burst out of the darkness and snow, waving axes, swords and maces above their heads.

'Form up, present to the front!' Kurt shouted at them, reining in behind the spearmen. They were slow to respond and the second rank was still ordering itself when the barbarians crashed into them. The spear wall almost buckled under the initial onslaught of the Norsemen, who drove like a wedge into their midst.

'Hold them!' Kurt commanded. 'Get round the back!'

The spearmen, outnumbering their opponents, started to encircle the marauders, and despite losing more of their number than they felled, the fight swung in their favour. Feeling confident that the breakthrough had been prevented, Kurt left the men-at-arms to finish off the Norscans and headed in the direction Viksson had indicated. On the way, he met up with Jakob, who was trotting through the snow with his arms wrapped around a bundle of lances.

'Here, I'll have one of those,' Kurt told him, reining in alongside. Sheathing his sword, the knight grabbed the shaft of one of the lances and pulled it free. 'Put them down and get my shield on.'

Jakob did as he was told, taking Kurt's shield from behind Heldred's saddle and offering it up.

'They was on us, before sentries shouted,' Jakob told him, moving back to the pile of lances. 'Came right through blizzard. Old Norscan trick, knew where we was. They was waiting for the snows to come.'

'Where are you going with those?' asked Kurt, walking Heldred forward alongside the retainer.

'Lord Lothar has gone for fifty knights for counter-attack, left squires and infantry to hold out,' explained Jakob. 'More than half of the knights aren't mounted yet.'

'Which way?' demanded Kurt, looking over his shoulder as Heldred broke into a canter.

'West, that way, other side of camp,' Jakob told him, waving a hand in a vague direction. Kurt gave him a nod and dug in his spurs again, riding past a row of burning tents towards the sounds of clashing weapons and shields.

The battle was a scrappy, disordered affair amongst the tents and fires. The fighting was perfectly suited to the more open style of the marauders, who roved in groups of ten to twenty warriors, hunting down and outflanking the more disciplined but less flexible blocks of halberdiers, swordsmen and spearmen. The squires, who had mounted quickly having no armour to put on, trotted around the edges, darting in with spear and sword where an opportunity presented itself, but neither skilled nor well armed enough for a proper full charge. Kurt rode up to the nearest group.

'You boys, come with me,' he commanded them. One, who he recognised as Leofe, squire to Lord Helfen, turned and looked at him with a scowl.

'Why?' Leofe rasped. Aggravated by the young man's insolence, Kurt slapped him across the face with his sheild, knocking the squire from his horse. Leofe scrabbled to his feet, his nose bleeding profusely, his left eye already beginning to swell.

'Helfen will hear about this, you'll pay for that!' spat Leofe, wiping blood from his chin.

'Disobey me again and I'll use my sword on you,' warned Kurt, looking at the others. Their fearful nods were all the sign he needed, and he kicked at Heldred, who jumped into a gallop, the squires hurriedly forming up around him. Kurt could not make out too much of the battle, but the largest concentration of men seemed to be to his left, gathered around three crude standards made out of animal skins and dangling bones.

'There'll be a fine reward for the man who takes that banner,' Kurt told the squires, using his lance to point out a massive totem decked with bells and carved bones, topped with an iron eight-pointed star.

Kurt allowed Heldred to forge ahead slightly, knowing that his lance and armour offered the best chance of ploughing a gap into the Norsemen for the small group of squires to dash into and wreak havoc with their spears. Snow churned up beneath Heldred's hooves and Kurt's ears were filled with the rushing of his own blood and his heart hammering at his ribs. Exaltation surged through him. This is why the Osterknacht existed: the glorious charge, the bite of lance through armour and flesh, the crash of sword on shield. He could feel the pull and release of Heldred's muscles and took joy in the power he felt. Like the breaking of a storm, Kurt fell on the Norscans.

'For the Osterknacht! For Lord Lothar!' he bellowed, the tip of his lance piercing the shield of a marauder who hurriedly turned at his battle cry, passing easily through the wood and punching into the bearded man's chest. Ripping the lance free he plunged it through the stomach of another marauder, then pulled it out and used the butt to stove in the face of a howling Norseman. He heard rather than saw the squires attacking just behind him. As the marauders turned to face him, he hurled the lance at the closest and pulled his sword free. Heldred reared and flailed his hooves as the Norse counter-attacked, his iron shoes smashing two of them from their feet while Kurt's sword cut through the thick leather breastplate of another.

Hacking left and right, unable to miss in the press of bodies, Kurt advanced through the enemy horde, Heldred stepping neatly over the dead and wounded. The squires followed in his bloody wake, protecting him from encirclement. Kurt's blade was slick with blood, but there was no relenting; the Norse hurled themselves at him with unflinching ferocity. A snarling northman with bristling blond whiskers came running at Kurt with a long axe gripped in both hands, and swung at Heldred's legs. The horse reared, nearly toppling Kurt, and swung around. The next blow smashed against Kurt's shield, threatening to unseat him, and Kurt struggled to bring Heldred back under control. Just then, a spear jutted out of the norseman's chest and Kurt looked up to see Sigurd, squire of Odel Dasteg. Parrying an axe blow, Kurt wheeled Heldred around to knock the man to the ground, trampling him beneath the horse's hooves. It was then that he realised Sigurd was not one of the squires who had ridden in with him; others had seen the attack and joined in, and looking around Kurt could see the mounted men battling their way through the throng of marauders.

There were now just a few Norsemen between Kurt and the standard he had chosen as his objective. They backed away as he closed in, clad in bristling furs, their faces covered with long plaited beards, helmets sprouting all manner of improbable horns and daemonic faces. One stood his ground a little longer, an axe in each hand, and Kurt spurred

Heldred towards him. With a shrieking cry, the marauder threw one of the axes, which buried itself into Kurt's shield and knocked him sideways. He grappled at the reins, causing Heldred to stumble in his stride, and fell to his right, rolling off the horse's back. The Norseman was on him as he got to his knees. Kurt's raised shield fended off the first two blows as he struggled to his feet and freed his sword from under him. The third blow swung low towards Kurt's knees but his sword was down to meet it. As the axe blade rang off his weapon, Kurt's cut upwards and the sword bounced off the metal horn protruding from the brow of the Norscan's helm, stunning the raider. A sweep with his shield put the northman on his back foot and Kurt moved in for the kill, driving his blade straight at the Norseman's throat.

At that moment, a dagger swept up towards Kurt's exposed armpit and he twisted quickly, catching it on his breastplate, his sword passing harmlessly over the northerner's head. Horrified, his gaze moved from the clawed fingers gripping the knife, up a twisted arm that pulsated with exposed muscle and connected just below the norseman's ribcage. How could he have not noticed the man had a third arm? His stomach churning with disgust, Kurt clumsily parried the next few blows on his shield, distracted and confused by what he had seen. He had heard tales that the northmen were brutal and ferocious fighters, but had ignored the more fantastical stories that claimed they were physically tainted. Face to face with the truth, he was unprepared for how revolting the sight was. His thoughts were focussed once more though, when the Norseman's axe clanged off his left shoulder, driving the plate into the flesh and onto the bone. Kurt could feel blood trickling into his armpit and the pain seared down his arm and across his chest.

To ignore the pain, Kurt concentrated on his foe's face. In a single glance, he took in every detail. The marauder was grinning with a few stubby teeth, despite the blood flowing from a cut in his forehead where Kurt's earlier blow had smashed his helm through the skin. The man's eyes were blood-shot and slightly askew, so that the knight was not sure where the marauder was looking. His beard was matted with filth, and Kurt noticed that the bindings that held the

plait in place were carved from bone. On each was inscribed
the eight-pointed star, mirroring the icon on the banner.
Shocked that he had not recognised it before, Kurt realised
the enemy was no natural foe, they were touched by the
curse that men in the south dared not name: Chaos.

With a shout that boiled up from the bottom of his lungs,
and was fuelled by disgust and righteous anger, Kurt cleaved
his sword towards the marauder's neck. The force of the
blow knocked aside the axe raised to parry the attack and
severed the man's head completely, sending it spinning
through the air, blood splashing across the churned and
muddy snow. Some of it spattered across Kurt's visor. The
unnatural stench that accompanied the blood made Kurt
gag and he fell to one knee, retching violently. He tore his
helmet free and gasped deeply. Tossing the helm aside, he
pushed himself to his feet just in time to see Leofe prising
the enemy standard from the dead grip of Sigurd.

Too weary to intervene, the pain from his shoulder dulling
him, Kurt cast his gaze around for a sign of Heldred. The
horse was well trained and would have broken clear of the
fighting, and would be waiting for Kurt to return.

As he picked his way through the corpses of marauders
and squires Kurt heard the chanting.

It was indistinct at first, masked by the noise of the wind,
but quickly grew in volume. The words were indistinguish-
able, shouted out in guttural syllables that struck a chill into
Kurt's heart. It was the language of the Chaos gods, the Dark
Tongue. Accompanied by the beating of drums and the crash
of weapons on shields, the prayer to the Dark Gods grew
louder and louder. Seeking the source of the cacophony,
Kurt peered through the snow and smoke, and saw a wall of
black advancing through the burning remnants of the camp.
To his right a horse whinnied in terror and bolted, hurling
the squire on its back to the ground.

Like a plague, the warriors of Chaos advanced closer. They
were a fearsome sight: clad head to foot in grime-encrusted
armour, carrying full length shields inscribed with twisted
markings, and armed with maces, axes, swords, cleavers and
flails. The air around them seemed darker and churned with
a life of its own. The sonorous chanting reached a peak,

accompanied by the clanging of metal, the thumping of drums, and the atonal ringing of brass bells. Kurt thought he would go deaf, such was the wall of sound that swept over him.

Kurt held his ground, though his legs felt weak from blood loss, and his stomach rebelled at the stench the wind swept to his nostrils. He saw a handful of the squires break and run, but the others mastered their nerves and formed up once more, prepared to meet the slowly advancing enemy. Hearing a shouted command, Kurt looked to his left and saw two ranks of crossbowmen, thirty in all, preparing to loose a volley. Their sergeant raised and then dropped his hand and red-feathered bolts flew through the night air. The dark cloud landed amidst the Chaos warriors, many of them bouncing harmlessly off their shields and armour. Kurt watched as bolts pierced the metal skin of one of the warriors, knocking him to the ground. The warrior pushed himself to his feet and ripped the bolts out of his torso, tossing them aside in derision.

The warriors were perhaps only thirty yards away, still advancing patiently, a few of their number felled by a second volley of bolts. Suddenly, the chanting stopped and they halted. The clamour of beaten shields reached a crescendo, a deafening artificial thunder, and ragged banners rose up from the ranks, daubed with savage runes and symbols of the dark gods. As one, the armoured warriors broke into a run. Kurt stood transfixed by fear as the wall of spiked, distorted metal rushed towards him. The ground trembled under the weight of the massive warriors hurtling themselves across the blood-spattered snow.

Their leader, at the front of the charge, was half as tall again as Kurt, a veritable giant of a man whose broad shoulders were wider than a horse's. On one arm he carried a shield almost as tall as a man, with three circles of crude rivets set in a triangular pattern. A massive mace was held high above his head, and fumes of smoke seemed to issue from cracks in the weapon. His face was bare, and Kurt looked in horror at the glowing green eyes that stared back at him. The warrior was shouting, displaying teeth filed into pointed fangs, and his face was a criss-cross of scars, boils and scabs.

When the warrior was only half a dozen strides away, Kurt realised that the man's teeth were actually proper fangs, longer than a dog's and dripping with black saliva. The darkness around the warriors was real and tangible, and a great buzzing filled Kurt's ears as the cloud of flies swept around him. His vision blocked, his nose and ears clogged with the flies, Kurt flailed around for a moment, completely disorientated. Something charged through the living fog only a yard away and Kurt flung up his shield just as the warrior's mace crashed against it, hurling him from his feet.

The force of the blow had winded Kurt and he desperately rolled through the snow and mud as the warrior loomed over him. A metal-booted foot crashed into his right arm, numbing his shoulder, as the other warriors pressed forward, heedless of the knight. His shield deflected another blow wide, the force of the attack jarring Kurt's left arm. Pain lanced up from his elbow, and he panicked for a moment thinking it was broken. Swinging wildly with his sword to give him a momentary respite, Kurt glanced at his arm and saw that one of the spikes of the warrior's mace had pierced his shield and was stuck in his arm. The Chaos warrior almost wrenched Kurt's arm off as he tried to pull his weapon free, but gritting his teeth against the pain the Imperial knight twisted and pulled the warrior downwards.

With a wordless snarl on his lips, Kurt struck out with his sword, every ounce of his dissipating strength behind the blow. The blade crashed against the Chaos warrior's body, shards of the sword's metal splintering into the air, opening a rent in the chest plate. A fountain of thick black fluid gushed from the wound, spilling on to the ground where it hissed and sputtered in the snow. The warrior let go of the mace and clasped a gauntleted hand to the bleeding gash to stem the flow. Mustering what little power he had left, Kurt hauled himself to one knee and chopped at the Chaos follower's legs, the dented and blunted edge of his sword biting halfway into an armoured knee and toppling the giant.

All around Kurt were screams, groans, grunting and shouts as the fight carried on in full fury. He heard the sound of a horn and the ground began to tremble. Kurt pushed himself to his feet, fearful of what horror the northmen would unleash upon them next. His fears were to prove misplaced.

With a mighty splintering of wood and the screech of tearing metal, the lances of fifty knights of the Osterknacht crashed into the warriors of Norsca. Spitted bodies were hurled to the ground to be trampled by the hooves of the knight's horses, the blaring of the horn beautiful and sweet in Kurt's ears.

Lord Lothar himself was there, swinging left and right with a sword that glowed with a red light, each touch of its blade slicing through armour as if it were paper, severing limbs and decapitating heads. Under the full force of the Empire Knights' charge the warriors of Chaos broke, and tried to flee. The knights were much swifter, riding down the twisted Norsemen with lance and sword, leaving none alive. As the knights swept past him, Kurt let out a shout of triumph before his legs gave way and he collapsed into the snow, his sword dropping from his unconscious grasp.

THE NEXT NIGHT, Kurt was wandering around the camp, his wounds freshly bandaged and sore, but otherwise he had not paid too dearly for his bravery. He bumped into Lord Militant Trevigar relieving himself just outside the perimeter of the tents. He turned to walk away but Trevigar called out to him.

'Yes, my lord?' Kurt asked turning back to the ageing knight.

'That was one of the damnedest things I've ever seen, and I've been campaigning for over thirty years,' the lord militant told him, running a hand through his coarse grey whiskers. He was heavily built but shorter than Kurt, and even without his armour gave an impression of stocky power and stubbornness.

'What was, my lord?' Kurt asked, confused. Trevigar walked up to him and clapped a hand on Kurt's shoulder.

'A knight leading a charge of squires!' laughed the lord militant. 'Never seen such foolishness and courage at the same time.'

'I... Thank you, my lord, I did what was necessary,' stammered Kurt. It was the first time he had ever spoken to a lord militant, and to be praised gave him a moment of heady pride.

'Yes you did, and more the credit to you for seeing that,' Trevigar agreed. 'What with that business back in Bechafen and now this, you're presenting us with a bit of a problem.'

'Us, my lord? I don't understand.' Kurt fidgeted under the scrutiny of his commander's deputy, thinking perhaps that his duel with Bayen continued to be viewed badly.

'Well, young man,' Trevigar said, laying an arm across Kurt's shoulder and walking him back towards the camp, 'we had you down as a bit of a troublemaker. I mean, picking a fight with the count's cousin, you'd have to have been kicked in the head as a babe.'

'I was well–' started Kurt.

'I don't care if you were right or wrong, it was still a stupid thing to do,' Trevigar cut him off. 'Being a knight isn't just about flashing a sword around and riding a horse well. It's political these days as well. The Osterknacht is a powerful organisation even now, and he who commands it wields great power and responsibility. But that's another matter. We think you a bit of a fool and troublemaker, and what do you then go and do?'

'I don't know, my lord,' Kurt replied weakly.

'You rally a bunch of squires and lead an attack on the enemy almost single-handedly,' explained the lord militant. 'You showed just the kind of bravery and initiative that we need in the higher ranks, but you'll have to calm your temper a bit.'

'I'm not sure if I can, my lord,' admitted Kurt. 'Not on some subjects.'

'Ah, your woman,' Trevigar said with a nod. 'Well, you're young and hot-headed, that's to be expected. But if you want to climb up the order, you'll have to show some patience. Either marry her and be done with it, or find someone more suitable.'

Kurt did not particularly like Trevigar's advice, and they walked on in silence for a bit, passing one of the many campfires, when something occurred to Kurt.

'May I ask a question?' he said.

'Of course, but that doesn't mean I have to answer it!' joked Trevigar.

'Why did Lord Lothar not order a pursuit last night or today?' Kurt had been surprised that they had not harried the northmen to prevent them gathering again and becoming a threat once more.

'Well, between you and me, we've got new orders,' Trevigar winked conspiratorially. 'It seems there's some growing trouble back near the capital. A messenger arrived yesterday saying that growing unrest in some of the towns around Bechafen is threatening to become a full blown riot. Who can tell what might spread from that, and what will happen at the capital? Lord Lothar received word from the count that he wants the Osterknacht to return to restore some sense of peace.'

'What sort of trouble, if you don't mind my asking, my lord?' Kurt's first thought was for Ursula. If there was trouble near Bechafen, it could easily spread to Badenhof.

'It's been a very harsh winter, famine is threatening the whole northern Ostermark,' explained Trevigar, stopping and looking at the flames of the fire, his gaze distant. 'Not only are the people in danger of rising up, we have to maintain supplies for the count and the order. And into this mess enters more trouble in the form of a witch hunter who's crossed over the border from Ostland. Word has it that he's heading to Badenhof to root out some cult or other.'

'A witch hunter?' Kurt whispered, a sudden shiver of fear passing down his spine.

'That's right, some rowdy fellow by the name of Marius van Diesl,' confirmed Trevigar. 'Sounds like he's from the Wastelands, name like that.'

Trevigar continued talking but Kurt heard none of it. His mind was a sudden storm of thoughts. Was van Diesl coming after him? Would he learn of Kurt's connection with Ursula? A sudden panic filled Kurt, his heart trembling with foreboding. There was only one thing he could do, but he was afraid to do it. With sudden resolve, he realised that he had no real choice in the matter, and with the decision made he felt better for it, whether it turned out for good or ill.

'...listening to me, Leitzig?' Trevigar asked with a scowl.

'Sorry, my lord, I am still fatigued from yesterday's battle,' Kurt apologised quickly, hoping his dismay had not been too obvious.

'I said that I'll put you in the detachment we send to Badenhof,' Trevigar repeated himself. 'You'll be going home a lot sooner than you thought.'

Not soon enough, Kurt thought to himself, making his excuses and leaving the bemused lord militant standing alone.

'WHO'S THERE?' A heavily accented voice called from the darkness. Kurt halted, his grip on Heldred's reins tightening with anxiety.

'Keep your voice down, Jakob, it's me, Kurt,' the knight hissed, pulling his horse towards the sound of the servant's voice.

'Leaving?' Jakob asked shrewdly as his moustached face appeared out of the darkness.

'None of your business,' snapped Kurt, shouldering the half-Kislevite aside.

'You'll be flogged and quartered for desertion,' Jakob told him in a whisper.

'What concern of yours is it?' Kurt snarled back, agitated at the delay.

Jakob hesitated, glancing around into the darkness, before stepping closer. 'I'll come with you,' he said suddenly, looking Kurt in the eye.

'What?' Kurt said, taken aback. 'Why do you want to leave?'

'Doesn't matter, I tell later,' Jakob said. 'What your reasons?'

'My reasons?' Kurt hissed, recollection flaring painfully. 'Oh, I have very good reasons.'

Jakob looked at him for a long time, disbelief on his face.

'I have to return to Badenhof,' Kurt told quickly Jakob. 'Ursula, my lady, is in great danger. But why should I care about you?'

Jakob looked at Kurt for a moment more before stepping back.

'It would be a shame if someone discovers you are leaving,' the servant said slowly, his meaning clear.

'You wouldn't!' growled Kurt, nudging Heldred forward. Jakob's shrug effectively conveyed that he would. 'Alright, meet me half a mile to the east, but I won't wait long.'

KURT'S NERVES WERE raw as he waited in the darkness, illuminated only slightly by the distant campfires. The slightest hint of a noise caused him to jump in the saddle, setting Heldred's harness jangling and causing Kurt more worry. He was about to head off without Jakob when his ear caught the distinctive sound of a horse approaching. He glanced behind him and saw a dun steed nosing through the snow, and he recognised it as Bayen's horse. His hand reached to his sword and partly drew it, but his grip relaxed when he saw the rider was not the knight, but Jakob.

'You stole Achelka? Are you mad? Bayen will be after you like the wrath of Ulric!' Kurt berated the half-Kislevite.

'He deserves it,' snorted Jakob. 'He is fine horse. Bayen will be angry, will confuse pursuit with his interference.'

'Perhaps,' Kurt agreed, knowing that the noble would demand to lead the hunt, a task he was not particularly qualified to do. 'Let's get going, we have to put as much distance as we can between us and the camp. The snow should cover our tracks before anyone notices we've gone.'

CHAPTER SIX
Trial
Badenhof, Winter early 1709

URSULA WOKE WITH a start and sat up abruptly. A trickle of
cold water from the thawing snow had run through the window and along the floor, before pooling under her feet.
Shaking the droplets free, she stood up, causing scurried
movements in the far corner of the cell. Raking her fingers
through her knotted hair, she padded barefoot across the
cell. The rat scurried for the door but she was quicker,
pouncing on the rodent and grabbing it around the neck.
With a crack, she snapped its spine and tossed the twitching
corpse onto the small pile in the corner along with the rest
of the week's haul. Two and a half shillings she'd earned,
more even than last week when it had seemed the whole
gaol had been swarming with vermin. Glancing out of the
window, she judged from the cold, watery light that it was
not long after daybreak. It was time for her prayers and she
creaked open the cell door and slipped out, trying not to disturb the other prisoners.

She wasn't sure how many other unfortunates were in
here with her; the lower levels of the dungeon were a warren
of oubliettes, corridors and cells. Most seemed to keep to

their cells, occasionally she would see one of them in the exercise yard, pale-faced, thin and weary. Some muttered to themselves, others seemed sane enough but avoided her. Then there was the one who screamed in her sleep, screeched profanities at the empty air, talked to the shadows and gibbered about having rats for friends. She had asked Lowl about her, and had found out that she was called Aliss and had been locked up here for years, long before he took over a little under a decade ago. She decided not to inquire further.

It had been two months now since her incarceration had begun. After her initial fear and anger, she had settled into a routine, just as she had with every other adverse situation with which her unfortunate life had seen fit to burden her. The warden, Dirk Lowl, had proved to be true to his word and life in the dungeon had been uncomfortable but bearable. It was not the worse time she had ever experienced, she had been hungrier and colder before, and she wasn't beaten regularly as she had been when she had lived with her grandparents.

She walked down the corridor, up a short flight of steps and out through the rusted gateway into the small exercise yard. Her skin prickled in the cold air. The ground was awash with snow that numbed her feet, beginning to melt as the first touches of winter's end began to take hold. She took a few deep breaths of air, fresh in comparison to the dank squalor of the gaol, and noticed the distinctive smell of smoke. Looking up above the high wall, she saw a pillar of darkness rising into the air. It was the third fire in as many days, and she resolved to quiz Lowl about it when he did his rounds at midday. Putting thoughts of the violent disturbances beyond the walls to the back of her mind, she set to her task.

There were no flowers here in the prison, but using her fingernails, she scraped the red moss from out of the cracks between the stones of the building. When she had a handful, way into the old Sigmarite shrine. It was a small, low room, barely high enough for her to stand, no more than a few yards square. The room was dim, lit only by two smoking wicks in small bowls of animal fat. Lowl had laughed when she had presented her first dozen rats and asked that he use the proceeds to procure her the lamp wicks and tinderbox for the shrine. He had said that the protection of a blanket and a hot meal would serve her better than the protection of a distant god. She had replied that now was the time she needed Sigmar the most, to look after her when it seemed everyone else had forsaken her. He had been silent then and the next day had returned with the tinder and cheap lamps.

Her cold, cramped fingers clumsily wove the strands of moss together into a wreath no larger than a bracelet. Kneeling in front of the far wall, she looked at the scrubbed walls and the chipped relief insignia of Sigmar's hammer. Clasping the moss token to her chest in both hands, she began her prayers. As she spoke the words, the cold flowed from her body as if the tiny flame of the lamps were a warm fire. She concentrated on the hammer, but her eye was drawn to the flickering flames as they danced fitfully in the chilling breeze. There was a brief moment of blazing flame and warmth in her eyes, shaking her and filling her nose with the imagined stench of burning flesh. Startled, she stood up quickly, banging her head on the ceiling, which set her ears ringing. Dazed for a second, she staggered and gave a shriek as someone grabbed her arm. Whirling around, her fingers clawed to rake the face of her assailant, she stopped herself just before she gouged at Dirk Lowl's eyes.

'Easy there!' he exclaimed, letting go and stepping back. 'I'm sorry if I startled you.'

'I… sorry, I banged my head,' she said lamely.

'Yes, I saw,' admitted Lowl. He seemed distracted. 'There's someone here to see you.'

'To see me?' Ursula replied quietly. Her heart skipped when she thought that perhaps Kurt had finally returned. 'Take me to him!'

With a nod, Lowl led her back through the exercise yard, down the steps and along the corridor between the cells and back into the entrance hall at the bottom of the steps. Unlocking the gate, he ushered her through into the chamber.

'In there,' the jailer told her, waving a hand towards his office. Ursula pushed open the door and darted into the small room, a smile creeping across her face, but the smile disappeared as soon as she saw that it was not Kurt waiting for her.

The small room contained Dirk's desk and a couple of chairs. On a shelf on one wall was a row of empty bottles, the stubs of used candles protruding from their necks. Bent over Lowl's desk was a tall man, absently picking through the papers there. He was dressed in a long black leather cloak with a dark shirt and breeches underneath, and his greying hair was pulled back in a short ponytail. His face was scarred and weathered, his eyes dark and calculating as he looked over his shoulder at her. Next to him on the desk was a wide-brimmed hat from which a black feather protruded.

HEARING URSULA ENTER, Marius van Diesl straightened and turned, giving her a cool look. She was young and very pretty, even with her scraggly hair and prison rags. She certainly did not look at all like the ugly hag of common folklore, but he knew better than to let appearances deceive him. Still, if his instinct was worth anything, it was telling him that this was a dead-end in his investigations. He had come to Badenhof searching for signs of skaven, and had been immediately greeted with hysterical accusations against this woman. He had spoken with the magistrate, the priest and other locals, and though the charges levelled were serious he had yet to hear or see any kind of evidence to support them.

'Who are you?' the woman demanded. 'Why are you here?'

He didn't reply immediately, taken aback slightly by her forthright manner. He marvelled at her spirit – here she was, locked in prison, taken to meet a complete stranger, all but defenceless, and yet somehow she had claimed the advantage and was questioning him! Such a strong mind might well be capable of the sort of deviant behaviour she was charged with.

'I am Marius van Diesl,' he told her with a slight bow, hoping she did not take it as mockery.

'The witch hunter?' she asked, not at all perturbed.

'Some call me that, yes,' he admitted, shutting the door. He was uncomfortable with the title and many of its connotations amongst the suspicious people of the Empire. 'I prefer to think myself a defender of purity and a seeker of truth.'

'Do you think I am a witch?' Ursula said bluntly, seeming to have ignored his reply. 'Is that why you are here?'

'I have not decided yet what you are,' he told her truthfully. Certainly witchcraft was becoming more prevalent, but for every one true witch he had burned, there had been ten innocent men and women accused who he had set free. 'I am here to divine the truth of this matter.'

'And just how do you propose to do that?' asked Ursula with an accusing tone in her voice, wary perhaps of torture or other violent interrogation.

'I am simply going to talk to you,' Marius replied calmly, indicating the chair in the corner of the room with a wave of his hand. Ursula sat down hesitantly, and in a moment of self-consciousness patted ineffectively at her bedraggled hair and attempted to smooth the creases in her tattered skirt.

'Among other crimes, you were sent to this gaol on a charge of witchcraft,' stated Marius, sitting on the edge of the study table.

'It's all nonsense, just the bile of a twisted woman,' interjected Ursula hotly.

'But why make such an unfounded accusation?' asked Marius, putting emphasis on the word 'unfounded'.

'Because she is bitter that I am in love with a man she thinks should be wedding her daughter,' Ursula replied coldly. 'For two months I have been in this prison because of her scorn, and the conspiracies of her brother-in-law!'

'Conspiracies?' repeated Marius, jumping on the word like a hunting dog. 'Such a word is not to be used lightly.'

'Yes, conspiracy, that's what it is,' Ursula affirmed. 'He's the magistrate and almost told me to my face that he was locking me up so that he could be spared from his wife's nagging.'

'That seems such a frivolous cause of action, what makes you think I'll believe it?' Marius inquired, gazing around the room as if distracted, although his ears were intent on Ursula's reply for any hint of falsehood or hesitation.

'I can do nothing but tell the truth,' Ursula stated flatly.

'Is that your only defence?' Marius snorted in mock derision, testing the girl. 'In a court of law that would hold very little weight. The magistrate has told me all about you, and the crimes you have committed. Breach of the peace, disorderly behaviour, these are not to be taken lightly.'

'I can do nothing but tell the truth,' Ursula repeated slowly. 'I trust that Sigmar will guide my judges' thoughts, as he does mine. I may not be as pure as some, but I am no heretic or witch.'

'Trust in Sigmar is a rare commodity in these times. Perhaps you would prefer to place yourself in the protection of Shallya, or perhaps the old wolf himself, Ulric?' suggested Marius. He had heard from Lowl about her attention to the gaol shrine, but he had known some cunning people in his time, himself included, and would not put it past a resourceful woman to have constructed a tangle of deceits and lies concerning her affairs and beliefs.

'Old, barbaric gods,' Ursula dismissed Marius's suggestion. 'Where were they when the orcs killed our forefathers and the northmen ravaged the lands and sacrificed our ancestors to their bloodthirsty masters? No, it was Sigmar who triumphed over these evils, and it is Sigmar who will triumph over the evil that currently attacks me. Can you not see I am a victim of jealousy, and local spite?'

'In time I will see what is what and who is who,' Marius replied enigmatically, using one of his favourite lines.

'And what does that mean?' snapped Ursula testily. 'What gives you the right to judge me any more than the superstitious peasants and gossiping hags in this town?'

Marius smiled grimly in response, though inside he was impressed by the girl's forthright nature. She wasn't defensive at all, but not aggressive either. Either of the two would have set his suspicions running, because they were a good sign that the other person was trying to hide something with evasion or bluster. But with this girl, it was something else. There was a fiery confidence in her that was quite refreshing, and it made her all the more attractive. Turning his mind from such thoughts, he stood and walked around the table to sit in the chair behind it, buying himself a few moments of time to think.

'I am actually an ordained priest of Sigmar,' he told her, completely truthfully. He had actually passed his Holy Orders in the great cathedral of Nuln when he was a young man, some twenty-five years ago. 'Perhaps with that knowledge, you will trust me.'

Ursula remained quiet, which perplexed Marius. He had expected some kind of retort challenging his legitimacy or another accusation against his aims, but nothing was forthcoming. Looking at her, he saw that Ursula's eyes were cast down at the floor, and she began to fidget with her skirt. For a moment, he thought that this was the sign of guilt he was waiting to see. As he watched her, he changed his mind; this was not fear, it was acquiescence. Well, perhaps not acquiescence, but it was certainly devout obedience. He had simply claimed to have been a priest and her entire manner had changed.

'Does it frighten you?' he asked her gently. 'The fact that I am a priest?'

'No,' she replied looking up and meeting his gaze. 'If you are a brother of Sigmar as you say you are, then you will know that He protects those who love Him, and so I have nothing to fear from you or anyone.'

'I spoke to Brother Theobald,' Marius told her, keenly watching her reaction, but there was nothing to speak of, no furtive glance, and no avoidance of his gaze. 'He told me of your little morning ritual, and the warder here informs me that you've been doing the same since your arrival.'

'I have made no secret of it,' she said levelly. 'It is nothing wrong, merely a practice that I picked up when I was a child.'

'Yes, I have seen versions of it before, but not within many miles of Badenhof,' he admitted. 'You must have travelled far in your short life.'

'Yes,' Ursula concurred, and for the first time there was hesitation, the timbre of her voice had changed slightly.

'You're holding something back!' he shouted, slapping his hand on the table and startling Ursula. Changing his

approach, he strode round the table and confronted her.
'What is it? What are you not telling me?'

'Nothing,' she replied, her gaze dropping immediately to
the floor again. 'I'm an orphan; I spent many years wandering, looking for happiness. I thought I had found it here, but
it seems what little I had has been taken away from me.'

Marius half expected a tear to roll down her cheeks, or
similar theatrics, but there was nothing else, just a bland
statement of fact. Relentlessly, he pushed her further.

'And that is all?' he demanded, grabbing her chin between
two fingers and forcing her to look into his eyes. 'You have
never secretly cursed someone, never perhaps offered up
prayers to proscribed powers in the hope that they might
deliver you when Sigmar seems to have deserted you.'

'Sigmar has not deserted me!' she replied, snatching his
hand away and standing up. 'Priests are supposed to offer
succour, but you taunt me with the failures of my life and
accuse me of terrible things of which I know nothing. What
kind of priest are you?'

Now tears did gather in her eyes; tears of sadness and frustration. In a moment of weakness he almost reached out a
hand to hold her close, so strong and yet vulnerable she
looked. But Marius steeled himself, feeling he was getting
close to the truth.

'And have you ever wished harm on anyone?' he asked
harshly. Ursula scowled at him.

'Of course I have, who hasn't?' she admitted, still crying.
'When my parents died and my grandfather beat me for the
first time I went to my bed praying to Sigmar that a great
twin-tailed comet would crash into his head. When I was
poor and starving and wandering the roads, I wished ruin
and poverty on the heads of the rich nobles who clattered
past in their carriages and splashed me with mud. Yes, I have
wished ill for other people, but only in anger and misery,
not out of genuine desire to see them hurt. If you believe
that is evil, then you can do what you like to me.'

It was a fine answer, and if he thought himself any judge
of the truth, Marius believed her. But there was one final test
he would make to be sure. He plucked the hammer symbol
of Sigmar from under his shirt, where it hung on a silver

chain. It was small, no larger than his thumb, and as he hooked it over his head he saw Ursula's eyes flickering between the symbol and his face, trying to tell what would happen next.

'Take this in your hand,' he said, thrusting the miniature hammer towards Ursula. She did so with trembling fingers while he watched her face intently. There was no reaction, no sign of pain or anguish, just nervousness. He took the holy talisman back and put in back on, turning away from the girl. There was nothing here for her to answer for, except perhaps a slight freeness of spirit and lack of manners brought about by a life of little social contact. If he was fit at all for this calling, she was no witch. But his intuition told him there was something more to this than first seemed. Why was she, of all the town's inhabitants, the one picked out for this persecution? And why had this only come to light now, just a matter of weeks before he arrived? Perhaps he was right to come here to Badenhof, maybe there was more to this parochial town than met the eye. Looking at Ursula, he saw she was shaking, a tear rolling down her cheek.

'Is it over?' she asked hesitantly, her eyes fearful.

'Yes, you have nothing more to prove to me,' he said, and she stepped in towards him.

'Thank you, thank you,' she said, burrowing her head in his chest. He let himself relax, and put an arm around her shoulder. She sobbed for only a few moments before she stepped back and wiped the moisture from her cheeks.

'Sigmar protects,' Marius muttered, remembering the massive gold-inlaid words carved above the main gates to the Nuln cathedral. This was not some random incident, he decided. He would keep the girl close, gain her confidence and see what happened. While he was doing that, he would do well to keep her safe from whomever was trying to distract him from his real task. He had a feeling that Badenhof could be a key to unlocking the skaven mystery.

A COLD WIND blew in through the door of the house as Marius stepped inside, kicking slushy snow from his riding boots. He hung his hat and cloak on a hook on the wall and slammed shut the ill-fitting door with a bang. Ursula looked over at him and smiled, before spooning hot broth into a cup from the pot hanging in the fireplace. She took the steaming soup over to the table whilst the witch hunter pulled off his boots with a groan. She heard the heavy foot-steps of Ruprecht coming down the stairs and hurried back to the pot to ladle out another serving. The two of them sat down and ate in silence while Ursula busied herself fetching bread and cheese.

For ten days now she had acted as housekeeper to the pair after Marius had arranged her release from the gaol, in a small abandoned cottage just a little further out from the shrine along the Sigmarstrasse. The rest of the witch hunter's men were berthed in inns and homes throughout Badenhof, while they continued searching for the conspirators within the town. She had heard the whispers when she had gone shopping for food, and seen the jealous glances of the other townsfolk, yet so far the protection of the intimidating Marius seemed to have kept her from further harm. Every day she had gone to the shrine to pray, for Kurt's safe return and speedy end to the town's woes, and she had been met with frosty stares and silent derision from Frau Linde, who waited for Ursula by her door every morning.

When he had finished, Ruprecht pushed away his dish, belched loudly and leaned his chair back on its legs.

'Darius found the body of Herr Stein,' he reported, with a glance at Ursula, who bustled back to the kitchen to leave them in some privacy. As she clattered with the pans, she caught snippets of their conversation.

'Where was it?' Marius asked.

'That's the thing, it was on the other side of town from his warehouse.' Ruprecht said. 'And it was not a pretty sight. We kept it covered up and the watch don't know, but it was plague-ridden.'

'But he died of a heart failure. How in Sigmar's name did he get plague after he was dead?' said Marius.

'I haven't any idea,' muttered Ruprecht, slurping the rem-nants of his soup. 'Perhaps he wasn't dead at first.'

'Not dead?' said Marius. 'I suppose if you want your activ-ities to remain hidden, there's little better alibi than being in your grave, but why bring this to everyone's attention by having that grave dug up?'

'I don't have all the answers,' Ruprecht said.

'No, of course you don't, neither of us do,' admitted Marius. 'Two weeks we've been here and hardly a sniff of any skaven activity other than my suspicions and some odd events. Any other successes today?'

'Still nothing to be found in the south district,' the big man complained as Ursula returned with a plate of baked potatoes and turnips. 'It's like a horde of orcs have been through there, one building in five is a smouldering ruin. The whole Suidenstrasse is a pile of rubble. When the towns-folk heard plague victims were living there they put the whole street to the torch before the watch turned up. Even the grave diggers are complaining there's too much work at the moment.'

'Has everyone gone mad?' Ursula asked bitterly, spooning the food out onto the men's plates.

'In a sense, yes,' admitted Marius, wiping the last drops of broth from the bottom of his cup with a hunk of bread and dragging the vegetable meal in front of him. 'People are like sheep and need good shepherding. Badenhof is in the grip of a strange disease, whose symptoms are fear and suspicion. Hungry and cold, isolated from the outside, its people are terrified and are looking for some solution to their woes. A few individuals have lashed out and the others have latched on to this. It is a hysteria that is sweeping through the town, fuelled by uncertainty. While the town leaders do nothing, it will continue to grow until the town tears itself apart.'

'We've seen it before,' Ruprecht confirmed with a sorrow-ful shake of his head. 'And the real problem is that it does nothing but hinder our work here. While everyone cries "witch" and points at their neighbours, the real culprits for these crimes and disturbances can hide behind the confu-sion and anarchy.'

'So surely you have to find out who profits best from this mess,' suggested Ursula. 'Perhaps I could help if you told me more about why you are here.'

'Perhaps, but perhaps not,' Marius replied solemnly. 'Not only are the original instigators involved in this, but all manner of opportunists will have exploited the situation to their advantage. Petty-minded people try to settle scores, like Frau Linde and you. In many ways, I fear my presence has accelerated the decay and disorder, giving the people even more of a focus to direct their suspicions to, I'm inundated by accusations and complaints every day. It is better that you stay out of affairs as much as possible, the feelings you arouse might simply complicate matters.'

'Our presence can even trigger off this madness,' added Ruprecht. 'One sniff of a witch hunter and suddenly everyone starts wondering why we're there and their prejudices and superstitions are brought to the fore.'

'So how do you thread through all of this tangle?' asked Ursula with a frown, annoyed that they did not trust her.

'To be honest, in this sort of situation things are far beyond a simple remedy,' Marius admitted forlornly. 'We have to be patient, and a little lucky. There may be nothing amiss apart from hunger and disease and disaffected people, in which case we will move on. But if there is something else, we have to be sure of ourselves before we move.'

'And we have to be watchful!' put in Ruprecht with more optimism. 'If we're diligent then somebody may slip up. The important thing is to be prepared for when that happens, so we can act swiftly.'

'Be lucky? Be prepared? Wait for them to slip up?' exclaimed Ursula in exasperation. 'What good is that?'

Marius and Ruprecht looked at her and then at each other and shrugged. There was nothing else to say.

NEARLY A THIRD of Badenhof was now in ruins and almost all control had been lost in the poorer areas. Some of the watch were little better than the bloodthirsty crowds and looters they were supposed to be keeping in order. Ursula herself had been told by Marius not to venture out. Ruprecht had also confided in her that he was concerned for her safety, and he seemed convinced that it was not just the petty-minded gossiping and vitriol of Frau Linde that directed the ire of the superstitious townsfolk. He had told her, after some coercion by the persistent redhead, that someone behind the scenes appeared to be using all of the disturbance and violence to mask their own nefarious activities, but Marius and his band were no closer to locating or identifying that person. Ursula was not unduly worried, for she knew she was innocent of any crime and whatever her enemies tried to do, Sigmar would keep her safe.

Two more days passed without significant event, as Ursula continued her housekeeping duties for the witch hunter and his comrade. Others in the group dropped by occasionally to report their findings, but there seemed to be little real activity to report and most complained of the constant distractions caused by the local watch, the wildfire mob violence and the ineptitude or complacency of the town officials. News arrived daily that nearby towns were suffering similar outbreaks of violence, and the whole of northern Ostermark seemed on the verge of outright revolt.

Ursula did not realise just how bad things had got until Marius burst through the door shortly before lunchtime, quickly followed by Ruprecht and another two of his men. Ursula was cleaning down the floor in front of the wood stove and stood up, startled.

'What's wrong?' she asked.

'It's getting serious,' growled Ruprecht, 'very bad indeed. Get something warm on, we have to move you out of here.'

'Why?' Ursula demanded indignantly. 'What am I supposed to be running from?'

'No arguments!' snapped Marius. 'Events have taken a turn for the worse for all of us, our enemies are being very manipulative. It seems their interest in you has not passed, and they are going to try to use that against me. I suspect you have been put up as a scapegoat ever since I arrived, and I am more convinced than ever that there is something dark afoot in this town. Now, get ready to leave.'

'I'm not going anywhere until you explain what is going on,' Ursula told the group, crossing her arms stubbornly.

'Accusations have been made concerning our, ah, arrangements here,' Marius mumbled, glancing out of the window. The sound of shouting grew louder outside.

'Our arrangements?' Ursula's voice rose to a shriek. 'I can just imagine the kind of hateful rantings of witches like Emerelde, they never believe anything good of me. I've seen their looks and heard the whispering when I've been out. Well, I've had enough of it!'

'The prattling of old wives I could live with,' Marius replied with a sour look, gesturing her to stand next to him and look out of the heavily leaded window.

Turning her gaze outside, Ursula saw a group of around fifteen men running down the Sigmarstrasse. Amongst them, she spotted a few red armbands, indicating that members of the town watch were present. She spun on her heel and strode towards the door, slapping away Ruprecht's outstretched arm as he tried to intercept her. Throwing open the door she stood on the step and waited for the crowd to get to the gate into the small garden at the front of the cottage.

'Haven't you all got work to do?' Ursula asked them scornfully.

'You may have cast your glamours on the witch hunter, bitch, but you'll not cloud our minds!' The speaker was a middle-aged man at the front of the crowd. He was short and wiry, with a prominent boil on the left side of his nose that gave his face a lop-sided look.

Ruprecht shoved past Ursula and began remonstrating with the mob, as Marius pulled her back through the doorway.

'Let us handle this, you impetuous girl!' the witch hunter hissed in her ear, feeling that events were about to overtake him if he didn't take control. Ursula's rashness could put them all in serious danger. 'That is Eiger Winckler, the senior court usher. There's more to this than just a noisy crowd you stupid child!'

Marius's sharp words stung Ursula and she stepped back as if slapped in the face. She stood silent for a moment before thrusting Marius back out of the way and charging past Ruprecht.

'What do you people want from me?' she shouted at the crowd, a few members of which, including Winckler, had now moved into the garden. 'I've done nothing wrong!'

'Then you won't mind facing a proper public trial then,' Winckler responded, stepping forward, a sly look on his face. 'You know the charges.'

'A trial?' spat Ursula. 'It would be a mockery of justice.'

'Don't do this—' warned Ruprecht at her shoulder. 'Be careful—'

'Magistrate Fenster foresaw such an argument,' Winckler told her, now a little ahead of the mob, his hands clasped in front of him like a rodent guarding its food. 'To dismiss your doubts, and also to give Herr van Diesl an opportunity to protect his own name, Magistrate Fenster proposes that the witch hunter officiates the proceedings.'

'What nonsense is this?' Marius exclaimed from the doorway, and then turned to Ursula. 'We have nothing to prove here. Someone is trying to trick you.'

'What have they been saying?' she asked the witch hunter, glancing back at Winckler.

'It isn't important, lass,' Ruprecht told.

'What are they saying about us?' Ursula's voice was little more than dangerous hiss.

'That I'm protecting you in return for, well, for certain physical favours,' Marius replied after a pause. 'You have bewitched me into agreeing this arrangement. Pay it no heed, though!' he insisted.

Ursula's fury was incandescent. She rounded on the crowd, her face flushed, and stalked up to Winckler.

'I'll stand trial!' Ursula spat, thrusting her face into his. 'This town will learn just who's responsible for this whole mess, and when the time comes I'll be there for when the judge at their trial sends them to prison to rot!'

'Well, that's us buggered then,' she heard Ruprecht mutter from behind her.

CHAPTER SEVEN
Fugitive
The Kislev Road, Winter early 1709

'WE STILL HAVE to work out where we'll cross the Urskoy,' Kurt pointed out, tossing another twig on to the small campfire Jakob had built.

'We should follow river for bridge or ford, road too risky,' agreed Jakob, pulling off his mittens and warming his hands at the growing blaze.

For the last few weeks, they had moved southwards as quickly as they could, but the harsh weather and the need to keep their route secret had hampered their speed. Now they would be crossing over into Ostland within the next day or two if they could, and from there turn south-east towards Badenhof.

'We'll have to be careful,' warned Kurt, following the servant's example. 'Those places will all have settlements, and who knows what might be waiting for us. I suppose you can try and get some of your people to help us.'

'My people?' Jakob answered with a frown. 'Not understand your meaning.'

'Well, this is your country after all,' Kurt explained. 'Are you from this area?'

105

Jakob was silent, poking at the fire with a stick.

'You've said hardly a word since we left,' Kurt complained. 'You won't even tell me why you insisted on coming with me.'

Still Jakob refused to comment, his expression surly.

'Give me one good reason not to leave you here and now!' demanded Kurt, rising to his feet.

Jakob shook his head slowly, still staring at the fire, and Kurt stomped off through the small copse of trees in which they had chosen to make their campsite. He snapped a twig from one of the snow-laden branches and twisted it between his fingers in agitation. The whole flight south had grated on his nerves. The need for stealth constantly warred with his desire to gallop to Badenhof as quickly as possible. Several times they had doubled back and circled to confuse the trail they left, and on one occasion had actually seen a small party of knights in the distance. Now Kurt was even more worried. The delay in finding a crossing point of the Urskoy, which would take them the wrong side of the river and hopefully throw off their pursuers, meant that there was no way of telling if the pair were still ahead of the hunt, or if any of the Osterknacht had overtaken them in the wilds.

The young knight was desperately worried about Ursula. He knew in his heart that she was capable, resourceful and able to take care of herself. She had done so for years. And yet, he felt responsible for her. Whether she could look after herself or not, he wanted to look after her, to free her from worries and cares. He wanted her to have a life worth living, and share in her fortunes and woes, regardless of whether they were his doing or not. He longed desperately to wake up and find that this had all been a bizarre dream, but the chill of the wind and the cracking of the icy snow underfoot was all too real.

A movement in the periphery of his vision and a quiet rustle drew his attention to his left. Kurt's hand strayed to the sword hanging at his belt and he stepped up to a tree to conceal himself.

'Master?' he heard Jakob call softly, and Kurt stepped out.

'I'm over here. Why aren't you watching the horses?' he asked.

Jakob picked his way through the snow-buried tree roots and rocks until he was stood a few feet from the knight.

'I wish to be sorry,' Jakob told him, avoiding Kurt's gaze. 'Not meaning to anger you, am afraid.'

'We're both afraid,' agreed Kurt, offering a hand of friendship, which Jakob took with a smile. 'But you don't have to be afraid of me, I'm not the enemy.'

'Not yet,' Jakob said sadly, letting go of Kurt's hand, hanging his head.

'What do you mean, "not yet"?' asked Kurt, growing suspicious. 'What have you done?'

'Cannot say why leaving the knights,' mumbled Jakob, kicking at the snow. Suddenly he looked up at the knight. 'Why you leave? You never say.'

Kurt thought for a moment, looking at the weary manservant. Could he trust Jakob? Then again, he thought, he couldn't expect Jakob to trust him with his secrets if he concealed his own. A sudden urge grew within Kurt to tell Jakob just what it was that had set him on this seemingly mad path. For too many years only he had known the full truth of his life, and here in the wilderness, isolated and hunted, it seemed fitting that the man who was his only companion should know the full truth about his travelling partner.

'Walk with me back to the fire, and I will tell you,' offered Kurt, receiving a look and a nod from Jakob. 'I have never told this to anyone, not even Ursula, and you must swear to secrecy.'

'Yes, I swear, as you when I tell the tale of me,' Jakob said.

'I agree, this shall by our pact.' Kurt replied, walking through the snow. After a moment, Jakob followed.

Kurt was quiet for a moment, the silence broken by a distant owl and the creak of branches under the weight of snow. He could recall the scene in every minute detail. The flicker of the fire through the trees made the memory all the more clear, and Kurt glanced at Jakob beside him. The man was watching intently, concentrating on the knight's words.

A DISTANT NOISE *in the night's silence woke Kurt from a dream of sunlit meadows. It was a dog's bark, the young boy noted as the noise sounded again, closer and louder. More than one, he* realised as a chorus of howls and barks erupted, drawing him from his bed. The night felt still and cold, despite the fire still dying in the grate and the warmth of the wooden panelling of the bedchamber. Brushing aside the light curtain of the four poster bed he stepped across to the window, his bare feet shrinking from the coolness of the bare flagstones. Pulling aside the left-hand shutter, he looked out over the ground of his father's estates.

In the distance, something glowed in the moonless dark. A ruddy halo approached through the trees, and more yapping and barking echoed towards the ancient family house. Fear gripped Kurt, the pit of his stomach tightening, as he listened to the clamour approaching, the noise swelled by the voices of men as well as hounds.

Behind him, the door crashed open and he span, a shriek about to erupt from his throat. Kurt relaxed when he saw it was Renchsel, his father's gamekeeper, with a shielded lantern in his hand. The man was sweating hard, his face red and puffy, and his eyes darted side-to-side nervously.

'Grab some clothes, young master, and quickly,' Renchsel told him, trying obviously to keep his voice calm.

'What's happening?' demanded Kurt, not moving. 'Where's my father?'

'He's downstairs, young master, now don't tarry, get something to wear.' The gamekeeper's voice became insistent and Kurt took a few steps towards the large wardrobe opposite the foot of the bed. He stopped and turned back to Renchsel.

'Is it trouble?' he asked, his stomach churning again. 'Who is out there?'

'Yes, lad, it's trouble,' Renchsel replied, wiping sweat from his forehead with his sleeve. 'Now stop dawdling or you'll be out in the cold in just your nightshirt, young master.'

Kurt hurried to the wardrobe and flung the door open. He paused self-consciously for a moment before flinging aside his linen night robe and grabbing a pair of breeches from one of the shelves inside. He grabbed a thick woollen shirt, deep red like the covers on his bed, and pulled it over his head. Lastly he pulled on some riding boots, scuffing the skin of his feet on the tight leather and wincing to himself.

'I'll grab a cloak from the hall downstairs,' Kurt told the gamekeeper as the two of them headed out the door. They were on the *landing above the reception hall, twin stairways arcing down gracefully to either side of the main doors. Barely half the torches were lit in their sconces, giving the hallway a lopsided shadow that left the feet of the stairs in darkness. Below he saw his father running out of the door to the servants' scullery and he was about to call out when something boomed against the thick oak doors and made them rock in the hinges.*

'What was that?' Kurt asked querously, snapping a glance at his father, who had stopped in mid-stride.

'No more questions,' Renchsel replied hoarsely, grabbing the seven-year old by the arm and dragging him down the stairway. His father, Lord Leitzig, met them at the bottom, dressed in full travelling clothes, a cloak over one shoulder. In his left hand he carried a heavy bag, and he grasped a thin fencing sword in the right.

'Pay that no heed, son,' Lord Leitzig reassured his son with a wink. 'Just the neighbours getting jealous. Follow me, your ma and Katherina are waiting in the west chamber.'

Another boom shook the main doors, and for the first time Kurt noticed that the ancient iron braces had been lowered into place, barring the entrance. Not since his great grandfather had been besieged by the army of Baron Klein of Ostland had the defences been used. The thought worried the boy even more, and he gripped Renchsel's hand tightly as the two adults led him through the door under the landing into the centre of the mansion. Turning left, they followed a narrow passage between the kitchens and the dining room, coming out to the chamber that dominated the west wing. Kurt's mother and sister were waiting there, a few candles lit on the massive candelabra that swung above their heads barely relieving the gloom. Low armchairs huddled in the shadows, filling the air with the fragrance of old leather. Wisps of candle smoke drifted lazily in a draught from the large windows that looked out on the gardens.

Kurt let go of Renchsel and ran to his mother, throwing his arms around her waist and burrowing his face in the soft folds of her skirt. He felt like he was going to cry, but then felt a hand on his shoulder and looked up. Katherina was there, six years older than him, as much a parent as his real mother.

'Everything's going to be all right, little weasel!' she said with a smile. 'Pa will get us out of here.'

He smiled back and pulled himself together. He was seven, not a baby, and if everyone else was going to be brave so was he. His new-found confidence disappeared instantly when the sound of crashing glass resounded along the corridor. A moment later he heard the dull clatter of metal on metal and matched it to the noise made when he was at sword practice. Someone was fighting!

'They're inside!' hissed Renschel, putting the lamp down on a low table and pulling a heavy sword from his belt. 'Get out, I'll guard your backs, milord.'

'Is it the Ostlanders again, pa?' Kurt asked as his mother grabbed his hand and pulled him towards the door at the opposite end of the room.

'It's not Ostlanders, no,' his father replied from just behind him, his gaze flicking between his young son and the other doorway, now filled by the bulk of Renschel.

'Hurry, my love,' his mother urged, squeezing his hand tighter and giving his arm a yank. Katherina grabbed his other hand and all four of them slipped through the door into the darkness of the stairwell leading down to the wine cellar.

Kurt heard Renschel bellowing but couldn't make out the words, and the sound of fighting erupted from the next room. His heart quickened and he thought he was going to cry out, but a reassuring squeeze from Katherina quelled the sob in his throat. He sniffed instead, ignoring the tears now welling up in his eyes.

'Where we going, ma?' Kurt asked pensively as his father opened the door to the cellar. Stone steps led down into the darkness, barely lit by the glimmering light from the room behind them. Kurt shrank back from the gloom, afraid of what might be down there.

'There's a secret passage my grandfather built down here,' Lord Leitzig said. 'For just this purpose, the crafty old goat. If we hurry, we'll be out and away before they realise we've gone.'

But at that moment, a heavy thumping sounded from down the stairs, followed quickly by the crash of splintering wood. A sudden cold breeze wafted up from the cellar and Kurt's skin prickled at the chill. His father snarled wordlessly and pushed them towards the open doorway to the servant's quarters.

'Just run!' he snapped, shoving Kurt through the opening. The young boy needed no more encouragement, and with tears streaming down his cheeks, nearly threw himself down the spi-ralling stairs, scraping his arm against the rough stone wall as he almost lost his footing. Proceeding less hastily, he heard the foot-steps of someone else behind him, then his father shouted something.

Reaching the bottom, Kurt found himself in a scullery, with a door leading left and right. He had played down here before, and knew his way around, but where was he supposed to be going? He stopped and looked back up the stairs, expecting to see his mother or sister. A flickering shadow descended around the bend, and the heir to the Leitzig Lordship was confronted by a barrel-chested man dressed in hunting leathers and a deep red cloak. His face was torn from his top lip to his left ear by a fresh wound, and his blunt nose trickled with blood as well. Under a thick shock of dark curly hair, deep brown eyes glared menacingly at Kurt.

With a shriek Kurt spun and darted to the left, which would take him past the servants' bedrooms and back towards the recep-tion hall. He slammed through the door, sobbing to himself, and sped along the narrow corridor with the man pounding behind him. Kurt burst through the door at the far end and stopped to look back. The man was barely five yards away, and the boy slammed the door home, and hared off again, across the small chamber back to the stairs leading to the entrance hall. He was halfway up when he heard the door behind him wrenched open, and redoubled his efforts, his breath being torn from his young lungs by the exertion.

Skidding into the reception hall, Kurt headed straight for the main stairs, realising that the pounding on the main doors had stopped. Their attackers had evidently given up hope of breaking through the sturdy portal. The chamber was empty, but Kurt could hear sounds of fighting from the nearby rooms and paused only for a moment to make sure no one was lurking in the shadows upstairs before breaking into a run again, taking the stairs as quickly as his short legs allowed.

'The boy's come this way!' he heard the man chasing him shout out, and he ducked behind one of the pillars supporting the high roof, peering out from his hiding place on the landing to see the man prowling around downstairs, looking for a sign of where the boy had got to. Kurt pulled his boots from his feet and laid them down out of sight before padding from shadow to shadow, holding his breath for fear of being heard. He reached the door to his room just as he heard several people thundering up the stair behind him.

With a gasp, Kurt leapt into the room. Where could he hide? Under the bed, he thought at first, but that seemed too obvious. His eyes fell on the large wardrobe and as the clamour from outside came closer he made his decision, climbing into the large cabinet and pulling the door almost closed behind him just a moment before the first man entered the room.

Now bursting for breath and red in the face, Kurt watched anxiously through the narrow gap between the doors as two more men, both vicious thugs by the look of them, came into the room.

'I'll swear by Sigmar's hammer he's in here somewhere,' the first growled, the one who had chased him from the servant's quarters.

He took a step towards the bed, pulling a hunting knife from his belt, and stooped to look under it. Grunting, he straightened and looked around, his eyes settling on the wardrobe. Fear gripped Kurt even more, though he wouldn't have believed it possible, and his stomach tossed and jumped so much he felt like being sick. The man took one step, then another, and was almost in reach of the door handle when a woman's shrieking attracted his attention to the window.

It was Katherina, Kurt recognised her high-pitched voice. He couldn't understand what she was screaming, if anything, and for a moment he almost rushed out to see. But he stopped himself just in time, as the three men looked at each other and laughed, turning away and moving out of the room.

There was more screaming, from his mother and sister. As well as shouted curses from his father. But Kurt waited, not sure if the ugly men would return for him. For ages he seemed to wait, listening to the sounds of his family in distress, and soon his fear of what was happening to them outweighed his terror of the men, and he ventured out. Crossing quickly to the window, Kurt gasped in horror as he saw that four poles had been planted outside, in the middle of the northern lawn, with branches and broken furniture stacked at their bases. Crying fitfully, he watched as his mother, father and sister were tied to the stakes by a mob of rough-looking commoners, helpless to do anything, feeling utterly wretched and sick with foreboding.

Then someone else walked into view. He was tall and straight, much better dressed than the others with a heavy cloak of black *leather hanging from his shoulders, riding breeches and boots, and a dark hat with a long black feather tucked into the rim on the left hand side. In his hand, the man carried a guttering torch, and slowly paced towards Kurt's family, who had fallen silent now, their expressions of dumb shock and uncomprehending horror. His father seemed to stir himself and spat at the man, who said something and then thrust the torch into the bundle of wood. The pyre went up like a firework, obviously doused in oil or something similar.*

Kurt threw up then, unable to stomach the horror any longer as first the cries of his father, then his mother, then his sister filled his ears. He was shaking and cold, his whole body numb, and he fell to his knees and retched again and again until his stomach cramped with agony. The stench drifted through the window and, despite every fibre of himself telling him not to look, Kurt gazed out the window again at the charring corpses on the stakes.

His tears stopped, and Kurt felt a stillness in himself. Something deeply profound passed through him. In that moment, he looked upon the silhouette of the man with the black feather in his hat, and for the first time knew true hatred. Like the fire that was consuming his parents, the loathing and disgust began to burn away his innocence as he looked upon his family's murderer.

The moment passed when Kurt's nostrils detected a different smell in the smoke now clouding the view from the window. Glancing down, he saw the flicker of orange flames from the manse itself, and realised that they had given up looking for him and were going to burn the whole mansion down.

No longer scared, but filled with the desire to save himself so that one day others might know what happened here, Kurt left the room. Smoke filled the landing, and as he passed towards the stairs, he could see the glow of flames beginning to creep across the entrance hall. Pulling his boots on quickly from where he had hid them, feeling a little foolish now for having taken them off, Kurt decided nobody else would be stupid enough to stay in a burning house. He dashed down the stairs as the flames began to lick up the walls of the chamber, setting fire to the animal heads hung as hunting trophies. He gazed for a moment in morbid fascination as the fire consumed the head of a proud stag and then jumped flickering to the bear's head next to it. Pulling himself

*from the trance, Kurt headed back towards the stairs to the cellar
and the secret door to the outside.*

He gave a silent prayer that no one was guarding it.

'THAT WAS WHEN I decided that I would never let anyone harm
my loved ones again,' Kurt said. 'I was too young to have the
words to express it at the time, and it's only been in the long
years since that I've been able to put it that way, but it was at
that moment I decided I would not mourn my family, I
would avenge them. Looking upon the silhouette of the
man with the black feather in his hat, for the first time I
knew true hatred. Like the fire that was consuming my parents, the loathing and disgust began to burn away at me as I
watched my family's murderer.'

'You know him?' Jakob asked, his eyes wide, amazed by
the horrifying finale to Kurt's tale.

'I found out later who he was, much later,' Kurt confirmed.

'You got away,' Jakob pointed out. 'You are here now.'

'Yes,' Kurt replied. 'There was no guard and just before
dawn I ran across the gardens, into the fields and then hid in
the woods on the borders of my father's lands. I crossed the
Talabec a couple of days later and lost myself in Ostland.'

'But who the man with the feather?' repeated Jakob. 'Who
the evil man?'

'My family was killed by a witch hunter,' Kurt told Jakob
with a snarl. 'A man called Marius van Diesl. Eight years
later, before I met Lord Gerhardt, I was with a group of sell-
swords, under a man called Captain Feigas. I heard from
him about van Diesl. He was looking to hire men. Feigas
was going to sign us up and I left, it was too soon to confront van Diesl.'

'He is one who goes to your town?' asked Jakob.

'Yes, the same man,' Kurt said. 'I don't know if he's there
for me, but I must stop him doing the same thing to Ursula
that he did to my family.'

'And kill him, yes?' urged Jakob.

'If I get the chance,' Kurt replied grimly, his eyes misted
with tears.

* * *

JAKOB DIDN'T COMMENT further. It was Jakob's turn for first watch and he rooted out more wood from under the snow to keep himself awake. Kurt's story had touched a chord, and although he didn't fully understand what could drive the young knight to abandon the Osterknacht, he could see that the trauma of his childhood was still having its effect a decade and a half later.

He thought of Kurt's devotion to his woman, Ursula, and wished that he had known that kind of love in his life. Staring at the sleeping Kurt, the firelight flickering over his handsome young face, Jakob could see why this girl had fallen in love. There was genuine strength there, as shown by the young knight's bravery, stubbornness and headstrong nature. It was what had drawn Jakob to the young knight, and to make himself known when he had carried the boy's banner for him at the duel. There was a certain destiny surrounding Kurt that Jakob could feel. Kurt was a catalyst, things happened around him, and Jakob planned to use that to his advantage. Also, with the revelation of the horrendous death of Kurt's parents, Jakob had seen where the youth's weakness and vulnerability was. That would prove useful in the future, the old retainer was sure. For too long Jakob had been scraping a rough semblance of a life, wherever he could. With Kurt to provide the muscle for his plans, Jakob was sure he could actually achieve something. Though his long years had not been easy on his mind and body, Jakob was sure that with his experience, he would be able to use Kurt to get the power and prestige he craved.

Jakob allowed Kurt to sleep through until dawn, instead of waking him when his watch should have started.

'Why didn't you wake me?' demanded Kurt, as he pulled on his garments, anxious that he should not be accused of failing to pull his weight.

'You needed sleep, was hard, difficult night for you,' Jakob replied, waving away the young man's concerns. He waggled a strip of salted beef in front of Kurt's face and grinned, exposing his missing and uneven teeth. 'Breakfast ready.'

They had eaten and mounted before the sun was fully over the horizon, and Jakob had opted to lead them westwards towards the Urskoy. They could follow the eastern

bank until they reached a village with a crossing. Not only
was it their greatest chance of losing any pursuit, it would
also increase their travelling time by at least a week. That
would give Jakob more time to establish himself with Kurt,
earn his trust and respect, and be in a position to exert his
influence over the lad. It also had the added benefit that the
longer they took, the more likely that they would arrive too
late to save Ursula, and that would leave Kurt open to whatever course of action Jakob cared to propose.

'Thank you for your story,' Jakob said suddenly, as the two
of them rode through the mud and snow following the
ancient frozen ruts of an old farm track. 'Owe you story of
me now.'

'I hope you would trust me after last night,' Kurt admitted
with a glance at his companion.

'I have lies too,' Jakob confided. 'Not Kislevite, father from
the Skaeldings.'

'The Skaeldings?' asked Kurt, confused, for he had never
heard the term before. 'Where is that?'

'Skaeldings people, not place,' Jakob laughed at the young
man's error. 'Skaeldings live in the north, land you call
Norsca.'

Kurt reined in his horse and looked aghast at Jakob, who
stopped his stolen steed a few paces farther on and looked
back over his shoulder.

'You're a northman?' the knight asked. 'Your people are
like those twisted things we fought a few weeks ago?'

'Yes, northman me,' confirmed Jakob. 'Not all touched by
the gods, most untouched like me.'

'I can see why you'd masquerade as a Kislevite!' snarled
Kurt. 'Just what devilment have you been up to?'

'Cannot control my birth,' Jakob replied, trying to look as
hurt as he possibly could. 'You evil, because a witch hunter
want to burn you?'

'My parents weren't witches!' Kurt said vehemently, before
realisation dawned on him. 'Sorry, I see why the subterfuge
was necessary, just like mine. People would not understand.'

'Yes, though I not as innocent as you,' Jakob told Kurt,
wheeling his horse around to ride a little closer. 'Perhaps
you understand a little. My people are my people and many

things said about them are true. Our gods are not your gods, our gods demand more from us than yours, but our gods are also stronger than yours.'

'I have no time for any gods. Where were they when my parents and sister were being scorched by the flames?' Jakob's heart soared as he heard the bitterness in Kurt's voice. Truly, here was a pupil worthy of the wisdom that lay within the old Norscan's mind.

'Our gods sometimes answer, sometimes not,' said Jakob philosophically. 'It matters not, they are the gods and we do not judge them. We earn reward by our deeds and thoughts and make lives our own. If the gods mark one out, then he is fortunate, but those who are chosen must still prove their worth.'

'I don't really understand what you are saying,' confessed Kurt, confused by Jakob's talk of marked men and chosen ones.

'Then I teach you,' Jakob promised with a friendly smile.

'But how did you come to be a servant in the Osterknacht?' asked Kurt. 'Why are you not still with your people?'

'Mother from your people, taken on a raid by the Skaeldings,' explained Jakob as the two started their horses walking again. 'Father was important warrior, but half-breed like me, not much standing. Only father stopped Jakob being slave for Skaeldings.'

'You're half-Norscan, then?' asked Kurt, digesting this information. 'What happened?'

'When father died I was alone,' Jakob continued. 'No food, no begging or be beaten, so I hunt and teach myself the ways of snow and mountain. I learn to tell story from village leaders. I sit in their hall out of sight and listen to their words. I watch them talk to gods and learn the words too. Sometime I have called on the gods, for little things. I light a fire with their help, or maybe kill a deer. Small rituals, but I know many of the words to call upon them for bigger magic. Ten year ago, I ask to become Elder for Skaeldings and I show them my power, but I am laughed at. Not welcome, I leave, but no other will take me, not Bearsonlings, not Feijgardssons, not others. Decide that land of mother will be new home, but is same there. I learn that Norsca not good home to have when you are in Empire, and I learn the name for this land, Kislev, and say I come from there. That make life easier.'

'Well, if my own reaction was anything to go by, I can see why you had to do that not to be stoned out of hand,' conceded Kurt.

'Yes, I not want to be stoned,' said Jakob with a shake of his head. 'Move around, end up in Osterknacht. Not good life, but quiet mostly.'

'So why the change of heart, why come with me?' asked Kurt.

'Need change of heart,' Jakob said, mimicking Kurt's words. 'You that change, perhaps. I see you stand up to Bayen, I like you. The gods like you too, so I come with you.'

'The gods like me?' Kurt inquired. 'What makes you say that, considering the life I've had?'

'You still alive, yes?' asked Jakob with a sombre expression.

'Yes,' Kurt admitted with a shrug. 'So?'

'Family die, you live, that a good sign the gods like you,' explained the northman with an emphatic nod of his head. 'You see family die, that bad sign, but I see you live, that good sign.'

'I think I understand, though I don't think I agree,' Kurt replied. 'I would rather die than see Ursula taken from me the same way my family were.'

Jakob grunted in a non-committal fashion and they rode on for the rest of the morning in silence. Just before noon, they saw the glittering waters of the Urskoy in the distance. Turning southwards, they followed the river for a few more miles and started coming across the first signs of civilisation since they had given Erengrad a wide berth a month earlier. The dark buildings of scattered farms stood out in stark contrast to the white blanket of snow, and low stone walls began to appear across their route.

'Farms mean town soon, Maersko, I think,' announced Jakob as they steered their horses on to a muddy track that curved away towards the river. Sure enough, by mid afternoon a cluster of low buildings could be seen on the banks of the river and the town of Maersko spread along the river's banks. It was not a large settlement, perhaps a hundred buildings at most, but it did obviously have a bridge or ferry.

'We should get more supplies,' Kurt said as they entered the outskirts of the town. 'Perhaps we could even stay the night, it would be good to have a proper bed for at least a single night.'

'Yes, warm bed, hot food, that would be good,' agreed Jakob with a grin. 'Find alehouse for beer!'

'Let's not get too carried away,' cautioned Kurt. 'We still can't relax, the Osterknacht could be only a few days behind us for all we know.'

'But beer?' asked Jakob, with concern on his face.

'Yes,' laughed Kurt, 'we can have a beer or two but no more than that, we may need our wits about us.'

THEY RODE TO the centre of Maersko, which was dominated by a large open place around a long stone bridge across the river. The buildings were all single-storey, built of roughly cut stones and roofed with slate – thatch was a rare commodity in Kislev. The people in the streets were dressed in heavy winter furs, and shuffled through the chill with suspicious looks at the pair. They found an inn close to the bridge with stables at the back. With Jakob's rudimentary skills with the language, picked up when he travelled south from Norsca, they were able to secure a room for the night, tankards of thick frothy ale, and bowls of steaming stew. The innkeeper, a pot-bellied, balding man with a long bristling beard, came over and spoke briefly to Jakob as the pair sat down to eat.

'What did he want?' Kurt asked as the man left, casting a glance at the man's back as he returned to the bar.

'Strange thing, he say,' Jakob told the knight. 'He say that we staying in wrong place, that other knights staying at inn on other side of river.'

'Other knights?' gasped Kurt, before lowering his voice. 'The Osterknacht are already here?'

'There are three, I asked him,' confirmed Jakob. 'What we do?'

'Well, we have to leave!' exclaimed Kurt, darting a look around the smoky room as if expecting hidden spies to be looking at them right there and then.

'Not only choice,' countered Jakob, his eyes narrowing. 'Osterknacht think this town safe, they have men here. We kill men, we escape and Osterknacht not know.'

'Kill them?' hissed Kurt. 'Don't be stupid! I've deserted but I'm not about to turn into a murderer. No, we turn back, go back the way we came and find another way across further south.'

'More south, more people, more danger,' argued Jakob with a frown. 'More knights too, maybe. Knights will learn that we here, or have gone, like we learn they are here. They will know where we go and more knights come this way soon.'

'I'll not spill the blood of a fellow knight,' Kurt said vehemently.

'You not knight any more,' Jakob pointed out, pushing away his empty bowl.

'Not by law, but the ideals I swore to, I still believe in,' Kurt replied. 'We leave before dawn, any earlier will cause comment,' he added before looking away and steadfastly ignoring Jakob to indicate the conversation was over.

THE HORSES' HOOVES sounded loudly on the stones of the bridge as Kurt and Jakob rode over the river in the still, pre-dawn hours. Kurt was nervous, his concern about the presence of the other knights heightened by the silence and gloom that enveloped the town. A mist drifted up from the banks of the sluggishly moving Urskoy, shrouding the far end of the bridge. Glancing at Jakob, Kurt saw that the northman was also tense, his head craned forward as his eyes strained to penetrate the shadowy mist ahead. The monotonous clop-clop-clop of the horses also grated on Kurt's nerves, each tread sounding like a booming alarm call.

They passed off the bridge into the far half of the town, and once amongst the darker blocks of the buildings and streets Kurt relaxed a little, feeling less exposed than when he was on the bridge. The mud and snow muffled the tread of the horses and they moved through the twisting fog like mounted ghosts.

It was only when they had moved out of the town itself that the pair felt safer, and picked up speed to put distance between them and their pursuers. As the sun started to burn off the morning mist, they galloped along the road that meandered westwards over a range of low hills. A few miles out of town, they came across a large building beside the road. It consisted of a central two storey building from which two wings came forward towards the road, creating a courtyard. The wing to their left was a row of stables, the other seemed to be some kind of storage sheds. Spying a well, Jakob suggested they pause for a few minutes for the horses to have a drink and to take some breakfast themselves – they had slipped quietly out of the inn before the cooking fires had been lit.

Jakob was busying himself at the well as Kurt strolled across the yard of the building, which was laid out in a u-shape facing the road. He was pleased to stretch his legs. For weeks now he had been sat in the saddle, and spending last night on a straw-stuffed mattress had only served to accentuate the woes of his bones and muscles rather than alleviate them. The door creaked open and a yawning figure walked out, head bowed and stretching his arms wide. Kurt froze. The man was dressed in full plate armour, and when he looked up, Kurt saw that it was Bayen.

'Come on move your lazy bones, I want to be back with the others before nightfall!' Bayen shouted back into the open door, before turning towards Kurt, almost stumbling to the ground in surprise. The two of them stood there for several heartbeats just staring at each other.

'Vermin!' bellowed Bayen, ripping his sword free and sprinting across the yard.

Kurt's blade was still hung on his horse, and he dropped into a crouching stance as Bayen closed in. The other knight gripped his sword two-handed and swung it in an overhand chop towards Kurt's shoulder. Leaning to the left, Kurt reached out, his hands shot up and grabbed Bayen's wrists, forcing the blow aside. Twisting like an eel, Bayen broke free and stepped back, but Kurt gave him no time to prepare for another strike, barrelling into the man, shouldering him in the stomach and hurling the pair of them to the ground. They scrabbled and rolled around on the frozen mud, fighting for a grip on the sword, as Bayen spat curses into Kurt's face.

Ramming his elbow into Bayen's chin, Kurt stunned the knight and brought his knee down on his arm, pinning it to the ground. He smashed a gauntleted hand into Bayen's nose, and then made a grab for the sword. It skittered out of both of their grasps and slid through the snow. Bayen was bleeding from two cuts to his face now, his lips twisted in a mask of fury. With a grunt, he got his foot underneath Kurt and pushed him off, rolling to the side. Kurt slipped in the snow, and the pair of them lunged towards the sword at the same time.

Kurt's hand closed around the grip of the weapon and he swung it low and to his right, its tip ringing off Bayen's breastplate. Panic entered the eyes of the count's cousin, and he back-pedalled away from Kurt, eyes flicking left and right seeking an escape. Anger welled up inside Kurt as he advanced grimly, the sword held ready before him.

With an incoherent yell, Bayen threw himself at Kurt, who reacted without thought, putting his weight on his forward foot and driving forward with all his strength. The sword plunged through the stomach of Bayen and he took two faltering steps before falling to his knees, pulling the sword from Kurt's numbed grasp. The knight's eyes looked up at Kurt in accusation and disbelief before he slumped sideways into the snow, which was turning red as blood spilled from the fatal wound.

Pulling the sword free and averting his gaze from Bayen's staring eyes, Kurt stepped away, shocked by the encounter. It had been over in a matter of moments, though it seemed hours ago that he had first seen the knight walk out of the building. With that thought came the realisation that the other two knights were probably there as well. He looked up at the dark windows, seeking any sign of alarm or movement, but there was none. Not sure what to do, he ran from the courtyard and called softly for Jakob. The Norscan was by the well feeding Heldred, and looked up at Kurt's subdued shout.

'The knights are here!' Kurt gasped breathlessly. 'We have to get out of here!'

'Wait, wait!' Jakob hissed, grabbing Kurt's arm and pulling him back as he tried to mount Heldred. 'Too late to run.'

'What?' Kurt demanded.

'Other knights will find body, will chase us down,' explained Jakob hurriedly. 'Can you fight two knights?'

'No, of course I can't, I'm not that good,' answered Kurt. 'That's why we must get out of here!'

'Hunt will get worse, you wanted for murder now on top of deserter,' Jakob continued.

'He attacked me!' said Kurt, exasperated.

'Not matter,' Jakob waved away Kurt's argument. 'Other knights must die. We hide the bodies, then run. Be far away before found, if they found at all.'

'I can't just kill them in cold blood,' argued Kurt.

'Must, for sake of Ursula,' Jakob responded, which made Kurt visibly flinch. 'Now we must speed, but cannot hide and run fast. We must kill them.'

Kurt hesitated, confused and dazed by the turn of events. He wasn't sure what to do, his own thoughts were in turmoil.

'Come, we do it now!' snapped Jakob, sensing Kurt's uncertainty and grabbing his arm.

They ran around back to the courtyard where Bayen's body was quickly cooling in the snow. Ignoring it, Jakob pointed to the door and they both went in. It was dark inside the coaching inn, the lanterns not yet lit, and Jakob prowled around the room, listening at the three adjoining doors. With a gesture, he indicated one particular room.

At that moment, the sound of footsteps sounded from a corridor leading off to their left and a short, skinny man, dressed only in his trousers, walked into view. Jakob sprung towards him and clamped a hand around his mouth, whispering urgently into the man's ear.

'What are you saying?' hissed Kurt.

'Told him the knights were deserters, we here to kill them,' Jakob answered quietly, letting go of the man who looked wide-eyed at Kurt. He turned to Jakob and spoke some more, pointing back the way he came.

At that moment, someone else came into view from where the man was pointing. It was Vikkson, rubbing his head in a half-daze. He too was dressed in his armour, his sword at his side.

'Leitzig!' the knight gasped when he saw the pair, and turned to run. Kurt was faster, tackling the man to the ground with a crash of armour. Vikkson rammed his elbow back into Kurt's chin, stunning him for a moment. The master sergeant got to one knee before Jakob jumped forward, his hand clamping around the knight's neck. With his free hand, he plunged his dagger up into Vikkson's chin, spilling blood down the front of his armour. He let the body slump to the ground and stood up, eyes narrowed dangerously. The owner of the coaching inn gave a yell and bolted for the front door. Jakob took a step after him, but Kurt held out an arm and stopped the Norscan.

'Leave him be,' Kurt said, panting heavily. 'There's still one more knight here.'

'Where?' asked Jakob.

Kurt walked down the corridor from which Vikkson had emerged, and listened at the first door. Shaking his head, he moved to the next one and held up his hand when he heard signs of movement. Drawing his sword, he flung open the door. The room had four beds, one of which was still made, obviously unused. A shuttered window blocked out almost all the light, and dust motes swirled in the draft. Standing in the centre of the room, still strapping on his armour, was the other knight. He was no older than Kurt, and his bright blue eyes gaped at Kurt as he entered. The man's attention became fixed on the point of Kurt's bloody sword.

'What have you done with the others?' the knight asked with an accusing stare, letting his breastplate drop to the ground. He started trembling, and his eyes darted around the room, looking for some avenue of escape.

'They're dead,' Kurt replied, glaring straight back at the other man.

'Murdering filth!' the knight spat, leaping forward. Kurt smashed the pommel of his sword into the knight's chin, hurling him onto one of the beds. The man stood back up, eyeing Kurt cautiously.

'Why are you doing this, Kurt?' he asked, meeting his gaze.

'You have to finish it,' said Jakob, walking in behind Kurt. 'If you don't, might never see Ursula again.'

'Turn around and kneel down,' Kurt told the knight quietly, pointing to the floor. Shaking, the man did as he was told.

'Don't do this,' the man begged, before bowing his head, a quiet prayer spilling from his lips. Steeling himself, Jakob's words still ringing in his ears, Kurt gripped his sword tighter and swung it down…

The man dead, Kurt looked away, the sword dropping to the floor from his numb grasp.

'We could take their horses,' Jakob suggested, not giving the corpse a second glance. 'Perhaps they have money.'

'I'm not going to loot the dead,' Kurt replied softly. 'Set the horses free, and dump the men and all their possessions in the river.'

'But is a waste,' complained Jakob, but he fell silent as Kurt rounded on him.

'Just do as I say,' Kurt hissed slowly.

With a shrug, Jakob grabbed the dead knight under the shoulders and dragged him out of the door. The young man's head flopped down onto his chest, his dead eyes staring up at Kurt. He heard the Norscan grunting and groaning as he manhandled the body down the corridor. Closing the door, Kurt was alone in the room, his sword lying in the pool of blood on the floor. There he sat on the fresh bed in the darkness, his head in his hands, and wept for what he had done.

CHAPTER EIGHT
Revelations
Badenhof, Winter early 1709

As THE NEWS spread of Ursula's trial, it had a strange effect on the town. A calm that seemed unnatural after the months of rioting and violence descended on Badenhof. There was still much hostility in the air, and if anything the antagonism towards Ursula became even greater, as though those who had sought to blame others had finally bowed to popular opinion and now found Ursula the guilty party.

Marius fretted and did little to hide the fact that being entangled in the legal proceedings of the town's court left him no time to pursue his real foe. As he told Ursula and Ruprecht the morning the whole sorry affair was due to start, this was probably the entire reason for the whole farcical episode. All three were sat in the Sigmarite shrine in whose grounds Ursula had lived. The pews had been formed into a horseshoe shape around the altar and more desks and chairs had been brought in to give it the semblance of a courtroom. This had been just one of the many niggling details that had plagued Marius for the last few days – as a priest and witch hunter he could not preside over a secular trial, and so had been forced to invoke his religious authority and try Ursula by Sigmarite

law. Along with Marius, her judges were to be Brother
Theobald and Magistrate Fenster. Fenster had insisted that
Ursula be tried for her lesser crimes at the same time as she
was answering to the charges of heresy and witchcraft.

'While I'm running around signing records and talking to
ushers, the real evildoers in the town are being given free
rein,' the witch hunter moaned. 'There are lists of witnesses
and character witnesses to be reviewed apparently. And all
the time priests and beggars, watchmen and merchants, the
magistrate himself, the guildmaster's agents, the burgomeister's spokesman, are all tugging at my coat tails for my time.'

'But it does tell us something,' Ruprecht said.

'And what's that?' snapped van Diesl. 'That petty towns
and their petty bureaucracies are no substitute for the genuine justice we deal in?'

'No,' replied Ruprecht with a scowl at the pessimistic
witch hunter. 'Whoever our conspirators are, they must have
good connections. From what we know of the other towns,
the men involved were civic and trade leaders. It seems that's
the case here as well.'

'Yes, you're right,' sighed Marius, pinching the bridge of
his nose. 'I've had no time to think these last few days. It's
just what they want, too! That gives us a few suspects at
least, which is more than we had a week ago.'

Footsteps echoing along the shrine hushed them into
silence. It was Magistrate Fenster, stalking towards them,
bent over with his head swaying from side to side like a carrion scavenger.

'It is most perturbing that a judge of this trial should be in
consultation with the defendant and a possible witness
before proceedings begin,' rasped the old magistrate.

'Until I'm sworn in at the start of the trial, I am free to do
as I wish,' Marius said in reply, standing up. 'What time is
the farce supposed to begin?'

'A farce is it?' said Fenster with a sour look. 'Your interference and cavalier overturning of my earlier judgement in
this matter was the farce. Just who do you think you are,
arriving in our town like this and disturbing our peace?'

'Disturbing your peace?' Ruprecht laughed bitterly. 'There
was almost a daily riot here, and all the while you great

leaders of men sat in the town hall and wrung your hands and waited for us to arrive.'

'Your constant refusal to condemn that girl as the witch she is has added fuel to the fires of our recent worries,' said Fenster, walking past towards the long table where the three judges were to sit. 'This whole matter would have been avoided if you had respected my position and judgement.'

'How long before we start?' asked Ursula.

'Not long now,' Ruprecht told her, glancing through the window at the crowd gathering outside.

IT ACTUALLY TOOK a further two days for the trial to begin properly, and all the formalities to be completed. There was the swearing-in of the judges, the re-sanctifying of the church, the specific charges to be levelled, the reading of ancient texts. The whole matter of Ursula's lack of a next-of-kin took nearly half a day to resolve thanks to the pedantic attention to detail shown by Winckler, the head usher. All the while, Marius was exceedingly vexed, because in the back of his mind he knew this was all a smokescreen to keep him from performing his proper investigations. Ruprecht was coping as best he could, but the whole event had turned into a circus of sorts. Every day, despite the bitter cold, hundreds of townsfolk gathered outside the shrine, listening to the reports of the proceedings from people stationed at the doors.

There was a strange atmosphere surrounding the crowd; a macabre festivity that lent the proceedings an unreal air. There were storytellers, beer merchants, fire-breathers, jugglers and beggars, all using the presence of so many people to earn an odd penny. Some had even erected tents in the church grounds to save themselves the trip back through the streets each day. It had been over two hundred years since the town had last held a witch trial, and the people of Badenhof were making the most of the occasion. On the positive side, the violence had all but died out and an uneasy calm had settled on the town. For Ruprecht though, the presence of so many people gave him cause for concern, as he explained to Marius during one of the many recesses, having shouldered his way through the crowd amidst damning cries of being a witch sympathiser and heretic.

'It's almost dead out there,' Ruprecht said. 'There's hardly a soul on the streets. Your men can't be everywhere, and I reckon that's just what the cultists wanted. With so few eyes and ears around, they could be doing all manner of harm with no one to see them. I think they'll take this opportunity to further their operation, whatever it is.'

'I fear you are right,' replied Marius. 'The longer the trial goes on, the better it is for our enemy. But that also gives us a weapon. I'll be endeavouring to make this as speedy as possible, and whoever seems to be doing the most to procrastinate and exaggerate this sorry affair is most likely one of our prime suspects. Already, I have my suspicions about Magistrate Fenster, and going by recent history the guild-master must surely have some stake in this.'

'Well,' said Ruprecht, 'there's not much I can do outside that the other men aren't doing. I'll keep an eye on our local dignitaries. If they're hoping to keep your hands full so that you don't notice what they're up to, I'll be here to see the things you can't. If it is Fenster, Koln or Kirche, they have a lot of support in Badenhof, and elsewhere. I don't think we can just tie them to a stake and have done with it, we'll need some hard evidence.'

'Very good, Ruprecht,' said Marius, with an almost fatherly smile, though he was barely five years older than his companion. 'I know I can trust you to get what we need. You're a good man.'

'Only because you taught me how to be,' Ruprecht admitted with a grin.

'I wish this wasn't going to take too long,' Marius said with a grimace. 'But I have a feeling that our foes have other plans for me.'

Marius's prediction was proven correct over the following four days. A progression of townsfolk appeared before the three judges, each proclaiming some real or perceived grievance against Ursula. Amongst the veritable throng of people who offered their testimony to damn Ursula, there was the butcher who said that she had caused a rash to appear all over his body after he had turned her down for employment.

Then there was the carpenter who had cut off his thumb with a chisel just days after she had accused him of improper advances towards her. On top of this was the vague testimony of three market stallholders claiming she had cursed them and caused their food to rot after arguments over prices, forcing them to sell bad food and driving them out of business. At each turn, Marius countered these accusations. He pointed out that the reason the butcher had become infected was by illegally buying meat from plagued stock. He told the court of how his investigations had revealed that the carpenter had been in frequent arguments with his wife over his adulterous behaviour, and it was she who had cut off his thumb out of revenge. He revealed that the market traders had been selling poor fruit and vegetables for many years, constantly over-charging their customers for inferior produce, and Ursula had caused a scene in the market one day, highlighting the fact to all within earshot.

Then there were other oddities. There was the farmer from several miles out of town, who brought in a pig that had a front trotter shaped like a human hand. He claimed it was down to the malevolent spirits that Ursula called upon. For all his vehement questioning, Marius could find no way to disprove the theory other than to state that Ursula had no connection with the farmer whatsoever. There were also those who came forward whose cows had refused to give milk for several weeks, or whose goats passed blood from their udders. One woman even went as far to say that Ursula had placed a hex on her baby, and that because of her it had been born with different coloured eyes. One by one over the four days the witnesses gave their testimonies. They were subjected to the questioning of the judges, and the evidence was laboriously written down in the trial records by Winckler, and Marius fretted more and more.

On the morning of the seventh day of the trial, the mid-morning prayer recess ended and the first of the day's witnesses was called to present her evidence. All eyes turned to the doors of the church as Winckler led in Frau Emerelde Linde. Hobbling up the aisle, her heavy skirts dragging wet mud across the floor, a lacy shawl wrapped tight around her, she took her place before the three judges and swore an oath to Ulric.

'Frau Emerelde,' began Marius before either of the other two could start, 'is it not true that you are related to Magistrate Fenster by marriage?'

'Yes, yes it is true, there's no secret about that,' she answered with a confused expression. 'He's my brother-in-law.'

'What has this got to do with the Schek woman?' asked Fenster testily, but Marius ignored him and continued.

'And is it not also the case,' Marius said, 'that you are using that relationship to settle your own personal vendetta against Ursula Schek, the woman accused today?'

'That's a slur on my character!' interjected the magistrate. 'What are you saying?'

'I have to concur with Magistrate Fenster,' added Theobald. 'I fail to see the relevance of this line of questioning.'

'For two years now, Frau Emerelde has waged a petty, spiteful campaign against Fraulein Schek,' explained Marius. 'This culminated in her arrest and supposed trial some months ago, after which she was imprisoned. It is only her false imprisonment that has led to any accusation being levelled. I believe that the witness is prejudiced and her testimony should not be submitted to this court.'

'She is an evil-hearted harlot!' snapped Emerelde, pointing a finger at Ursula. 'She bewitched that fine knight in this very shrine, and has done the same to live off immoral money from the cursed pact she has made with the dark powers.'

'What is this immoral money you refer to?' asked Brother Theobald.

'Why, the keep she earned from Kurt Leitzig, and now from this impostor who calls himself Marius van Diesl.' Her accusing finger swung around to point at the witch hunter. The church and the crowd outside erupted with jeers, and handfuls of rotten fruit were tossed from near the door to splatter on the heads of the people who had crammed into the church as far as they could.

'Silence, all of you!' rasped Fenster, banging the table with his silver hammer. 'No trial over which I preside will have

accusations being levelled at the judges sitting it, myself
included. The accused is one Ursula Schek, the redheaded
woman standing over there in case you are not acquainted.
No one else, including the witnesses, Herr van Diesl, is on
trial here, and the questions put to the witnesses should be
only for the purpose of divining the guilt or innocence of
the accused.'

'You are right, magistrate,' Marius said with a gracious nod
before turning his attention back to Frau Linde. 'Ignoring
this business of immoral earnings for now, what are these
dark pacts of which you speak?'

'Every morning, she comes in here and defiles the statue
of Sigmar,' said Linde, and a rippling murmur spread
through the shrine and the crowd outside.

'Defiles it?' asked Theobald. 'Be aware that this is my
shrine, and mindful of what you say next.'

'You have seen her, hanging flowers and whatnot on the
statue,' said Emerelde. 'Now, I'm not a Sigmarite by nature,
but I never seen nothing like that going on. I never seen anyone doing that afore she came here, not in this shrine.'

'Is this true?' Fenster asked, turning to Brother Theobald.

'I can find no passages or laws that proscribe the practice,'
Theobald answered heavily.

'Indeed, it is a ceremony I have seen in other places of
worship,' said Marius. 'Though not from these parts.'

'But picking flowers from graves and putting them on
Sigmar, that says something, doesn't it?' Emerelde insisted.

'You will answer questions, not offer opinions,' barked
Marius, causing the housewife to flinch, and dart a glance at
Fenster, who merely returned her entreating look with a
scowl. 'The charge of heresy is a very serious one, bringing
with it the threat of death by hanging. I ask you now, to
reconsider this accusation. Ask yourself if it is merely
brought about by your ongoing rivalry with the accused, and
to consider your own motives in this affair. Is such a thing
worth the death of Fraulein Schek?'

'I've seen her consorting with spirits!' hissed Frau Linde,
eliciting another shocked reaction from the audience and a
disbelieving gasp from Ursula, who up until now had held
her temper in check and remained silent.

'Frau Linde!' snapped Brother Theobald. 'I will remind you of Herr van Diesl's words from a moment ago and add that false accusation of such a crime as you describe also brings the penalty of death by hanging.'

'I have seen it, I swear by Ulric!' insisted Emerelde, wringing her hands around the knot that tied her black shawl around her shoulders. 'Why, not two days before the snows came, she was in here and I was at that very door listening to her. It was like she was talking with someone.'

'Could she not have been praying, Frau Linde? It is a very common occurrence in a shrine, I hear,' Marius said and in the silence that followed he heard Ruprecht's deep chuckle.

'No, she was having a conversation, clear as day,' Emerelde replied. 'She was talking *with* someone, not *to* someone.'

'And what was the subject of this unnatural conversation?' asked Brother Theobald, leaning forward on his elbows.

'I didn't rightly hear all of it,' admitted Emerelde. 'But what I did hear concerned fires. She was talking about fires against the cold, and burning something. I think she was putting a spell on the town, what started all this violence and fire-starting.'

'You believe she bewitched the entire town?' Marius said. 'She must indeed be a potent sorceress to do such a thing, and only nineteen years of age as well.'

'She might be older than that if this is true,' countered Brother Theobald, looking curiously at Ursula.

'Surely you do not believe this, brother?' Marius said.

'And why not? The annals of this town include many strange things which were proven to be true,' Theobald said. 'Beef cattle who rotted as soon as slaughtered when cursed by a rival farmer. The wilting of the crops on the north fields by a scorching hot wind in the middle of winter. Emilie Langstrom was burned here three hundred years ago for bringing down a fever that killed half the young children of Badenhof.'

'In your labours as a protector of our lives and souls, have you ever encountered such a thing, Herr van Diesl?' asked Fenster.

'Well, similar occurrences, certainly,' admitted Marius. 'The foul arts of necromancy can be used to commune with the spirits of the dead, and some say to entreat them to act upon the living. The *Book of Neselrus* claims that the soul of a person can be attacked by an unquiet spirit and much harm can be caused. But these I have witnessed with my own eyes.'

'As Frau Linde may have done,' Brother Theobald pointed out. 'So far I have heard nothing to invalidate her testimony.'

'As priest of this shrine, you must have been long aware of the antagonism between Ursula and Emerelde,' Marius said, glancing at the two women in turn.

'Certainly, Frau Linde has entreated me on numerous occasions to cast out the accused from the rough dwelling the laws of my church say I must provide for the pure yet needy,' Theobald said. 'You argue that her accusations are fuelled by her dislike of the accused, but I ask is it not possible that her dislike of the accused is fuelled by the fact that she is indeed a witch?'

'Fellow judges,' spoke Fenster. 'This is getting us nowhere, and we still have many witnesses to interview. Unless definite evidence comes to light that persuades us Frau Linde is either of unsound mind or driven by illicit motive and her testimony is invalid, let the records remain as they are and her evidence be retained.'

'But there is no evidence,' said Marius, exasperated. 'Merely hearsay and speculation. And I fear we shall see nothing more tangible in the way of proof over the entire course of this trial.'

'You will not prejudice this trial with unwarranted statements like this!' snapped Fenster. 'It shall remain to be seen what evidence comes before us. And remember that though weight of opinion does not sway the law, weight of recurring testimony does, following the adage that there is no blood without a wound.'

MARIUS'S PATIENCE FINALLY ran out that afternoon when the next witness to be called was Aliss Kieller, the delirious inmate at the town gaol. She was brought in to the shrine manacled hand and foot, her thin, starved frame barely covered with tattered rags. Her staring eyes roved everywhere

from under a tangle of matted black hair, and lesions and
scabs marked her skin all over.

'And what in the name of Sigmar is this creature doing
here?' he demanded from Fenster as the woman was
brought before them. 'Are we now to be subjected to the testimony of a mad woman?'

'It has come to my attention that during her stay at the
prison, the accused performed certain acts witnessed by Frau
Kieller,' explained Fenster.

'And just what are these acts?' Marius asked her. She looked
around the shrine once more before focussing her attention
on him. In a hoarse whisper, she began her testimony.

'Aliss sees the witch girl every day,' the inmate said. 'She
sees what she does. Yes she does, day and night. In the dark
places. Rats. She eats them, she eats the rats, Aliss saw it!
Bites off their heads, piles of bloody furry bodies everywhere. Aliss is scared, the rats are her friends, but Aliss
doesn't listen to them any more, no she doesn't.'

'What is this raving?' asked Marius, turning to Fenster. 'I
cannot understand a word she is saying.'

'Drinks the blood of the rats, Aliss sees her every night,'
the mad woman continued, oblivious to Marius's anger.
'Snip-snap, their necks broken, and the feast begins. Aliss
also heard her talking to someone when she kills the rats.
She hears the voices that Aliss can't hear, telling her to eat
the rats, lick up their blood on her lovely tongue. Snap!
Necks all broken for the pile. Aliss has seen it, with these
eyes, like the bad times when the sacrifices were burnt.'

'This is very grave indeed,' Brother Theobald said, listening
intently to Aliss's words.

'You believe this lunatic?' Marius asked.

'When she was a child, Aliss lived in on a farmstead several miles outside the town walls,' replied Brother Theobald.
'The farm was sacked by half-beast creatures of the dark
gods, that came from out of the woods. She was left for
dead, and saw the beastmen pile up the corpses of her family and their workers in a sacrifice to their foul gods. It sent
her mad, as you can see, but I think she is saying that Ursula
was repeating this unholy ceremony on a smaller scale. That
was why she was so afraid.'

'Afraid yes,' interrupted Aliss, who had been listening intently to the priest. 'Aliss's neck, snip-snap and on the pyre for the bloody one. And the chattering, the voices Aliss can't hear tell the evil girl to do the bad things.'

'Get this pitiful creature out of here, for Sigmar's sake!' ordered Marius, but as the guards closed in on Aliss, the woman began a deafening shriek.

'Aliss saw them, the rats were unhappy, they told Aliss, yes they did,' she wailed. 'In the shadows, the red eyes looking at Aliss, and scared of the red girl, the bad girl who eats rats. Aliss heard them whispering and squeaking to each other, saying evil things. They was walking on their back legs and dancing, Aliss saw it!'

'Surely the ravings of a woman who we all accept to be touched cannot be entered as evidence?' asked Marius when Aliss had been unceremoniously bundled out of the church.

'I certainly advise that we consider her state of mind when weighing up the evidence,' Fenster said smoothly, stroking his bristled chin with a long fingernail.

'And who is to be the next witness,' Marius said. 'Perhaps we should talk to the rats? Or perhaps we should cut through to the heart of the matter and speak to the accused, Fraulein Ursula Schek?'

'Very well, the accused stands as witness after a short break for food,' conceded Fenster.

URSULA DID NOT know whether to cry or laugh. The trial was a travesty of common sense and justice, and yet she knew that the parade of petty-minded, selfish witnesses would have their way unless she defended herself properly. Marius had called for her to be the next witness, and as she sat there in the shrine, she looked up at the statue of Sigmar that seemed to loom behind the judges' table. As the bustling ushers busied themselves around her shuffling papers, scraping back chairs, talking loudly to each other, she found herself in a small zone of silence. For a moment, she felt utterly calm as she looked upon the caring features of Sigmar. Give me strength, she whispered to herself. The moment passed and once more she was caught in the dizzying activity around her.

She was called to stand in front of the judges, and rose from her chair, head held proud as she stared down her accusers. She would show them the type of woman she was. She was not some fishwife to be battered and bullied into submission. She wasn't some loose-tongued gossiper or immoral harlot. She felt confidence flow through her as she strode in front of the statue. Bending to one knee, she made her oath.

'I swear by the blood in my veins and the love of the Lord Sigmar that my testimony shall be the truth,' she said before standing up.

This time Brother Theobald spoke first, though every previous examination had been pretty much carried out by Marius.

'Tell the court of the particulars of our first encounter,' the priest said.

'Just over two years ago, I was travelling north, thinking perhaps to seek a living in Bechafen,' she said, shifting her gaze equally between the attentive eyes of the three judges. 'It was a stormy night, the skies themselves wept and lightning ripped the clouds.'

'Spare us the theatrical prose, Fraulein Schek,' snapped the magistrate. 'Just tell us the facts.'

'The first night I was here, there was a great storm,' continued Ursula. 'I knocked on the doors of several houses, wet to my skin, and asked for shelter, but none was offered. I worked my way up the Sigmarstrasse until I reached this very church. The doors were open and I let myself in and slept the night at the foot of Sigmar himself. In the morning, Brother Theobald arrived as is his duty and found me there.'

'And tell us what happened next,' Fenster said.

'The revered brother asked who I was and how I came to be here,' Ursula answered. 'I told him that I had spent many years wandering and I hoped that I might make a home for myself here. He said that there were enough poor folk in the town and I should move on.'

'And what was your reply to that?' Brother Theobald asked. 'Why did you ignore my good advice?'

'I know that priests are sworn to uphold the rights of the needy and offer succour to those who ask for it,' Ursula answered, and she saw a faint glimmer of a smile quiver on Marius's lips for a moment.

'And since then?' pressed Fenster.

'Since then I have tried all that I can to find employment in this town and yet the people snub me and until imprisoned I still relied upon the charity of Holy Sigmar.' Ursula turned an accusing look towards the crowds pressing in through the shrine's doors, receiving a chorus of whistles and hisses in return.

'So people have been suspicious of you ever since you arrived,' asked Marius, hoping to steer the conversation to more profitable ground.

'Yes,' Ursula said. 'The prejudice of this town is greater than any other I have encountered, and I have met many prejudiced people in my life.'

Snarls and catcalls echoed from the gathered townsfolk at this statement, until the chief usher was shouting for quiet.

'And what is the basis for this suspicion?' asked Marius when some semblance of order had been restored.

'There is no basis for it,' said Ursula. 'I have tried to find employment, I have prayed every day, and I have tried my best to live alongside my neighbours in peace.'

'And what of your relationship with the knight Kurt Leitzig?' asked Brother Theobald. 'Do you not concede that it is odd that a fine man who has lived in this town for several years, during which he has shown no sign of seeking a relationship with a woman, decides within a month of your arrival to seek your hand in marriage?'

'The ways of the heart can be odd,' admitted Ursula. 'You would have to ask Kurt about his feelings.'

'Enough of this,' said Fenster. 'What do you say of the accusations levelled against you? '

'I cannot answer that until the accusations are made clearer,' Ursula replied.

'Clearer?' the magistrate retorted. 'You have been accused of communing with evil spirits. We have testimony that you perform unholy rituals, both in this shrine and during your period of incarceration. Did you or did you not bewitch this young man?'

'I admit that I killed rats whilst in prison,' said Ursula. 'I did it to earn the money to pay for soap and a brush to clean the prison shrine, and to buy candles to light there. I broke their necks, that is true, but I never drank their blood nor made any sacrifice of them. The idea is abhorrent. I would never foul a sacred place with such blasphemous behaviour. I did not use sorcery on Kurt, that is equally disgusting.'

'Abhorrent indeed,' agreed Brother Theobald with a glance at Fenster. 'But what of the voices it is said that you hear.'

Ursula did not reply straight away, choosing her words carefully.

'I do not commune with evil spirits,' she said.

'Remember that you have sworn an oath to Sigmar to tell the truth,' Theobald continued. 'In light of that, do you also swear that the tales we have heard of voices that speak to you are untrue?'

'I swear by Sigmar that I do not participate in any evil or unholy practice,' Ursula replied evenly.

'Answer the question, woman,' snapped Fenster. 'Do you, or do you not hear voices that others cannot?'

Ursula hesitated and her heart palpitated wildly. She looked at the statue of Sigmar again, at his serene face, and remembered her oath.

'Sigmar protects and guides me,' she said. Marius glanced in alarm at Ruprecht.

'What does that mean?' he asked with a frown.

'I hear the voice of Sigmar,' replied Ursula, and the shrine erupted into pandemonium.

CHAPTER NINE
Conspiracy
Badenhof, Winter early 1709

MARIUS STARED IN disbelief at Ursula as the two of them sat in a secluded antechamber of the shrine, while outside his men combined forces with the watch to drive out the mob who had piled in through the doors following Ursula's simple statement.

Mastering his anger, he stood up and started to pace back and forth across the small room, looking at the faded mosaics of the triumphs of Sigmar that adorned the floor.

'I'm sorry,' Ursula said. 'He asked me a direct question and I had sworn not to lie. What else was I to do?'

'You did not mention this in our conversation at the gaol, or at any other time,' Marius replied heavily. 'You've played straight into their hands, you realise that? You have played me for a fool as well, it seems.'

'I have faith that Sigmar will see me prevail over my enemies,' Ursula said. 'I did not mention it because there is nothing wrong with it. Believe me, I knew this would happen, that I would end up on trial if this came out, but I am not evil. It is Sigmar who talks to me, nothing else!'

'Well, you'll need a bloody miracle now,' said Ruprecht, pushing through the doorway. 'The church has been emptied. You're to remain under guard here, Marius has to go to the town hall to speak to the burgomeister and the guildmaster. One of our men is here as well, for your protection.'

'Say nothing to anyone,' warned Marius. 'Pray if you like, but say nothing to anyone else.'

'I will pray,' Ursula said with a nod.

With a last glance, Marius closed the door behind him before stalking out of the shrine. Outside the mob was still in full voice, shouting derisive comments at him and Ruprecht as Marius's men literally beat a path through the crowd. A wagon was waiting for them by the shrine's main gates and they jumped aboard as a light drizzle began to fall from the sky.

'Does it seem odd to you that the town councillors, particularly the burgomeister, have failed to attend such an important trial,' Marius said to Ruprecht as the drivers whipped the horses into a canter that had the cart bouncing and swaying over the uneven stones of the road.

'Aye, I smell something for sure,' agreed Ruprecht, pulling his hood up to ward off the growing rain. Marius did not notice the worsening weather, so lost was he in his dark thoughts. Neither of them said any more as the wagon clattered along the Sigmarstrasse to the central square.

Leaping off in front of the town hall, the pair found a small detachment of the watch awaiting them. The five men guided them through the huge oak doors into a reception hall beyond, lit by a massive chandelier that hung from a ceiling covered in peeling gold leaf. Down a corridor they were led, into the bowels of the council chambers, until they were brought before the burgomeister himself. He was seated behind a low desk ornamented with all manner of strange artefacts. There was a bird skull on one corner with a sheaf of papers in its mouth; at the other end was a three-pronged candelabra, which spat cheap wax onto the wooden surface. A dried toad used as a paperweight squatted next to a bone-handled letter knife, and behind the clutter sat the flabby figure of Burgomeister Koln. His black velvet jacket was haphazardly buttoned across the huge expanse of his stomach, failing to conceal a food-stained red shirt. Crumbs littered his lap, and as the two entered, he was chewing on a rind of pork, his jaws working monotonously like a cow chewing cud. Behind and to one side stood Kirche, the skeletal guild-master. The two were an incongruous pair, and to Marius it looked as if Koln had somehow sucked all the fat from the guildmaster and added it to his own bulk.

'This is the witch hunter,' announced Kirche, glowering at Marius.

'Ah, of course it is,' Koln said as he leaned forward with a huffing breath and offered a podgy hand in welcome. 'It is a shame that we could not have met earlier under more pleas-ant circumstances.'

'And what are the unpleasant circumstances?' asked Marius, ignoring the burgomeister's offer of greeting.

'Shall we cut to the chase, as the hunters say?' the bur-gomeister said, leaning back with a wheeze, his smile replaced by a shrewd look. 'We all know that you are here to spy for agents of the elector count of Ostland.'

'What?' sputtered Ruprecht. 'Spies? Us?'

Marius waved him to be quiet before turning his full stare on Koln. He was distracted when a scratching at the open doorway heralded the arrival of a fat black rat. It hobbled quickly into the room, bounded lopsidedly onto the desk and then into the burgomeister's lap. In its right front paw, it clasped a small scroll.

'What in Sigmar's name?' exclaimed Marius, stepping back in horror.

'Oh, this is just Ranuld,' Koln said, stroking the rat's bald-ing head. 'They're very clever, you know, smarter than dogs by my reckoning. He runs little errands for me, that's all.'

'Tread carefully, Herr Koln,' Marius whispered, trying to regain his composure. 'I think that there are two men in this room who would not appreciate careful scrutiny of their business and affairs.'

'Are you threatening us, van Diesl?' snorted Kirche, step-ping out from behind the chair to stand directly in front of the witch hunter. His neck craned down like a stork to look into Marius's face. In turn, the witch hunter had to look up at an awkward angle.

'It is not a threat,' the witch hunter said. 'You can try all you like to smother what you are doing behind this trial, but if you are behind the woes of this town, you will be punished for it.'

'You should leave before I call for a guard,' snapped Kirche.

'Now, now,' interjected the burgomeister. 'Herr van Diesl is merely carrying out his vocation, so leave him be. On your part, my good witch hunter, your efforts to protect the interests of my town and its people are remarkable, but this antagonism has got to stop.'

'Antagonism?' Marius asked, his eyes narrowed with suspicion.

'The people want to see the girl strung up or burnt,' Koln continued lazily. 'Just give them what they want and things will quieten down. If it wasn't for the meddling of that idiot Fenster, this would have been sorted out without any bother at all.'

'You want me to sacrifice an innocent girl to that mob out there?' spat Marius, pushing past Kirche and leaning over the desk. 'What makes you so sure their bloodthirst won't turn on someone else if we feed it?'

'Oh, rest assured that once the girl is dealt with the town's problems will all be solved,' Kirche replied. 'You won't be needed here any longer and you would do well not to stretch the hospitality with which Badenhof has welcomed you.'

'The trial will be conducted fairly and a true verdict reached,' declared Marius. 'I'll not kill an innocent.'

'Are you so sure that you haven't done so already?' asked Kirche. 'I mean, I have heard a lot about you these recent days. You are a busy man. Over three hundred executions you have presided over, not to mention the amount of blood spilt by your own hand in so-called battle.'

Without a word, Marius stormed out, Ruprecht trailing in his wake. The pair of them waited until they were escorted to the wagon and on their way back to their lodgings before saying anything.

'Treacherous… Lying…' Marius was so angry he could not speak for several more minutes, and Ruprecht stayed silent as the witch hunter fumed. With visible effort, Marius calmed himself, took a deep breath and then looked at his companion with a shake of his head.

'By Ulric's fangs, what was that about?' asked Ruprecht, confident that the clatter of horses' hooves and the grinding of the poorly oiled axle masked their words from the driver.

'I'm not sure, but I think it was a threat,' said Marius, scratching at his cheek. 'An empty one at that.'

'People with power like they have don't tend to make empty threats,' Ruprecht pointed out. 'They can cause serious trouble for us.'

'They won't,' Marius assured his friend. 'I even think perhaps they're panicking. Whatever scheme it is they're up to, they're scared I'll find out. Ever since we got here, it has been one wild chase after another. We've been facing misdirection, interference, incitement by the watch, no support for our investigations, rabble-rousing, and stalling. The very fact that it's come down to a personal confrontation means that they're losing confidence. All this time I've been worried about the time I've wasted, but actually, they've played it all wrong. They're used to manipulating the guilds and townsfolk, and getting their way with the local council, but I've turned up as an unknown element and it's thrown them. All this time, they've been getting more and more worried and desperate. Keep a close eye on them, they may do something stupid.'

With a nod, Ruprecht jumped from the back of the wagon and began to walk back up the road towards the town hall.

THE NEXT MORNING, the crowd outside the shrine was larger than before and the mood was tense and angry. Marius barged his way into the church amidst shouted accusations. Threats were called out, and he was only kept from harm by the presence of ten of his men armed with cudgels and the sword hanging from his belt. Ruprecht was waiting for him on the steps.

'So, what of Koln and Kirche?' Marius asked, striding up the steps two at a time. 'What have they been up to?'

'Nothing outside the town hall, as far as I know,' Ruprecht told him. 'I stayed the whole night and had three men out the back as well, and they didn't come out during the night.'

'So where are they now?' asked Marius.

'Well, that's the thing, isn't it?' said Ruprecht, leading Marius to the door and pointing inside. The two town leaders were sat to one side of the temporary court, talking to Theobald and Fenster.

'We got here just before you,' Ruprecht added as the two walked inside. As they entered, Fenster looked up and grimaced in their direction before he and Brother Theobald took their places behind the main table.

'Watch them like a hawk,' Marius told Ruprecht.

'Be careful,' warned Ruprecht. 'There's scores of guildsmen outside. They haven't been here before.'

'Kirche might be planning something. Make sure the men are ready if need be,' said Marius before leaving his second-in-command and sitting down beside his fellow judges.

It took a while to get the proceedings started, but eventually Ursula was brought out of the antechamber to stand before the judges and at her appearance, the crowd broke into raucous shouting and chanting for her to burn. Ursula steadfastly ignored the mob and stood quietly, waiting for the questions to start again. Marius stood and leaned forward on the table, about to begin, when Guildmaster Kirche interrupted.

'If I may make a small interjection before matters progress,' he said, walking forward.

'What can we do for you, guildmaster?' asked Fenster.

'I was reviewing the records of the trial last night, and a small but important detail seems to have been overlooked,' Kirche continued.

'A detail?' said Marius.

'Well, it seems we have denied a certain right to the accused.' Kirche turned and looked at Ursula as he spoke. 'Under the laws of the church of Sigmar, the defendant may, if she wishes, forego a judgement of the court in favour of a higher power.'

'I don't follow you,' said Marius, searching Kirche's face for some sign of what the guildmaster intended. 'What is this higher power you speak of? Perhaps the court of the count in Bechafen?'

'Oh, much higher than that,' replied Kirche, pointing towards the statue dominating the shrine. 'I refer to great Sigmar himself.'

'And how might an individual do such a thing?' asked Marius. In reply, Kirche simply looked at Brother Theobald, who gave an almost imperceptible nod before standing up and addressing the gathered people.

'It is written in the book of Sigmar's life that he once proved his strength by holding back two horses,' said the priest. 'Any man, or in this case woman, who can truly call upon the strength of Sigmar should be able to repeat the feat.'

'You expect Ursula to be able to hold back a pair of horses by herself!' Marius retorted.

'Indeed, there are several precedents of such a trial by strength being undertaken by members of the faithful community,' Theobald said. 'The defendant is tied to the two horses and if they can hold them in place for the turning of a minute-glass they are deemed innocent.'

'And at what point may the defendant opt for this trial by strength?' asked Marius, looking towards Ursula, who was listening attentively to the exchange.

'Well,' replied Kirche. 'Strictly speaking, she should have taken the trial before proceedings began. After all, we would not wish this to be used as some kind of trick to avoid the judgement of the court once the details of the presented evidence had become known. However, I think we can perhaps be flexible in this case, considering that it was bad form not to inform Fraulein Schek and the court at the outset.'

'I have nothing to fear from the judgement of Sigmar,' said Ursula, breaking her silence.

'Such confidence,' smiled Fenster. 'Of course, judging by your revelation of yesterday, Sigmar will guide you and give you his strength.'

'He will,' Ursula replied.

'This is nonsense!' snapped Marius. 'This is just another attempt to confuse this trial, stall any progress that may be made, and hinder our efforts to locate and punish the real perpetrators of the hideous crimes that have been committed in this town.'

'You refuse to acknowledge the right of Ursula to undertake the trial by strength?' asked Fenster, returning the witch hunter's icy stare.

Before Marius could reply, he found that Ruprecht was standing next to him. The big man motioned the witch hunter to step aside and bent down to whisper in his ear.

'Koln has gone,' Ruprecht said. 'For a fat man he can move quietly.'

'Find him!' hissed Marius, glancing at the now empty pew where the burgomeister had been seated. 'I'll handle whatever Kirche is up to, you find out where he's gone.'

'There can't be too many nooks and crannies he'd fit into,' said Ruprecht as he turned to leave. 'We'll find him.'

Watching Ruprecht leave, Marius's mind was racing. Kirche was trying to trap Ursula into accepting the trial by strength, knowing that the chance to prove her faith in Sigmar would be almost irresistible to the young woman. The question was how Marius could persuade her otherwise. And once he did that, how was he going to get the trial finished so that he could concentrate his efforts on the burgomeister and guildmaster?

BORROWING A HORSE, it did not take Ruprecht long to find the wagon Koln had used to leave. As he had said to Ursula the week before, if they were patient enough, their prey would slip up sooner or later. It looked like the waiting was over. It was no surprise to Ruprecht that he found the wagon concealed amongst the storehouses and abandoned sheds of the Bergmund district, next to the Stein warehouses. Initially, they had watched this part of town day and night, but after the first week, it seemed that whatever had taken place with Stein was in the past, and Marius had told them to move on to other leads.

Ruprecht dismounted and approached cautiously. Scouting around for a while, he spotted two guards trying to hide in the shadows of doorways, near to the wagon. Fortunately for him, they were not positioned well. They could not see each other, and both had at least two approaches to their positions that they could not watch at the same time. Ruprecht paused to consider whether he should go back for more men, but decided against it. He was here to observe, not to fight. Marius had been quite specific in their regular talks that to move against the enemy before they were sure would invite resistance from the local populace.

Ruprecht skirted around the corner of a building towards the closest sentry. Climbing through an open window, he found himself inside a warehouse that was empty except for a few sagging sacks. Crossing the floor quickly, he stood next to the side door, on the other side from the guard outside. He could hear the man's boots scraping on the stone step. Choosing his moment, he flung open the door. The man's back was to Ruprecht and as he turned, a swinging right hook connected with the guard's jaw and flung him to the ground. Stooping, Ruprecht confirmed that the sentry was out cold, and dragged his unconscious form back through the door. Wrapping the man in sacks, he left him there before exiting the building.

The other guard was positioned on the far side of the warehouse, standing next to Koln's wagon. He was pacing back and forth by the horses and it was an easy matter for Ruprecht to sneak up on the blind side when the sentry's back was turned. Just as before, a solid punch from Ruprecht silenced the man, who he bundled into the back of the wagon.

The door to the Stein store was latched shut with a knotted rope around a nail. The whole building was dilapidated and bore the marks of neglect across the wooden boards of the walls. The hinges were rusted and Ruprecht decided against trying to gain entry that way; it was unlikely that he could open the door with any kind of stealth. Looking for another means of access, Ruprecht found a set of doors leading down to a cellar. To his experienced eye, there were signs of recent use: the hinges were oiled, and the mud showed scrape marks and footprints. Easing open one of the doors, he found a set of wooden steps leading down into the dark. Taking a couple of steps, he peered into the gloom and could make out the flickering red light of a flame in the depths of the cellar.

Cautiously navigating the steps, Ruprecht came into a long, low room filled with broken shelving. Heading towards the flame, he eased his way between the shelves and quietly slipped his hammer from his belt. A few yards closer and Ruprecht could hear the sound of voices, in particular the voice of Koln. Ruprecht worked his way around the end of a collapsed shelf for a better vantage point. Koln was stood holding a burning torch and talking to a shadowy figure, though Ruprecht could not make out the actual words spoken. As Koln shifted, Ruprecht saw something that caused his heart to miss a beat. Talking to the burgomeister was a short, hunched figure swathed in a robe. A twitching rat-like nose protruded from its hood and thin, clawed hands reached forward, holding something that glittered in the firelight. Beady red eyes reflected the torchlight in the depths of the hood. It was unmistakeably a skaven.

A scratching sound caused Ruprecht to turn quickly, and he just managed to raise his hammer in time to deflect a dagger arcing down towards his neck. The skaven was wrapped in black rags, and it held a notched blade in each hand. Ruprecht rammed the head of the hammer into its face, sending it sprawling into the shelf behind it in a shower of splinters. There was a shout from Koln and a hiss, and Ruprecht glanced over to see a blade that glowed with a faint green light appear. Koln gave a gurgled scream as the skaven sliced open his throat and leapt towards Ruprecht. With no thought other than to get out, Ruprecht turned and ran. He barrelled past another skaven who jumped in his way, leaving it squirming on the floor with a knife sticking from its chest.

Bursting out into the light, Ruprecht leapt onto the driver's board of Koln's wagon and whipped at the horses. The wagon clattered onto the main street, almost throwing him from his place, as a handful of furred creatures raced from the cellar.

'Oh, bugger!' Ruprecht cursed as he steered the wagon towards the shrine.

MARIUS WATCHED DISCONSOLATELY as the crowd parted to allow Brother Theobald to lead the horses through the gates of the shrine and into the gardens surrounding the outhouses. It was sheer folly, but he had been unable to persuade Ursula not to take part. It mattered not that she risked being torn apart by the two powerful stallions. The crowd were waiting in excited silence, and Marius had been alarmed to see Kirche walking amongst them, talking to a number of his men. The witch hunter was certain that whatever happened, the guildmaster would make sure he had the result he wanted.

Ursula was kneeling on the steps up to the church doors behind Marius, her head bowed in prayer. She had argued vehemently with Marius, and as far as he could tell, she honestly believed that Sigmar would grant her the strength she needed. Although once a priest of Sigmar, and still a believer in his heart, Marius had seen too much to have the fervent, unwavering faith that she possessed. There had been a slight change in the strategy of Kirche and Koln. They had moved from trying to procrastinate and delay the trial to focus attention away from themselves. Now Kirche had tried to coerce Marius into offering up Ursula as a sacrifice, and had presented a way for the trial to be quickly and unquestionably ended. Of course, Kirche wanted Ursula to fail so that suspicion would be allayed and the town could return to some semblance of normality. To Marius, this could only mean that the secretive cartel operating within Badenhof had all but completed whatever it was they were doing and would disappear again, far from the reach of any retribution he might want to visit upon them.

Winckler approached from across the gardens, now reduced to a churned mire by the feet of hundreds of onlookers.

'The trial by strength is ready to begin,' he announced. Ursula looked up and gazed out over the crowd. Most of them had been cleared out of the church grounds, and were now packed into the Sigmarstrasse, or sitting and standing atop the surrounding wall to get a good view of the proceedings. She strode down the steps, erect and dignified. Marius fell in a few paces behind her. The sombre procession made its way along the path towards Brother Theobald, who stood by the carthorses procured for the trial by strength. Holding their reins with one hand, the priest was reading from a book held by one of his lay assistants. They stopped just short of the priest and Ursula stepped forward.

'Are you ready to undergo this trial?' asked Theobald when Ursula knelt before him.

A distant shout interrupted proceedings and an angry murmur spread through the crowd. There was a great deal of commotion and part of the crowd surged forward, trampling each other in their efforts to get out of the way of something. As space cleared, Ruprecht crashed the wagon into one of the gate posts, knocking splinters of stone flying in all directions.

'Marius!' he bellowed, leaping down from the driver's position. He crashed like a bull through the mob who were between him and the witch hunter, sending guildsmen, children and housewives sprawling to the ground. Marius saw that he held his hammer in his hand, and there was blood on it. The big man was panting hard and his eyes were wide with fear.

'Koln's dead!' said Ruprecht, trying to catch his breath. There was a shocked gasp from those within earshot and the news spread out through the mob.

'What is this?' demanded Kirche, pushing through the crowd that had gathered around the witch hunter.

'Your allies have betrayed you!' hissed Ruprecht, grabbing hold of Kirche's coat. 'They slit his throat.'

'Betrayed?' said Kirche, aghast.

'This sham trial ends now,' said Marius, pulling Ruprecht away and confronting the guildmaster.

'The witch hunter is a traitor!' Kirche called out. 'He's an agent of Ostland! He wants the trial to end!'

Screams and cries of panic cut through the air, from further up the Sigmarstrasse.

'What devilry is this?' demanded Marius, his hand reaching for the hilt of his sword. The crowd was surging forward even further. Marius pushed past Theobald, bullied his way through the crowd and leapt up onto the back of the wagon. Looking out over the heaving crowd, he saw a carpet of brown moving down the road. It was a moment before he realised that it was a tide of rats, thousands of them, pouring towards the churchyard from every cellar and alley, sweeping over everything in its path.

'She's summoned a daemon swarm to save her!' someone shouted out.

'Burn the witch!' a voice called out from the crowd, to be taken up by dozens of other throats.

The mob surged forward, clambering over the walls and pressing in around Marius, who jumped clear and battered his way back towards Ursula. She shrieked as hands grabbed at her. Marius pulled out his sword and the blade swept downwards, cutting into a man's arm. Ruprecht leapt in, swinging his hammer, and everything descended into chaos.

CHAPTER TEN
Saviour
Badenhof, Winter early 1709

As THEIR HORSES trotted through the gate along the Bechafenstrasse, Kurt and Jakob gazed around in horrified astonishment. They had seen the haze of smoke from a few miles away and ridden swiftly, and the scene that greeted them was not at all the homecoming Kurt had imagined. The buildings showed the scars of burning and looting, even here on the outskirts. For a moment he thought he saw someone looking furtively at the pair of them from a shattered window, but the figure scuttled out of sight. Jakob pointed out a charred body in the ruins of one burnt-out shell of a warehouse and Kurt quickened the pace.

The town was strangely quiet and as they progressed the signs of the violence that had engulfed Badenhof became more evident. It was not long though before the eerie silence was broken by the distant sound of shouting. Spurring Heldred into gallop, Kurt raced out onto the Sigmarstrasse where he was confronted by a scene from a nightmare.

Hundreds of people were running in all directions and the streets swarmed with rats, some of them as large as dogs. The vermin were biting and clawing at everything in their way, and Kurt watched in horror as people fell and disappeared beneath the tide of rodents. He tried to ride through the mayhem, but the press of bodies was too much for Heldred and he dismounted, slapping the horse's rump to make him run clear. Jakob appeared beside him, a bow in his hands. They exchanged glances.

'What's happening?' Jakob shouted over the din of the shouting mob.

'I have no idea!' Kurt bellowed back, drawing his sword. 'We must find Ursula!'

The two of them pushed against the throng that was now moving down the Sigmarstrasse towards the outskirts of the town. A rat scurried over Kurt's foot and he kicked it away. He was being buffeted left and right by the fleeing crowd, and someone made a grab for his sword. He smashed his fist into the face of the bearded man responsible and flung him aside. They pushed their way towards the side of the road where there was a little more space. The panicked townsfolk were making no attempt to hide, they were simply fleeing down the road as fast as they could.

'Ursula might be at the shrine,' Kurt said to Jakob. 'It's a little further up this way.'

The pair punched and barged their way through the mob, who seemed more interested in getting clear than fighting. The rats were everywhere, crawling across bloodied corpses, in people's hair, clawing at faces and causing mayhem. They scurried underfoot, making Kurt stumble on more than one occasion, and their keening squeaks drowned out the cries of distress and pain that surrounded the knight.

Further up the street, the crowd suddenly thinned and Kurt got his first view of the shrine and the churchyard. There were still a sizeable number of men standing at the walls of the church. Many of them were fighting off the rats with sticks and other improvised weapons, but others were intent on something or someone inside the shrine itself. He saw the tall guildmaster, Kirche, striding back and forth, shouting out instructions, directing the armed mob. Pointing back to the church, he called something out and then disappeared through the gateway. The street was littered with corpses of rats and people, and the shouts and noise of fighting rang from the walls of the houses nearby.

MARIUS WAS ON the shrine's steps with Ursula behind him, swiping at the mob with his sword.

'Get back!' he roared, smashing a man from his feet and kicking him down the steps. The majority of the men were followers of Kirche, and it was now evident by the number of clubs, hammers and other weapons they carried that they had come prepared for a fight. The guildmaster himself disappeared once the fray had started, and Ruprecht had gone after him. Marius and a handful of his men were holding the steps, but unless Ruprecht returned with more help, they would be overwhelmed before long.

A man with a short black beard and an eye patch ran yelling up the steps, brandishing a wood cutter's axe. Marius easily parried his clumsy attack and ran his sword through the man's arm, making him drop the weapon.

'Cease this stupidity!' bellowed Marius, shoving the screaming man aside. 'There are more dangerous foes in this town than this woman!'

'She's the spawn of the dark gods!' a man yelled.

'She's brought plague to the town!' came another accusation.

The crowd surged forward again and Marius's men charged, their swords cutting through the untrained guildsmen and hurling them back.

Suddenly the shouts of anger turned to cries of fear. From his vantage point on the steps, Marius saw black-furred bodies moving out of the houses along the Sigmarstrasse and attacking the men at the wall of the shrine's grounds. The skaven were attacking in force! The verminous creatures leapt forward with astounding speed, a tide of rats around them, and hacked into the men around the church with serrated daggers and crude spears. Unaware of the peril behind them, the guildsmen inside the garden rushed the steps again, taking Marius by surprise. He hastily blocked a cudgel swung at his head and was bowled over by the impetus of the man's attack. As he scrabbled around trying to free himself, Ursula loomed over the pair of them and kicked the guildsman square in the face, sending him tumbling into the legs of those that followed.

'Get inside, you impetuous girl!' snarled Marius, clambering to his feet.

His men were outnumbered and falling back when something else caught his eye. One of the corpses in the grass had a black-feathered arrow sticking out from its back. Looking around, Marius caught sight of a man who had climbed onto one of the statues for a better vantage point and was now loosing arrows into the crowd. His targets were not random though, and Marius watched as a man clad in full armour cut his way through the guildsmen with swift and strong sword strokes.

'Kurt!' Ursula shrieked with joy.

'Kurt?' Marius asked, turning to Ursula with a questioning look.

'Yes, it must be him!' she laughed.

Just then someone came out of the doors behind them and Marius spun quickly, sword raised. He relaxed slightly when he saw that it was Ruprecht.

'The other doors are barricaded. Kirche is dead,' the burly man reported.

'How?' asked Marius, to which Ruprecht just grinned and hefted his hammer meaningfully.

With the other dozen men accompanying Ruprecht, the witch hunter and his band were able to fight their way down the steps and push the mob back into the gardens. As he chopped through the neck of a man wielding a rusting sword, Marius came face to face with Kurt. Marius halted as if struck. The man in front of him was a vision from his past. His eyes, his nose, his chin: it was unmistakeably Baron Leitzig, who Marius had put to death many years before.

'Bastard!' the knight shouted, smashing a gauntleted fist into the witch hunter's face and knocking him down. Kurt raised his sword for the finishing blow, but Ruprecht intervened, causing the knight to step back with a swing of his hammer.

Ursula threw herself between the two men and Kurt grabbed her around the waist.

'What are you doing?' she screamed.

'Rescuing you, now shut up!' snapped Kurt, lunging once more at Marius.

'Leave him be, he was trying to protect me!' Ursula shouted in his ear, but he ignored her.

Marius just sat there, dazed by the blow to his cheek, while Ruprecht interposed himself between the knight and the witch hunter.

At that moment, a short wiry man emerged from the throng, a bloodied knife in one hand.

'We go now!' he shouted, dragging Kurt away by the shoulder and the three of them disappeared into the turmoil.

'After him!' screamed Marius, throwing himself into the mass of fighting men, indiscriminately striking left and right with his sword.

Ruprecht lunged after him and grabbed his collar, hauling him back out of harm's way.

'Have you gone mad?' the big man said, dragging the struggling witch hunter back up the steps. 'What's got into you?'

'Leitzig!' snarled Marius, gazing at the armoured figure cutting through the throng and escaping. He was still dazed from Kurt's blow. 'That's Baron Leitzig.'

'Who?' Ruprecht demanded, pulling Marius further up the steps.

'No, not the baron,' Marius said, wiping at the blood dribbling from his split lip. 'He's the son of Baron Leitzig. I didn't register the name earlier, but seeing him face to face, I'm sure it's him. That man must be the son of Baron Leitzig.'

'And just who is Baron Leitzig?' asked Ruprecht, following Marius's gaze and seeing the retreating back of the Osterknacht knight.

'He's the daemon-worshipper I killed for murdering my wife,' Marius replied, his face a mask of hatred.

URSULA WAS PROTESTING loudly, but Kurt ignored her. He flung her over Heldred's back and mounted quickly with the help of Jakob, who then ran off in search of his own stolen steed. Already the horrific rat creatures were running down the street after them. The sea of red eyes and pointed teeth came

rushing towards them, it was like nothing he had seen
before. Terrified by the rat swarm, Heldred whinnied and
broke into a gallop with the merest touch of Kurt's spurs,
and the three of them raced down the street. At the next
junction Jakob joined them. Letting go of his reins, he
unslung his bow, nocked an arrow and turned in the saddle.
The arrow flew straight into the chest of one of the pursuing
creatures, spinning it into the beast skittering forward alongside. Turning a corner, they disappeared from view and sped
towards the town gates as fast as they could.

BOOK TWO

CHAPTER ONE
Northwards
Kislev, Autumn 1709

URSULA WAS TIRED and cold. As far as she could see, the desolate, icy wasteland stretched in every direction, broken only by thin, scattered woods and rocky outcrops. She stood at the mouth of a small shelter formed by three boulders atop one another, leaving a space inside just big enough for the three of them to light a fire and lie down for some sleep. She had no idea how the stones had come to be in the middle of the snowy plain, but the faint remains of carvings inside suggested that it was by human, or inhuman, hands.

She pulled her furs tighter around her shoulders as the strong wind eddied around the rocks in a gust that set her hair flapping across her face. She could hear the droning of Jakob's voice echoing from inside and she grimaced to herself. She was reluctant to go back in and listen to the blasphemies that he was trying to teach Kurt, and she knew she would get angry if she did so. But it was bitterly cold out here and hunger gnawed at her empty stomach. Making her decision, she turned and ducked inside.

The small fire was enough to warm the inside of the cave, allowing her to shrug off the furs and use them as a cushion to sit on. Kurt and Jakob were sitting on the other side of the fire, talking to each other in low tones. She tried to ignore them, but with no other distraction found herself listening in to the conversation.

'And Kjarl was great warrior of our people,' Jakob was saying. 'Khar gifted him with the strength of a bear and he led many raids against neighbouring people.'

'You have mentioned Khar many times, but often speak of there being many gods,' said Kurt.

'There many gods, yes,' Jakob said. 'I speak of warriors, and Khar their god. He gives strength and bravery, and in battle, we call on him. But there is also Slaeresh, and in the bed and at the council fire we ask for him. Jaenz is the god of shamans and leaders, and he sees all we do. Many worship him, but few are cunning enough to prosper, for Jaenz changes favours often. Last of the great gods is Nierg, and he brings sickness and to him we offer sacrifice to look away from our children. The men you fought here last winter, they were men of Nierg.'

'These gods you speak of are abhorrent things, worthy only of hate,' spat Ursula. 'I have heard of them but they are known by different names in civilised lands. The blood god, the dark prince, the lord of change and the lord of decay. Barbaric, bestial things that are best forgotten. Kurt, why do you let him fill your head with this?'

'My gods are strong, where is Sigmar when you need him?' Jakob taunted her.

'Sigmar sent you and Kurt to me,' she replied, turning away. 'Perhaps if you had not interfered he may have saved me another way.'

'Will you two stop bickering?' exclaimed Kurt, getting to his feet. 'I have had to listen to you arguing for months now.'

'Must you encourage him though?' complained Ursula. 'You never ask me about Sigmar.'

'I have had Sigmar rammed down my throat since I was a child,' Kurt said. 'What has he ever done to alleviate the burdens of my life? I saw my family killed, and I almost lost you. In fact, Sigmar has done nothing for me.'

'Exactly!' said Jakob, punctuating his remark with a waved fist. 'Fight in his armies and he gives you nothing. You see our warriors. They are brave and strong, and the gods bless them.'

'Kurt, you know I don't like this, why do you always take his side?' said Ursula.

The former knight crossed over the cave and laid an arm across Ursula's shoulders.

'I left the Osterknacht, rode through wind and snow and rescued you from the jaws of death,' he pointed out. 'What more proof do you need that I love you?'

'And now what are we doing?' she said, shrugging off his arm and stepping away. 'I am cold. I am tired. I am hungry. Why have you brought me to this Sigmar-forsaken place? What love is that?'

'What else was I to do?' exclaimed Kurt, throwing up his hands. 'How many times do I have to tell you? We had to leave the Ostermark, that devil van Diesl would have found us anyway. We couldn't go to Ostland, we can't cross the mountains, so that left north. Why do you keep asking me the same question?'

'Because I still don't know where we're going,' replied Ursula, flopping back down on her furs and hanging her head. 'I want to know when we can stop running.'

'We head north,' Jakob said. 'I take you to my people.'

'What?' Kurt said sharply. 'I never agreed to that! Your people threw you out, what makes you think I want to go there, or that they'll take you back?'

'I bring wisdom,' declared Jakob. 'I spend time in the south. You be great warrior that I also bring to them. We shall be welcome as chosen of the gods.'

'I am not going to Norsca,' Ursula stated coldly.

'No, we're not,' Kurt assured her, darting an angry glance at Jakob. 'We'll find somewhere to hide for the winter and then head south again.'

'I know town, not far,' Jakob told them. 'Tungask, hunters and traders, some of my people, some of Kislev there.'

'So we winter in Tungask, head east to the mountains and go south again,' declared Kurt. 'Marius will never find us; we'll head to Stirland. The whole province is in ruins anyway, we can start afresh there.'

'You said that about Novestok, and Marius almost caught up with us,' said Ursula with a disconsolate sigh. 'And the same about Verigrad.'

'Yes, but it's been summer,' Kurt said. 'Three people like us can move in the winter, but Marius and the Osterknacht cannot. I learnt that last year.'

'And what sort of reception will we get in this town?' asked Ursula.

'We safe there,' Jakob assured them. 'Peaceful town.'

'How far is it?' Kurt asked, moving over to sit down next to Ursula.

'Not sure,' admitted Jakob. 'Perhaps two days, perhaps week.'

'And you're sure you can find it?' Kurt continued.

'I am,' Jakob said. 'I have ways of knowing things; things the gods tell me.'

'But why do we have to run like this?' Ursula asked. 'I keep trying to tell you that Marius is our ally. He defended me, and it was Marius who tried to make sure my trial was fair.'

'It was just a trap, to lure me in, I'm sure,' Kurt said. 'Fourteen years and he's still hunting me, is he a madman?'

'I still say we should turn back and submit to the mercy of Sigmar,' Ursula told them. 'We have done nothing wrong. It would be better than this self-imposed exile. I thought I had a home, and we were going to get married. Now I feel like I am just wandering again, not sure where my life will end up and I don't know why.'

'Sigmar perhaps show mercy because he is weak like all your gods, but not van Diesl,' snorted Jakob. 'Cut our throats when he see us.'

'Jakob's right,' said Kurt. 'The man is evil. I told you what he did to my family, and you still think he would show us any kind of justice. And what about the Osterknacht? We know they have given him men, we saw them. Do you think they would deal kindly with two deserters and murderers?'

'You brought that on yourself!' Ursula said scornfully. 'You are the madman. What got into your head to make you run off like that? And killing those knights? The Kurt I first met would not have done that.'

'I did it for you!' Kurt said plaintively. 'I knew you were in danger. How many times must I say this?'

'And I'm not in danger now?' Ursula snapped.

'You have good man,' Jakob butted in. 'You not see that?'

'I *had* a good man,' Ursula replied, with a look at Kurt, who was staring into the flames of the low fire. 'You've done something to him, he's changed.'

'I am here, you know!' Kurt said suddenly, his distraction broken. 'Don't talk about me as if I wasn't. We're all tired, and I suggest we get some sleep and not head out too early in the morning. Some extra rest will heal some of the ills we feel.'

IT WAS FIVE days later when they came across a tributary to the Lynsk. They had been forced to sell the horses in Novestok and had travelled on foot ever since. The going had been hard, over rough, inhospitable terrain. Jakob had taught them how to hunt and set snares, and Kurt and Ursula had become adept at skinning the foxes, hares and other animals they had caught. They were exhausted and hungry still. The last time they had any quantity of food had been over a month ago, when Jakob had managed to bring down a small deer with his bow. The one consolation that Kurt felt was that any difficulties they were facing were multiplied many times over for Marius and his men.

In Verigrad, the three of them had been staying in the small fishing town for barely a few days when knights of the Osterknacht had ridden in, searching for them. Jakob had reported that they were as weary as the fugitives, demanding food from the locals for dozens of men. They had fled that night, hoping that the knights would not be too eager to pursue them, and it seemed to have proven true.

However, twenty days later in Novestok they had rested again and had considered staying for a while. Their money from the horses was enough to get them board and food for several weeks if necessary. But four days after arriving, a scouting party from Marius's band had arrived. It was only four men, and Jakob and Kurt had ambushed them the next morning as they rode back out of town. They would have

taken the horses if they could, but the locals interfered and
they were forced to flee again.

'Maybe west of here,' stated Jakob, standing by the stream
and looking around.

'Maybe?' said Ursula. 'You don't sound very confident.'

'Ursula's right,' Kurt added. 'Is it west or is it east?'

'Look around!' snapped Jakob. 'What you see?'

Kurt gazed over the wintry landscape. The low cloud
spread from horizon to horizon and the only features were
some rising hills to the north.

'I don't see anything in particular,' Kurt said.

'You find small town in north of Kislev with no land-
marks?' asked Jakob. 'No roads here to follow. These are not
my lands, but we are closer to them. I tell you the gods show
me the way, but you do not believe me.'

'Yes, you're right,' Kurt apologised. 'We head west. If nothing else that will lead us towards the Lynsk and the coast
where we can perhaps find somewhere, even if it isn't
Tungask.'

With a dark look at Kurt and Ursula, Jakob shouldered his
pack and started off to the left, walking along the bank of
the stream. The two of them watched him for a while before
following.

'Why do you hate Jakob so much?' Kurt asked. Ursula
didn't answer for a while and they tramped on in silence.

'He scares me,' she admittedly finally. 'The things he says,
the way he looks at me, the way he looks at you. I don't trust
him.'

'But he's looked after us well, he could have left us any
time he liked,' Kurt pointed out.

'But why?' Ursula said pointedly. She had never been
happy with Jakob's explanation that he wanted to leave the
Osterknacht and had looked to Kurt for protection. He
seemed more than capable of fending for himself, more
than either Kurt or herself could in this barren wilderness.
'He admitted the other night that he wants to go back to
Norsca. He's using you as a trophy.'

'He's never lied about that to me,' said Kurt. 'He thinks
I am marked by the gods and he wants to stay close to
me.'

'His gods are vile,' Ursula spat. 'I saw him writing symbols on the ground with rabbit's blood. Did you see the things he carved from that deer's horns? They were dark symbols, unholy things!'

'And how would you know?' Kurt asked. 'When did you become such a scholar?'

'You know what he talks about, about the gods of the north,' she said fearfully, glancing around as if the mere mention of the gods of Chaos would bring doom down upon her and Kurt. 'I've heard about them in prayer sessions, the tales that the priests tell of the Dark Gods who will damn your soul. You have seen the creatures that live at the roof of the world, the sort of men that worship the gods of the north. You cannot want to be like them!'

'I would rather believe Jakob than the mutterings of old priests who have never seen the things of which they speak,' Kurt said, gazing into the icy waters of the brook. 'You should listen to what he says. I have never had much time for any gods, but if you listen to him, you will see why I believe him. These are harsh lands, and further north it is even worse. His people are crude, I grant you that. But they are strong, not just in body but in mind and faith. Remember, I have fought these people. I have seen them, has van Diesl? They may have brutal gods, but these are brutal times and brutal places.'

'But you said they were tainted,' Ursula argued. 'How can you worship a god that does that to his people?'

'How can I worship a god that allowed you to come to such harm?' countered Kurt. 'You have been faithful and fervent your whole life, and yet Sigmar has watched on as you were cast out from town after town, ridiculed, reviled, and beaten.'

'There is something I must tell you,' Ursula said quietly, and the tone of her voice caused Kurt to stop.

'What is it?' he said.

Ursula hesitated. Could she really trust Kurt with her secret? The thought made her almost burst out laughing. It was no secret since the trial, she had stood there and admitted it to everyone in that church. If she could do that, then surely she could tell her loved one. Feeling more confident, she took a deep breath, looked Kurt square in the eye.

'Sigmar has guided me,' she told him, examining his face for some sign of horror or disgust. 'I sometimes have visions.'

'Visions?' asked Kurt, looking interested but not unduly worried. 'What sort of visions?'

'Visions,' Ursula said simply, slightly disappointed by Kurt's lack of reaction. She had expected surprise, awe, loathing, but not indifference. 'Like waking dreams. He warns me and guides me. You don't seem at all bothered by it.'

'And when was the last of these visions?' Kurt asked, ignoring her question and looping his arm through hers. He started walking again, but she held him back.

'Don't you believe me? Are you mocking me?' she said, a scowl creasing her brow.

'No!' Kurt replied with a shake of his head. 'I believe you, and I want to know all about it. But if we don't walk we'll lose sight of Jakob.'

Indeed, the Norscan was disappearing over the crest of a hill some distance ahead now, forging forward with some speed. The two of them broke into a brisk hike to try to catch up.

'So, when was the last vision you had?' Kurt asked again.

'Back when I was in prison,' Ursula told him and paused before continuing. 'Aren't you angry that I kept this secret from you?'

'I may have done things I regret these past few months, but I have yet to turn into a hypocrite,' he said with a bitter smile. 'It would be unfair of me to judge you when I kept so much secret as well. Let's just be open with each other from now on, eh?'

'Yes, let's,' she replied with a smile, hugging Kurt's arm tighter.

IT WAS MID-AFTERNOON the next day when Jakob let out a laugh and pointed to a dense forest a few miles distant.

'Tungask, other side of trees,' he said with a grin. 'You trust me now?'

'When we're sat in front of fire with some food in our stomachs, I'll be more forgiving,' Ursula said.

'How much further?' Kurt asked, eyeing the forest. 'It looks quite large.'

'We cut through corner,' Jakob said, indicating the southwest outskirts of the wood where the setting sun glittered on the winding trail of the stream. 'Be there just after night falls.'

'Good, then let's keep the pace up,' Kurt said, striding ahead.

They reached the edges of the trees as the sun was setting. Tall pines rose up into the sky far above their heads, and between their trunks was a thin carpet of bracken and ferns. At first the going was fast, the undergrowth little hindrance as they followed the course of the stream. However, as darkness fell, the way became more obstructed until finally they had to abandon the watercourse as they could no longer negotiate the tangle of roots and leaves that snaked across their route. Turning slightly southwards and then west again, they tried to keep the stream in sight as much as possible, but the ground rose and fell steeply in places and soon Kurt thought they were lost.

'We still head west, we still find Tungask,' Jakob assured Kurt.

'But which way is west, I can't see any stars at all,' Kurt replied, looking up into the thick web of branches above their heads. Ursula walked away, kicking at sticks, muttering to herself.

'Don't stray too far, who knows what's in these woods,' Kurt called out after her. She gave him a sour glance over her shoulder and threw her pack down at the base of a tree before sitting on it.

'Why you let your woman treat you like this?' Jakob asked, looking over at Ursula. 'My people like strong women, but they still behave.'

'Leave her alone, and remember your place as well,' Kurt said angrily.

'How many arrows do you have left, Jakob?' Ursula called out quietly.

The Norscan walked over to her, unhooked his bow and pulled a shaft from the quiver strapped to his pack. Kurt followed, and saw that not far off was a small clearing. It was dark, the clouds thick enough to block out the moonlight, but he could see something moving in the gloom.

'Wolf,' Jakob whispered, notching the arrow and stalking forward.

The pair watched as he advanced in a crouch, moving from tree to tree to get closer. Kurt kept an eye on the wolf, which was just pacing to and fro as far as he could tell. Jakob had settled against the bole of a smaller pine, and raised his bow.

'Watch out!' shouted Ursula, jumping to her feet and pulling free her hunting knife before sprinting forward, throwing up clouds of dead pine needles. Kurt was taken by surprise and it was a couple of heartbeats before he reacted and ran after her. Jakob had turned round to see what the commotion was. It was then that Kurt saw the two low, lupine shapes running through the undergrowth to Jakob's left, just a dozen yards from the northman. Ursula pointed with her knife and Jakob looked up.

Kurt pulled his sword free and surged past Ursula, heading to intercept the beasts.

'Look out for the one in the clearing!' he called out, noticing that the wolf they had first seen was now stalking in towards the three of them.

Jakob loosed his arrow at one of the two wolves running at him, catching it in the shoulder. It tripped and fell, and then pulled itself to its feet. As Kurt ran towards the closest one, he realised how big the beasts were, their shoulders came up to above his waist, and there was an unnatural sheen about their fur. Kurt was in front of the beast by a few yards and turned to face it. He looked at its slavering jaws as the beast raced towards him, and took a wide-footed stance, bracing himself for the beast to leap at him. Instead, the beast veered to Kurt's right and circled him, slowing its pace.

Kurt turned to keep it in sight and it leapt forward with surprising speed, and dived at Kurt's leg, his sword swing passing over it. Its teeth scraped across the greaves of Kurt's armour and he heard a yelp, but the impact was enough to unbalance him and he fell to one knee. Springing away, the wolf shook its head and then attacked again, jaws lashing out at Kurt's face. He rolled onto his back and thrust with his sword, its tip scoring a bloody line across the creature's left shoulder and forcing it clear. Rolling to his feet, Kurt prepared to defend himself again when a massive weight crashed into his back and hurled him forwards.

Stunned, he glanced back to see the wounded wolf grappling with his legs. Suddenly Ursula was there, screaming at the top of her voice. She dived head on at the wolf, her knife sinking into its back, forcing it to let go of Kurt's leg. It writhed on the ground to snap its jaws at Ursula, but she dragged her knife free and plunged it down again. A growl snatched Kurt's attention back to the other creature. It was bleeding heavily now and slinking warily forward with its head low. As a howl echoed through the air, it looked up and then turned and ran into the darkness. Checking on Ursula, Kurt saw that she was lying on her back, breathing heavily, the corpse of the wolf lying over her legs.

'Jakob?' he called out.

'I'm here,' the Norscan replied, jogging through the shadows, bow in hand. 'The other ran away.'

'And what do you think you were doing?' Kurt snapped at Ursula. He pointed to the slender sword that hung in its scabbard from her belt. 'Why didn't you use that?'

'I…' she started, crestfallen. 'It's going to take me a while to get used to it. And I'd like you to take more time to teach me how to use it properly. I don't feel comfortable yet waving it around.'

'Alright,' Kurt said, pulling Ursula to her feet and hugging her tightly. 'We'll spend some more time with sword practice once we're settled in Tungask.'

The three of them rested for a while, sitting down under a tree and keeping a sharp lookout in case the wolves returned.

'Was it just me, or were they even more cunning than normal wolves?' Kurt broke the silence, pulling himself to his feet and putting his pack on.

'You in north now,' Jakob replied, also standing. He leant down to pull up Ursula, but she snatched her hand back and pushed herself to her feet. With a shrug, Jakob continued. 'Breath of the gods spread across the northlands, and all

breathe it: men, plants, animals, birds. All more intelligent,
all stronger. You not in the Empire now.'

'No, we're not,' Ursula said sombrely.

THE THREE OF them were battered and weary when they
limped across the bridge to Tungask, not long before midnight. The town was made up of low log cabins, and the
warm flicker of firelight shone out from narrow windows.
Jakob led them through the town, past a massive pine trunk
planted in the centre of the town. The space around the trading post was circled with two storey buildings, and it was to
one of these that Jakob took them. Pushing open the door,
the crackling of fire and hubbub of conversation flowed out
to the travellers to welcome them in.

Inside, the floor was strewn with sawdust and the furniture made up of barrels and planks of all shapes and sizes.
Pipe smoke hung heavily in the air and cheery laughter
greeted them. They made for the roaring fire, but few of the
tavern's customers paid them much heed. Jakob went to the
counter – a row of waist-high kegs topped with a rough pine
plank, and spoke briefly to the man behind it. He returned
to Ursula and Kurt with a grin.

'Lars is son of Hengrist, who ran this place when I first
here,' he said. 'His father tell him many tales of me, he say,
and we welcome to stay as long as wish.'

'Seems friendly enough,' Ursula commented, looking
around. 'Can we please get something to eat?'

'We have good food for nothing tonight,' Jakob clapped
Kurt on the shoulder. 'Come, we sit and rest.'

They seated themselves on a bench by a table near the fire
and pulled off their muddied furs. Jakob wandered off to
talk to a group of blonde-haired northmen drinking from
long drinking horns on the other side of the room, saying he
would get what news had reached this far removed settlement. Kurt inspected the scratches to his leg, but it was
nothing serious, just some grazes at the back of his knee
where his armour strapping offered little protection. Ursula
had a scratch across her chin, and she asked for water to
wash it clean. Taking the cloth, Kurt dabbed at her face with
a smile.

'That was a very brave and very stupid thing to do,' he said, slipping the cloth back into the bowl, a mix of blood and mud rinsing out into the water.

'What was?' Ursula asked, wincing as he applied pressure to the cut once more.

'Attacking that wolf like you did,' Kurt told her.

'It would have been stupid if I had thought about it,' Ursula told him. 'There wasn't time to think, though. I just saw it coming for you and acted. To tell you the truth, I was terrified.'

'We all get scared. It's what we do that counts, not how we feel,' Kurt reassured her. 'I'm so proud of you, I can see how you survived for so long on your own now.'

'You know that we forgot my birthday?' she said. 'Not long after we crossed the border into Kislev.'

'I didn't realise, I'm sorry,' Kurt said, putting the cloth down and taking hold of her hand. 'You know, we could get our own room here, Jakob won't be around.'

'I know what you're saying, but we're not married yet,' Ursula smiled back.

'Married?' Kurt laughed bitterly. 'How can we get married now? Come on, I'm not in the Osterknacht any more, we're not in the Empire. We can do what we like. Damn their laws and rules!'

Ursula snatched her hand away and looked into the fire.

'And that was the only reason?' she asked. 'Because of the Osterknacht? What about love and respect for me? Didn't that ever matter?'

'Of course,' Kurt laid a hand on her shoulder but she turned away further and he pulled it back angrily. 'You've done nothing but complain and blame me since we left Badenhof. Come on, we're free now, I love you. What is the real problem?'

Ursula looked back at him and there was a tear in her eye.

'We're in the far north, miles from where we lived, surrounded by strangers and barbarians,' she told him. 'But I would like to think that some of that life we had can still survive. You said we'd go to Stirland and start again. Why not wait until then?'

'You used to be so warm and approachable,' Kurt replied. 'Now I fear the bitter wind has frozen more than just your skin, it's frozen your heart.'

'That's a horrid thing to say!' snapped Ursula. 'You've changed, and not for the better. That Jakob has been telling you all kinds of nonsense. You really shouldn't listen to him.'

'Oh, so we're back to Jakob again,' sighed Kurt. 'There's no point in talking to you when this mood is upon you. I'm not the only one who has changed. This has affected all of us and we'd best just start living with some of the consequences of what happened.'

Ursula stood up and looked back at Kurt.

'I'll get Jakob to ask for a separate room for me,' she said slowly. 'You can warm yourself by the fire tonight.' And with that, she walked away.

CHAPTER TWO
Hounds
Kislev, Autumn 1709

'BRING THAT BEARDED coward in here!' roared Marius, hurling his goblet of wine at the knight standing by the doorway. The young soldier looked at Ruprecht, who gestured him to leave with a flick of his head.

Marius and his band were camped in the ruins of an old watchtower, some twenty miles south of the Lynsk, while the Osterknacht were in their tents outside the tumbled stones. He and Ruprecht were in the remains of the upper guardhouse, rain dripping through the splintered wooden roof, despite the hasty repairs that had been attempted earlier. Marius paced up and down, clenching and unclenching his right fist and staring at the floor. He retrieved the goblet, wiped the rim with his sleeve and then picked up the bottle lying on the floor next to the rough pallet he was using for a bed. Pouring the last few drops from the bottle, he gave a growl and hurled away the empty vessel, which shattered on the stone walls into small pieces of green glass.

'Calm down, Marius,' Ruprecht said. 'You've been drinking since nightfall, and you're tired. Get some rest and we'll think about what to do in the morning.'

'Fetch Filandantis for me, Ruprecht,' Marius said quietly. 'Please, most loyal of my men. These knights have no respect for me, I see it in their eyes.'

'They have sworn to serve you and hunt the traitor down, Marius,' Ruprecht tried to soothe his master's fears. 'Filandantis is tired, as are we all. Perhaps by morning, he will have regained his strength. He is an old man, the march and the cold exhaust him.'

'I am no longer a young man, either,' exclaimed Marius loudly, draining the last of the wine. 'Do you hear me complain? No! The justice of our hunt gives me strength. Do I cower like a whipped dog when the rains and wind come? No! The elements are not my foe, for as they hinder me, they hinder my quarry.'

'You are a great man, and driven by your quest for vengeance,' Ruprecht admitted. 'However, we are merely ordinary men, and though you are a shining example to us all, we need to rest and we need food.'

'And what would you have me do?' cried Marius. 'Tarry and delay while our enemies make their way back to the heartland of darkness in the north?'

'We should have stayed a few days at Novestok,' Ruprecht said bluntly. 'You are driving us all too hard.'

'I thought you supported me,' Marius growled, slumping on to the pallet and dropping the goblet to the floor. 'Now you argue against me.'

'I am worried for you, Marius,' Ruprecht said softly, and the witch hunter looked up at him and saw his honest, open face.

'I am sorry Ruprecht, truly I am,' Marius said finally, dropping his head. 'You are right, this need for justice is like a fever inside me. It makes my blood run hot but it consumes me as well.'

'That is not the only fever you have suffered,' Ruprecht said. 'How is the wound?'

In the fighting at Badenhof, the skaven had butchered many of the townsfolk and Marius and his men had been forced to fight their way clear and abandon the town. The witch hunter had been cut by a ratman blade and the wound had festered for several weeks until Ruprecht had forced

Marius to visit a priestess of Shallya in Erengrad. Several days after the skaven had forced them to flee, a detachment of the Osterknacht had arrived. Marius had told them Badenhof was irrecoverably tainted, and invoking the ancient power of his position ordered the whole town put to the torch. Ruprecht shuddered at the memory when he recalled the mask of hatred that had been the witch hunter's face as he had poured oil down the sewers of the town and thrown a burning brand onto the fuel.

There had been a mad gleam in Marius's eye when he had personally taken an axe to the pews in the shrine of Sigmar and built a great pyre. Brother Theobald had escaped the skaven attack, but documents found in the town hall had shown that the money the cult had been taking from the skaven in exchange for secrecy and food had found its way into the priest's coffers. Ruprecht suspected that it was the priest who had put forward Ursula as the scapegoat for the conspirators' activities.

Marius had found Theobald hiding out in the loft where Ursula used to live. When the witch hunter had uncovered him, he dragged Theobald screaming into the shrine and tied him to the statue of his god, leaving the priest shrieking prayers of repentance to Sigmar as the flames engulfed the buildings. Never before had Ruprecht seen the witch hunter so harsh and so possessed by a need for violence. He had seen Marius do some cruel things, and had himself shown few qualms in torturing a man to speak his dark secrets. But over the last months, Marius's madness had grown, and no matter how hard Ruprecht tried to shield the men from it, they were growing suspicious about their leader's state of mind.

'It is sore but no longer troubles me overly,' Marius said, unconsciously rubbing at the scar on his arm. 'It is the wound in my soul that cuts deeper. The betrayal of that accursed woman! All the time playing me like a fool, in league with Leitzig and his minions. How could I have been so blind to the truth?'

'She fooled us all, Marius,' Ruprecht said, though in his heart he doubted that the great conspiracy that Marius feared was actually real. He seriously thought Ursula an unwitting pawn in the whole affair, but dared not confront Marius on the subject given the foul, almost murderous, mood he had been in since Kurt Leitzig had turned up and tried to kill him. Any mention of the former knight's name sent Marius into a raving fit or silent melancholy, and except for the first admission of his wife's death, he had offered no further justification for his hatred. Ruprecht was wise enough to know that many fears haunted a man, and perhaps the reminder of his earlier failure to kill off the Leitzig line had opened up a wound in Marius's soul that had never truly healed.

A rasping snore snapped Ruprecht from his thoughts and he saw that the witch hunter was curled up on the bier, sound asleep. With a shake of his head, Ruprecht went and sat on his own bedding by the door and leaned back against the wall. Tiredness welled up inside him, and it was not long before his head lolled forward and his snores joined the slumbering noises of his master.

THE NEXT MORNING Marius awoke to a throbbing head. Wiping at his bleary eyes he rolled off his pallet and struggled to his feet. There was a pitcher of brackish water by his bed and he poured it over his head. Ruprecht was still asleep by the door. Marius walked over to him and let the last few drips of water fall on his face. Spluttering, Ruprecht's eyes snapped open.

'Some guard you are!' laughed Marius. 'I thought you slept at my door to protect me from treachery from my own men!'

'More likely to bloody well stop you waking them at this ungodly hour,' Ruprecht grumbled back, looking up at the holes in the roof to see a dark sky beyond. 'Why so early?'

'I had a dream last night,' Marius said, his voice dropping. 'There were storm clouds in the sky, and a great bolt of lightning stuck me. Rather than being killed, I was lifted up into the air, and the energy flowed through me.'

'Very good,' Ruprecht sighed, pulling himself to his feet with a grunt. He was used to these high moments, which had characterised Marius's personality recently as much as his black moods. It was this unpredictability that was the most worrying aspect of Marius's changed personality.

'Don't you see it as a sign, my good friend?' Marius asked, slightly downhearted by Ruprecht's reaction.

'I can't eat signs,' Ruprecht told his master. 'Now, if you said you had been given a sheep, I might be more jovial.'

'Can you not feed on faith, big man?' Marius joked, slapping Ruprecht's diminished but still considerable stomach with the back of his hand.

'I worship Ulric, remember?' replied Ruprecht, sorrowfully pulling out the waist of his trousers to demonstrate how much weight he had lost. 'He loves the winter, and he loves wolves. A poor man like me has to make do with food to feed upon.'

'We'll spend another day here and send out the hunters,' Marius declared, to the surprise of Ruprecht. Seeing his companion's expression, Marius shook his head. 'I may have been drunk, but I wasn't insensible. I remember what you said, and I thank you for saying it. Men who march on empty stomachs cannot fight and will grumble like old wives. But in return for this kindness I expect every man to drive northwards hard, once that doddering fool Filandantis tells us where we should be going.'

'Let the seer rest today,' Ruprecht advised. 'You have called on him many times since we crossed into these barren lands.'

'What use is a seer who can't scry?' asked Marius, walking towards the door. 'Bring him up here after breakfast and I will talk to him.'

'Breakfast?' laughed Ruprecht. 'Cold beef and bad water, that's what we'll be having.'

'Feed on faith, Ruprecht,' Marius said. 'Feed on faith.'

MANY WITCH HUNTERS were wary of using seers, seeing them as little better than the tainted creatures they hunted. Marius was more pragmatic. He had first met Filandantis in Nuln, where he had come to the witch hunter with news of a cult of the pleasure god operating from inside the count's own palaces. He had subjected the seer to the Seven Tests of Purity: swearing an oath on the Book of Sigmar; dousing his head with blessed water; recounting the fourteen trials of Sigmar whilst holding a holy icon; spending a day fasting before feeding on a loaf baked with flour from a cathedral's mills; a drop of his blood was weighed against a drop of blessed water and found to be the same; after a day of prayer he passed his hand unflinching through the flame of a shrine candle; and slicing his hand with a silver dagger, the wound being inspected the next day for signs of putrefaction. All of these things Marius subjected him to once a year, and by the traditions of the Sigmarite church and his own order, the seer was deemed untouched by the dark gods. Still, there were those in the church who would not sanction the use of magic for any purpose. Marius thought them fools for being shortsighted.

In the end, Marius decided to go down and see the visionary rather than wait for him to be brought up. Filandantis was camping in a small white, conical tent slightly away from the knights. Pulling open the tent flap, Marius was greeted by a waft of incense smoke. It was one of the sources of irritation to the witch hunter that an entire pack pony was needed for the mystic's supplies, but there was little Marius could do if he wanted to retain the man's services.

The seer was sitting on a prayer mat in the middle of the tent, a burning incense pot in front of him. He had a thin face, heavily wrinkled, and a wispy moustache and beard hung down to his chest. He was swathed in woollen robes and cloaks, though his feet were bare and looked frostbitten. His eyes were open but unfocussed, and Marius knew that Filandantis was not looking at him as he entered. He sat down next to the seer and waited. There was no point breaking the trance, there were too many tales of daemonic possession, madness and physical injury caused by such a rash act. As it was, it was not long before the seer's glazed look disappeared and he blinked heavily several times before looking at Marius.

'Why are you here?' the old man snapped.

'You are the seer, don't you know?' Marius replied.

'I don't need my gift to know you are here to pester me for another sight of the witch and her lover,' muttered Filandantis. 'You have badgered and hounded me for this last week, and I tell you, as I told you yesterday and the day before and the day before that, I cannot see again yet. My gift is like a well. If you drink too much from it, you risk running it dry. It needs time to fill again, and for that I must rest, which is a commodity I have had precious little of these last four months.'

'You complain endlessly about the poor conditions, and yet you still come with me,' remarked Marius, standing up.

'I can't very well make it back on my own now, can I?' said the seer, closing his eyes. 'Besides, I could have stayed in Nuln all those years ago, but I suspect that by now I would have been strapped to a stake by an overzealous member of your order.'

'Your time is running out, we head off tomorrow and I need to know where we march,' Marius warned him.

'That's easy, if you were just to think for a moment,' Filandantis replied. 'We have headed northwards for two months now, with hardly a change. Head north, van Diesl, and you will be getting closer to your prey.'

CHAPTER THREE
Beasts
Troll Country, Early winter 1709

'I STILL SAY you panic,' said Jakob, dusting snow from his furs and dropping a pile of sticks at Kurt's feet. 'It one dream, it mean nothing.'

'I trust Ursula,' Kurt argued, sitting up on his blanket. 'She tells me that her visions have always come true, and there's no reason to doubt it this time. Every vision she has had so far has proven true.'

'She just say she see you fighting the witch hunter,' Jakob said. 'Does not mean he find us at Tungask, no need to run so soon. Why you believe her? Why you trust Sigmar? Have I not proven my gods are the strong ones? Did I lead you to Tungask with their help? Where Sigmar then? You let that woman lead you by the nose like pony.'

'I don't know why she didn't have any visions until yesterday,' Kurt said, exasperated. 'You both keep telling me to believe in this, or trust you. I don't know what to think.'

'Even if vision true,' Jakob conceded with a deep shrug, 'does not mean you lose fight with Marius.'

'I will not risk Ursula again!' Kurt said, stepping away. 'I want her as far away from that monster as possible.'

'She trouble, she keep saying to turn back,' Jakob said, grabbing Kurt's shoulder and turning him round. The former knight shoved him away with a growl.

'Never say that again!' he said. 'Remember that she's the reason I left the Osterknacht, and she's the reason I have been running all this time. Not you! You have helped us to survive, but I have never asked you to stay.'

Jakob muttered something inaudible, grabbed the firewood and ducked out of the tent. Outside it was bitterly cold and he could smell more snow on the wind. Already it was knee deep, and the winter was just beginning. It was a bad time to head north; Jakob knew that. He had come south this way in the summer and had found it difficult, even though he had been raised in the mountains of Norsca and was used to months without the sun and freezing conditions.

He looked with contempt at the smaller of the two tents, where Ursula slept. She had demanded that she not share with either of the men. Kurt was a fool for letting her lead him round by the nose. A good beating would soon quell her fierce spirit and allow the ex-knight to bed her. But he was still smitten with her, and Jakob knew that if he so much as lifted a fist against the wench Kurt would do him great injury. He also knew that there might be some truth to these visions she claimed to have. There was a definite air about her, a vibrancy close to her that he could feel. Raised in the north and used to the power of great warriors and sorcerers, it was a slightly sickly sensation he felt when she was close.

A howl in the distance attracted Jakob's attention and he listened to the night for a few moments. It was repeated, from further north, where a dark forest stretched across their route. They were camped in a small dell rimmed with pines, a tiny spring at its centre. He had heard the elders of his people speak of a great place to the south where there was no water and the ground was as dry as bone. His forefathers had sailed that far south and sacked the cities of the land called Arbarec, which he had learnt was called Araby in the Empire. The waterless sea was known as desert, and the sands stretched for weeks in every direction. The copse they were staying in reminded him of the oases he had learnt about, a small paradise of water and shelter in a desolate wilderness.

He would like to see a real oasis, Jakob decided. When he returned with Kurt to his tribe, he would teach the warrior how to fight properly, in true Norse style. Then he would get Kurt to challenge for leadership, and when he won, he would become the chieftain, with Jakob as his shaman. When that happened he would use his influence to get Kurt to sail south and take the gold and gems from the Arabians and live in luxury. It was a good dream, but one that was unlikely to come true as long as the red-headed bitch still argued against Jakob's plan. He needed Kurt to be malleable, easily influenced. At first he had simply accompanied the knight because he had felt a touch of greatness about him. Now Jakob was more certain that Kurt could achieve remarkable things if taught well. And Jakob would be there to reap the rewards when the time came.

There was little Jakob could do though, while the girl remained under Kurt's protection. He had tried all he could to divide the two, and though they bickered and fought more than ever, he felt that the bond between them was still strong. Other than that, Kurt had proved to be an able student, despite the protestations of his woman. He had learned Jakob's language well, and he could curse like a sailor in the Skaerling tongue. Jakob could feel the gods' favour growing; there were powers surrounding the young warrior that even Kurt was beginning to sense. Here in the north, under the breath of the gods, great men could become greater.

For all the bad memories of his childhood and exile, Jakob felt proud to be returning. The air here was clear, and tonight the cloudless night was bright with the light of the twin moons. There was Esdra, the white moon; the eye of the wolf that Kurt called Mannslieb. Esdra was the sailor's moon, predictable and constant to navigate by. Then there was Jandra, the red moon; the sorcerer's baleful eye that was known in the south as Morrslieb, after the god of death. Jakob had laughed when he had heard that Jandra shone green in the south, but it had been true. Perhaps, like the Norse themselves, the shaman's guide looked down on the southern lands with jealousy.

It was while he was meditating on the strange ways of the world that his attention was drawn to the chorus of howls erupting from the woods. Instantly alerted, he recognised the wolf calls as warnings to each other. There was something in the woods that had spooked the packs and they were shouting to each other to get out of its way. Fearing the worst, Jakob called for Kurt and Ursula.

The pair poked their heads out of the tents at almost the same time.

'Listen,' Jakob told them, and they did as he said for a short while.

'You think the wolves might attack?' Ursula asked, stepping out of the tent.

'No, they're scared,' Kurt corrected her, ducking back into the tent and emerging with his sword belt and shield.

'You hear that?' Jakob asked, eyes wide with awe.

'It's this place, I can feel their fear in the air,' Kurt answered. He looked up into the skies and closed his eyes, resting his shield at his feet and strapping on his sword. There was another flurry of howls and then the air fell silent.

'It's left the forest,' Kurt announced, opening his eyes. 'The wolves are glad to see it go.'

'Kurt, you're scaring me,' Ursula said, cautiously approaching him. He looked at her and smiled.

'Get your sword and remember what I taught you,' he said. 'You know how to look after yourself.'

'I didn't mean that,' Ursula said, looking at him oddly. '*You* are scaring me, not whatever is coming this way. Something is happening to you.'

'Do you remember your first vision?' Kurt asked, walking towards the lip of the wide dell.

'Yes, it was painful, like my eyes were on fire,' Ursula told him. 'Why?'

'I feel a bit like that,' Kurt told her. 'I feel like I'm waking up, after a life of being half-asleep. This place, it feels like home.'

'It is not your home!' she said shrilly, grabbing her sword from inside the flap of her tent. It had a narrower blade than Kurt's broadsword, useful for someone of her slender build and natural speed.

'I didn't say that,' Kurt called back. 'Don't worry, we'll head south after the winter snows pass. Now, get up the other side and keep watch. Kharghash, where's Jakob got to?'

The Norscan was nowhere to be seen, though a line of footprints led out between the tents and out of sight.

'What did you say?' Ursula said sharply.

'Did you see where Jakob went?' he repeated.

'No, that word you used,' Ursula said.

'Word?' Kurt paused to recollect what he had said. 'Oh, I'm sorry, it's just a curse Jakob taught me. It means Khar's blood.'

'Well don't say it again, it sounds like blasphemy to me,' she snapped back.

They waited in tense silence as clouds swept across the skies and the howling of the wind grew louder. The chill air had turned and Kurt moved out of the dell, taking Ursula with him, walking a short way north-east.

'Where are we going?' she asked as they hid amongst the snowdrifts.

'Wind's shifted,' he explained quietly. 'It'll attack from downwind, which means that whatever is out there will probably come this way if he can smell the camp. I'd rather catch it out here in the open.'

'Any sign of Jakob?' Ursula asked, looking around.

Kurt didn't answer. There was a scent on the air, very faint, but still noticeable. It was the stench of rotting flesh. Rising from his hiding place, he looked around. The fitful moonlight did little to relieve the gloom, but there was something moving out of the darkness. Over the noise of the wind, Kurt's ears caught the sound of sniffing and growling.

'Stay here,' he whispered before moving forward, crouching low. He advanced slowly through the snow, sword ready, all his attention focussed on the lighter shadow that stood out against the blackness of the distant forest. It was large, taller than him, and moving at some pace. When the creature stopped, he saw that it was in fact stooped over and running on all fours. Getting closer, he saw that the thing was covered in patches of long fur, its arms almost reaching to its knees.

The monster lifted its head and sniffed the air. Kurt froze. The beast's head swayed to the left and right, searching the

breeze, before dropping back on all fours. It was undoubt-
edly a troll. Though he had never seen one, Kurt had
listened to Jakob's descriptions of the semi-intelligent
beasts. The gangling limbs, the horns and long claws, all
were matched by the creature in front of him. Kurt began to
relax as the troll started to shuffle away, when suddenly
Ursula's voice cut through the air, calling for him. The troll
reared up once more, growling loudly. It gave a strange barking shout, which Kurt realised was more a crude language
than just an animal cry, and started lumbering straight
towards him. There was an answering roar from behind,
where Ursula was, and Kurt suddenly realised that was the
reason Ursula had cried out. There was at least one other
troll out there.

Cursing himself for a fool, Kurt rose and ran. He heard a
roar from behind him and glanced back to see the troll lumbering forward before dropping to all fours and bounding
through the snow with surprising speed.

'This way!' he shouted out, plunging through a snowdrift
and almost losing his footing. Ursula raced out of the darkness, her pale face twisted with fear. They were barely ten
yards apart when a massive shape loomed up behind her,
three long arms held high, one clawed hand gripping a
crude club.

'Watch out!' screamed Kurt as he hurled himself forward
even faster, his lungs fit to burst. Ursula dived forwards and
rolled through the snow, the club thumping down in a
shower of snow and frozen dirt. She rolled to her feet and
sprang forward as a claw swiped through the air just behind
her. The two of them ended up back to back, and a guttural
shout to Kurt's right heralded the approach of a third troll.
He wracked his brains to remember what Jakob had told
him.

'Jakob said that we have to keep moving, they're not very
quick on their feet,' Kurt told Ursula, shifting his grip on his
shield and stepping forward. 'Circle round them, keep them
turning.'

The trolls closed in more slowly now that their prey had
slowed, grunting to each other in their basic tongue, pawing
at the ground and throwing clods of earth into the air.

'What are they doing?' Ursula asked.

'Sizing each other up, I think,' Kurt said. When he had gone hunting as a child, he had once watched two bears confront each other. They had reared up on their hind legs and stretched to their full height to see who was biggest. 'They're not a pack, they've all followed the scent separately.'

'Can we run for it?' Ursula asked, backing away to her right, away from the troll approaching her, just half a dozen yards away.

'No, they'll beat us over open ground,' Kurt replied, trying to circle to keep the other trolls in view at the same time. 'We should have stayed amongst the trees.'

The stand-off lasted for a few heartbeats more and then the troll in front of Kurt took a jump forward.

'We'll go for your one!' snapped Kurt, spinning around and charging towards the troll behind him.

Ursula split to the left while he headed right, and the creature was confused for a moment, unsure which of them to go for. Kurt shouted to attract its attention and its heavy head swung his way, its mouth opening to reveal a ragged row of fangs dripping with bloody saliva. The smell was terrible this close to the carnivores, but Kurt concentrated on his attack, swinging his sword high towards the monster's arm. It swung up a fist to block the attack and the blade cut deep, slicing through the flesh and spilling dark blood across the snow. The creature did not even pause, swinging it claws in a backhand sweep that slammed into Kurt's shield and threw him to his back. It loomed over him, but Ursula ducked in and slashed at its calves before leaping away again, giving Kurt time to regain his footing. There was a rip scored into his shield across its entire width, the splinters of metal scattered over the snow.

The second troll came charging in, and Kurt scrabbled through the snow, to put the wounded troll in the way. Coming face to face with each other, the two trolls roared at one another and the wounded one lashed out. Kurt noticed that it was no longer bleeding, and a thick scab was already forming over the cut. Jakob had said they were tough to kill, but they seemed nearly indestructible.

Kurt jumped at the wounded troll and drove his sword halfway to the hilt into its back. It gave a howl and spun, but Kurt had plenty of time to drag his sword free and leap clear. More thick blood splashed into the snow for a second, but the flow stopped within moments. Sidestepping to his right, Kurt circled quickly and brought his sword down in a vicious slash that carved into the troll's shoulder. It gave a grunt of pain and turned, but Kurt could see that like the first wound, the cut was already beginning to heal. Trying again, he dodged under a backhanded swipe by the beast and drove his swords into its gut. Only the tip of his blade penetrated its thick skin, and a tiny dribble of thick blood oozed out. Kurt realised they were in serious trouble. He and Ursula might have been able to kill one of the beasts, but three of them were going to be all but impossible.

A flickering light caught Kurt's attention, and that of the trolls. Out of the darkness flew a bolt of fire, and as it slammed into the stomach of the closest troll Kurt saw that it was a flaming arrow. The flames spread across its body and it gave a keening cry and dropped to the snow. Seeing his opportunity, Kurt rushed forward and hacked at the screeching beast. It paid him no attention and he struck repeatedly, his sword biting into its arms, neck and legs as it thrashed around. More flaming arrows came flickering into the battle, a couple of them falling wide, but more catching their mark and setting fire to the trolls. Kurt reversed his sword and gripped it in both hands, ramming the point through the troll's neck, pinioning it to the ground. Ripping the sword free, Kurt gave a shout of triumph, a bellow that roared from his throat louder than the calls of the trolls.

Strength surged through him, boiling through his veins, rushing through his heart making it beat like a blacksmith's hammer. With his sword still gripped in both hands, Kurt charged through the snow towards the wounded troll. It was no longer on fire, its body covered in a smattering of snow where it had doused the flames. It bellowed at Kurt and he answered the challenge with a shout of his own, cleaving his sword through the air. The blade ripped through an outstretched arm, the clawed hand spinning away, scattering droplets of blood across Kurt. The beast howled into the sky and Kurt's rush continued, driving his sword through its chest up the hilt, the impetus of his attack making him barrel into its collapsing form. Taking no chances, he tore his sword out and slashed across its neck, severing its head.

Panting hard, he turned to finish off the last troll, but its corpse was burning fitfully a few yards away, Ursula standing over it with a blood-slicked blade. The energy Kurt felt started to drain away, leaving his limbs leaden and his lungs aching. From the darkness, he heard Jakob shout, and Ursula called back that it was safe.

'Where were you?' Kurt demanded when Jakob appeared, running through the snow.

'I go to forest, to fetch tree resin to light,' the Norscan explained, picking an arrow out of its quiver. 'Troll cannot heal burns, fire best weapon against them.'

'You could have told me that before,' Kurt said, turning away. 'We almost died here.'

'Is it safe to go back to the camp?' Ursula asked, looking at Jakob who looked at Kurt. The former knight sniffed the air, but all he could smell was blood and burning flesh.

'The stench will carry a long way,' he said, sheathing his sword. 'The gods only know what it might bring from the north. It is not safe, tonight we keep double watch, and tomorrow we go back to Tungask. If the gods demand that I fight Marius, then I will be there, waiting for him to come to me, not running away like a coward.'

CHAPTER FOUR
Warband
Kislev, Early winter 1709

'THE SEER SAYS we have turned too far north,' Ruprecht told Marius as the small army prepared for the day's march. 'We need to go more westerly and south, towards the Lynsk.'

'I don't suppose he cared to mention on which bank of the river we need to be?' grumbled Marius, rubbing his hands to warm them before slipping on the sheepskin mittens he had picked up in Erengrad.

'He didn't say,' Ruprecht said, ignoring his master's tone. 'The scouts reported some forest about twelve miles to the west. The road leads through it, or we can go around the southern edges.'

'Why would we want to go further south than necessary?' asked Marius, mounting the longhaired pony he had bought for the journey into the harsh northlands.

'We are almost north of the Lynsk, Marius,' Ruprecht warned. He pointed northwards. 'That's Troll Country up there, and in harsh winters like we've been having, all sorts of beasts and men are driven south in search of food. That forest is a dangerous place, there could be all manner of beasts lurking within the treeline.'

'It would be a foolish creature who attacked us, my friend,' laughed Marius, waving an arm to encompass the three dozen knights and fifty men who now accompanied him. 'I have enough men here to fight off any number of trolls. Or perhaps you are afraid of dragons? Or manticores? Or the grimgralkin living under your bed that used to terrify you when you were young?'

'You still think these things are children's stories, when you have seen the things we've seen.' Ruprecht said. 'We have fought creatures that were half beast and half man, who fed on raw flesh. We've faced the walking dead, for Ulric's sake! And what about the skaven? Most people in the Empire would think you mad if you started talking about rats that walked on their hind legs and were the size of a small man. No, there is truth to those old stories, they don't pass into legend for no reason.'

'Well goblins and skaven I have seen, but I've yet to see a dragon and until I do, then a myth they shall remain,' said Marius before kicking his heels into the pony's flanks and riding off towards the road. 'We go through the forest!' he called back.

MARIUS'S FORCE HAD set off early and made good speed along the road, so it was just before noon when the first trees began to appear, scattered thinly at first, but after a mile or so, they started to crowd together until the horizon was thick with a dark swathe of pine trees. The road itself twisted and meandered into hollows and around hillocks, so that for every straight mile travelled, the column had to ride or walk a mile and a half.

With the trees to shelter them from the constant bitter winds, it seemed deadly silent within the looming trunks of the trees. The air was filled with the scent of pine resin and rotting mulch, and not a sound could be heard above the sighing of the breeze through the treetops. The state of the road began to deteriorate as well, soon turning into little more than a muddy track with the trees pressing close on both sides.

Ruprecht felt his hackles rising as he walked through the stillness of the forest, and pulled his hammer from the sling at his back. A couple of the men noticed him arming himself and looked around for signs of danger.

'Don't mind me, lads,' the big mercenary said. 'I just feel more comfortable with it in my hands rather than slapping my backside.'

His joke fell flat and there was no laughing. The mood of the whole column was subdued, from the knights to the squires and the warrior band of Marius: everyone felt the same tenseness and air of danger.

About three miles into the forest a stream trickled under the road ahead, and a small wooden bridge had been built. Some of the men dismounted and began to lead their horses down to the bank when Ruprecht stopped them with a shout.'

'Hold it there, men!' he called, striding towards the front of the column. 'Have you not brains in your heads?'

'What's the problem here?' demanded Marius, trotting over on his pony. 'What's the delay?'

'The men were going to water at the stream,' Ruprecht explained.

'So?' said Marius.

Ruprecht said nothing. Jumping off his horse, he gestured for Marius to follow him. The witch hunter dismounted and the two of them strode down to the water's edge.

'Look at it!' snapped Ruprecht in exasperation. Marius and some of the men did so, and gasped at what they saw. The stream was running with a thick red liquid, like blood, and a slight smell of rotting flesh could be detected.

'What's this?' Marius said, looking around in alarm. 'How did you know?'

'I told you! We're as good as in Troll Country now,' Ruprecht said. 'Things are not as we are used to this far north. I used to take my boat up the Talabec as far as the Urksoy sometimes and spoke to traders from these parts and a little further north. When the wind is from the north, they call it the *dovoiska petrenya*; the breath of the dark lords. Any river that flows from the north can be tainted, some like this, others with tar, or oil, or seething with fish that walk on legs and birds with no wings. These are strange places, we should not tarry here!'

Marius gave Ruprecht an odd look after his outburst and then seemed to dismiss whatever thought was passing through his mind at the time.

'Move along, you men!' he called out to the knights at the front who had stopped. 'I want to be out of these woods by nightfall.'

'We can hope,' muttered Ruprecht, tightening his grip on the warhammer and stalking off through the snow.

AS THE SUN, faint behind the winter clouds, dipped towards the treetops, the forest was bathed in long shadows. The path the group followed had long given up any semblance of being a true road, and had disappeared altogether over the last mile or so. Now the band was making its way between the trunks of the pine trees themselves. They were incredibly ancient, soaring high above the heads of the mounted men, their thick trunks too wide for even a big man like Ruprecht to put his arms all the way round. Their bark was dark and craggy, and the snowdrifts beneath the branches were littered with dead pine needles.

Ruprecht's attention was attracted to one tree in particular, as he ploughed his boots through the thick layer of snow. It was just to his left and seemed to be reddish in colour, or perhaps it was red resin oozing from the cracks in the bark. He strayed slightly from the column to investigate, his suspicions aroused.

Sure enough, there was something thick and red seeping from the tree, and touching a finger to it, Ruprecht was convinced it was blood. Perhaps there was some dead animal under the roots, he thought and then he glanced up. Over his head, in the lower branches some ten feet higher above him, hung a corpse. Its head was battered and bloody and it was bound to the trunk and branches by thick rope studded with flint blades. It was then that Ruprecht realised that the man was wearing the colours of the Osterknacht; he was one of their scouts. And as a gurgling sound issued from the corpse's throat Ruprecht also realised with horror that it was not a corpse at all, but a living man.

'Ware! Ware!' shouted Ruprecht, breaking into a run. 'To arms! Prepare yourselves!'

As he ran back towards the others, Ruprecht tripped through a snowdrift and heard a shout. Amazed, the burly Talabeclander watched the drift rise up, to reveal a heavily muscled man swathed in a cloak. Snow stuck to his long blond hair and plaited beard, and except for boots, cloak and a loincloth, he was naked to the elements. He was pale-skinned and covered in tattoos made from swirling blue patterns. The man grinned, shouted something in a foreign tongue and then swung his axe at Ruprecht's head.

'Ambush!' Ruprecht bellowed, throwing himself clear of the blow and rolling to his feet. Dozens more figures were now rising up through the snow, similarly garbed, wearing an assortment of horned helmets, scraps of leather and mail, and wielding axes and maces. They screamed hoarse battle cries as they raced through the trees towards the straggling knights, dragging them off their horses and staving in their heads and chests with their brutal weapons.

Ruprecht had little time to pity the dead knights as he lifted his hammer to parry another axe blow aimed for his chest. Metal rang on metal and jarred his arm as the blow was deflected away.

'Norse scum!' growled Ruprecht, shoulder charging into the marauder and hurling him into a nearby tree. The Norscan ducked Ruprecht's swing with his hammer; the head of the weapon smashing loose a clump of bark and wood just above his enemy. The Norseman struck out quickly with his axe, trying to rip through his groin, but Ruprecht just managed to get the haft of the hammer in the way to prevent a fatal injury. Bringing down the heavy head of the hammer, he slammed it into the Norseman's stomach, smashing him to one side with a cracking of ribs. The Norscan vomited blood into the snow and Ruprecht pressed forward, his hammer dashing the marauder's brains out over the tree's roots.

Ruprecht saw that most of the knights had dismounted now, the trees making it impossible to fight properly from horseback. Marius's men and the squires were firing ragged volleys of arrows and crossbow bolts at the attacking marauders, though few shots were finding their mark amongst the shadowy trunks. Ruprecht charged into the fray, bellowing Ulric's name, his hammer snapping the spine of one Norscan who failed to turn in time and smashing the mace from the hand of another who was too slow to dodge Ruprecht's next attack.

Over the Norscan's shoulder Ruprecht could see Marius battling with two more marauders, deftly parrying their attacks with his sword, wearing them down ready for a counter-attack. The Norseman fighting Ruprecht made a dive for his mace, half-buried in the snow, but Ruprecht kicked him squarely in the stomach as he went past, spinning him onto his back. He didn't have time for the finishing blow though, as a throwing axe spun towards him, forcing him to dodge to the right as it skimmed past his head. The snow underfoot was slippery and Ruprecht had to take a moment to steady himself, by which time the Norseman on the floor had clambered to his feet and was holding a wickedly long hunting knife in his left hand. His other hand hung loosely by his side, and his face was twisted with the pain of his broken fingers.

'Back to the hell that spawned you,' snarled Ruprecht, swinging low with his hammer. The Norseman nimbly jumped back, and then stepped forward with his knife thrust forward, burying it an inch into Ruprecht's chest. Grunting away the pain, Ruprecht wedged his hammer between the two of them to lever away his attacker, but was stunned by a head butt that crashed against the bridge of his nose, breaking it. He could taste blood running over his lips and brought his knee up sharply, ramming it into the groin of the marauder, who collapsed to the ground again.

'Spoil my good looks, would you?' spat Ruprecht through the blood and phlegm in his throat, before driving his hammer into the man's chest, bludgeoning into his heart and lungs.

The rest of the men were faring well now that they were over the shock of being ambushed. The marauders wore little or no armour and their clumsy axes and maces were poorly matched against the deft swords wielded by the fully armoured Osterknacht. Ruprecht saw shadowy shapes slinking off through the woods as the more sensible members of the warband made a bid to escape.

'Follow them, they're getting away!' bellowed Marius, two dead marauders at his feet, their blood cooling in the glinting snow.

'We'll never catch them on horseback,' called back Trevigar. The lord militant had volunteered to lead the force sent after the renegade, Kurt Leitzig, when he had met Marius outside Badenhof. He had been almost as obsessed as Marius at the start, as if the traitor had done him some personal slight, but Ruprecht had never felt comfortable about pursuing the matter further. Now, though, Trevigar was just as weary and tired as the rest of them and did what he could to temper the effect on his men when Marius was in one of his manic moods.

A dozen or so marauders were left, battling on for a little while longer against impossible odds. They were foolishly brave, thought Ruprecht, but then again if he had been in the same position, would he actually have the stomach to turn and run rather than facing the gods' judgement?

'Find me at least one that's alive,' commanded Marius, striding through the corpses, inspecting them for signs of life. 'I want to know where Leitzig is!'

'HE'S TRYING TO pretend he doesn't understand Reikspiel,' Ruprecht told Marius, striding out of the witch hunter's tent, wiping blood from his hands on a ragged remnant of the marauder's clothing.

'You can get nothing out of him?' Marius asked, not turning from where he was stood, gazing into the red depths of one of the camp's cooking fires.

'He just keeps spouting Norscan nonsense, as far as I can tell,' Ruprecht said, tossing the rag onto the fire where it hissed and sputtered in the heat before being consumed by the flames.

'No reaction to Leitzig's name?' pressed Marius, now actually turning to face his second-in-command.

'He doesn't seem to recognise it, just like the other two,' said Ruprecht.

'What could he have possibly offered them to make them so tight-lipped, I wonder?' said Marius. 'Gold? No, he was not rich unless he has stolen something since he fled from me. Honour? Pride? Glory? How has he made them so loyal?'

'Perhaps he has nothing to do with them,' suggested Ruprecht, turning to look back at the tent where the marauder was still bound to the central pole, leaking blood from dozens of small cuts inflicted by the witch hunter's burly interrogator.

'Nothing to do with them?' asked Marius, with an edge to his voice that Ruprecht had now learnt meant that he was on the verge of launching into another lengthy tirade. 'They just happened to be lying in wait for us, eh? Leitzig didn't send them back to attack us, is that what you are saying?'

'Many things are driven south by the bad winters, perhaps these northerners come south looking for easy pickings,' suggest Ruprecht. 'In which case, they should have chosen a more defenceless prey.'

'No, they're not that stupid,' announced Marius. 'These are hardened raiders, used to feeding off soft merchants and stupid peasants from coastal villages. They know better than to attack knights and men-at-arms. No, Leitzig must have sent them to waylay us, there's no other reason why they would attack such an obviously difficult target.'

'You may be right,' Ruprecht conceded. 'I have sent a couple of trackers to follow their trail through the woods. They'll be back by morning to tell us which way they went. We can follow them right back to their camp if you wish.'

'Yes, we should get some rest now, it's been a hard day,' said Marius, closing his eyes and all of a sudden looking like the tired, battered old man that he really was. 'But we march out at first light, I want this whole affair settled before the real winter snows come. I want to be in a house with a warm fire and a soft bed when the north winds start howling.'

'Don't we all, Marius, don't we all?' agreed Ruprecht, stooping to pick a stick from the fire, its end glowing red-hot. 'Anyway, I'll give this one another chance to tell us everything,' he said, blowing on the stick to make the ember flicker into flame again.

CHAPTER FIVE
Betrayal
Tungask, Early winter 1709

URSULA SIGHED HEAVILY, earning a smile of understanding
from the Kislevite housewife sitting at the next table. The
pair of them watched as Jakob, Kurt, the woman's husband
and two Norscans argued in the corner, remonstrating with
each other in a language neither Ursula nor her companion
could understand. Ursula couldn't fathom why Kurt would
want to learn such a disgusting, tainted tongue. Worse than
that, she had no idea why they had come this far north in
the first place. Every time she had argued for turning east or
west, or, Sigmar forbid, actually heading south again, Jakob
had been there with reasons why they could not turn from
their course. Now the winter was setting in and the likeli-
hood that she could leave Tungask before the spring thaws
had all but vanished, and who could tell how long that
would be?

The young woman just wished that this whole sorry turn
of events hadn't taken place. Kurt had become so stubborn
lately, and listened far too much to the advice of the crude
little Norscan, rather than to the words of his loved one. His
continued insistence to practise the strange rituals of the

northern gods, and to learn the Norse language, was offensive in the extreme, and Ursula felt this did not bode well for the future. If she did nothing, Jakob would eventually have his way and they would end up in Norsca, living amongst the barbarian tribes. Ursula shuddered slightly at the thought. Soon she would have to make up her mind: would she keep blindly following Kurt, trying to save him from himself and the manipulation of Jakob, or should she go her own way? She resolved to have another talk with Kurt later, and see what happened.

Pushing away her mug of hot goat's milk, Ursula stood up, nodded at the housewife, and made her way upstairs to her room. She realised it had been too long since she had prayed, her once inviolable morning routine had been shattered by their speedy escape from Badenhof, but she told herself that now, more than ever before, she needed to renew and rejuvenate her faith in the true god, Sigmar. Amongst these heathens and heretics, she would remain pure, and hopefully with that purity she would be able to pull Kurt back from the dark precipice towards which he was moving. She feared for his soul, and when she knelt down to pray beside her bed, her first words were to ask Sigmar to protect her beloved.

She had not been there long when she heard a commotion from the tavern room downstairs. There was shouting and the door banged open, making her jump with fright.

'MARIUS IS CLOSE,' Kurt said, walking in to the room and seeing Ursula knelt beside her bed. 'You should come downstairs and see this.'

'What is it?' Ursula asked, pushing herself to her feet and dusting off her dress, which was grubby from where she had been kneeling on the bare wood of the floor.

'Twelve Norse have arrived, Fjaergardians, and they say they fought with a man with a black feather in his hat.'

She followed Kurt back down the stairs and into the common room. Jakob was talking hurriedly to a group of muscular, bearded men, who she had not seen before. They were not like the Norse of Tungask, they were taller and heavier built. They wore few clothes, even though the temperature outside was freezing, and were openly armed with maces and axes. One carried a shield with a twisting Norse rune of the front, clumsily daubed in red paint over the beaten metal.

'Who are they?' asked Ursula, as Kurt listened in to the conversation.

'They're of the Fjaergard,' he said, brow furrowed in concentration. 'From what I can remember, they're quite a way from home. They come from southern Norsca. They sailed across the Sea of Claws to raid, but a storm almost wrecked their longship and forced them to beach further north than they planned. They couldn't get the ship afloat again and were stranded. Their chieftain, Hrolfgar, the big man with the shield and the gold on his helmet, wanted to lead them back north, but his brother, Bjordrin, the smaller man with the black beard, had an argument with him.'

Kurt paused and said something in Norscan to Jakob. The marauders turned and looked at him, then burst out laughing, slapping Jakob on the shoulder and almost sending him sprawling to the floor.

'What is so funny?' asked Ursula, who was intimidated by the hulking men, who stood half a head taller even than Kurt, who was not a short man.

'Jakob has been telling them who I am, they think it funny to hear their own tongue spoken by a man of the Empire,' Kurt explained.

'What did you say to them?' Ursula asked, pursing her lips in irritation. 'Why can't you speak Reikspiel when I'm around, it's very rude of you to ignore me like that.'

'They don't understand Reikspiel,' Kurt said, glancing at Ursula with an annoyed look. 'And there's no point me asking things through Jakob all the time when I'm getting to grips with the language now. I need the practice. Now, be quiet a moment, I'm trying to hear what they are saying.'

Kurt walked closer and listened intently, his gaze passing from one Norseman to the next as each spoke in turn and carried on the tale of how they came to be there. As the tale continued, drinks were passed around, and the talking got heartier, making it more difficult for Kurt to understand. Sitting at the next table, he did his best to translate the story to Ursula. The Norseman explained how Bjordrin, with the support of the rest of the raiding party, had persuaded Hrolfgar to head further inland. Heading south-east, they had decided to follow the Lynsk. They came across one Kislevite village and looted it, and an encouraged Hrolfgar had decided to press on. They had travelled for many days, when one of the group had remembered a tale of a Norscan settlement this far south. He had heard rumours about Tungask, and Hrolfgar had resolved to find it. However, to get there they had come across the large forest to the south of the Lynsk. They had come across the tracks of many men and horses, which piqued Hrolfgar's interest. Wanting to arrive in Tungask in triumph and glory, Bjordrin had come up with a plan for the warband to lie in wait in the forest ahead of what they thought to be a traders' caravan. To this Hrolfgar had readily agreed, keen to get more loot for himself.

Unfortunately, the first people to come along had been Marius and his force, and they thought them a contingent despatched to hunt them down. The Norse had killed their scouts to leave them without any clue of who else was in the woods, and then decided to try to destroy the interlopers. Hrolfgar had reasoned that all the while the soldiers were there, they would be looking over their shoulders to see if they were safe. At first Bjordrin had argued that they should just leave. After all, there were some three dozen mounted knights, and twice as many men on foot. It was a small army by Norse standards, much more numerous than the survivors of their raiding party. Hrolfgar had disagreed. He thought it better to ambush the armed men and have the surprise, than have the enemy stumble on the marauders, or worse still catch up with them in Tungask. Not wanting to feel like cowards, the rest of the warriors had backed Hrolfgar. The attack had faltered when one of the soldiers had stumbled on the body of a captured scout, and the attack had ended up failing dismally. Hrolfgar had lost thirty men that day, and three more died from their injuries the following day, while the survivors headed to Tungask as fast as they could.

All this Kurt relayed to Ursula as he heard it, and her expression grew increasingly horrified as the story progressed.

'Why are you looking at them like that?' Kurt asked when he had finished, seeing the venomous glare Ursula was directing towards the Norsemen.

'Thieves, murderers and rapists, that's what they are!' hissed Ursula. 'You said they had come to attack the coast, and that they sacked a village not long ago. What blood-thirsty barbarians. The last time you came to Kislev was to fight these types of animals!'

'The last time I came to Kislev I wasn't being hounded like a dog by an insane witch hunter,' Kurt replied. 'I have more in common with these men than I ever had with the Osterknacht. They are brave and strong, they are honourable and they strive for glory. What is so wrong with that?'

'You condone the raping and pillaging they do in the name of those hideous gods they worship?' Ursula snapped, her voice rising. Jakob heard her and came over, waving at the newcomers to seat themselves by the fire. The wiry Norscan had fitted into Tungask very well, his knowledge of both the common languages proving useful, and as Kurt and Ursula's only guide, they had given him most of the money they had.

'I hear what you say,' Jakob said with a frown. 'You do not understand the way of the north. It is right that we raid and take from these lands, and the lands where you were born. The wolf hunts the sheep so that it may live. If the shepherd is strong, he kills the wolves, and if he is weak, the wolves will eat. Your soldiers are made strong because they must fight us! We give you strong shepherds to protect your towns and your cities from the sword and the burning torch.'

'Don't you think it is obscene?' Ursula said, turning her attention to Kurt.

'The northmen have lived this way since Sigmar himself walked these lands,' Kurt replied with a shrug. 'We share the same ancestors, and though the Empire has forgotten the old ways and the old gods, and hidden itself from its history, those times of legends and heroes still exist here in the north. What these men do is little different to what Sigmar did before he was Emperor.'

Ursula slapped Kurt hard across the face, attracting the attention of everyone in the room. Hrolfgar said something and his warriors laughed aloud, making Kurt flush red.

'He calls me *sutenmjar*,' Kurt rasped at Ursula, grabbing her wrists and pulling her forward. 'It means southern pup. He says I cannot even control my woman.'

'No you can't,' Ursula spat, wrenching her hands free. She ran out into the snow-filled night outside, slamming the door shut behind her.

'I should go after her–' Kurt suggested, glancing at Jakob for advice.

'What, and beat her?' Jakob asked, looking at the closed door. 'It would not be too soon.'

'No!' Kurt snapped, shoving Jakob away from him.

'Then you will be laughed at more,' Jakob said, looking over at Hrolfgar and his men. 'At the moment they are happy for you to be here because you entertain, but if Ursula insults them and they understand, they kill her.'

'If any of them so much as thinks about harming her, I'll butcher them all,' growled Kurt. 'I'm going after Ursula.'

'Leave her be,' Jakob advised, putting his hand on Kurt's arm as he made to leave. 'She angry and upset, you cannot change that yet. Talk with Hrolfgar and his men, learn of Marius's soldiers and make amends to Ursula in morning time.'

Kurt paused and thought it over for a moment. Jakob was right, as he usually was. Ursula would be in no mood for reconciliation for a long while, and it would be better done elsewhere, where Hrolfgar and his warriors were not close by.

'I am sorry, my friend,' Kurt said, grabbing Jakob's shoulder and giving it a comradely squeeze. 'Let's see what Hrolfgar has to say.'

As Kurt turned his back on Jakob and stepped towards the raiders, the ex-servant could not stop the sly smile that twisted his thin lips.

JAKOB AWOKE TO a heavy pounding on his door, which was matched by the pounding in his head. He and Kurt had spent the night talking to Hrolfgar and his men, swapping stories of battles, and washing the evening away with koidva, a local spirit distilled in the back room of the tavern.

He pushed back his blankets and sat up groggily, his head swimming and his stomach threatening to rebel. He ignored the nausea and forced himself to stand up on wobbling legs, clutching his head in his hands as if to block out the pain. He unlatched the door and it slammed open, knocking the Norscan to the floor.

'She's gone!' Kurt said as he burst into the room, his expression as dark as a thundercloud.

Dazed and dizzy, Jakob sat there for a moment, uncomprehending.

'What?' he asked as Kurt helped him to his feet.

'Ursula's missing!' insisted Kurt. 'Get dressed and help me look for her.'

'She knows the town, she not lost,' protested Jakob, who tottered back towards his bed. Kurt grabbed him by the arm and dragged him to the window. Opening the shutter, snowflakes started to drift inside and the blast of chill seared through Jakob's fugue, waking him immediately.

'Her bed wasn't slept in,' Kurt said impatiently, pushing Jakob back towards his clothes. 'It's mid-morning, I've already been across town twice, checking if she stayed over anywhere else. She hasn't, she isn't in the town.'

'She a strong girl, she look after herself,' Jakob replied, silently thanking the gods for this wondrous turn of events.

'I don't care,' snapped Kurt. 'Meet me downstairs quickly, I want to find out where she went.'

When Kurt had left, Jakob struggled into his rough woollen breeches and shirt before donning a thick fur coat he had bought from one of the Kislevite traders in the town. He dragged on his fur-lined boots and pulled his bow and arrows out from under the bed. Stomping downstairs, still feeling like there were hot nails driven into his skull, Jakob found Kurt waiting at the tavern door, fully dressed and carrying his sword.

'Boris Ytselva saw her walking towards the bridge last night, we'll start there,' Kurt said, opening the door.

THEY HAD SPENT much of the day searching for Ursula in Tungask, but other than the single sighting of the night before, there was no news. They had circled the town for

some other sign of where she might be. There were slight
tracks by the bridge that Jakob could see; the snow had been
light the night before and had left a clue that Ursula had
passed that way. He concluded that she had gone into the
woods, the edge of which could be seen a mile or so away.
Looking up at Kurt, he saw the ex-knight staring into the distance as if willing Ursula to come into view. A plan began to
form in Jakob's mind. Here was an opportunity to be rid of
the barb-tongued woman for all time.

'Give me a moment,' he said to the knight. Sitting cross-
legged in the snow, he pulled the small bag of hair and fox
bones from his belt, tipped them into his hand and began
to mumble nonsense words to himself – an old rhyme he
had learnt as a child, the names of the village elders who
had scorned him, and the constellations that rose in the
north. With a dramatic shout, he threw the bones into the
air and let them scatter onto the snow in front of him. He
pretended to study the pattern for a little while, umming
and tutting to himself as he did so. Grunting, he looked up
at Kurt, who was staring at the Norscan with fascination.

'There is some sign that she went out onto the plains,'
Jakob lied, pointing in the direction Kurt was looking. 'If
you go that way I shall go into the woods to make sure I am
not mistaken.'

Without any further acknowledgement, Kurt began to
stride away purposefully. Jakob allowed himself a smile. He
could not fail here. Marius was somewhere in the forest as
well. If he found Ursula, he would most likely kill her. If
Jakob could prove this the case, then there would be no
more argument from Kurt against going north to Jakob's
homeland. If Jakob found Ursula then he would despatch
her himself and blame it on Marius. In either case, the
blame fell on Marius and although the headstrong Kurt
would demand an opportunity to exact vengeance, Jakob
could forestall any attempt. He would talk with the Norse
of the town, warn them of Marius's approach and advise
them to banish Kurt for fear of what the witch hunter might
do to them for harbouring such a dangerous renegade. If
Ursula wasn't found, then the chances were that she would
be dead already, and Jakob's task would be even easier.

With a light heart, he shouldered his bow and set off towards the forest.

AS NIGHT FELL, Kurt's mood became even bleaker. He had searched all day across the icy wasteland for a sign of Ursula, but had found none. The weather had worsened and he had been forced to seek shelter in a small cave amongst the foothills roughly ten miles south-west of Tungask. It was little more than a dell really, the cave barely deep enough for him to lie down and keep his feet out of the snow. He feared for Ursula in such appalling conditions, and his guilt lay heavy on his mind and his heart. It was he who had turned her away so roughly, and he realised the truth of her words in the argument of the previous night. He did listen to Jakob too much and he ignored her, even though he knew and trusted her more than anyone else in the world. The lands themselves were also having an effect on him, he could feel it in his blood and his bones. He was worried, but at the same time, Jakob had reassured him that this was natural, and that the men of the north felt this quickening of their pulse and this keenness of the senses all the time.

For the moment though, he was just as concerned for his own safety. The snow and wind had frozen his face and hair, and his fingers and toes had been numb for some time. He wasn't even sure exactly where he was; he had stumbled half-blind through the blizzard until he had found a little respite in the valley between the hills which had led him here. Cursing himself for an idiot, Kurt realised he had brought nothing with him with which to light a fire. He would more than likely freeze out here, and Ursula would suffer a similar fate. As he resigned himself to his short future, Kurt recalled the night they had spent in the cave formed by the overlapping boulders. He remembered how Jakob had taught him the names of the gods, and the way in which they could be asked for power. He had half-heartedly tried a few of these rituals with little success, but now the words came unbidden to his mind again. He remembered them more clearly than he had done before. Feeling slightly foolish, but with no better idea, he cut some of the fur from his cloak and laid it in front of him. Sitting crossed-legged, as he had seen Jakob do, Kurt began to chant, focussing his attention on the fur and picturing the small rag as an undying flame. Kurt concentrated on what he had to do, remembering Jakob's warning that calling on the gods had its dangers. Attracting their attention was never straightforward, even with a ritual as insignificant as the one Kurt wanted to perform.

Closing his eyes, Kurt concentrated harder, the words spilling from his lips in a steady stream. In his mind's eye he could see the flickering red of the magical fire he wanted to create. Chanting louder and louder, Kurt felt something inside him change. It was if a breath of wind had passed through his body. His limbs tingled and he felt a warm flush on his face. It was a moment before he realised the heat was genuine and not a phantasm of his imagination. He opened his eyes to see a red and green flame burning the scrap of fur in front of him. The gods had answered him! With a shout of joy, Kurt punched the air. This was a good sign, as Jakob would say. The gods would keep him alive to find Ursula.

As HE DRIFTED off to sleep, his flame still burning happily beside him, Kurt's ears picked up a noise from outside the cave. It was a loud snuffling sound, as if a large creature was sniffing close to the entrance. Instantly awake, his heart racing, Kurt sat up. In the flickering light of the fire, he could see something bulky moving around outside. It looked like a bear, but as Kurt rose to a crouch, he saw that it was no ordinary animal. It was like a bear, only larger and stranger. It was easily twice as tall as he was, and five twisted and curved horns sprouted from its head. Its teeth were as long as Kurt's fingers and dripped with saliva that hissed and spat as it dropped on to the snow. Pulling his sword from his sheath, Kurt rose to his full height.

The beast turned and looked directly at him, its large black eyes reflecting the magical flame. A deep growl issued from its throat that reverberated around the cave. Kurt felt utterly calm as the creature took a step into the cave, its bulk almost too much to fit through the entrance.

'Come on then, you ugly thing!' hissed Kurt, raising his sword to a position from which he could thrust or cut.

The beast sniffed the air again, its head turning first towards the fire and then back at Kurt.

'Come on!' Kurt shouted, taking a step forward, sword ready.

The beast gave a grunt and shuffled backwards quickly despite its bulk, a plaintive moaning escaping its throat. Kurt took another step forward and it turned and bolted, ploughing through the snow at some speed. Kurt stood and watched it disappear into the darkness, bemused by this turn of events. He bowed and sniffed the flame. He could smell nothing unusual. In fact, the flame didn't smell of anything at all, not even the burning fur. With a shrug, Kurt propped up his sword against the cave wall and settled back under his furs, wishing for sleep to come, but his tumultuous thoughts of Ursula kept it at bay.

CHAPTER SIX
Falsehoods
South of Tungask, Early winter 1709

SNOW DRIFTED FROM the branches of the trees, scattering like white dust over Ursula. She woke with a start. Her joints ached from the bitter cold and her skin was pinched with the first touches of frostbite. She had made herself a rough bier out of branches and bark, and the fire she had built still smoked fitfully beside her. With a moan of pain, she forced herself to sit up, her frozen limbs protesting at the movement. Standing, she shook off the fine layer of snow that covered her. Her hair was stiff with ice as well, and her face felt numb. Thanking Sigmar for seeing her safely through the night, she gently blew on the fire to get it burning again, her breath coming out as a fine mist. It was still dark under the canopy of the trees, and Ursula had no way of telling how long she had slept. With horror she realised that she might not have woken at all; if she had slept longer, the cold may have pulled her into a painless death.

Cursing herself for running away the night before, Ursula added a few small twigs to the fire. She looked around, but there was nothing recognisable within sight. Last night she had run from the town, her eyes filled with tears, and had headed unthinkingly for the promise of safety offered by the forest. In hindsight, that might have saved her, for out on the plains with no shelter from the snow or protection from the bitter north wind, she may well have succumbed to the freezing cold.

She felt like a silly young girl now, for last night she had been driven by the urge to run away from her sadness, the same instinct that had made her leave home all those years ago and pushed her from town to town throughout her childhood. It seemed ridiculous, as she was cold and hungry now. Suddenly, Ursula thought of Kurt, and the tears welled up again. He had been so angry, so concerned about what the savage Norsemen thought, he had scared Ursula. At the same time, Ursula wondered if her loved one even knew she had left Tungask. Was he looking for her now, or was he no longer concerned?

In her heart, she knew that Kurt still loved her and would be mortally worried, but there had been little evidence of his love lately. For a long while he had been growing more distant, as if the distance from the Empire was somehow connected to the closeness he felt with Ursula. The two of them had reacted in opposite ways to the situation. Kurt had been pragmatic about their exile at first, and now seemed to embrace it as a great adventure. Ursula, however, had become more and more homesick and worried as their exodus had continued. She had little experienced a true home in her life, and to be driven from the one place where she had actually found a small measure of happiness cut her to the soul.

And Kurt was not the only person she was missing. Apart from the solitary vision of Marius and Kurt fighting that she had experienced in Tungask, she had not felt the presence of Sigmar since she had left Badenhof. She had been given little time to pray, and felt that perhaps finally her god had abandoned her. Even now, lost and alone as she had been so many times in her life, Sigmar was silent. Had she strayed too far from him? Had her acceptance of the wickedness of Jakob and his corrupting influence on Kurt turned Sigmar against her?

As she fed more wood to the crackling fire, her sadness turned to grim resolve, as it often had during her most miserable periods of life. She would see the Empire again, she would pray again in a proper church, and she would fight for Kurt to be with her. But she realised that the two of them faced a choice now. As much as she loved him, she could not go north with Kurt and start a life amongst the barbaric Norse. Her heart was in the south and the warmer lands. She wanted contentment and safety, not a constant fight against the elements and the scorn of the people she would be living with. Kurt had to choose if he wanted to share that life with her, or if the strange calling he felt from the north was more important to him.

With this resolve in her heart, Ursula stood up and looked around again. There was no way yet of telling which way was north, south, east or west. The forest looked the same in every direction. In her mind, Ursula had a debate with herself. Would it be better to just choose a direction and strike out, or to remain where she was and hope that others found her?

Almost instantly, she made her decision. She was not the sort of person to wait on others; she would take control of her life. The fitful smoke from the fire was drifting in the breeze and she took this as a sign that she should head downwind. She couldn't explain why this seemed the right choice, and wished that perhaps Sigmar, in his great wisdom, would have granted her a vision of what to do, as he had done in the past. However, he had not, and so with no other better course of action evident, she set off with the wind at her back. As she walked, she thought of other reasons why it was better to keep moving. Firstly, if she stayed in one place too long, there was no way of knowing what sort of animals might be drawn by her fire and her own scent. Secondly, if she walked, she would leave a trail that another person might find and follow, whereas if she stayed where she had been, any searchers would have to come across her, almost by chance. Happier in her heart that she was doing the right thing, she strode more quickly through the snow and bracken.

* * *

IT WAS NEARLY noon and Jakob had scoured the outskirts of the forest with little success. Already a whole night and day had passed without finding Ursula and he was trying to work out how long he should search before returning to Tungask to break the news to Kurt. The sooner he quit looking, the less likely she was to be found alive. However, whenever he decided to confront Kurt with the truth, the ex-knight would not be happy and Jakob knew that the longer he stayed out here in the cold, the better his defence against accusations that he had not tried hard enough. He would have to judge it carefully, but decided that if he had found no sign of the wretched woman by sundown, he would turn back tomorrow morning. If he could not find her to deal with her, then the chances were the cruel northern lands had already done his grim task for him. He would be able to go back to Kurt and report her death, and then they could go north. It seemed strange, the path the gods had laid out for him. Only a few days ago he had been arguing to stay in Tungask, wary of travelling in the height of winter. Now here he was, contemplating just that to avoid a confrontation with van Diesl.

Jakob worked as methodically as he could, doubling back and forth along stretches of the wood looking for signs of where Ursula might have been. He had been following a good trail for a while yesterday, but the ground had become rocky and more open to the sky, allowing the steady light fall of snow to obliterate whatever tracks she might have made. However, she had been travelling steadily south-east, away from Tungask, and it was in this direction that Jakob concentrated his efforts.

Another hour or so had passed when Jakob came across a clearing, and at its centre was a low log building, its roof sloping down to the ground at the back, with a low door and narrow windows. The stumps of trees all around the clearing showed that this was a logger's hut, but he could see no smoke issuing from the chimney and deemed the place to be empty, perhaps even deserted. Even so, he approached cautiously, noting the pile of firewood stacked up under the lee of the roof to the south, away from the prevailing wind, and the thickness of the snow in front of the door meant that no one had used it for several days, perhaps even weeks. He called out as he got closer, but there was no reply.

Knocking at the door, he shouldered it inwards, spilling snow across a packed earth floor. The inside of the hut was sparse, with an open fire pit in the centre, and a table with two low benches flanking it set to the left. There was no sign of plates or other utensils, and checking the small food store, he found only piles of salted meat. To Jakob, it was obvious that the hut wasn't used in the winter, but supplies of wood and food had been left here for anyone needing shelter at these inhospitable times. Grateful for the chance to rest and eat, Jakob started a fire in the pit using the driest wood from the pile outside, and sat at the bench to chew on a few strips of the cured meat.

As before, he was at a loss concerning what to do. He had only a short amount of light left to search, for this far north the nights were long during the winter. Not as long as in his homeland, where midwinter was shrouded in darkness for almost the entire day, and in the summer the sun still shone close to midnight. As he sat and ate, he considered his options. The logger's cabin was a good base and he would return here tonight if he could. That gave him a little extra time because he was an experienced woodsman and would be able to find his way back here, even after the sun had set. He also knew that Ursula was capable of looking after herself, she would be able to start a fire, and if he searched upwind again, towards the north, he might catch some scent of smoke.

Gulping down another piece of meat, Jakob stood up and stretched his tired legs. Yes, he told himself, a little more searching today, some hunting tomorrow and then he would return to Tungask and face Kurt.

DUSK WAS STARTING to darken the forest when Jakob came across the first signs of life that were not animal tracks. He was only a mile or so south from the logger's cabin, and had stumbled on the trail almost by accident. He had followed a narrow track from the cabin, which had led to a wider path between the trees. He had found a single trail to begin with and at first he thought it might be Ursula, but upon closer inspection, he decided the footprints were too large and the strides too long for a woman. Scouting around the area, he came across more tracks, those of other men and the hoof prints of horses. With a growing sense of unease, the Norseman guessed that the tracks were made by Marius and his warband, nobody else would be travelling in such numbers at this time of year, and that they had been made recently within the last day. There were at least thirty horses, most likely knights', and the same number again of pack ponies. More worrying perhaps, was the mess of footprints that indicated a sizeable force on foot as well. Quite how the witch hunter and his men had not run into Jakob was a mystery, but upon a careful examination of the tracks, Jakob was confident that they had also not captured Ursula because none of the footprints matched those he had seen the day before. That did not mean that she had not been discovered, merely that if they had found her, she had not been brought with them.

With Marius this close to Tungask, Jakob was forced to think through his plans once more. To stay in the town was to invite disaster, but he knew that without any solid news of Ursula, Kurt would not leave. Trying to convince him otherwise would be impossible.

Jakob decided that he must try to find Ursula, kill her and take her body back to the town. With such irrefutable evidence, and vulnerable because of his loss, Kurt would be more easily persuaded to quit the town and evade Marius again. Then a thought struck Jakob. Out on the plains after the troll attack, Kurt had already resolved to make a stand in the town against Marius and his men. If he thought the witch hunter guilty of killing Ursula, there was a good chance he would not listen to Jakob at all, but instead, driven by anger and grief, try to exact some vengeance on the witch hunter. And that would not be good either. For a moment, Jakob considered abandoning them altogether. He could easily slip away to the south and leave them to their fates. It was Kurt that Marius seemed intent upon, judging by the history the two of them shared, he would not be interested in pursuing Jakob, if he even knew who he was.

And yet, Jakob dismissed the idea. He was fully aware of his own shortcomings, and life had taught him that cunning and guile were his best abilities rather than the overblown sense of honour and courage that many of his people seemed to suffer from. Despite this, the gods had presented Jakob with an opportunity to return to his people, whom in his heart he still longed to be with, and to do so in triumph with a mighty warrior at his beck and call. Could he really give up this chance to make a good life for himself, and go back to his former existence scraping and surviving on the edge of society? Surely, the gods would laugh at him for his cowardice.

Resolving to find a way to make his plan work, Jakob followed the trail of Marius for a while, thinking hard about how to best turn the situation to his advantage. Somehow, he had to sever the link between Kurt and Ursula in such a way that the former knight would be happy to accompany Jakob back to his homeland. Saying she was dead, or actually killing her, would not do this. He had to make Kurt abandon her. It was while thinking along this line of reasoning that Jakob was struck by inspiration. One way he could get Kurt to give up on Ursula would be to convince him that she had already abandoned him first. But there was also the problem of Marius. Was there a way he could get rid of Ursula and the witch hunter at the same time?

It was getting dark now, and Jakob was running out of time. Tomorrow Marius and his men could be at Tungask, and there was little hope for Jakob once that happened. How could he forestall that event and at the same time locate Ursula? For once she was under Jakob's control, however reluctantly, it would be easier for him to enact whatever scheme he could devise to extricate himself and Kurt from the dangerous situation they were in. Wracking his brains for a solution, a sudden revelation struck Jakob that made him laugh aloud.

For months, he had been teaching Kurt many of the old ways, the traditional supplications to the gods for strength and guidance. He had even used a few of his powers before now, to guide them through the featureless tundra of the north. How could he have been so blind? The knowledge

Jakob needed was within his reach, he had been going about the whole matter in the wrong way. His time in the south had dulled his mind and instincts, he had should have been thinking like a northman rather than a southerner all this time. There was no need for all this back-tracking and searching; there was a riskier but quicker way.

Clearing himself a space in the deep snow beneath a towering pine tree, he sat down on the frozen earth. He pulled a pouch from his belt and emptied the contents into his hand: seven rune stones he had carved from whalebone when he had still lived in the north, copying the designs from those he had seen the elders use.

He held the rune stones, each roughly the size of his thumbnail, in both hands, and closed his eyes. Concentrating, he tried to recall the words he had heard spoken in guidance rituals all those years ago. He had attempted it once before, when he had first left the village, and had been unsuccessful. He knew there were dangers associated with calling on the gods in this manner, for they were fickle and not used to the demands of mere mortals.

Jakob hesitated for a moment, doubts suddenly filling his mind. This was more than just the small tricks that Kurt had so ably learned. This was old, dangerous magic. He snorted at himself in derision, for worrying. He was older and wiser now, and his strength of mind was greater than it had ever been. Though Kurt had some natural ability, Jakob had been dealing with the gods in this way for many years now. Focussing on Ursula, he began a low chant, the words barely a whisper, as he pictured the red-haired woman in his mind. He began to shake the rune stones in his hands, rattling out a rhythm in time to his heartbeat.

He felt the earth beneath him and the air around him closing in, threatening to swallow him, but he fought back his fear and increased the speed of the chanting and rattling. The rune stones began to warm in his grasp as the breath of the gods flowed through them, trying to give them a voice. Jakob's heart was palpitating wildly now and the words that flowed from his lips were of a language long dead and yet living on within the world around him: a primal tongue still spoken by the clouds and the trees, the mud beneath his feet, in the minds of worms and beetles, and in the hearts of men.

The heat from the rune stones flared suddenly, scorching Jakob's hands and he fought the urge to drop them, knowing that to do so would invite all sorts of danger from the backlash of divine power flowing through him. Resisting the pain, he grasped the stones tighter and focussed his thoughts even more, imprinting the image of Ursula into the runes carved on the bone chips.

Feeling the power of the gods passing through him into the stones, he scattered them onto the bare ground in front of him and opened his eyes. The runes were glowing red with energy, vibrating on the frozen ground, which steamed and bubbled beneath them. Calling on Tzeentch, the true name of the god his people knew as Jaenz, for the location of Ursula, he read out the names of the runes in the order they had been scattered, starting from the one furthest away and working towards himself. As he spoke each rune-name, the stone glowed stronger, and a web of flickering, multi-coloured light linked them together in a complex pattern that shifted and spun, impossible to remember from one moment to the next.

At the heart of the magical web, a cloud of energy began to coalesce, forming a vague shape. The mist rearranged itself into a vague facsimile of Ursula's face, static at first, and then growing into animated life. The picture began to shrink, until Jakob could see all of Ursula, walking through the woods, inspecting the ground. He could see the trees around her, picked out as shafts of shimmering light, and the snow on the ground sparkled within the vision.

With a thought, he commanded the magical picture to direct him towards them girl, and the energy dimmed for a moment, collapsing into a small ball of white that flickered occasionally with reds, blues and greens. It hovered above the stones and then began to stretch, seeping out over Jakob's shoulder and wavering between the trees to the west before vanishing.

Jakob reached out to pick up the stones, his hands prickling at the heat emanating from them. As his fist closed around the first one, the ground beneath them shimmered and glowed red, and a clawed hand shot out of the earth and grasped his wrist. With a scream, Jakob tried to wrench his hand away, but the grip was unnaturally strong. The glowing spread further and a form began to rise up in front of Jakob: an arm, then a shoulder and then the tip of a horn began to struggle through the portal he had unwittingly opened. Jakob sat there, paralysed with terror, as a daemonic figure began to push its way through the shimmering barrier. A long, thin face, with seven eyes that flicked with flames, surfaced and stared at him. A lipless mouth full of tiny pointed teeth smiled at him cruelly and the arm began to pull him closer.

'Foolish mortal,' a voice said inside his head, fluctuating disturbingly in pitch and volume. 'I will feed on your soul, for you have not paid for what you have taken.'

Panic flared through Jakob and he tried to get to his feet, but the emerging daemon dragged him forwards and another hand plunged through the magical mist grabbing hold of his throat. Jakob's mind was racing. What had he done wrong, what had he forgotten? Looking at the pulsing red light from which the daemon was emerging, its words still ringing inside his mind, he realised his mistake. He had not sealed the bargain with the daemon that had come to his summoning! With his free hand, he scrabbled at his belt and drew out his knife. He scored a deep cut into his other arm, and the blood ran freely over the daemon's fingers.

A long tongue lashed out and slurped at the wound, causing pain to rip through Jakob's arm. The blood flowed out even quicker than before, as the daemon drank deep. A wave of dizziness struck Jakob, and he could feel consciousness slipping away. With a final surge of energy, he pulled himself back, breaking the grasp of the daemon, which was nearly sated, weakened by its feasting. He took a few steps away and collapsed into the snow, looking back at the horrific apparition. The daemon faded back into the ground, dissolving into a cloud of writhing colours that drained back into the rune stones.

Waiting until he was sure the daemon had truly passed back to its own realm, Jakob lay in the snow, his head spinning and his heart thumping wildly. Such a foolish mistake, he chided himself, and yet he was also happy that his divination had been successful. Rolling over, he crawled back through the snow and gathered up the stones, noting that they were now icy cold to the touch and seemed to suck the heat from his hand. Their energy had been dissipated and it would take time for them to recover. There were rituals he could use, offering up his own blood to restore them to their power, but the daemon had already severely weakened him and there was little time left for him to find Ursula. The divination had told him to head westwards, but he had no idea how far away the girl was, or how long she would remain in that direction.

Shuddering with the memory of the near-fatal encounter, Jakob forced himself to his feet, steadying himself against the tree, whose bark was now burnt with an image of the daemon's twisted face like a permanent shadow. Jakob packed snow onto the wound he had cut into his arm and hobbled away in the direction the light had shown him.

URSULA POKED AT her little fire with a stick and sighed. She had wandered the forest for the whole day without being any surer of where she was. At times, her desperation and panic had returned, and she had almost given up, but digging into the reserve of strength she had cultivated through long years of wandering in her teenage years, she had pressed on. Now, with the sun setting, the forest filled with long shadows, and she decided that she must have headed in the wrong direction. There was no chance she could have gone so deep into the forest that first night. She thought she had only run amongst the trees for a short while. Tomorrow she would retrace her steps and head back the way she had come.

A noise out in the darkness caused her to reach for her sword, which was lying next to her. A darker shadow moved between the tree trunks and she rose to her feet, balancing herself the way Kurt had taught her. The pitiful light from her fire only illuminated the forest a few yards in each direction, and she glanced behind her for signs of other movement, but could see none.

'Put down your sword, it's me, Jakob,' she heard the Norseman call out, but she didn't relax. She saw him walk into the light, staggering slightly, his face gaunt, his eyelids drooping with fatigue.

'Where's Kurt?' she asked, still wary. She did not trust Jakob, and did not like the idea of being out here on her own with him, but her heart still fluttered with excitement as he walked closer. For all the scorn she had for the Norscan, he could lead her to safety and back to Kurt.

'A cabin,' replied Jakob, leaning against a tree. 'Not far away. He wait there for you. I take you there, give me time to get my strength.'

'Are you hurt?' she said, seeing the deep cut on his arm.

'Not important,' he waved away her concerns and straightened. 'We move now, not safe here. Marius close.'

'Marius is here?' she said, startled. She looked around as if expecting to see the witch hunter right there with them. 'In the forest, but not very near,' Jakob assured her, beckoning her to follow him and turning away. She sheathed her sword after a moment and followed.

The realisation that she could have blundered into the witch hunter during her aimless wandering made her legs weak and caused her stomach to tighten sickeningly. Perhaps Sigmar was still watching over her.

'Perhaps we should go to him, ask him for mercy?' she said. 'He's a priest, he would have to offer us shelter and sanctuary. We should ask Kurt when we find him.'

'Man who hunts us for half a year over river and through snow not likely to give us welcome,' Jakob pointed out, but Ursula's words had prompted a chain of thought. Perhaps there was a way he could dispense with Ursula once and for all, and persuade Kurt to go north at the same time.

THE NORSEMAN HAD not been lying, about half a mile from where he had found her there was a small log building, with a small wisp of smoke drifting from the chimney hole in the roof. Jakob muttered something in his own language and hurried forward. She followed him inside, eager to be reunited with Kurt, but apart from the two of them, there was no one else there.

'You said Kurt was waiting for me!' she said, grabbing the weary Jakob by the front of his furs. It had been the thought of seeing Kurt that had given her the strength to follow the Norscan through the thick snow, exhausted as she was from her day's travels.

'He very worried,' Jakob said, pulling himself free. 'He must be looking for you in the woods. I fetch him. Stay here and build fire. Use only dry wood, not too much smoke to see.'

Jakob pointed at a small pile of wood splints stacked a little way from the fire and then left without further comment. Ursula picked up a few of the staves and carefully placed them on the fire, blowing gently to make the flames catch. Happy that the fire would go for a while longer, she crossed the room to one of the benches and sat on it, resting her head on her arms on the table. Totally drained, both physically and emotionally, she drifted off to sleep.

WEARY TO THE bone, but driven on by his sense of purpose, it did not take too long for Jakob to find van Diesl's trail again. Following this for several miles, he became aware of a glow ahead in the forest, which was quite obviously coming from several large campfires. They shone out like a beacon to Jakob, and he slowed his pace, suddenly wary of his proximity to the enemy.

He approached the camp cautiously, circling it twice to locate their sentries. There were four, spread evenly around the tents. It was not too difficult for Jakob to stealthily make his way between them and get closer. There were no signs of life; the soldiers appeared to be sleeping. He could hear coughs and snores in the stillness of the night. Snow began to fall again, lightly settling on the branches above and drifting randomly down between the pines, dusting the grey tents with whiteness.

Confident that nobody was aware of him, Jakob stole from trunk to trunk, working his way towards the closest sentry. The man was leaning with his back against a tree, dozing fitfully, and it was a matter of moments for Jakob to sneak up behind him and plunge his hunting knife up under the man's ribcage, robbing him of air for a scream and

killing him silently. He dipped his hand in the blood
spilling from the man's chest, and soaked a corner of his furs
in the liquid as well. Making sure to spill plenty of the blood
on the ground, he set off towards the cabin, leaving deep
imprints in the snow as he ran, squeezing droplets of blood
from his coat at occasional intervals to ensure the trail was
clear.

CHAPTER SEVEN
Power
South of Tungask, Winter 1709

THE DOOR TO the cabin slammed open and woke Ursula with a start. She looked up, expecting to see Kurt, but framed against the door was Marius van Diesl.

'Thank Sigmar!' Ursula cried out, running towards the witch hunter. As she attempted to embrace him, he slapped her across the face, sending her sprawling to the floor.

'Enough of your lies, murdering witch!' he spat, grabbing for his sword.

'Marius, wait!' Ruprecht said from behind the witch hunter, his meaty hand closing around Marius's wrist.

'Stand back!' barked Marius, but Ruprecht's grip remained firm as he shouldered his way into the cabin. 'Unhand me or suffer the consequences!'

'Listen to him,' Ursula pleaded, sitting up. 'Listen to me!'

'So you can twist my mind with your insidious falsehoods again?' sneered Marius, pulling his arm from Ruprecht's grasp. 'I think not. You have avoided this fate for too long to distract me with your words now.'

'Hear her out,' Ruprecht insisted, stepping between the witch hunter and Ursula. 'She can't do any harm.'

'Harm?' Marius's voice was hoarse with anger. 'Badenhof lies in burnt ruins because of this one's vile ways and silken tongue.'

'Please, hear me, I'll explain everything,' begged Ursula, standing up.

Marius paused, glancing at the girl and Ruprecht, before sheathing his sword.

'If you try to lie, I will strike you down where you stand,' warned Marius, striding past Ursula.

'Kurt told me about what happened all those years ago,' Ursula began, and she saw Marius twitch at the memory. 'I was willing to stand trial against the accusations you heard, and all I ask is the same for Kurt.'

'That trial was a sham, and you know it,' Marius argued. 'You still seek to deceive me.'

'No!' Ursula insisted. 'The deception was not on my part, I swear by Sigmar. I'm telling the truth.'

'And again you invoke that holy name with your unholy lips,' said Marius.

'And I will for as long as I live, for he still remains my true guide and protector,' said Ursula, taking a step towards Marius and holding out her hand in supplication. 'Kurt is not an evil man, but he is misguided.'

'Misguided?' asked Ruprecht from behind her.

'Yes,' Ursula said. 'He is under the influence of a cruel northman, Jakob. This barbaric man has Kurt in his thrall somehow, and has driven him to the wicked acts you accuse him of. Give us a fair hearing, but spare no mercy for the barbarian, for he is unashamedly heathen, and worships the Dark Gods openly. I fear for Kurt while this man lives, and I beg you to help me free Kurt from his grasp.'

'You want my help?' asked Marius, his voice full of scorn. 'You expect my pity?'

'I do,' Ursula replied quietly. 'We need your pity as only a true man of Sigmar can give it.'

'Marius, let me talk to you outside for a moment,' Ruprecht said, looking curiously at Ursula. The witch hunter darted a venomous stare at the girl and then nodded, following Ruprecht outside.

Telling one of the squires at hand to go inside and guard the girl, Ruprecht turned to the witch hunter.

'You believe her?' asked Marius, his eyes searching Ruprecht's face for some sign of dishonesty.

'It doesn't matter what you or I believe,' answered Ruprecht after a moment. 'The important thing is how we can use this to our advantage. Listen to her, and we'll see what opportunities are presented. Kill her out of hand and we may never get Leitzig; keep her alive and she could give us some measure of power over him.'

'You think he still cares for her?' said Marius, looking back through the door at Ursula. 'Why is she here on her own then?'

'I don't have the answers to those questions; she has,' Ruprecht said. 'Let's hear what she has to say and then we'll think about what to do next.'

'I see your point,' Marius said with a nod. 'But if she proves useless I will kill her here and now.'

'If it comes to that, you'll get no argument from me,' agreed Ruprecht.

KURT WAS TORN between two courses of action. He wanted to continue the search for Ursula, but was also of a mind to return to Tungask to see if Jakob had found her. For nearly two days, he had looked for her without even the slightest sign that he might be close, and he could see there was little else he could do. He had no food left, and had not taken the time to do any hunting. Perhaps he could go back and rouse more of the Tungask townsfolk to help in the search, or maybe she had already returned of her own accord. He had tracked back and forth within ten miles of the town with no success, and did not think that Ursula would have gone further. Jakob may have misread the signs he had spotted, and Kurt was in the wrong place altogether. To the east was Tungask and further on the vast spread of pine alongside the Lynsk tributary. The stream itself, quite wide this side of the town, glittered in the last rays of the sun to his left. It was unlikely Ursula could have got lost out in this windswept expanse, whereas the forest was dark and forbidding and easily she could have turned astray. Deciding that his efforts were best directed in that area, he headed back towards Tungask.

As he marched through the snow, Kurt pondered the strange course of events that had led him to be searching for his love in the wild north of the world. How had things spun so far out his control? There was no mistaking the intentions of van Diesl; his relentless pursuit of Kurt proved that he had been the target of the witch hunter's plans all along. Only the freak comment by Trevigar to Kurt had allowed the ex-knight to head off whatever nefarious scheme the witch hunter had concocted. It seemed incredible to Kurt that van Diesl was pursuing his bloody vendetta so many years after their first encounter. What madness drove the witch hunter to slaughter a family and then spend his life searching out the surviving son? For his part, Kurt, though vowing that he would kill van Diesl if he ever had the chance, had tried to put the episode behind him, to draw on the experience to give him strength and resolve, and to create whatever type of life the gods permitted him. Now the witch hunter had once more destroyed everything Kurt held dear, shattering the fragile peace that had existed in Kurt's and Ursula's lives. Not only had he tried to kill Ursula, which was sin enough in Kurt's mind, he had destroyed whatever chance she may have had for living a normal life. Kurt had laboured so hard, had endured torment and hardship, to give her a life that she had never known. Now, Marius had taken that from Kurt as well, and he felt his anger rising and his step quickening as he forged through the snow along the bank of the stream.

Fuelled by his fury and desire to be reunited with Ursula, Kurt made good speed. He decided against returning to Tungask, and instead made directly for the forest, which spread out across the snowy plains a few miles distant. The sooner Ursula was safe, the sooner Kurt could begin to formulate a plan to combat the witch hunter and, if the gods willed it, to finally avenge his murdered family.

'SO YOU CLAIM that Leitzig never told you what happened to his family?' Marius said, pacing back and forth across the cabin floor, his feathered hat held in both hands behind his back. It was mid afternoon and he had been questioning Ursula for most of the day. 'He never confided his dark secret?'

'Ask any of the Osterknacht outside,' Ursula replied, sat on the edge of the table, her feet on the bench in front of her. 'He always claimed to come from a branch of the family in the south, he never told anyone he was heir to Baron Leitzig. Until I met Kurt, I had never even heard of the Leitzig family.'

'So when I came to Badenhof, you had no idea who I was?' continued Marius.

'I had heard that you were a witch hunter, but no more than that,' Ursula said. 'I have already told you all this, why must you ask me again?'

'I do not believe your story,' Marius said frankly, stopping his pacing and facing Ursula. 'Does not your flight act as proof of your guilt? If Kurt were as innocent as he claims, why would he drag you across the world, to these inhospitable climes? No, those are the actions of a man driven by guilt and fear.'

'Fear, yes,' agreed Ursula, pushing herself off the table and striding towards the witch hunter. 'Fear of you! Fear of what you would do to me! He saw you burn his family alive, and you expect him to be rational? You think he would feel safe were either he or I in your hands? I tried to explain to him that you were doing nothing but protecting me, but his grief for his family clouds his mind. You are both as blind as each other!'

'And you believe him?' sneered Marius, turning away again as if the sight of her offended him. 'He has lied to you, and now you are worried about his unnatural interest in the Dark Gods. Is it such a surprise? Has he not been raised under their gaze from birth? Chaos is in his blood.'

'I knew him for two years before you came,' Ursula argued. 'He was never a devout man, I admit, but he was never a worshipper of the powers we do not name. It was you, and what you did, that killed any faith he might have had in Sigmar. Jakob is maliciously filling that emptiness with his dark teachings. The Norscan is a vile, manipulative man. I am surprised that you have not found him in the woods; he was close by last night. He lied to me, and said that Kurt was here. Instead, I find myself waking to you and your ruffians. How did you find me, anyway?'

'We followed a trail here,' Ruprecht told her carefully, speaking for the first time since she had begun her version of the tale some time before.

'He led you here! Jakob!' cried Ursula, noticing the caution in his voice. It would be just like the Norscan to betray her; how else would they have found her tracks?

'You don't know that,' Ruprecht pointed out.

'The little weasel has constantly been trying to get rid of me, to belittle me in Kurt's eyes,' replied Ursula. 'Agh, I'd wring his scrawny neck if he were here. Without me to stand against him, who can tell what horrid influence he has on Kurt. We need to rescue Kurt as soon as we can!'

'Rescue Leitzig?' laughed Marius. 'From who?'

'From himself, and from Jakob,' Ursula said. 'Have you not listened to a word I said?'

'Marius, might I speak with you?' asked Ruprecht, nodding towards the door. The witch hunter stopped what he was about to say and looked at his large companion, and then nodded. Without a word, both of them left.

LOOKING UP AT the faint lightness of the sun behind the clouds, Kurt noted that sunset was a short time away. He had reached the outskirts of the forest, where he had parted company with Jakob, and was now trying to decide what to do next. The vast wood stretched out south and east, and he opted to go south at first, working along the outskirts of the forest before heading eastwards a little and turning north again. In this way, by the same time tomorrow he would be able to return to Tungask without too much difficulty. If he didn't find either Ursula or Jakob in that time, he would organise a wider hunt with the help of the town's inhabitants.

He had gone a few more miles into the forest when he sensed a change in the air. His sight, hearing and smell had been getting keener the further north he travelled, and there was a taint amongst the scent of the pine trees that caught his attention. Looking for a break in the trees, he located a small clearing and looked up. To the south-east, he could see a darker patch against the pale snow clouds, which were holding off the blizzard they contained for now, and realised the smell he had detected was smoke. He couldn't tell how far he was from the source, and drew his sword before heading in the direction of the smoke cloud.

It was maybe half a mile further when Kurt heard the sound of voices. The forest was otherwise quiet and the noise carried far in the stillness. Twilight gloom was beginning to descend on the trees, and Kurt halted and pressed himself up against a craggy trunk while he tried to locate the source of the sound. Scanning the woods for sign of movement, his eye was drawn to a brief flash of red to his right, quite some distance away. Moving as softly as his armour allowed, he stalked through the snow towards the movement, his sword ready.

About fifty yards away were two men. They had started a small fire, the flicker of movement Kurt had first noticed. They were definitely not Kislevites – their style of dress, even with their fur cloaks, reminded him of Imperial soldiers. Stepping a little closer, keeping the trees between him and the men, he recognised one of the men as the squire, Leofe. So, they were van Diesl's men, which meant that the fiend himself was close at hand. Mixed emotions warred inside Kurt for a moment. He was delighted that his enemy was nearby, for it gave him an opportunity to exact his revenge. On the other side, the presence of the witch hunter in such close proximity to where Ursula had last been seen increased Kurt's worries. Did Marius have her? Could he be holding her hostage, or was she dead already?

The men in front of him might be able to give him the answers to these questions, Kurt realised. If he could take one alive, he could gain the upper hand on Marius for the first time since he had rescued Ursula from the witch hunter's clutches almost half a year before. The problem was, how was he going to capture just one of the men?

His dilemma was solved when, as he closed on the pair, his foot slipped on a slick exposed root, and his shield banged against the bole of the tree he had been crouched behind. Leofe looked up and gave a startled shout. The two of them turned to run, and Kurt sprang out of his hiding place and sprinted after them. Despite the wearying search of the last two days, Kurt could feel energy flowing through him, his heart pounding strong in his chest. Leofe was the faster of the two squires and was still some ten yards ahead when Kurt caught up with the other man. With a single sweep of his sword, Kurt hacked through the man's leg, toppling him into the snow in a fountain of blood. Leofe was keeping just ahead. Kurt redoubled his efforts. He was closing the distance slowly when suddenly Leofe pitched to the ground, a black-feathered arrow protruding from his throat.

Kurt skidded to a stop, almost falling over in the slippery snow. Steadying himself, he walked over to Leofe to see if he still lived, but a quick glance at the ragged wound scored through the squire's throat quelled any such hope.

'Jakob!' Kurt bellowed, looking around. 'Come and show yourself!'

The Norscan appeared from behind a tree about two dozen yards in front of Kurt, another arrow notched to his bowstring. He advanced cautiously, head swivelling left and right as he scanned the trees for more enemies.

'We must go back to Tungask, is not safe here!' hissed Jakob when he was just a few yards away from Kurt.

'What of Ursula?' demanded Kurt, stepping towards Jakob, sword half-raised. 'Did you find her?'

'Marius's men everywhere,' insisted Jakob, looking beyond Kurt to check the surrounding woodland. 'We die if we stay. Tungask, then I tell you everything.'

Kurt hesitated for a moment, unsure what to do, but a look at the fear in Jakob's eyes convinced him of the truth to the Norseman's words.

'We go back, and then you tell me everything,' Kurt replied grimly.

'SHE MAKES PERFECT bait for a trap,' said Ruprecht, leaning against the logs of the cabin.

'What do we need a trap for?' replied Marius. 'She's already told us that he's in the town. We go in and kill him, it's simple.'

'Marius, don't be hastened by your need for blood,' Ruprecht warned. 'I may be overstepping my mark here, but I've known you for a long time now and it's time I said what I should have said months ago. I believe in your need for retribution, but don't let it cloud your judgement. It was you who taught me patience and guile, not to charge in without knowing your foe.'

Marius said nothing and turned and paced away towards the edge of the clearing. Ruprecht hurried after him.

'Marius, listen to me!' Ruprecht said, running in front of the witch hunter and stopping him. Marius was shaking, and held his head in his hands.

'I know you are right,' the witch hunter said quietly, looking his friend in the eye. 'I know we need to plan and think. But I want him dead, and to bury that part of my past that I thought was gone. At one time, I thought that I was over the death of my wife; that I could carry on. But how can I? How can I ignore the flesh and blood of the man who destroyed my life? A man whose evil has been reborn into his son who waits less than a day's travel from where I am standing now. I want him, I want his body ripped apart and his remains scattered to the corners of the world!'

'And you shall have it,' Ruprecht said, laying a firm hand on Marius's shoulder. 'To make sure you get your vengeance, we have to think. The girl is a weapon we can use against him. I believe her story, she is as much a victim here as you. But she need not know that just yet.'

'You think she is innocent?' asked Marius, signs of his anger returning.

'Perhaps, but that is of no account,' Ruprecht answered carefully. 'We can deal with her after Leitzig is dead, in whichever way we deem necessary. Until then, she is most useful to us alive. And so are you. Charging into Tungask heavy-handed will get us all killed, and then how will you get your revenge?'

'So what do you propose?' asked Marius.

CHAPTER EIGHT
Initiation
Tungask, Winter 1709

BACK IN THE town, Kurt and Jakob were both bent before a crackling fire in the tavern, warming their cold limbs. On the trip back, Jakob had told Kurt that Ursula had willingly turned herself over to the witch hunter, and it had been all the Norscan could do to rescue himself.

It had taken all of the Norscan's guile to persuade the knight not to head back then and there to attempt a rescue. Kurt had agreed to go back to Tungask with the condition that they try to entreat the aid of Hrolfgar and his men, who Kurt was sure would relish the chance to avenge those who fell in battle against the witch hunter in their last encounter.

The door to the tavern thumped open and Hrolfgar strode in, followed by Bjordrin and another of his men, a raven-haired warrior called Svelka. Hrolfgar eyed Kurt suspiciously as he entered, and turned and said something quietly to Bjordrin. The chieftain's brother walked up to the counter and helped himself to ale from the keg on the top, returning with three jugs brimming to the top with frothy beer. He handed one to Hrolfgar and another to Svelka, before taking

a draught of his own. Jakob nudged Kurt in the ribs to spur
him into action.

'Not drinking with us?' Kurt said in his best Norscan
accent.

'I heard you were asking after me,' Hrolfgar replied. 'I do
not like being summoned like a slave.'

'The witch hunter who killed your men, van Diesl, is less
than a day from this town,' Kurt told the Norse chieftain,
ignoring his complaint.

'What of it?' Bjordrin asked warily.

'He is looking for me, and will burn this town to the
ground if he finds me here,' Kurt explained, sitting at one of
the benches by the fire.

'Then be somewhere else and save us the trouble,' said
Hrolfgar.

'Perhaps your defeat by Marius and his men has dulled
your sense of honour,' Kurt said, meeting Hrolfgar's eye with
an accusing stare.

'What do you mean by that?' said Hrolfgar, taking an
angry step forward.

'I was told the Norse were brave warriors, who take pleasure in avenging their fallen kin and comrades,' Kurt
continued.

'You think me a coward?' growled Hrolfgar. 'Lesser men
than you have felt the kiss of my axe for such an insult.'

'And yet I am still here,' Kurt countered, unimpressed. He
stood up and strode slowly towards the chieftain. 'The gods
judge us by our deeds, not our words.'

'Then let them judge this!' roared Hrolfgar, dropping his
ale and swinging a meaty fist at Kurt, who ducked the slow
punch easily and rose from the crouch with an uppercut
that slammed into Hrolfgar's jaw, knocking him back two
steps.

'The gods favour me!' crowed Kurt. 'What will you do to
restore yourself in their eyes?'

Hrolfgar charged like a bull, hurling himself shoulder-first
at Kurt, who stepped quickly away to leave Hrolfgar
sprawled on the floor, spitting curses. As the Norscan picked
himself up, Kurt delivered a swift kick to the man's chin,
smashing him to his back.

'Will you drink with me now?' said Kurt, punching Hrolfgar on the nose with a short jab and then skipping back out of harm's way.

'I'd rather bed a mad wolf!' Hrolfgar snarled, getting to his feet. He pulled his axe from where it hung at his belt and advanced slowly towards Kurt.

'Hold it there, brother!' said Bjordrin, stepping between Hrolfgar and Kurt. 'Let's not offend our host with spilt blood!'

'Then tell this dog to step outside and I'll finish him quickly,' Hrolfgar replied, staring venomously at Kurt.

'Let us hear him out,' added Svelka. 'If he is wasting our time, then you can take your axe to his neck as much as you like.'

Hrolfgar looked at his two warriors and straightened up. He then turned his eyes back to Kurt and grinned, hooking his axe back on his belt.

'Make it good, sutenmjar,' Hrolfgar said, gesturing for Bjordrin to fetch him fresh beer and sitting at the bench where Kurt had been moments before.

'Marius has taken my woman,' Kurt said. 'I will kill him and take her back.'

'You?' laughed Hrolfgar, taking his mug from Bjordrin, who sat down beside the chieftain, contemplating Kurt with a wily look. 'You've no muscle, sutenmjar. You're better built for running, not fighting.'

'I beat you,' Kurt replied.

'I can take woman hits like that forever,' jeered Hrolfgar. He clenched his fist and waved it at Kurt. 'One of these hits you, you don't get back up again.'

'You are indeed strong,' admitted Kurt, sitting opposite Hrolfgar. 'That is why I want you to help me attack van Diesl. Do you not want a chance to settle the score for those of your men who are now food for the wolves in the forest?'

'I would settle the score, but not at the price of the warriors who survived our first battle with that southern devil,' Hrolfgar said. 'The pain of the loss is hard to bear, but I live. If I should lose all my men and die, what then will the gods do with me? They would send my soul back as a goat or a pig for such waste of life.'

'But what if I could show you that the gods look kindly upon this battle?' Kurt asked.

'I have no concern for what your weak gods think,' Hrolfgar said.

'No, I mean the true gods, the Dark Lords of the North, your gods,' Kurt said. 'I can feel their breath upon me, in these cold lands. I hear the whisper of their voices in the wind and thunder.'

'Nonsense!' laughed Svelka. 'You are full of more wind than a longship's sail.'

'Jakob, you said yourself that I was touched by the gods.' Kurt turned and spoke quietly to his companion. 'Why can they not see it, like you?'

'Because I have a small amount of power, which gifts me the sight of such things on occasion,' Jakob told him. 'They do not have the sight.'

'You are not strong enough to fight this battle,' Hrolfgar interrupted, standing up. 'If, as you say, this man will come to burn down this town, then we will get ready to leave.'

'We shall come with you,' Jakob said quickly, also rising to his feet. 'For too long I have been away from the mountains of my birth, and I long to smell the sweet air of the sea by my village.'

'And why would we let a runt like you come with us?' asked Bjordrin. 'At least the southerner can fight. I see you carrying that bow. We have no need of more hunters.'

'We're not going with them,' Kurt said, suddenly realising what Jakob intended. 'I'll not leave Ursula in the hands of that man.'

'She's betrayed you, Kurt,' Jakob argued. 'Even now she is probably plotting with van Diesl. If not, then she is dead.'

'I'll not give up hope,' Kurt said, turning away. Jakob followed him and spoke quietly in Reikspiel so that the Norsemen would not understand.

'Nothing two of us can do,' Jakob said. 'We not save her by ourselves.'

'Van Diesl will burn Tungask to the ground for harbouring me,' Kurt said, head bowed. 'The people will fight alongside us to prevent that.'

'There are some hunters,' replied Jakob. 'Only true warriors, Hrolfgar and his warband. These people merchants and woodsmen, not fighters.'

'Then you must help me convince Hrolfgar,' insisted Kurt. He looked up at the muscled warrior, who was laughing with his men and pointing towards the door. 'If he fights with us and we win, then I promise you that we head north.'

'What of promise to girl that we return to Empire?' asked Jakob, remembering Kurt's earlier vehemence that they were not travelling to Norsca.

'For months now I had been pulled this way and that by you and her,' Kurt said slowly. 'Well, no more of it, I say! Give me a way to bend Hrolfgar to my will, give me the strength I need to fight van Diesl and his men.'

'You one man, I have not the power,' Jakob said, fearing what Kurt intended.

'You said yourself that the gods have marked me out for greatness,' Kurt reminded the Norscan. 'That's why you wanted to accompany me, is it not?'

'Yes,' admitted Jakob with a shake of his head. 'But not follow you to die in fight we cannot win.'

'Then give me a way to win it, damn you!' snarled Kurt. He turned to Hrolfgar as he was about to leave.

'If I can prove to you that the gods favour me, will you follow me?' he asked the muscular northman.

'And how do you think you will prove this, sutenmjar?' Bjordrin replied for his brother, the group of them looking at Kurt with interest now.

'Amongst your people, how do you know those who are chosen from those who are not?' Kurt asked, his desperation growing.

'The elders can see it, and they prove it through their deeds,' Svelka said, crossing his arms across his broad chest. 'Your pet shaman says you have the power, but he must prove it.'

Hrolfgar glanced at his two men and then looked back at Kurt. He walked forwards and slapped a meaty hand onto Kurt's shoulder.

'You say you feel the breath of the gods within you?' Hrolfgar said. 'Get your wise man to summon forth the voices of the gods, get him to use his power to show us this, and I will fight alongside you against the man who killed my kin.'

'It cannot be done!' interrupted Jakob, stalking forward, scratching at his long moustaches. 'The gods are not there at our beck and call, they would strike me down for such an affront. And I said I have some gift, not that I am a shaman.'

'Then we will leave you to die in this town,' Bjordrin said, stepping up beside his brother.

URSULA STOOD BETWEEN Ruprecht and Marius as the war-band set up camp on the plains not far from the outskirts of the wood, beside the road that led to Tungask. The seer, Filandantis, was sitting on a mat not far from them, humming gently to himself. Ursula was intrigued by the strange little man, and slightly repulsed by him at the same time. She had heard of sorcerers, hedge wizards and foul necromancers, but the idea of such a tainted person working for the church of Sigmar was new to her. Ruprecht had told her that the seer was spiritually pure, proven by many painful tests, but she still felt on edge standing this close to the man while he performed his rites. She had overheard Jakob telling Kurt about the dangers of using magic, and how the risks increased the further north the practitioner was – or the closer to the gods you came, as Jakob had put it.

'I see him,' the seer murmured. 'He is in the town, in a building made of logs.'

'Where is he?' asked Ruprecht. 'Which part of the town?'

'He is not far,' Filandantis replied. 'There is song and laughter. There is a large fire.'

'That's the tavern where we were staying,' Ursula explained with a glance at Marius, whose attention was directed solely at the seer.

'What else do you see?' Marius asked, leaning forward eagerly. 'Are they readying for battle, preparing to flee?'

'I am not sure,' the seer said in a melancholy voice. 'He is hard to see. There is another close by. He has power.' A sudden note of panic entered Filandantis's voice. 'He feels my presence, he is looking back into my mind!'

With a hiss, Filandantis opened his eyes, and the orbs were a pure blood red. He started quivering, and his face twisted into a cruel snarl.

'*Turn back, Sigmarite dog!*' snarled the seer, rising effortlessly to his feet. He stepped purposefully towards Marius, and Ursula noted with horror that he was walking on top of the snow, leaving only the faintest of prints. When he was within a few paces of the group, the seer reached out a hand towards the three of them. Knights and men-at-arms close by had stopped to watch the horrifying scene unfold, staring spellbound at the jerking, spasmodic advance of the possessed seer. '*Go back to your warm lands, he is ours now.*'

'What do you mean?' Ursula asked, her voice hoarse with fear.

'Kill it!' snapped Marius, drawing his sword. Ruprecht swung his hammer two-handed, the head connecting with the seer's chin, snapping his neck in an instant. The body stood there for a few heartbeats more, the head lolling back unnaturally, and took another hesitant step forward before collapsing.

'We attack at nightfall!' Marius declared loudly. The sun was already on the horizon and dipping fast. 'We will burn the town to the ground and take the traitor's body from the ashes.'

'No!' shouted Ursula, turning to Marius. 'You said you would give us a chance, you would hear our side of the story.'

'Marius, remember what we discussed?' asked Ruprecht, taking the witch hunter by the arm and walking a few steps away, out of earshot from Ursula. 'If we can take Leitzig without a fight, all the better. Get ready for the attack, but first we try the other plan.'

'He won't come,' Marius stated flatly, stalking off into the camp. Ruprecht took that as a sign of assent and walked back to Ursula.

'How do you think you'll convince him to come out?' Ruprecht asked her. He knew that Marius planned to kill Kurt and her as soon as the renegade knight was in his power, but Ruprecht would try to stay his hand and ensure they were properly tried, as Ursula had requested. Though he had helped Marius hunt her for the best part of half a year, Ruprecht was convinced by her story. She was nothing more than an unwitting pawn between the two men, and had no malice in her. Marius could do what he liked with Kurt; whatever else he was still a deserter and a murderer. The girl, on the other hand, had simply been swept up in events beyond her control, or so Ruprecht believed.

'Kurt has been lost for so many months now, listening to me or Jakob, it won't be difficult to convince him,' said Ursula. 'As long as I can speak to him away from the weasel, Jakob, there should be no problems.'

'You make him sound weak-willed for someone who has gone to such extraordinary lengths to protect you,' Ruprecht countered. 'I don't think you know him as well as you say.'

'He has no idea what he is really doing,' Ursula confided. 'He completely imagined the danger I was in, and dashed off to rescue me without any thought. He hasn't got a plan, he doesn't know what he wants to do. Like me, he's just tired of running. I can persuade him to put down his sword and offer himself up to the mercy of Sigmar. I know I can.'

'I hope you're right, because if not, there's only going to be one of three ways to end this,' Ruprecht said.

'And what are they?' asked Ursula.

'Either Marius kills Kurt,' Ruprecht explained. 'Or Kurt kills Marius.'

'And the third option?' Ursula asked.

'They kill each other,' Ruprecht replied bluntly, avoiding her gaze.

'Then all the more reason for me to get him to come peacefully, for I do not want any more blood on my hands,' Ursula said confidently.

'I really do hope you're right,' Ruprecht said again. 'For five months I've trailed you through fen and forest, and from what you say, it is because of nothing.'

'Nothing to us,' Ursula corrected him. 'Don't forget that Marius did kill Kurt's family. In many ways, he has brought this all down upon us.'

'Don't blame Marius for this,' argued Ruprecht. 'He's only said it once, but he told me that his wife was killed by Kurt's father. I don't know the details, but I've never known Marius to be wrong in these matters, and I have followed him for many years.'

'Let us not argue over events over which we have no control, and which we know nothing about,' said Ursula. 'As you say, Kurt and Marius cannot resolve this, it is up to those of us, you and I, with more level heads and less at stake.'

'Your life is still at stake should you go on trial,' Ruprecht pointed out.

'I trust in Sigmar,' Ursula replied. 'He will continue to protect me.'

But will he continue to protect Kurt, thought Ruprecht. Not if Marius had his way.

KURT WAS DOZING on his bed in the room above the tavern when an urgent knocking at his door broke his slumber. The red haze of sunset was glowing through the unshuttered window. He had been sleeping since midday. He was tired to the bone, and sadness over his inability to rescue Ursula wrapped his soul like the blankets covering his body. He had argued long with the Norscans but had been unable to persuade them to stay. Frustrated and exhausted, he had gone to bed and left Jakob to convince them that fleeing was not an option. Now Jakob pushed the door open and poked his head through.

'I have answer,' the Norscan said cautiously as Kurt sat up and beckoned him in.

'You do?' Kurt said, throwing back the bedclothes and swinging his legs free.

'I speak to others of my people in Tungask,' explained Jakob, though without much enthusiasm. 'Most born here, but some of older men move here from Norsca. We talk about what you say earlier. I think there way to get gods to reveal their will to us.'

'There is?' Kurt asked, standing up quickly and grabbing his shirt from the chair next to the bed.

'Very dangerous,' warned Jakob. 'You might die. I might die. With the gods, everyone might die, there is no saying.'

'As things stand, Marius will kill us all, anyway,' Kurt pointed out. 'I will risk whatever is necessary to even the odds against us.'

'Greatest danger to you,' Jakob said, though he was more concerned about the risks he would be facing. His close brush with the daemon in the forests only the day before was still fresh in his mind.

'Tell me what I need to do,' Kurt insisted as he finished getting dressed.

'You come with me,' Jakob said. 'I know you say yes, so I tell others to start preparing for ceremony.'

'What ceremony?' Kurt asked, suddenly suspicious.

'We ask gods to make you protector for us,' Jakob explained. 'They give you power.'

'The gods do not give gifts freely, that much I learnt from you,' said Kurt, picking up his breastplate.

'Not need armour, need spirit,' said Jakob, striding across the room and taking Kurt's armour from him. 'Armour your mind, not your body.'

'What is this ceremony?' Kurt asked again. 'What do I have to do?'

'You follow me, must be quick, I send scouts in woods to watch witch hunter, and they say he is close,' Jakob said, pulling Kurt towards the door. 'We already have made preparations.'

The Norscan led Kurt down the stairs and out of the tavern into the snow-swept open area around the trading post. Kurt saw that many of the Norscans of the town were busy building a great fire, piling logs into a pyre in the middle of the open ground. Hrolfgar and his men were standing to one side watching the proceedings. The other northmen and women gave Kurt curious glances of fear, distrust and hope. He couldn't blame them. He had brought this madman from the south to their homes, and was now offering himself up as their only salvation from the terrible blood and fire of vengeance that van Diesl would visit upon the town.

'You're doing this right here, in the middle of town?' asked Kurt. 'What are you planning to do?'

'This not great secret like in Empire,' Jakob explained hurriedly, pushing Kurt out into the square. 'This great ceremony in honour of gods, like the southern holy days.'

'Tell me what I have to do,' insisted Kurt as Jakob led him towards the fire.

'Take off clothes,' Jakob said, pulling at Kurt's shirt.

'I'll freeze,' Kurt complained, yanking Jakob's arm away.

'Warrior of the gods not frightened by snow,' sneered Jakob. 'Must be stronger than this if you want to rescue your woman. Worse than freezing can happen to you tonight.'

Stung by Jakob's words, Kurt divested himself of his clothes and stood shivering in the cold, self-conscious under the gaze of the gathered Norscans. It was not long before the great fire was lit, and as the flames began to spread and tower into the air their warmth swept over Kurt. Jakob was consulting with some of the oldest Norscans, wizened old men whose hair and beards were long and flowing and woven into intricate plaits. The skinny Norseman returned with a long knife, its blade carved with odd runes. In his other hand, he held a pouch.

'What have you got there?' asked Kurt, reaching for the pouch, but Jakob snatched it away.

'No more talk, concentrate, think of the gods,' Jakob chided him. He knelt down in the snow and using the point of the dagger cut a swirling line into Kurt's foot. Blood welled up from the cut and ran in drops down into the snow. Kurt closed his eyes and ignored the bite of the knife as Jakob continued his bloody work, cutting thin, delicate lines and shapes into Kurt's flesh. Soon Kurt could feel blood dribbling down over his legs, chest and arms. He opened his eyes again when Jakob started on his face, but held himself still as the northman carved a rune onto each cheek and onto Kurt's forehead. Blood began to stream into his eyes and congeal on his lips, the taste bitter.

Kurt had been concentrating on the knife so much he had not heard the slow beat of drums beginning. Glancing around, he saw three of the Norscans pounding out a slow beat, in time to his own heart. Jakob began to chant to the time of the drums, grabbing the rune stones from his pouch and holding them in his hands. He saw warm light spilling from between Jakob's fingers as he spoke in a tongue that Kurt could not understand, and could barely make out the words. He did however recognise four words: the names of the Dark Gods of the north; Khar, the lord of skulls and god of battle; Jaenz, the changer of the ways, god of magic; Slaeresh, the dark prince, god of passions and pleasure, and finally, there was Nierg, lord of decay, god of plague and famine.

Looking at Jakob's face, he saw that the shaman was sweating blood; it dripped in small amounts from his forehead, prickling on his skin. The flames of the fire began to burn with different colours, the orange flames tainted by greens and blues. The drumming grew louder and Kurt felt the cuts in his skin begin to burn, gently at first, but growing more painful. He closed his eyes and gritted his teeth and the fire began to eat its way through the cuts into his veins.

CHANTING LOUDER AND louder, accompanied by the drumbeats and prayers of the other Norsemen, Jakob circled Kurt, spilling the rune stones from his hands in a rough circle around the chosen warrior. They glowed with bright blue light, more powerful than before, and the snow hissed and steamed. He could feel the breath of the gods blowing stronger, at the back of his eyes seeing wisps of energy coalescing around Kurt. The power seethed up from the ground beneath Jakob, and down from the cloud-heavy skies above. A break in the clouds allowed the light of Morrslieb to shine through, emitting an eerie green light that bathed the whole town in its glow, and Jakob felt a rush of energy.

Jakob spasmed with the power that flooded through his limbs and mind, falling to his knees, and swirling images filled his head. He saw endless ranks of warriors marching through bloody snow, their axes and swords drenched in gore. He saw strange beasts bellowing praise into the night and skeletons dressed in ornate gold armour stalking across ancient sandstone ruins. He heard the cries of wild creatures surging beneath the waves of the Great Ocean. All of this flashed through Jakob's mind in an instant, the intensity, the sight, the smell and the touch of it so vividly real, he felt himself trembling. Pushing the images away, he looked at Kurt, and concentrated on the words he had to say to bind the power of the gods into this mortal vessel before him.

THE FIRE WITHIN his blood writhed through Kurt, burning his heart, searing his lungs and scorching his brain. His whole body was awash with pain, and he cried out through gritted teeth. Opening his eyes, he looked at the burning pyre, at the leaping flames that swirled in and out of focus. The buildings around him began to swim in his vision, merging with the flames into a vortex of magical flame and shadow. Still the internal fire burned within him, growing in strength, surging through his veins, through his muscles, into his fingers and out of his eyes.

The spinning landscape began to coalesce into strange forms: flitting three-headed fish, amorphous clouds of energy with teeth, and leering faces with burning eyes of flame. A shadowy creature swept at him out of the light, its lashing claws aimed for his face. He ducked as it dived towards him, throwing himself to the ground as it swept overhead. Something touched his leg and he looked to see a twin-headed serpent coiling around his thigh, its skin barbed with hundreds of tiny hooks that tore at his flesh. Ripping his leg free in a shower of blood, Kurt forced himself to stand again, and looked down at his own naked body. The runes Jakob had drawn on him were burning with energy, each a fine line of pulsing magical power that crawled across his skin. Another daemonic creature flew at him, a jewel-eyed woman with long flowing fangs and scything claws. He raised his fist and the creature veered aside at the last moment, dissipating into a scented mist that rose into the air leaving behind the smell of flowers and blood.

Kurt felt the circle of creatures closing in around him, and could sense their hunger for his flesh and spirit. As fear crept into his mind, he felt the fire within him beginning to dull. The runes began to flicker and fade, and he realised this was the danger Jakob had warned him of. His was filled with the power of the gods and it protected him, but if he was to let it go, then the daemons would descend on him in a frenzied cloud and devour him.

Summoning all his energy and will, he concentrated on the fire that burned inside. He thought of it feeding off the breath of the gods as a normal fire feeds on a slight breeze. Once more, he felt the energy swirling into him. Mastering the pain, he began to laugh. He felt the breath of the gods and heard their whispers in the back of his mind. They taunted him. They praised him. They laughed. They bellowed in anger.

Kurt's vision began to clear and with a last effort, he reached out his right hand towards the emerging sight of the fire. He imagined the flames as his armour and sword and the multi-coloured fires leapt through the air towards him, surrounding him yet not burning him. The fire inside his body was hotter and he used that power he now felt to pull the flames into his flesh, the magical energies seeping into sinew and muscle, strengthening his bones, moulding into his eyes and ears and nose.

With a thunderous finale, the drumming crashed and then fell silent. Kurt collapsed to his knees, panting hard. Jakob lay next to him, unconscious, blood dribbling from his nose, ears and eyes. Kurt pushed himself to his feet, noticing as he did so that the cuts inflicted on him by Jakob were now no more than thin traces on his skin, a pinkish-red like the scar left by a burn. Glancing at the pyre, he saw that the fire was dead, nothing more than smouldering ashes as if it had been burning for many days rather than just a short while. The clouds were thinning as well, a strong northerly wind breaking them up to let through the rays of Morrslieb, the daemon moon. Disorientated, unsure how long he had been away from the world, Kurt looked around the assembled Norscans. His gaze fell on Hrolfgar. The tall marauder was stood with his arms crossed, his face impassive. Kurt strode across the bare ground, and the snow hissed into steam under his tread.

'Will you swear to follow me?' Kurt asked, and his voice was louder and deeper than before, carrying across the night sky like a thunderstrike.

'You have survived,' Hrolfgar admitted. 'But you must still prove your worth.'

'Which of your men would you have me challenge?' Kurt said, looking at the assembled warriors. Some looked eager for a fight, others met his gaze with looks of fear, while one of them, the chieftain's brother Bjordrin, had an exultant look on his face.

'I will fight you!' called out one named Kjarl, stepping forward. He was one of the youngest of the marauders, but Kurt could see that he was strong and fast. His face was covered with the first touches of a beard and he carried a sword in his hands, its hilt wrought in the shape of a coiling serpent.

'Then strike me,' Kurt said confident, arms spread wide. Kjarl glanced at Hrolfgar, who nodded, and then drove his sword towards Kurt's midriff. To Kurt the blow moved at a snail's pace, giving him plenty of time to react. Everything seemed to move slower now, or perhaps it was just that he could now move that much faster than a normal man. Kurt's hand flashed out and smashed the blade from Kjarl's grasp, flinging it into the snow. There was no mark on his hand.

'Try harder,' Kurt said, darting a sidelong glance at Hrolfgar, who remained unimpressed. Kjarl picked up his sword and stood in front of Kurt again. This time he attacked with an overhead cut aimed at Kurt's left shoulder, but Kurt swayed to one side and grabbed the blade in his fist. Blood trickled from between his fingers. Gripping his sword two-handed, Kjarl tried to pull it free, but Kurt stood there relaxed, and held the blade in a grip as tight as a blacksmith's vice. With a flick of his arm, he pulled the sword free, flipped it in the air and caught it by the hilt.

'One more chance,' Kurt said, tossing the sword back to Kjarl. The young Norscan advanced even more warily than before, and then shot forwards, lunging with sword outstretched. The blade punched into Kurt's stomach, ripping into his guts and forcing him back a step. Kjarl gave an exultant shout, but his look of joy turned to one of panic when Kurt slowly reached out and grabbed Kjarl's wrist, pulling the blade in further until it pushed through out of his back. Face to face, Kurt smiled at Kjarl and then smashed his free hand into the boy's chest, fingers spread like claws, his muscles feeling as tough as iron. Kjarl was hurled a dozen yards back by the blow, landing heavily in the snow, a howl of pain torn from his lips. The other marauders huddled around him and gasped when they saw the circle of five bloody holes in Kjarl's chest, each as deep as a spear wound. Kurt pulled out the sword, its blade slicked with black blood that oozed fitfully from the wound rather than poured, and tossed it into the ashes of the fire. He flicked Kjarl's blood from his fingertips into the snow and looked at Hrolfgar.

'The gods have spoken,' the chieftain cried out, striding forward and snatching up Kurt in a massive bear hug. 'You are one of the chosen!'

IN HIS CAMP on the outskirts of the forest, Marius heard a loud cheer break the stillness of the night. For a while now he had heard the faint pounding of drums, and had seen the flicker of firelight and a column of smoke at the far side of Tungask. They were obviously up to some devilry, he told himself. No matter, he would soon raze this miserable place to the ground and be done with these Sigmar-forsaken lands. He turned to Ruprecht beside him.

'Is everything ready?' he asked, receiving a nod in reply.

'Good,' Marius said. 'Send the girl in.'

CHAPTER NINE
Trap
Tungask, Winter 1709

URSULA THOUGHT THE town strangely quiet as she walked
through the deserted, snow-shrouded streets of Tungask.
The windows in the log houses were dark, and the only
sound was the quiet sighing of the north wind. She walked
slowly, trying to collect her thoughts. Earlier she had been
confident that Kurt would come with her, but now she was
not so sure. Ruprecht's words were etched on her mind.
Could she persuade Kurt to hand himself willingly over to
Marius? And what of herself? Now she was free of the witch
hunter, did she really think he would give them a fair trial?
Had too much blood been spilt now to ever resolve this
peacefully or would it, as Ruprecht had said, be a matter of
who survived the battle to come?

A shadow loping through the snow made her jump, but
she relaxed when she saw it was just a dog, hunting between
the buildings for vermin. It stopped and looked at her for a
moment, head cocked to one side, and then ran on, sniffing
the air, its ears flat against its head.

As she walked through the town, Ursula could smell
smoke. There were also the sounds of life up ahead: voices

talking and the ring of metal on metal. Walking into the open space in front of the tavern where they had stayed, she saw that many of the townsfolk were gathered here, both Norscan and Kislevite. She saw a group of Hrolfgar's marauders in front of the tavern door, and they noticed her too, drawing weapons as she approached. One of them said something in Norscan and held out a hand for her to stop. Another of them gave her a scowl and then opened the door and disappeared inside. The crowd, some hundred or so men, had fallen silent and now all eyes were on her. The remnants of a large fire smouldered to her left and she noticed the telltale red of blood in the snow. She looked at the gathered men and saw that they were all armed, with axes, swords, bows or knives. They were clearly preparing to fight. Looking at their faces, some familiar, others not, she hardened her resolve to avoid battle.

KURT WAS IN the main room of the tavern sharpening his sword when Svelka stepped inside and crossed over to him.

'The woman is outside,' the Norse warrior said.

'What?' Kurt asked, looking up.

'Your woman, she is outside,' the marauder repeated, glancing back at the door. 'Shall we bring her in?'

Kurt didn't reply, but sprang to his feet, the sword dropping from his hand as he ran to the door. He wrenched it open and shouldered his way through the Norscans gathered there. Sure enough, there stood Ursula. She looked beautiful, swathed in furs, her long hair blowing slightly in the wind. Her face was slightly red with the cold, her cheeks ruddy. He stood there for a moment longer before stepping forward and hugging her close, burying his face in her hair. He felt her arms encircle his waist and lifted her up, kissing her forehead lightly.

'How did you escape?' he asked with a grin, almost not believing his own eyes.

'We need to talk,' she replied, letting go of Kurt and stepping away. 'But not here, not in front of all these people.'

Kurt glanced around at the crowd, who were watching everything in silence, though most of them could not understand what was being said.

'Of course,' Kurt said. 'We'll go inside.'

'No!' Ursula said quickly. 'I want to walk for a while, in the fresh air.'

'I'll be back shortly,' Kurt said in Norscan to the men at the door. 'Hopefully she'll know where Marius is hiding. Then we can go on the attack rather than sit here waiting for him.'

The men nodded and grinned, eyeing Ursula with less suspicion now. Kurt ignored them and looped Ursula's arm around his own.

'You're getting ready to fight,' Ursula said as they walked out of the square, heading southwards towards the bridge.

'I have to kill van Diesl,' Kurt replied frankly. 'He isn't going to simply go away. And besides, do not forget that he murdered my mother, father and sister.'

'Do you think they would thank you for more killing?' Ursula asked quietly. 'Killing Marius will not bring them back. Would not they be more happy for justice?'

'Justice?' laughed Kurt. As they walked, the town got darker, and thicker clouds gathered overhead to obscure the newly rising moon of Mannslieb. 'My sword will give van Diesl the only type of justice he understands.'

'And what of us?' Ursula said. 'Assuming you don't die and leave me here in this bleak land on my own, what then? Do you think we could really go south again? Do you think that we would ever be safe?'

'No, we would not be safe in the Empire,' agreed Kurt. 'That's why we head north, with Jakob, back to his people.'

'I cannot live amongst these barbarians,' Ursula snapped, flicking her head in irritation and causing more strands to come loose from her plait. The dampness in the air made her red locks stick to her face in the same way it had when Kurt had first seen her.

'You give me no choices,' Kurt complained, ignoring the sudden memory. 'You say we cannot return home, and you are right, and yet you also say that you won't go north with me. What would you have me do?'

She didn't reply immediately, instead she quickened the pace, leading him by the arm through the streets of the town towards the bridge. The log huts on either side were quiet and dark, the people of Tungask having fled to the far side of the town in fear of Marius's attack.

'I said we couldn't return if you killed Marius, but there is another way,' said Ursula.

'I cannot see it,' said Kurt, stopping to let go of Ursula and face her.

'Give yourself over to the mercy of Sigmar,' Ursula told him, laying a hand on his chest.

'What does that mean?' Kurt laughed back.

'Marius has agreed to stay his hand if you come back peacefully,' Ursula said, her stomach tight with tension.

'He's lying,' hissed Kurt. 'You're a fool!'

'No, I believe him,' insisted Ursula. 'We go back and stand trial. We are innocent, and with our names cleared we can try to make another life for ourselves.'

'You may be innocent, but I am not,' Kurt replied with a shake of his head. 'I killed three knights, remember? I killed two of Marius's men in the woods yesterday.'

'You were only defending yourself,' Ursula said. 'That is no crime.'

'I'm a deserter,' Kurt added. 'Had you forgotten that? Do you think the Osterknacht will just agree to letting us go? I don't think so!'

'We have a chance, have a little faith in me,' Ursula said, her hand dropping to her side. 'Have some faith in Sigmar.'

'Sigmar had his chance,' Kurt replied. 'I fear it is too late for him now.'

'What do you mean?' Ursula asked sharply. She looked closely at Kurt and for the first time saw the faint scars on his face. His armour was also finely carved with swirling runes and crude pictograms, put there by Hrolfgar and his men while he slept in the afternoon. It was to be his gift from them if he passed the test, and if he had failed, Hrolfgar would have claimed the armour for himself. Kurt now looked more like the warrior of Chaos he was becoming than the proud knight of the Empire he once was. 'What have you done?' she demanded, pushing him away.

'You might get your strength from Sigmar, but I have found a better way,' Kurt said triumphantly. 'I am so much stronger now, faster. I was going to rescue you.'

'You're disgusting!' snapped Ursula. Immediately, her eyes dropped to the ground and she took a deep breath. When she looked at him again, her eyes were wide and pleading. A tear rolled down her cheek. 'But it's not too late,' she said quietly, stepping closer again.

'Not too late for what?' Kurt said, looking down at her.

'Not too late for you to renounce this evil that Jakob has put in your soul,' explained Ursula. 'Come with me back to Marius. Clear our name! Would you abandon me, after all this?'

'It was for you that I have done this,' Kurt insisted, frustration evident in his voice. 'For the last two years, it is you who has been my reason for living. Don't you see? I could have died, but I wanted to see you safe. I risked everything because I want you.'

'I did not want this,' Ursula replied. 'Did I ever ask you for any of this?'

Kurt said nothing, confused, his emotions whirling. He strode a few paces down the street, back towards the tavern, and then stopped and looked back at Ursula.

'Van Diesl has poisoned you against me!' he said suddenly. 'Jakob was right, you have betrayed me.'

'No, I haven't!' cried Ursula, running to him. 'I could never betray you, I love you!'

'I love you too, with every ounce of my soul,' Kurt replied, once more sweeping her into his arms. 'Can you not see that?'

'I don't think your soul is yours any more, is it?' came a voice from the shadows. They both looked up to see Marius van Diesl striding out of a sidestreet, blade in one hand and a torch in the other. More men closed in around Kurt, armed with crossbows. He recognised Lord Militant Trevigar, clad in his ornate Osterknacht armour, his naked sword held across his chest.

'Marius!' Ursula cried out. 'What are you doing here?'

'You traitor!' spat Kurt, hurling Ursula to the ground and reaching for his sword. But his weapon was on the floor of the tavern where he had dropped it. 'Was this your vile plan?'

'I swear this was not my doing!' begged Ursula, clutching at Kurt's leg.

'She brought me straight to you,' Marius laughed, walking closer.

'Why?' demanded Kurt, tearing his leg from Ursula's grasp.

'This was not how it was supposed to happen, please believe me,' Ursula said, crawling towards Jakob, shivering from the cold touch of the snow.

'Kill them both!' snapped Marius, motioning to the cross-bowmen with the blazing brand.

'No!' shouted Ruprecht, from behind Kurt. 'We take the girl back with us to stand trial, like you said!'

The men looked hesitantly between the two of them, one their leader, the other their true comrade-in-arms.

'Very well,' Marius said dismissively, sheathing his sword. 'Spare the girl.'

Ursula threw herself at Kurt with a shriek, putting herself between him and Marius's men.

'No!' she yelled. 'I won't allow this!'

A crossbow bolt sliced through the air, but Kurt reacted with preternatural speed, plucking it from the air barely inches from Ursula's chest.

'I'll make you swallow this,' he growled, tossing Ursula aside and striding towards the man-at-arms who was now backing away fearfully, frantically trying to reload his crossbow. Kurt felt something hit him in the side, and glanced down to see a quarrel sticking from his thigh. Gritting his teeth, he ripped it free and snapped it in his fist. 'You'll have to try harder,' he laughed, advancing quickly.

'Kurt!' he heard Ursula scream, and turned to see Marius dragging her off through the snow, his blade hovering at her throat. Another crossbow bolt slammed into his back, pitching him forward onto one knee. With a growl, he rose up and reached around to the bolt, snapping the shaft with his hand. He glanced back and forth between Ursula and the men-at-arms. Trevigar was backing away, sword held out in defence in front of him. Blood was dripping down Kurt's leg and back, and he began to feel the pain of the point lodged near his spine.

With a roar, he charged towards the closest man-at-arms, who flung down his crossbow and fled. With Kurt rushing towards them, the others fired hastily, their shots flying wide, and then they too were sprinting away into the darkness. Turning around, Kurt saw that van Diesl had disappeared, along with Trevigar.

'I will kill you all!' Kurt bellowed into the night, his voice echoing over the town. 'All of you!'

CHAPTER TEN
Judgement
Tungask, Winter 1709

RUPRECHT WATCHED AS the men kicked in the doors to the houses, tossing in burning torches. Behind him, a dozen homes were already burning steadily. There had been no opposition so far; most of the townsfolk had deserted their homes for safer buildings further from the bridge, or had fled Tungask altogether. The warrior band was steadily and methodically making its way through the town, razing everything, herding the inhabitants to the north. Ruprecht glanced ahead to Marius, who was standing with Ursula. It had taken all of Ruprecht's skills to dissuade the witch hunter from killing her out of hand. Ruprecht wanted no part of the bloodlust that was fuelling Marius, and had only stayed the witch hunter's hand by convincing him that Ursula was still more useful alive than dead. Luckily for Ursula, Marius wanted to kill Leitzig more than her, and while the ex-knight still lived, she had a stay of execution. After that, Ruprecht hoped Marius would be more reasonable and perhaps be persuaded to take the girl back to stand a proper trial. If not, he was unsure what he would have to do. But those were matters for later. For now, Ruprecht's attention was focussed on not being killed.

KURT STOOD IN the middle of the room. All around were babbling voices, from Hrolfgar, from Jakob, and from dozens of the townsfolk whose homes were now turning into smouldering ruins. He ignored them all. His mind was focussed on one thing, and one thing alone: Marius van Diesl. He pictured the witch hunter in his mind, every contour and line etched into his memory from when he was seven. Again, he would see that face against a backdrop of crackling flames. This time, it would be van Diesl who would suffer. And Kurt's wrath was not restricted to the witch hunter alone. He wanted to destroy the men who followed him, to wipe out the knights who accompanied the murderer.

'The witch hunter is mine!' declared Kurt, snapping out of his reverie. 'And the girl is not to be harmed.'

There were nods of assent from those around him. Kurt looked at Hrolfgar.

'We leave van Diesl until last,' the marauder chieftain told him. 'I want him to see his men being killed, just like I watched him butcher my men.'

'Good,' Kurt agreed. 'Are your men ready?'

'Hungry for it!' announced Hrolfgar with a grin. 'Almost as hungry as you, Sutenmjar.'

'Why do you insist on calling me that?' asked Kurt. 'Have I not proved that the gods are with me?'

'You are a southern whelp, nothing can change that!' laughed Hrolfgar. 'You are one of the sheep that the wolves of the north prey upon, but you are a sheep that has grown teeth!'

'No, I am not a wolf of the north,' Kurt said with a nod, 'but I shall be the lion amongst your wolf pack.'

'What is this lion you speak of?' asked Bjordrin.

'I saw one at a travelling circus once,' Kurt told them. 'It's a gigantic cat, as big as a man, and heavier. They have a great shaggy mane of fur, and eat the deer.'

'From where do these lions come from?' Bjordrin continued. 'I have raided your lands many times and never seen one.'

'They come from far to the south,' Jakob told him. 'Much further south than the Empire, further south than even Bretonnia. In the lands called Araby they can be found, and there are also other giant cats, such as the black-skinned panther, and the spotted leopard.'

'You speak as if you have been there,' Hrolfgar said.

'No, I have not seen the deserts, but I would like to some day,' Jakob replied, tightening the buckles on Kurt's vambraces.

'We go north first,' Kurt said. 'To the mountains and fjords.'

'Assuming we survive tonight,' muttered Jakob and a murmur of agreement rippled around the room. 'The witch hunter has a small army, with armoured knights and men with bows.'

'The knights will be on foot in the town, I have a way to deal with them,' Kurt said with confidence. 'And since when have archers scared the marauders of Norsca? Besides, we have hunters here, whose aim is better than any man who learnt his trade on the training field and did not rely on his eye for food for the night.'

'But we are few, they are many, and they already are halfway here,' Bjordrin pointed out. 'I am no coward, but the gods will not reward us for being foolish either.'

'We shall survive tonight,' Kurt assured his companions. 'I have a plan to deal with these troublesome knights. And as Jakob keeps telling me, are not the gods with us?'

THE FIRST ATTACK on Marius's warband was haphazard and desultory. Kislevites fired arrows at them from the windows of their houses, forcing Marius and his men to take cover in doorways and down behind walls. However, it was easy to send some of the squires and men-at-arms around side routes to come at the houses from the other side and toss brands through the windows. Marius laughed as he heard the screams of the people inside, and marched up the street brandishing his sword and dragging Ursula along by her furs.

'Come on you coward!' Marius shouted, waving his sword above his head. 'Are you man enough to face me? I'll kill her, you dog!'

Ruprecht felt uneasy. He had done more than his fair
share of dubious things in the past, including torture and
killing, but the sheer cold-bloodedness of Marius's attack
left Ruprecht feeling faintly sick. The witch hunter was
exhibiting a callousness that Ruprecht had never seen before
during his long years of service to Marius. He had always
known him to be a ruthless man, and gave him credit for it,
because the foes they faced were inhuman and merciless.
But this was something else entirely, and yet somehow
familiar. Since Marius had never spoken of it, Ruprecht had
asked Ursula to relate Kurt's account of the fateful encounter
between the two of them so many years ago. To Ruprecht,
the similarities were obvious, down to the burning of the
buildings to flush Kurt out of hiding. The problem was, this
time Kurt was not a frightened child, alone and scared. He
was a fully-grown man with warriors under his command.
Worse than that, Kurt himself was now a fearsome fighter in
his own right, and invested with the dread powers of Chaos.

A startled yell drew Ruprecht's attention behind him. The
door to one of the burning buildings slammed open and a
figure ran outside, screaming, hair and clothes ablaze. It hur-
tled towards the nearest soldier, knocking into him and
setting him on fire.

'Shoot it!' Ruprecht bellowed at the men standing around
him and the smoke-filled air sang with the sound of bow-
strings and crossbows. The burning figure and the soldier
were pinned by a flurry of bolts and arrows that knocked
them to the ground. Both the smoking bodies were still. As
if sensing the sudden confusion amongst the ranks of
Marius's men, three Norscans came rushing around a corner.
They each carried a throwing axe and picked their targets
well, the heavy-headed weapons burying themselves in the
backs of two knights, on foot within the confines of the
town, who had turned to watch the commotion. These were
proper warriors, clad in battle harness and carrying shields,
unlike the townsfolk they had run into previously. They
turned and ran back out of sight before the archers could fire
back, and several of the squires gave chase.

'Hold fast!' Ruprecht yelled, running after them, but they
didn't listen. Rounding the corner himself, he saw the three

Norscans hacking at the bodies, two of them with battleaxes, the third with a short sword. They looked up at him and grinned, and Ruprecht skidded to a stop a dozen yards up the road, realising he was on his own and outnumbered. He started walking backwards, his hammer in his hands, as they advanced towards him, their bloodstained weapons and round wooden shields held ready.

'To me! To me!' cried Ruprecht, glancing around for help. The three marauders jeered at him in their own tongue and joked with each other, laughing cruelly at Ruprecht's plight. Their humour soon vanished though when five Osterknacht ran around the corner, quickly followed by a handful of squires and men-at-arms.

'Not so brave now, are we boys?' laughed Ruprecht as the marauders in turn started to backtrack, their shields raised as the men-at-arms loosed arrows towards them. One of the Norse raiders was hit in the leg by a crossbow quarrel, and fell to one knee with a cry of pain. The other two stopped for a moment to help him up, but snarling in Norscan, he waved them away.

KJARL GRITTED HIS teeth against the pain, and dropped his axe to pull the crossbow quarrel out of his thigh. The wound was not particularly deep, though blood ran freely down his leg. He stood unsteadily and picked up his axe, looking over his shoulder to see if Koltan and Svelka were still moving away. Already wounded in the chest by the strange southerner, he was in no fit state to run any more. And besides, he told himself, he wasn't going to be weak with the gods watching on. He backed himself against a wall and took shelter behind his shield. More arrows flew at him, clattering off the logs, one of them punching through his shield and scratching his arm. He ignored the flesh wound.

'Come on, you dogs! Fight like men!' he screamed at them as the archers paused further down the street, stringing more arrows. 'Only cowards use bows!'

They fired another volley and Kjarl ducked behind his shield again. With a shout, he launched himself into a limping run, his heart hammering in his chest. Blood flowed from his wounds and he felt dizzy, but he pushed himself

forward, his eyes fixed on the giant with the hammer. He'd
seen him fighting in the woods, and he was the one who
had killed Kjarl's older brother, Sven. He'd see the burly
fighter dead before the gods took him. His heart surged with
pride at the thought of avenging his kin. They would sing a
tale around the fire about him, when Hrolfgar and the others got back to Norsca.

An arrow struck him in the shoulder and spun him to the
ground. Kjarl forced himself back to his feet and hobbled
forward, his axe raised in defiance.

'Your women will lament this day!' the young Norscan
shouted, limping forward, leaving a blood-filled furrow in
the snow from his wounded leg.

More arrows hit him, one in his right arm, the other in the
stomach, and he pitched forward to his knees, his axe dropping from his grasp. He scrabbled in the snow for his
weapon, and watched as the hammer-wielding giant finally
stepped forward, a grim look on his face. The bearded man
stopped a couple of paces away and raised the hammer
above his head.

'Don't kill me without my axe!' pleaded Kjarl, holding up
a hand, his other still searching through the snow for the
blade.

The southerner's uncomprehending face looked down at
him for a moment before his hammer descended in an arc
and smashed into Kjarl's temple, hurling him sideways. As
he fell, Kjarl saw the glimmer of metal in the firelight, just to
his right. He stretched out to reach it, but the giant stamped
on his hand, shattering his fingers.

'No...' sobbed Kjarl, trying to force himself towards the
axe, his vision swimming. He collapsed in the snow, the ice
stinging his face. Blood pooled around him and it was a
moment before he realised it was his own. 'The gods...'

The hammer swung again, and Kjarl's head was knocked
backwards, snapping his neck, his last, desperate thought
that the gods would curse his soul for not dying with a
weapon in his hand.

'THEY'RE STICKING TOGETHER like the herd of sheep they are,'
Svelka said to Kurt, as the Norscan warrior barged through

the door of the tavern. Kurt was sitting at one of the tables with a mug of ale in his hand. This was much to Svelka's annoyance, as he had watched the witch hunter's men kill Kjarl while this southerner had been sitting here in safety. 'There's twice as many of them as there are us altogether, and only a dozen of us are real warriors.'

'Then the dozen of us attack them head-on, the others get around their flanks and harass them as much as they can,' Kurt replied, getting up and walking towards the door.

'Did you not hear him?' said Hrolfgar, stepping in front of Kurt. 'There are knights, with armour. We cannot fight them.'

'Leave the knights to me,' Kurt said.

'What are you going to do?' Bjordrin asked, standing up and grabbing his axe from the table.

'I'm going to show you what it means to be the chosen of the gods,' Kurt replied.

He strode out of the door and into the cold outside. He looked at the smouldering pyre and remembered the ceremony that had taken place. It had only been held just after nightfall, not much time ago, though to Kurt it could have been a lifetime away. So much had changed in that time; he felt like a different person. He recalled the power he had felt as the breath of the gods had flowed into him. Even now, he could feel their presence, lingering inside him, looking down on him from the clouds above, listening to his words from the ground beneath his feet. The gods were indeed everywhere this far north, he could feel them ebbing and flowing around him. In the distance a growing red glow spread above Tungask as van Diesl torched the houses on this side of the river. Realising now was the time to act swiftly, Kurt strode across the square. He called for Jakob, who emerged from one of the nearby houses, bow in hand.

'I have two things for you to do,' Kurt told Jakob as he came closer.

'Of course, what do you want?' the wiry Norscan replied.

'You remember the ceremony when you called on the gods?' Kurt said. 'The daemons came, and tried to kill me.'

'They did?' Jakob asked, eyes wide in amazement. 'We saw you writhing on the ground, but there were no daemons.'

'They were there, believe me, perhaps only I could see them,' Kurt said. 'Anyway, I want you to bring them out again.'

'I am not powerful enough for such a thing,' Jakob said, waving his hands in disagreement. 'I have only summoned a daemon once and that was by mistake.'

'The power is in the rune stones,' Kurt said.

'But their power is gone, I am amazed they had enough energy for the ceremony, yesterday they were all but exhausted,' Jakob argued.

'You don't need much power, it is in the air, can't you feel it?' Kurt said, gazing up into the sky. 'Can't you hear their howling and laughter in the distance?'

Jakob paused and gazed around him, his eyes half closed.

'The blood and death brings them closer,' Jakob said after a while, his eyes still slightly glazed.

'Yes, and I will create more blood and death than has ever been seen in these parts,' Kurt grinned.

'Even if I can bring them through, I do not have the skill or power to control them once they arrive,' Jakob said. 'They are as likely to attack us as van Diesl and his men.'

'We'll worry about that if it happens,' said Kurt. 'At the moment we need to use everything we can to swing the balance.'

'Perhaps,' Jakob agreed cautiously. 'You said there were two things.'

'Ah, yes,' Kurt said with a sly grin. 'Let's go to the tavern to discuss that.'

MARIUS SMILED AT Ursula, who darted him an angry glance. All around them, the flames crackled high into the air, filling the sky with smoke. Nearly half the town was ablaze now, flushing the inhabitants out of hiding like vermin hiding in the cellar.

'I never thought you were a wicked man,' Ursula said, stumbling alongside the witch hunter with her hands tied at the wrists in front of her.

'I am a righteous man,' Marius said to her. 'The fire cleanses the world, I thought you would understand that. Is it not written in the Book of Sigmar that he burnt the villages of the

Norsci? As one of the devout faithful, don't you agree with me? Did you not say that these barbarians deserved death?'

'But not like this!' argued Ursula. 'Not this drawn out, agonising death.'

'It is the fear that is my weapon,' Marius explained as another house started to go up in flames further up the street. 'You saw it in Badenhof, the terror that my position brings with it. It is that fear that keeps normally good people from straying into the darkness. When their will is weak, it is the thought of the flames that keeps them pure.'

'I was almost killed by that fear in Badenhof,' snarled Ursula. 'You are a monster!'

Marius just laughed, but then fell silent as a solitary figure appeared ahead at the end of the street.

Sword drawn, the flames glittering off his armour, Kurt took a few steps forward.

'Murderer!' he called out, raising his sword to point at Marius. 'I will kill you! Your men's lives are also forfeit!'

'Any attack and the girl dies by my hand,' Marius warned, his voice raised to carry over the crackling flames.

'Cowards!' Kurt shouted in reply, his voice booming and unnatural. 'The woman has betrayed me, she means nothing to me!'

'He's bluffing,' Ruprecht muttered from behind Marius. 'Let me look after her, you'll need your sword arm free if they do attack.'

Marius paused for a moment, unsure, and then nodded, pushing Ursula back towards his lieutenant. Ruprecht took her by the arm and dragged her a little further from the front of the group. Looking up the road, he saw that Leitzig had disappeared from view.

'Where did he go?' he shouted out to Marius.

'The coward simply walked away again,' the witch hunter called back. 'I don't think he cares for the woman at all. Split the men into three groups, send two bands out to the flanks to encircle him. I don't want them slipping away.'

'Is it wise to divide our forces?' Ruprecht shouted back. 'We don't know how many of them there are, or where they are hiding!'

'Sweep the town, drive them out!' Marius bellowed, marching forward with his sword raised.

'Don't worry,' Ruprecht said quietly to Ursula as the two tagged behind a group of knights advancing after Marius. 'Stick close to me and I'll keep you safe.'

'Don't you think I deserve to die?' Ursula said, an accusing look on her face.

'No, Marius is not himself, hopefully he'll calm down after the battle,' Ruprecht replied.

'I can't believe he'd use me like that to trap Kurt,' she said.

'Would Kurt hesitate in holding me hostage if the positions were reversed?' Ruprecht asked. 'He isn't the Kurt you once knew. You saw him, pinned full of bolts and still walking. He isn't a normal man any more. It's too late to save him, you have to let Marius do this his way.'

'Kurt said I had betrayed him,' Ursula said with a disconsolate shake of her head. 'It's not true, and I won't give up on him now.'

'You're very faithful, girl, I'll give you that,' Ruprecht said after a short pause.

'You still follow Marius, though you accept he isn't really in control of himself,' Ursula pointed out. 'You hold out the same hope for him that I do for Kurt.'

'Yes, I guess you're right,' admitted Ruprecht. 'That just makes us both bloody fools.'

JAKOB'S HANDS SHOOK with fear as he crouched on the snow-covered roof of a house not far from where Marius's men were now fanning out through the town. For a moment he considered disobeying Kurt's orders, and to just tell him that the summoning had failed. At the back of his mind, though, was the doubt that somehow Kurt would know he was lying, and not just from the way the Norscan spoke or acted. Jakob knew that Kurt was now tapped into the flow of energy that spilled from the north, and could sense its pulses and eddies. He would be able to feel if Jakob tried to do any ritual, and would instinctively know if the attempt had been tried and failed, or not tried at all.

Jakob wished he could just hide up in this roof until it was all over. He was not a coward, but even though Kurt claimed to have fought off a pack of daemons during his initiation, he didn't really understand the horror he was asking Jakob to perform. Perhaps his time in the south had indeed softened him, Jakob thought. Then again, Kurt had never heard the tales of villages destroyed by ceremonies gone wrong, blasted from the face of the world without trace, or left as smashed ruins decorated with the corpses of their inhabitants by the creatures that were drawn to magic like hounds at a chase. Jakob's only consolation was that unless it went disastrously wrong, he was up here on the roof, and whatever he brought through from the realm of the gods would be down there on the ground.

In one hand, he held a pot filled with blood donated by Kurt, Hrolfgar and Bjordrin. Jakob's rune stones bobbed and sank unnaturally within the blood, soaking it up like sand absorbing water. Holding the pot over his head, Jakob began to chant, a variation on the rituals he had performed before. This time he called only upon a single god, Khorne the master of slaughter. Jakob hoped to bring forth the bloodletters, the servants of the blood god who were possessed by insatiable rage and the need to spill blood. In his hands, the pot began to vibrate, and after a couple of minutes, he could hear the rune stones rattling around in the now empty jar. His arms began to ache with the strain on them, and after a particularly violent shake, a crack appeared in the clay vessel. Jakob stuttered for a moment, his heart skipping a beat, and then concentrated more carefully, praying to Khorne for deliverance. The pot grew hot in his hands and smoke began to issue from the open top, bringing with it a stench Jakob knew only too well: the smell of burning flesh.

Looking down into the street, Jakob saw that a group of knights and men-at-arms were only about twenty yards or so away. They were advancing house by house, kicking in doors and setting fires. It would not be long until they reached the building on which Jakob was hiding. When they were only a few yards away, Jakob rose to his feet, holding the pot in one hand above his head.

'Arise, warriors of the blood of gods,' he cried out, hurling the pot into the midst of the knights. '*Khaos aqshyash aqshy'phak khaddar khardhaos!*'

The pot exploded in mid-air with a ball of writhing flames, scattering the rune stones like small comets that left trails of blazing sparks. Where each stone landed, the snow exploded into red steam and droplets of blood. The blood began to coalesce into a pool, multiplying and growing, rising from the ground. The men stood stock still with horrified faces, watching as the blood pools formed into columns, and then split into limbs and heads. Bestial faces grew out of the blood, and thick hair matted with gore sprouted from the daemons' backs. Reaching down into the ground, the daemons pulled out massive brazen axes and swords, inscribed with writhing runes of the blood god. Growling and snarling, the creatures raised themselves to their full height, towering a head taller than the men, their broad chests swelling with unnatural muscle. Throwing their heads back, the daemons howled in unison, a sound so terrifying that even Jakob started trembling. He stumbled back along the roof, almost disbelieving he had been successful.

One of the knights gave a shout and jumped forward, but his sword shattered against the skin of the nearest bloodletter. The daemon lunged forward, its hand smashing through the knight's face, flinging him into the wall of a house. The daemon swung its axe and beheaded the ragged mess that was left. The other daemons sprang forward, their weapons rising and falling in bloody arcs, accompanied by screams of panic and agony, and punctuated by growls and the snapping of bones. The attack was over in a matter of moments, as the daemons crouched down to feast on the bloody remnants of Marius's men. When they had slaked their blood thirst, the daemons stood up and sniffed the air, snarling and snapping at each other in their own inhuman tongue. Catching the scent of Jakob, they turned and looked up at the Norscan, who was cowering terrified on the roof. Never before had he unleashed such a creature, and what he had feared would happen looked as if it was about to come true.

The creatures padded quickly through the snow towards him, their glowing red eyes intent on Jakob. Their attention was drawn away though when a figure appeared at the end of the road. Howling with delight, they bounded forward,

hunched over, their weapons glittering with unholy light.
Jakob saw that the figure was Kurt, who simply raised a hand
as the bloodletters charged towards him, halting them in
their tracks. He then pointed back past the bloodletters and
said something Jakob could not hear. The bloodletters nodded and turned on their heels and sprinted away, barking
and growling with joy.

Jakob was stunned. He knew Kurt was special, marked by
the gods, but such power with so little knowledge and training was beyond anything the northman had ever seen or
heard about. Kurt looked up to where Jakob was still
crouched on the roof, and called out.

'Good, that should keep them busy for a while,' Kurt
shouted. 'It's time we dealt with our other problem.'

Jakob nodded and slipped down into the street, running
off into the darkness.

THE MEN AHEAD of Marius had no chance. The red, blood-
slicked daemons leapt out of the darkness with inhuman
speed, their axes and swords scything through the squires
and men-at-arms with ease, severing heads and limbs and
scattering them across the street in an orgy of destruction.
Shouts of terror echoed from the log walls of the houses
around them, and Marius stopped, a moment of fear gripping him. Then anger returned.

'See the abominations he unleashes upon us!' he cried
out. 'Sigmar give us strength!'

Marius charged forward, ducking beneath an axe blade
that would have cleaved him in two, and rammed his sword
into the chest of the first bloodletter. It gave a shriek of rage
and then exploded in a shower of bloody droplets, spatter-
ing Marius and the snow with crimson. Dragging the
hammer icon he wore as his badge of office from around his
neck, Marius thrust the holy device into the face of the next,
his fist exploding with white light which scorched the daemon, causing it to burst into flames that rapidly consumed
its magical body. Emboldened by the leadership of the witch
hunter, the other men attacked, and though another five fell
to the cruel weapons of the Khornate daemons, eventually
they managed to banish them back to the otherworldly

realm from which they had been summoned. By the end of the fight, Ruprecht was panting hard, his face and furs awash with gore. Marius had an exultant grin splitting his face.

'See how the spawn of the Dark Gods are no match for men of pure faith!' the witch hunter cried out, raising his sword in triumph. 'Mere mortals will bow before our fervour and skill!'

The knights formed up as a bodyguard in front of Marius, advancing warily, with Lord Militant Trevigar at the front of the small column. Ahead there was an open space, the smouldering remnants of a fire at its centre. Just before they reached the square though, Norscans and Kislevites appeared at the windows above them, and on the rooftops. They held jugs and bottles of koidva spirit, and hurled them down onto the knights, who tried to rush forward. One pot splashed over Marius, stinging his eyes, but otherwise not hurting him, and for a moment, he was confused about the purpose of the attack. The plan became all too evident though when burning brands and bottles of burning fuel followed in the next volley. Soon the street was wall to wall with knights screaming and burning as the crude alcohol caught fire, their armour no protection from the flames licking up their legs and arms, melting their skin and setting fire to their hair.

Ruprecht stayed where he was, backing into an empty doorway with Ursula behind him. Marius turned left, leading the remnants of his men, only twenty squires and men-at-arms after the carnage wrought by the bloodletters and firebombs, down the alley between two houses. They came onto a wider road. Waiting for them was Hrolfgar and his ten warriors, shields ready; axes, swords and maces, gripped tightly.

The barbarians charged forwards, screaming their battle cries. The men-at-arms fumbled with their bows and crossbows, but shaken by the earlier attacks and surprised by the ambush, only two of them managed to shoot before the marauders fell upon them, felling one of the Norscan warriors. The fight was going to be short-lived, the battle-hardened northmen would easily chop their way through the unarmoured young men. Marius hacked out a clear path, felling two of the marauders, and raced back to the alley, diving down the dark street, panic gripping his heart. It had all gone wrong, so horribly wrong. Skidding in the snow, he saw Ruprecht and the girl on the opposite side of the street. The enemy on the rooftops had disappeared, there was no one else in sight. The bodies of burning knights were scattered across the road as pools of koidva continued to flicker fitfully with blue fire. There was no way through to the square along that route.

Marius ran across the street and grabbed Ursula, putting his sword point to her throat.

'I know you can see me, Leitzig!' Marius called out, hauling the red-haired girl to her feet. Ruprecht stepped back, his eyes darting around the street uncertainly, his hammer in his hands.

Kurt stepped out from the alley Marius had used to try to circumnavigate the inferno in the street, his sword in his hand, his armour spattered with blood. He walked slowly through the reddened snow, the smoke from the burning knights drifting around him. The crunch of the snow underfoot seemed unnaturally loud, as did the jingling of his chainmail, the crackling of flames and the sighing of the wind.

'Leave the girl,' Kurt said, his voice low but carrying over all other noise.

'Never!' snarled Marius, pricking the skin of Ursula's throat with his sword. 'Another step and she dies.'

'To hell with you!' Ursula shouted, smashing her balled fists into Marius's face and leaping away. Ruprecht grabbed hold of her as she ran past, and the two of them fell to the ground. Kurt advanced slowly, a cruel smile on his lips.

They both attacked without a word, their swords clashing together as they attacked and parried, spinning away from each other and then leaping into the attack. The blows were fast and furious, a silvery weave of blades and ringing metal as they advanced and retreated back and forth across the street. Kurt saw a sudden opening as Marius backed into a building, his retreat stopped. Kurt thrust his sword forward with all his might, skewering Marius's right shoulder and ramming into the log of the cabin behind him, jarring the witch hunter's sword from his grasp.

'Kill me then, hellspawn!' spat Marius. 'Cut my damn head off if you wish.'

'I have something better in mind than that,' Kurt said, grinning wolfishly. 'I want you know the pain you brought to my family and the gods know how many other innocents.'

Kurt exerted his will, feeling the power inside himself. He could sense the burning fires of magic inside his veins and let it run free, coursing through his body. With a thought, he let it extend out through his fingertips, and it enveloped the sword as if it was an extension of Kurt's body.

'Burn!' Kurt spat, and the sword burst into flames, which caught on the koidva already soaking the witch hunter's coat so that he exploded into a raging blaze. Marius's death screams echoed along the streets, then the town was silent except for the crackling of the flames.

Kurt stepped back, his sword still in the witch hunter, and looked at Ruprecht.

'You're the last one,' Kurt said, stalking forwards, his fingers flexing. He grabbed Ursula and pulled her aside, and Ruprecht slammed a blow with his hammer into Kurt's midriff, but it barely halted the warrior of Chaos.

Contemptuously, he grabbed the haft of the hammer in one hand, twisted it from Ruprecht's grasp and then jabbed it into the warrior's chest, knocking him to the ground. Discarding the hammer, he advanced again, wanting to finish this with his bare hands. He grabbed Ruprecht by the throat, the big man's punches not even distracting him, and hauled him to his feet.

Suddenly pain exploded in the back of Kurt's head and he pitched forward, his vision swimming. Letting go of Ruprecht, he fell to his knees, dizzy. Glancing back, through ill-focussed eyes he could make out Ursula, Ruprecht's hammer in her hands.

'You're a monster!' she screamed, smashing the hammer into his face, hurling him to his back. 'You killed the man I loved.'

There was movement behind her as Hrolfgar and his men moved into the street. Ruprecht pushed himself to his feet and grabbed Ursula.

'Come on, we have to get out of here!' he told her, dragging her away. The two turned and ran down the street, disappearing into the flames and smoke clouds as Hrolfgar sprinted over to Kurt.

'Shall we go after them?' the chieftain asked, looking up at the retreating shadows.

'Leave them be, there'll be time enough later,' Kurt said, rubbing at his head, his own blood staining his hand.

TREVIGAR WAS PANTING hard: sweat slicked his forehead and his heart hammered into his chest. His armour felt even heavier than it should as he ran down the flame-lit street, his eyes darting from side to side looking for signs of the foe. There were none that he could see, and he stopped for a moment to catch his breath.

It had all gone disastrously wrong. The impetuous attack of the witch hunter had seen three dozen of his knights killed. He had only escaped the fiery ambush by smashing his way through a door and fleeing through a window at the opposite side of the cabin. Separated, he had decided there was nothing he could do but get back to the camp and warn the few men left there as guards to pack up and leave. Leitzig would not pursue them, he was sure. No, the ex-Osterknacht's vengeance would be sated if he was not killed by Marius.

And perhaps Marius might win. After all, Trevigar had seen van Diesl battling against the daemons of the blood god and he had been a fearsome warrior, stronger and faster than his age would suggest. Feeling slightly more encouraged, he decided he would go back to the camp, muster the men to leave but remain close by in case the witch hunter returned triumphantly. As he settled on this course of action, the sound of crunching snow caught his attention. Looking over his shoulder, he saw a figure walking through the smoke, carrying a bow with arrow nocked. At first, it looked like one of the men-at-arms.

'Who's there?' Trevigar called out, straightening up and brandishing his sword with what strength he had left.

'Your humble servant, lord militant,' a strangely-accented voice called back.

'Name yourself,' Trevigar said, lowering his sword slightly. He vaguely recognised the man who walked out of the gloom. He was middle-aged, his face thin and worn and long moustaches drooped past his chin. He was dressed in furs, a small pack over one shoulder and tied with a belt hung with a variety of pouches.

'Who are you? One of the Kislevite guides?' Trevigar asked again, slightly perturbed at the man's appearance.

'Not Kislevite,' the man said with a vicious smile, raising his bow. Trevigar opened his mouth to shout just as Jakob loosed his arrow, which flew straight at the knight, its point glittering in the firelight. The arrow took the lord militant just below the chin, in the gap between his helmet and chest plate, punching through his mail coif and pitching him backwards. Blood gurgled up into his throat, choking him to death, as Jakob turned away and disappeared back into the night.

KURT STOOD ON the snow-covered hill and watched the burning ruins of Tungask collapsing to the ground. The Kislevites of the town were already heading southwards to other settlements. The Norse stood with him and Jakob, along with Hrolfgar and his men, ready for the journey north. Around him, the flaming remnants of van Diesl's camp whirled into the sky on columns of thick smoke.

'What do we do now?' Jakob asked, seeing the faraway gaze in his master's eyes. 'Do you want to go after her?'

Kurt didn't reply straight away, staring into the distance, his mind elsewhere. With a blink, he looked at Jakob as if seeing him for the first time.

'Yes,' he said. 'But not yet. I will go north and fulfil my pact with the gods. Then I will return at the head of an army, and I will raze the whole Empire until I see her head on a pole.'

Jakob smiled to himself. He would be going home soon.

ABOUT THE AUTHOR

Gav Thorpe works for Games Workshop in his capacity as Warhammer Loremaster (whatever that is). Something to do with making stuff up and designing games, apparently. He has written an armful of short stories for Inferno! magazine, and people constantly nag him for more Last Chancers stuff. For those who have followed the soap opera of his life over recent years, you'll be pleased to know that Dennis now has replacement batteries and is enjoying a new lease of life.

More Gav Thorpe from the Black Library

13th LEGION
A Last Chancers novel

GLANCING OVER MY shoulder I see that we're at the steps to the command tower now. You can follow the trail of our retreat, five dead Last Chancers lie among more than two dozen alien bodies and a swathe of shotgun cases and bolt pistol cartridges litters the floor. A few eldar manage to dart through our fusillade, almost naked except for a few pieces of bladed red armour strapped across vital body parts. Almost skipping with light steps, they duck left and right with unnatural speed. In their hands they hold vicious-looking whips and two-bladed daggers that drip with some kind of venom that smokes as it drops to the metal decking. Their fierce grins show exquisitely white teeth as they close for the kill, their bright oval eyes burning with unholy passion.

ACROSS A HUNDRED blasted war-zones upon a dozen bloody worlds, the convict soldiers of the 13th Penal Legion fight a desperate battle for redemption in the eyes of the immortal Emperor. In this endless war against savage orks, merciless eldar and the insidious threat of Chaos, Lieutenant Kage and the Last Chancers must fight, not to win, but merely to survive!

More Gav Thorpe from the Black Library

KILL TEAM
A Last Chancers novel

THE COLONEL COUGHS purposefully. He really hasn't changed a bit. Still that strong, clean shaven jaw, sharp cheek bones and the piercing glare of his ice-blue eyes. Eyes that can bore into your soul and burn through you sharper than a las-cutter. 'There is another mission,' he begins.

'I figured as much,' I reply.

'There is not much time, relatively speaking,' he continues, his gaze constant. 'You will assemble and train a team to assassinate an alien military commander...'

LANGUISHING IN AN *Imperial detention centre, Lieutenant Kage – convict soldier of the 13th Penal Legion – is at the end of the line. That is, until his ruthless old commanding officer returns with one more deadly assignment. Now Kage must whip into shape a new team of the very worst the Imperial Guard has to offer, before leading them on their one and only mission: to assassinate a warmongering enemy general, one of the mysterious alien Tau!*

More Warhammer from the Black Library

The Gotrek & Felix novels
by William King

THE DWARF TROLLSLAYER *Gotrek Gurnisson and his long-suffering human companion Felix Jaeger are arguably the most infamous heroes of the Warhammer World. Follow their exploits in these novels from the Black Library.*

TROLLSLAYER

TROLLSLAYER IS THE first part of the death saga of Gotrek Gurnisson, as retold by his travelling companion Felix Jaeger. Set in the darkly gothic world of Warhammer, TROLLSLAYER is an episodic novel featuring some of the most extraordinary adventures of this deadly pair of heroes. Monsters, daemons, sorcerers, mutants, orcs, beastmen and worse are to be found as Gotrek strives to achieve a noble death in battle. Felix, of course, only has to survive to tell the tale.

SKAVENSLAYER

THE SECOND GOTREK and Felix adventure – SKAVENSLAYER – is set in the mighty city of Nuln. Seeking to undermine the very fabric of the Empire with their arcane warp-sorcery, the skaven, twisted Chaos rat-men, are at large in the reeking sewers beneath the ancient city. Led by Grey Seer Thanquol, the servants of the Horned Rat are determined to overthrow this bastion of humanity. Against such forces, what possible threat can just two hard-bitten adventurers pose?

DAEMONSLAYER

FOLLOWING THEIR adventures in Nuln, Gotrek and Felix join
an expedition northwards in search of the long-lost dwarf
hall of Karag Dum. Setting forth for the hideous Realms of
Chaos in an experimental dwarf airship, Gotrek and Felix are
sworn to succeed or die in the attempt. But greater and more
sinister energies are coming into play, as a daemonic power
is awoken to fulfil its ancient, deadly promise.

DRAGONSLAYER

IN THE FOURTH instalment in the death-seeking saga of
Gotrek and Felix, the fearless duo find themselves pursued
by the insidious and ruthless skaven-lord, Grey Seer
Thanquol. DRAGONSLAYER sees the fearless Slayer and his
sworn companion back aboard an arcane dwarf airship in a
search for a golden hoard – and its deadly guardian.

BEASTSLAYER

STORM CLOUDS GATHER around the icy city of Praag as the foul
hordes of Chaos lay ruinous siege to northern lands of
Kislev. Will the presence of Gotrek and Felix be enough to
prevent this ancient city from being overwhelmed by the
massed forces of Chaos and their fearsome leader, Arek
Daemonclaw?

VAMPIRESLAYER

AS THE FORCES of Chaos gather in the north to threaten the
Old World, the Slayer Gotrek and his companion Felix are
beset by a new, terrible foe. An evil is forming in darkest
Sylvania which threatens to reach out and tear the heart
from our band of intrepid heroes. The gripping saga of
Gotrek & Felix continues in this epic tale of deadly battle
and soul-rending tragedy.

More Warhammer from the Black Library

DRACHENFELS
A Genevieve novel
by Kim Newman writing as Jack Yeovil

NOW CONRADIN WAS dead. Sieur Jehan was dead.
Heinroth was dead. Ueli was dead. And before the
night was over, others – maybe all of the party –
would be joining them. Genevieve hadn't thought
about dying for a long time. Perhaps tonight
Drachenfels would finish Chandagnac's Dark Kiss,
and push her at last over the border between life and
death.

DETLEF SIERCK, *the self-proclaimed greatest playwright in
the world, has declared that his next production will be a
recreation of the end of the Great Enchanter Drachenfels
– to be staged at the very site of his death, the Fortress of
Drachenfels itself. But the castle's dark walls still hide a
terrible and deadly secret which may make the first night
of Detlef's masterpiece the last of his life.*

More Warhammer from the Black Library

ZAVANT
by Gordon Rennie

'You HAVE EXAMINED the corpse, no doubt?' Graf Otto rasped, looking at Zavant Konniger. 'What are your conclusions?'

Konniger set down his wine glass and composed himself before answering. 'Foul play has been committed, certainly. But it was not a robbery-turned-murder. The victim's killer left a full purse of gold behind him. And Altdorf's footpads and cut-purses may be a bloodthirsty lot, but I have yet to meet one who would make a habit of ripping out his victims' throats with his bare teeth.'

'Surely it is the work of some wild animal, then? Some beast loose within the city walls?'

Konniger paused, sensing that he was being tested. 'Animals kill for food. Whatever killed this poor unfortunate did so only for its own savage pleasure.'

THE OLD WORLD *is a dark and dangerous place, and even the towns and cities offer little shelter, for the evil that stalks their fog-shrouded streets is as deadly as it is elusive. Enter Zavant Konniger, the great sage-detective of Altdorf. Accompanied by his trusty halfling manservant, Vido, this most brilliant scholar must use his incredible powers of deduction to solve the most sinister mysteries of the day.*

INFERNO! is the indispensable guide to the worlds of Warhammer and Warhammer 40,000 and the cornerstone of the Black Library. Every issue is crammed full of action packed stories, comic strips and artwork from a growing network of awesome writers and artists including:

- William King
- Brian Craig
- Gav Thorpe
- Dan Abnett
- Barrington J. Bayley
- Gordon Rennie

and many more

Presented every two months, Inferno! magazine brings the Warhammer worlds to life in ways you never thought possible.

For subscription details ring:
US: 1-800-394-GAME   UK: (0115) 91 40000

For more information see our website:
http://www.blacklibrary.co.uk/inferno